Entanglement

Juliet Bressan

POOLBEG

Published 2009
by Poolbeg Press Ltd
123 Grange Hill, Baldoyle
Dublin 13, Ireland
E-mail: poolbeg@poolbeg.com

Typesetting, layout, design © Poolbeg Press Ltd.

1 3 5 7 9 10 8 6 4 2

A catalogue record for this book is available from the British Library.

ISBN 978-1-84223-351-1

Typeset by Patricia Hope in Bembo 11/14.5
Printed by
Litografia Rosés, S.A., Spain

www.poolbeg.com

About the Author

Juliet Bressan is a novelist, doctor and author of the bestselling novel *Snow White Turtle Doves*. She lives in Dublin, is married and has two daughters. She is a tutor in creative writing at the Irish Writers' Centre, a medical journalist and a script advisor to the award-winning RTÉ drama series *The Clinic*.

For further information on the author see
www.julietbressan.com

Acknowledgements

Yet again I am deeply indebted to Gaye Shortland for her unfailing enthusiasm, and to Paula Campbell, Sarah Ormston, Niamh Fitzgerald, David Prendergast and all at Poolbeg for all their wisdom and support.

To my mum, Jacqueline Bressan, for giving me so much support in this and in everything I've ever written, and my dad, Dino Bressan, for his honesty, generosity, and incredibly patient translation of an enormous number of documents of the French medico-legal system. To my daughters: to Molly, for coming to visit the Paris morgue with me (seriously, how many daughters would do that for their mum?), and to Jessica for her superb sense of humour and the constancy of her love. To Nicola, Pat, Ina, Maree and especially Jennifer Kelly for their lifelong friendship, inspiration and their forgiveness. To Miriam and Sam McCallum for so much support and fun always, and for giving me the title for this book. To Siobhan Herron, Barry Brophy and especially baby Mae Brophy for long lunches, lots of fun and a very special friendship. To Conor Bowman, novelist and Barrister-at-Law, for his creativity, friendship and imaginative legal expertise. To David Wheelahan, Barrister-at-Law, and Grace Wheelahan for their very thorough explanation of the fiddliness of the Irish legal system (which I then completely ignored), and for being such very forgiving friends. To Dr Peadar O'Grady MRCPsych, for his invaluable assistance with political research and a very thorough knowledge of Africa. To the staff of the Institut Médico-Légal de Paris and the Police Judiciaire of the 12th Arrondissement for their patience with my awful French, their generosity in allowing me access to visit the Institut, and for their absolute charm. Any remaining errors are entirely my own. To the wonderful Dr Patrick Harrold, writer and physician, for his lifelong friendship and generosity. To my dear colleague, the writer Shaun Doyle, for his tremendous kindness in taking on the appalling task of proofreading the manuscript and for being the only person whom I can trust to see all the trees in the wood. To Kieran Grimes, Paula Molroe, Marigold Joy, Peter McKenna, Shay Keating, Katie Davies, Ciaran Hayden, Jonathan Curling and all of the creative team at Parallel Films/ *The Clinic* for their kindness, creativity and most of all their friendship. To all the staff of Tyrone Guthrie Centre at Annaghmakerrig, and to the artists Michelle Jackson, Ger Mills, Jean O'Brien, Elizabeth Greisman and Conor Kostick for an unforgettable summer residence. To all the team at Implementek, Belgrade, Serbia and especially to the writer, epidemiologist, IT queen and Renaissance woman Mary E Black. And to the writer and artist Donal

O'Dea for his considered approval of those first three very tentatively written chapters – his masculine assessment of the embryo of a novel gave a handful of nervous ideas a proper nudge that turned them into a real story.

A very special debt of gratitude goes to Dr Dominic Rowley MRCP, of the Health Service Executive Addiction Services, and to Eimear Faughnan PA, without whose intelligence, creativity and wonderful sense of humour this book could never have been written. And very grateful thanks to Justin Gleeson, Midwife, Rotunda Hospital and HSE Addiction Services for all his assistance with the medical research.

And finally to Peter, my dearest, with whom I am unforgivably entangled – another book that you don't have to read!

To the two cities that inspire writers,
Dublin and Paris.
With absolutely all my love.

1

Tuesday Morning, 4.a.m.

"Doctor Gilmore to the labour ward. Labour ward, Kate. Come urgently, please. Labour ward, Kate, thank you."

She was wide awake. She had the light switched on almost before the bleeper's siren had finished. But Doctor Kate Gilmore was quite used to switching from dreamless deepest sleep to a hyper-alert state of wakefulness, then jumping out of bed and grabbing her clogs to make it down into the labour ward in under a minute. The transition was almost automatic to her now, after seven years of obstetric training.

She slipped swiftly out of the single on-call bed and ran her fingers through her short dark hair that sleep had left all askew. Kate kept her hair deliberately short and in an almost boyish haircut, because it was so much easier to leap out of bed and be in the labour ward in seconds if she didn't have to brush it down. The tight short cut suited her smooth olive skin and heart-shaped face with its wide cheekbones, enhancing her elfin neat appearance.

She quickly smoothed her sleep-creased theatre scrubs across her chest, feeling underneath the bed for clogs while the labour ward sister's low-toned voice summoned her across the pager back to work. She checked her watch. It was almost four o'clock. When she'd been getting into bed, it had said three. She'd only had an hour's sleep.

Kate strode very rapidly now, down the shockingly bright corridor towards the labour ward. It was never a good idea to *run* anywhere in clogs, and the kind of doctors who *ran* about the hospital rather than walked were generally the headless-chicken type. And that was the last thing Kate would ever have wanted anyone to think about her.

Natasha, the labour-ward midwife, was standing at the nurses' station with the patient's notes all ready for Kate.

"What's the story?" Kate raised her eyebrows and kept on walking briskly, towards the room that the midwife had indicated. The room was full of noise of oxygen hissing, trolley cot sides clanging, instructions being called.

"Twenty-nine-year-old para 0 plus II at thirty-four weeks with PV bleed and low BP," said Natasha. "Foetal heart right down. It looks like an abruption."

Kate took the case notes out of the midwife's hand and whipped them open. The file was empty of written notes. "Unbooked patient, yes?"

The midwife indicated yes. Kate bit her lip and flipped the case file over and went straight to the labour chart. Probably a drug addict or undocumented migrant, if she was unbooked. She stood a moment studying the labour notes and then the tocograph, while the midwife tended to the woman who was on the trolley, lying on her side, desperately inhaling nitrous-oxide gas.

"Hello there, I'm Kate Gilmore. I'm the doctor on duty tonight. It seems that you will need to go to theatre straight away now, I'm afraid, Mrs . . ." Kate flipped the chart over to the front. "Mrs – Le Normand." She turned to Natasha. "French?" she mouthed.

"She gave us a next-of-kin address in Switzerland," the midwife said quietly, while she checked the continuous-blood-pressure monitor.

Kate nodded, watching the midwife work. Natasha took another large pad from underneath the trolley while she spoke quietly to the woman.

Kate quickly calculated the extent of this emergency. The blood pressure was dropping. But there was a foetal heart of ninety-five.

Kate glanced at Natasha. "Looks like the placental haemorrhage is concealed."

Natasha nodded back. It was time to go to theatre.

Kate let the midwife slide out of the way and then stepped up to the woman on the trolley, showing her the consent form to sign.

"*Bonjour, Madame. Pardon, je ne parle pas Français. Je suis médecin*. Can you please sign the consent form for

3

Caesarean section? *Nous voulons prendre le bébé, vers le . . . le . . .*"

Mme Le Normand was nodding in between deep moans, the black mask clamped firmly to her face. It was impossible to see much of her behind the mask but her long brown hair was soaked with sweat and her skin was very pale.

"I can speak English!" she said breathlessly – and with a mild American accent, Kate thought.

"Good. Thank you." Kate touched the woman gently on her arm. "Madame, I need to take the baby out immediately. Can you just sign the consent form here? Thank you."

The woman grasped the pen and signed the line that Kate had marked with a generous X.

"Thank you," said Kate. "Very good. Thank you." She turned to speak to the midwife again. "BP?"

"A hundred over forty now."

"Okay. Good." Kate snapped the case notes shut and placed them on the trolley at the woman's feet. "Let's go. Have we grouped and cross-matched blood?"

"Six units and twenty of fresh frozen plasma on the way."

"Foetal heart?"

"Almost down to eighty-five."

Kate frowned.

"Nick Farrelly is in theatre already," Natasha added.

"Good." Kate stood back to let them out. Nick was the anaesthetist she liked to work with best.

Kate put a hand out to touch the woman's arm very briefly as they pushed the trolley into the lift. "Don't worry, I am going to deliver your baby very quickly now."

But the woman's hands were shaking as she held the rubber mask to her face, dark hair sticking to her neck with sweat. She groaned and Kate met Natasha's eyes as the lift door closed between them.

Kate turned rapidly to take the stairs. Thirty-four weeks. In this hospital, without the placental bleed the baby would have been a good enough gestation to deliver in the labour ward. But with the mother in shock the situation was much more severe. Everything depended on keeping the mother as well as possible now. She took the stairs two steps at a time, wooden clogs tapping loudly in the night.

Kate pulled a cotton theatre hat out of the box that was in the hallway just outside the operating room and grabbed a mask to tie around her mouth. There was the sound of metal clanging against metal, instruments being unwrapped, nurses' voices over one another. She stood back to let Natasha leave and then pulled two plastic shoe-covers over her clogs before walking backwards into the operating theatre, letting the doors flap shut behind her.

At four o'clock in the morning, gynae theatre was alive, crashing with the noise and light – nurses flapping drapes, the wheeze of anaesthetic machines, the snarl of suction. The patient was already parked and undergoing anaesthetic, in the centre of the long wide room. Kate caught the familiar earthy smell of iodine and sour liquor that was the night-time delivery smell of new birth.

Across the theatre underneath the window the nurses were quickly unwrapping and counting instruments and towels. Normally, as soon as you walked into this theatre you were struck by the beautiful view over the Dublin Mountains through the long wide windows on the far wall. Tonight, the sky was thickly black outside.

Nick Farrelly the anaesthetist was working rapidly, fixing Mme Le Normand with a central line.

"Hi, Nick. Glad you're on tonight. This is a tricky case here. Unbooked patient. Is Paeds out of bed yet?"

God damn it – Nick mustn't have been able to get another vein if he was going straight into the major vessel just above the heart. The woman must be quite shut down.

"Shit, Nick, does she need a central line already?" Kate said quietly over her shoulder as she passed him on her way to the scrub area. Not waiting for his reply, she whacked the two taps on at the scrub sink and began to briskly lather up.

"Aw, I don't know, but who's going to wait around to find out?" Nick grinned at her over his shoulder and Kate smiled back at him from the scrub room through the glass.

"I just love putting clever things in, you know." He shrugged his shoulders while he taped the central line in place, briskly attaching it to the IV. Despite the tension Kate couldn't help smiling at Nick while she scrubbed her fingernails. Nick worked very briskly but he was always very careful and neat, with his black-rimmed glasses and slightly protruding, ever-smiling teeth. Everybody loved Nick Farrelly, the anaesthetist.

"Well, do something even cleverer and get her oxygen sats in good nick for me, there's a good man," Kate called to him over the noise of the nurse's counting.

"Paeds on the way, Kate – Ronan's nearly here." Nick was starting up another unit of fresh frozen plasma. "And the patient's under. We are all ready for you now, Kate."

Kate spread her arms out to the theatre nurse who opened out the gown, twirling her around to tie the wrap-around while she snapped on rubber gloves from the box that was kept specially for her on the window-ledge beside the scrub sink. Kate Gilmore was the only member of the hospital theatre staff who needed sterile gloves in a size *extra small*.

"How's the patient's oxygen saturation, Nick?" Kate asked him now, as she took the scalpel from the theatre nurse. One neat swipe and the skin was open. Kate clamped the incision open and the uterus was visible instantly. "Okay, opening up the uterus now . . . suction please and we can get a look in . . ." The suction vacutainer was filling rapidly. "Christ, Nick, we're going to need a lot more volume. Look at the loss just since we've started and there's more going down there . . . gosh, this is a small baby for thirty-four weeks, Sharon." Kate looked up at the theatre nurse who stood by with a green towel draped across her arms, ready to take the newborn.

"Is the Paeds here yet?" Kate went on, talking rapidly as she worked. "Oh, good. Hi, Ronan. Brilliant. Very tiny baby, Ronan. Here we go. A bit still as well. Heart rate is right down." Kate neatly clamped and cut the cord. "Okay, there you are, she's all yours." She handed the silent, slippery newborn child to Sharon Guinness who whisked the child away towards the paediatric station in the green theatre towel.

"I'll rub her up for you, Ronan, and then I think you'll have to intubate." Sharon Guinness wiped the baby carefully and placed her on the resuscitaire for Ronan Clare the paediatrician to examine.

"How's the Apgar, Ronan?" Kate called over to him, but he did not reply.

I'm rushing him, thought Kate. Steady on. Take your time. Ronan's in charge there now.

She checked Nick Farrelly's eyes over his theatre mask for signs of worry. Behind his black-rimmed spectacles, Nick looked his usual placid self. But then Nick was never jumpy or emotional. Kate slid her hand around the cavity one more time, desperately trying to make sure she had it emptied completely. The uterus was empty all right but it was boggy and unresponsive.

Kate could feel her heart begin to thump.

"This placenta is all over the place," she said, looking at Nick.

"Okay, Kate, no problem, honey." Nick looked at her, reassuring her with calm eyes behind his glasses. "You just work away. I've got her saturated enough for the moment. But I'd stick another unit of packed red cells on now, Sharon, and maybe some ergometrine?"

"Apgar four at one minute," said Ronan. "But don't worry, she's responding to oxygen by mask. And crying now. There you go, little baby!" He rubbed the tiny infant's chest to make her gasp. "She's really pinking up now."

"Good man, Ronan!" Sharon nodded over to him.

They were needing all the signs of life that they could find.

The theatre went silent for a moment. Kate removed the last remnants of the torn placenta and handed it to Sharon to weigh.

The familiar warm-blood dampness of the crash gynae theatre was soaking into her gown and she scolded herself inwardly yet again for forgetting to put a rubber apron on. She would be soaked in this woman's blood afterwards. And her scrubs (which she had slept in) would be soaked right through.

Kate was always forgetting to get a rubber apron on for a crash section. It was the one mistake she consistently made, and the only person who suffered for it was herself, and now she'd have to take another shower before she could get back into bed tonight. And it was already nearly time to get up again.

She stood back to examine her work and check the progress of contraction. There was no contraction happening. The woman's uterus lay where she'd placed it outside the abdomen on the green drape like a limp hoodie, its open mouth tiny now that the small newborn person it had housed had been delivered.

Kate glanced sharply at Nick, to see if the anaesthetist had noticed. "Nick, what do you think about the blood loss? I can't seem to get stasis from this uterus at all."

Nick squinted at the volume that had already gathered in the vacutainer. It was almost four litres. It was more than enough to need a hysterectomy and if they didn't make a very quick decision, the woman would no longer be able to tolerate the numbers of units of fresh frozen plasma and the packed red cells and would start using up all her blood-clotting factors – which could be fatal.

Nick looked at Kate now, and she searched his face to see what he was thinking.

"How many units of packed red cells has she had?" she asked him.

"Four."

"In what length of time?"

"In twenty minutes."

"If we keep going, there is a risk of disseminated intravascular coagulopathy, isn't there? And then we'll lose her altogether."

"Of course there is. Isn't she contracting down at all?"

"We've given two infusions of oxytocin," said Sharon Guinness, shooting a warning glance at Kate who was desperately squeezing on the uterus. "Kate, the fluids are just flying in and they're flying right out again through that uterine wall."

"Kate. You can squeeze it all you want, but if it keeps on bleeding –"

"I know, Nick." Kate spoke quietly but her mouth felt as though it were full of cotton wool. "Sharon," she said, "is her husband still outside?"

Sharon looked questioningly at the others.

"Does anybody know where this lady's husband is?" Kate's voice was sharper now. "Or partner? Did she come in with someone, or come in alone?"

In the echoey theatre her voice was shrill with nerves. Steady on, she told herself. This is a team decision. Nobody is alone here. And this is about life and death. Do the right thing, and do it well. That's all you need to do. She flared her nostrils to calm her eyes and breathed a deep, liquor-scented breath.

Ronan Clare the paediatrician was happy with the baby's Apgar now and was settling her up underneath the lights. The baby seemed to be breathing spontaneously, her tiny head fast asleep beside the continuous-oxygen mask that Ronan had set beside her. Ronan usually liked to avoid intubation if at all possible at resuscitation, pushing babies hard to breathe on their own.

"Good little girl, that's a good baby, take a big deep breath, and have some nice cold oxygen." Ronan chatted to the baby while he held the mask in front of her face.

Normally Kate would smile to hear Ronan yapping away behind her as she worked, but tonight her face was frozen.

"I'll pop outside, shall I, and see if there's anybody

11

with her?" Ronan offered. "Thanks, Ronan," said Kate. "Please do that."

"Sharon, you just keep an eye on *le bébé*," said Ronan.

Sharon's expression of anxiety as she passed Kate on the way over to the resuscitaire said it all. They would have to make a quick decision, and every second counted now. Above the theatre masks, four pairs of eyes blinked, searching one another for an answer.

"We'll give her one more unit," said Kate, "and then if there's no stasis after two more minutes we'll make a decision then."

It was a plan, at any rate. And it was a decision.

Kate stood still for a moment, waiting for the packed red cells to run in through Nick Farrelly's central line. God help her, thought Kate, while she tried to pack the woman's still-flaccid uterus again with yet another towel.

An unknown patient, here on holidays, having a disastrous delivery in a strange hospital. Please God, let there be a husband outside! She felt her neck becoming tense; her nostrils flared. Every second was an agony.

Kate tried to rub a contraction up again and packed the uterus with another towel. It was as flaccid as a burst balloon.

"Shall we have some music on?" Sharon suggested. "How about a bit of Lyric FM?"

"That would be lovely, Sharon," Kate smiled at her gratefully.

Nick began to hum along with Mozart's Clarinet Concerto. They stood silently, waiting. Blood and liquor dripping from the soaked green drapes into the bucket underneath, running off the operating table like a thick black rain. Mozart and the hum of theatre lights, and the wheeze of ventilation machines.

Ronan poked his head around the doorway of the theatre. "She is alone," he said. "I checked with them downstairs too. They have a phone number for her next of kin and they've been ringing it all night. They got through and left a message earlier but now there's no reply. They think she was visiting Dublin on business."

"Her sats are very low now, Kate. And the BP is not responding." Nick's brown eyes looked at her solidly.

"Okay, Nick. Thanks. I appreciate that." Kate looked at Sharon.

"Do you want to ring the Prof?" Sharon asked her.

"There isn't time," Kate heard Nick quietly say.

"All right," she said. She turned to the trolley and changed her gloves briskly for new dry ones. Size extra small.

"Let's go then, Nick. Clamp by two then, please, Sharon?"

The theatre nurse handed her forceps, and she tied off the uterine vessels one by one.

They worked rapidly, heads bent together, her dark hair under one theatre hat, Sharon's strawberry curls like a cherubic halo under hers. Four gloved hands moving swiftly as they passed sutures and clamps, in silence – the only noise the wheezing of machines, the snarl of suction, and the Mozart lightly in the background.

"Don't you just love the clarinet?" said Kate. Although they couldn't see her mouth behind the paper mask, her eyes revealed the creases of a clearly very distressed smile. She held her hand out to Sharon for the scalpel.

"Don't worry, Kate, you're doing the right thing," Nick told her. Behind his glasses, dark brown eyes full of kindness.

Sharon closed her eyes and opened them again, looking at Kate above the theatre mask as if to send her a small silent message of goodwill.

Kate lifted the woman's womb away from her anaesthetised body, for good.

Tuesday morning, 5.45 a.m.

"Prof, it's Kate Gilmore."

"Kate."

"Prof – we had a very difficult delivery in theatre just now. Unbooked patient Para II. She's stable now. But we've had to do a hysterectomy."

There was a very long pause.

"Is the infant alive?"

"Yes. Apgar four and nine. Thirty-four weeks. Patient is in ICU."

There was a longer pause.

"I'll see you soon, then."

Leaning against the wall, she replaced the receiver. Her green operating gown discarded, she sat down. She sat for half an hour alone in crumpled, stained pale-blue theatre scrubs in the dressing-room, exhaustion overwhelming her like a wave.

Professor Dennis Crowe arrived into the ICU at seven smelling of a musky aftershave and soap. He and Kate sat side by side at the big desk in the nurses' station while the sisters did their round. He calmly read through her theatre notes, picking through them like a haystack in which a vitally important needle might be found. He ran a finger over the labour chart as he silently scrutinised each word she'd written in her theatre notes, taking what she assumed were mental notes. This was Professor Crowe's idea of debriefing. Silent scrutiny followed by withdrawal. She sat patiently and waited for him to get through the notes. The noise of an unanswered phone punctuating the silence made her jump. The wheeze of a computer printing methodically in the background grated on her nerves.

"We'll need to present this to the M and M on Thursday," said the Prof.

Every tough delivery was audited in a question-and-answer style presentation by the entire maternity hospital staff at a meeting called the monthly Morbidity and Mortality meeting. Evidence-based medicine was what it was all about. And a pretty good thing it was too, Kate usually felt, and normally she looked forward to her monthly task of presenting the hospital statistics for these meetings. But now, after this disastrous delivery, the last thing she wanted in the entire world was to have to go through last night's events in theatre in front of the staff of the entire hospital.

"Yes, of course," she said. But her heart was as low as it could be. "I'll get a PowerPoint demonstration ready tomorrow," she said, wondering in her over-tiredness how she'd summon up the energy to even *look* at a computer screen. And then suddenly something caught her eye – Jesus, was this even the right chart? Yes. Of course it was. But surely . . . she'd been convinced that she'd delivered a Para *two* last night – and yet this chart was yellow – which meant it was the woman's first pregnancy. This didn't make sense. She was sure the midwife had said that the woman had been on her third pregnancy and midwives didn't make those kinds of mistakes – unless – was there any chance that she could have made that kind of mistake herself? She shook her head and tried to focus her memory on the events of last night – but her over-tired state of fuzziness was drawing a complete blank. The chart the professor was holding was a yellow one, primagravida. And then she noticed, there at the top right-hand corner of the theatre notes, in the midwife's handwriting: Para 0 +II. Two previous pregnancies – both miscarriages.

She glanced sideways at the Prof's face to try to read his thoughts and desperately tried to re-run last night's events of the emergency in the labour ward – to see if she could remember what she'd read in the admission notes. She *seemed* to remember Natasha saying to her that the patient was a Para II – which *would* have meant two live births. Kate closed her eyes for a moment and tried as hard as possible to remember what she'd heard the midwife say. But fifteen hours later and after only one hour's sleep it was all a fuzzy blur.

Perhaps it had been a language problem, she thought, glancing sideways at the Professor's face again as his finger underlined the words *Para 0 plus II*. Perhaps the patient had misunderstood, she thought, and we muddled the history in the emergency last night. Even with perfect English, in a state of distress *she* might have got things slightly mixed up.

But Professor Crowe had a face that told her nothing. He continued to read through the notes with one finger underlining each word, as if he were marking an exam. The only sound that she could hear while he read was his breathing, deep exhalations through his nostrils that sounded like a wind tunnel. That, and the thumping of her heart.

Mme Le Normand was under heavy post-op sedation and Kate would only be able to speak to her properly when she'd woken up. And the most important thing Kate would have to tell her was that she wouldn't be able to have any more pregnancies.

Kate leaned her elbows on the desk and rubbed her temples with her eyes closed. Talking to the patient about the delivery and having to explain everything that went wrong was a major anxiety to face. But having to present it in front of the entire staff – that was like having to rub her own nose into it.

"All right," said Dennis Crowe eventually, standing up. "You've done enough. I'll go and see the patient." And he turned to march away, carrying the case notes with him underneath his arm, as if they were a weapon.

Tuesday evening, 7 p.m.

All she could hear all day long going around in her head was Mozart's Clarinet Concerto, second movement. Normally it would have been a beautiful piece of music to have fastened into the brain, but today it was like a toothache that wouldn't go away.

Kate decided to take one last run through the charts in ICU while the nurses were busy. In the quiet of the nurses' station while the evening medicine trolley was going round she flipped through the trolley full of files. It was very difficult to concentrate now. The familiar buzzing feeling in her cheeks and hairline meant that she was not only running short on sleep but running short on patience too. She clenched her jaw and steadied herself to read the case notes on the patient one more time. But her mind didn't seem to be able to absorb the information any more.

She shivered and yawned widely and noisily, and then wondered if she ought to just go home and try to forget about everything till morning when she'd had some sleep. It was after seven, the traffic would be hell outside and she couldn't do much more tonight. And yet she felt that she couldn't leave the hospital.

If only there were someone she could talk to about all this, about how awful she was feeling now – that was all she needed, someone who knew the significance of what she'd been through but who'd want to make her feel instantly better. She'd been trying to ring her husband Dave all day. But Dave was an anaesthetist doing a list on the other side of the hospital, and he was uncontactable.

It was pitch dark outside now and a light rain was beginning to streak the window just above the nurses' station. Freezing out tonight, Kate thought, her head spinning with the tiredness. Kate had plenty of good friends in the maternity hospital and everyone had been so kind to her today, knowing what had happened for her in the gynae theatre last night. But what she really wanted was to be able to talk it through with someone she loved.

And Dave seemed to be held back later and later every evening these days as the cases in his theatre piled up because of bed shortages and he always seemed to have someone difficult in ICU himself. It was still worth trying to give him one last bell, though. She dialled his mobile number from the ward, just in case he'd already left and might be on his way home.

But Dave's mobile was still switched off.

Kate stood a moment by the desk in the nurses' station and gathered her thoughts together. She would still have to go back down to the on-call room to get her bag anyway and then head out into the carpark and face the blustery December night. Perhaps Dave was still in theatre. Perhaps he'd been caught up in an emergency too.

She yawned and then shivered again suddenly. She could ring the ENT theatre of course, on the other side of the hospital where Dave had been doing a list earlier on, and see what stage they were at and ask if he was still in there. But that would mean going through the petty nosey-parker theatre porters again, who took messages down all wrong and got people's names mixed up and pretended that they couldn't recognise anybody in a theatre mask. It might be more trouble than it was worth.

"Jesus, are you still at it? And I thought *I* had no life!" Ronan Clare grinned at her as he ambled into the office.

She smiled. "I have a life all right, Ronan – it's just a bit rubbish at the moment, that's all."

Poor Ronan had been up all night too and Baby Le Normand was struggling as well.

"How is the French – I mean Swiss baby, Ro?" she asked him now.

Ronan shrugged his drooping shoulders and sat down in the nurses' station, putting his feet up on the desk. "Quite up and down, really, now. IV feeding, which is to be expected. But he, oh no, it's a she – she was actually a bit more shocked than I'd realised. Jittery today, and we had to do an X-ray. And we might be ventilating in an hour. I'm waiting to hear back from the lab about the blood gases and then I'll decide – but I've a feeling that we'll be intubating and going for full-on ventilation."

"Oh. I'm so sorry, Ronan. That's a bummer. Are you knackered out?" Kate could feel the clang of anxiety come over her again. She closed her eyes for just a moment. Thursday M and M to prepare tomorrow – having to talk to the Prof today was bad enough – what if the baby doesn't do well either? But that's not my problem, she carefully reminded herself. The Paeds are responsible there from now on. I've kept my patient alive, we delivered a live infant. I've got to keep on telling myself that.

She opened her eyes brightly instead, to smile at Ronan.

"I guess there's no point in worrying any more about it for tonight," she said. "We should just go home and get some rest, Ro. I feel like have done enough for this week anyway."

"Well, I could do with a pint but I'm not going home for a while – do you want to pop over for one later on when I've got the baby settled?" he asked her hopefully.

Poor Ronan is so sweet, she thought. But I'm not up for hospital gossip now. It's been a hell of a night and a very long day trying to make it right again. She shook her head.

"I'm going to go on home, Ro. Try to see my husband, get something to eat and hit the sack. But maybe later in the week, if you're still around?"

"That would be great." Ronan nodded and yawned

at the same time. He suddenly beamed. "Let's go to the Clarence after the meeting on Thursday night and get absolutely pissed!"

Kate laughed and clapped him on the back.

Ronan looked up at her. "You did the right thing, Kate, you had no choice. Last night, I mean. It was really tough on you."

"Yeah, I know." She sat down again with him. "My head's all over the place, Ronan. I'm sure this case has gone as well as we could have expected in the circumstances, but I can't seem to think straight any more. The other thing is that I won't feel better about it until I've talked to the patient to counsel her. Prof went to talk to her this afternoon but she's still very heavily sedated. She won't be taking a lot of it in yet." She looked at him. "Ronan, I'm normally quite good at talking to patients, aren't I? I mean, I'm good at breaking bad news to patients, aren't I?"

"You're the best. You put a lot of time into it," Ronan grinned. "And I know a lot of Obs and Gynaes who wouldn't, so I'm sure it will all go well."

"You're a pal," she said, squeezing his hand where it rested on the table.

But the truth was that she had never felt more alone. What she longed for more than anything was to have somebody at home who would talk her through her horrendous night, who'd know exactly what to say to make everything all right again, who'd understand completely all the tough decisions doctors have to make and who would love her for it – and that person should have been Dave. But Dave just wasn't there for her in that way any more. He was completely absorbed in his own work issues. And here she was, staying back late at work when she could hardly think any more, just to have someone to talk to.

Kate normally felt quite confident about her career, about her ability to get things right – but the more responsibility she had at work, the more tough decisions she was going to have to make. And although she didn't want to be a wimp, there were some things that happened in hospital life that were almost impossible to deal with without support. Colleagues just weren't the same. They couldn't be detached and still supportive at the same time because they were also involved in the case. Dave was the one person who could have been there for her – another doctor, an anaesthetist, someone who had known her all her life, someone who loved her no matter what, someone who understood the responsibility for life and death. But Dave was the one person who wasn't there for her tonight. And the empty hole that left in her confidence was beginning to yawn wider.

"Here," Ronan put his arms around her, "give us a hug, Katie-cakes."

He took the wind out of her with his crushing bear hug and Kate squealed, wriggling away.

"I'll see you in the morning. But thanks for the pep talk, Ronan." She was about to add, "I really need somebody to talk to now" but that made her sound pathetic.

"Don't mention it!" Ronan waved at her and pulled the *Lancet* towards him, putting up his feet again. "Jesus," he yawned again and grumbled in a tired voice. "When is that flipping lab going to ring me with that baby's sats?"

"You won't be able to have any more children, I'm afraid. We did the best we could but sometimes things happen during emergencies that are out of our control."

Marianne Le Normand looked at the head of the man that was talking to her – and saw two of them. He was speaking English.

This is – yes, I am in the hospital in Dublin. The baby – yes. That's the nurse. She's the one who told me about the baby. I have had the baby. The baby has been born, and it's a girl. The nurse who told me, that's her over there – and she said I'd see the baby soon. It's in a special place. A special baby place. The nurse has blonde hair, strawberry blonde, that's what the Americans call it, reddish gold, like a Botticelli painting. She's so beautiful. And this place. It's very noisy, this place now, and what's this tubing on my hand? Oh. Medical equipment. But the man is speaking again. His head is saying things. Both his heads are, actually.

"Things go wrong very quickly in obstetrics."

His mouth is moving – both his mouths – and saying the words.

"You will need some more time to come to terms

with it. But the main thing is that the baby is quite well and that you are making progress too. We'll answer any questions that you ask."

Well. That's very nice of them.

Her lips were trying to move but she didn't seem to be able to operate them fully. She tried to speak – "Mweeh!" – but no, that wasn't a real word at all. Not in any language.

Try again, Marianne. Say something nice to the doctor, now.

"Thank you, *docteur*." She smiled at both his heads and then, with relief, they merged back into one. But the one head had horns growing out of it.

What? What's happening to his head? No, that's not horns. That's his soul, it's a halo around his head. Oh! And the nurse has one too. Well.

That's beautiful.

She closed her eyes.

"We'll talk to her when her husband gets here, too," she heard the man's voice say.

"He'll be here tomorrow night," said the nurse.

In her sleep, she stepped onto a boat, gently, gently, with her newborn baby in her arms.

Veronique.

Her name is Veronique.

And the boat rocked both of them together.

The carpark was almost empty when Kate scuttled across it in her duffle coat, head down against the icy drizzle. She beeped her pale grey Mini Cooper open and slammed herself inside, rubbing her hands against the cold before she started up the engine.

A blast of music boomed Kate's small car across the empty carpark in the hard night rain. Kate always left the radio on whenever she parked her car – she liked the fact that as soon as she turned the key in the ignition, music played. Starting up the engine and the radio at the same time would run down the battery, Dave would grumble furiously at her if she left the radio on in *his* car. But in her own car, she could leave whatever the hell she liked on, and do whatever she wanted to the battery.

'Cos I know how I feel about you now! sang the Sugababes and Kate waved her head in time to the music, singing as loudly as she could as she swung the Mini out into the traffic jam, trying to put the hospital and the ICU and Mme Le Normand and the disastrous night on call that she had had as far away from her memory as was possible.

2

Kate's first year as a senior registrar had gone pretty well so far. She was getting on quite well with Professor Crowe, even though he could be very old-fashioned sometimes. But Kate was smart enough to know which side her bread was buttered on and so she refrained from engaging in any kind of feminist discussion with the rather opinionated Prof. And most of the other maternity hospital staff seemed to like her. It hadn't been too difficult to fit in so far.

It was kind of weird at first, coming back to work in Ireland after five years in Australia – but Kate had been the one who had wanted to come home. Dave would have been pretty happy to stay on in Melbourne pretty much forever. But Kate was desperately homesick.

Everybody who was over there seemed at some level to be planning to come back to Ireland in the end, anyway. Kate convinced herself that they would be better off to come back as soon as possible. Dave's fair skin didn't suit the heat, she told herself. They spent December to February virtually indoors, Dave sweating miserably, sinking one cold beer after another. He was beginning to find it difficult to sleep at night. Kate was quite convinced that as soon as they got back to Ireland Dave's moods would improve. But her expectations had been disappointed.

Dave had found himself a senior-reg job in anaesthetics but the rota was much more severe than he had been used to in Australia. And the sleep disturbance did not improve in the cooler climate. If anything, Dave's sleeping habits were worse now than they had ever been. And even though they'd both been lucky enough to find posts at St Xavier's, Dave didn't seem to have found the happiness that Kate had so desperately hoped he would. He seemed to be working longer and longer hours, to be becoming more and more exhausted, and as a couple they were spending less time together than they had ever done.

Kate fiddled with the radio now while she sat at a traffic light and tried to find her favourite station, Lyric FM. Although she liked to start the car up with loud rock sounds, what Kate really liked was jazz and there was often a good evening jazz programme on at night on Lyric. She needed soothing sounds to chillax her now, after the shit night on call she'd had.

She tapped her fingers on the steering wheel, but the

images of last night's theatre kept bundling back into her mind again.

It was the first time since she'd started in this hospital that she'd had to do a Caesarean hysterectomy. And it was the first time since she'd started in this hospital that she'd ended up with a patient in ICU. And Professor Crowe had been so unhelpful and cold. His silence that morning had felt worse, almost, than any kind of censure.

She found the radio station at last but there was no jazz music at this hour, just some light classical sounds. She blasted up the cheesy Luciano Paverotti solo any way and loudly sang along. Anything to keep her mind distracted from work now.

She sat impatiently at another red traffic light. Traffic was very heavy tonight, even though it was after eight o'clock by now. Must be the rain, and bloody Christmas shopping, she thought. There was only one more week to go till Christmas. The car crawled another fifty metres forward and was stopped.

I'll try to phone Dave again, she decided, at the next set of red lights, and pressed the speed dial on her phone, turning on the loudspeaker. This time he answered promptly enough.

"Are you finished, sweetheart?"

"No. Not for another fucking hour or more. Kate, please don't ring me on the mobile when I'm in theatre."

"But I couldn't get through when you were in theatre! You had it switched off all afternoon for God's sake, Dave! I only got your voicemail."

"Oh, for Christs's sake! Now you're blaming me! You are unreal, Kate. I'm at work, for Christ's sake. *You're* at home by now, I suppose?"

"No, I'm not! I've only just finished too. I've had a hell of a night as well, you know!"

She felt humiliated but she didn't want a row, not while driving the car and making an illegal mobile-phone call at the same time. And she didn't know if Dave was talking to her in theatre or not – but the background sounded far too jolly for it to be an operation. He could be in the Res or in the dressing-room and anybody could be listening. He did sound knackered though.

"Dave, forget about it," she said miserably. "Hang up now. Ring me later when you're coming home. I only wanted to see if you'd like to do something for dinner."

Dave sighed deeply. "Look, you sort yourself out. I'm stuck here and I don't know when I'll be home."

"Oh. All right."

She hung up, furious, but powerless. Bastard, she thought.

And then regretted it.

He's stressed out.

Anaesthetics is a brutal job.

Dave often got no sleep at all, working all night in ICU and then doing a theatre list in the morning. But not all anaesthetists were like him . . . she thought of Nick Farrelly, her lovely camp gay anaesthetist friend.

Nick was always cool as shit. He never seemed to get into a state like Dave did. Perhaps gynae theatre was less stressful than general surgical, which was what Dave was always grumbling. Although when you thought about it, she and Nick and Ronan the paediatrician were up at night just as often as Dave. More often sometimes.

Nick Farrelly was smaller and much slighter than Dave, who at six feet tall and with broad rugby-playing shoulders probably needed much more sleep and better nutrition than Nick, she told herself. *Maybe us littlies have an advantage when it comes to going without sleep and living on hospital toast and crisps.* She swung the car over the bridge on Baggot Street and then towards home in Percy Place. It was probably much better anyway if she had the house to herself for a couple of hours and then got an early night, she decided as she parked the car.

Once, when Dave and Kate had been married for just over a year and they were living in Australia, they took a long drive out of Melbourne to Apollo Bay, a seaside resort in South Victoria, for a weekend's break. Dave was doing the driving. Dave had always liked to drive with his legs thrust out to meet the automatic pedal of the car with just the tip of his toes, and he liked to steer the car with just one finger. So Dave *loved* driving in Australia.

At that point in their life, Dave's one-finger driving didn't bother Kate at all. She found it quite romantic that he loved to hold her hand and drive at the same time, or caress the inside of her thigh, or run his hand up her legs and rummage underneath her skirt. And the long Australian highways were monotonous and poker-straight. Driving an automatic car on a long unbending road was something you could almost do in your sleep.

But on that one long drive from Melbourne to Geelong and then onto the meandering Great Ocean Road, Kate had suddenly noticed that there was another car coming towards them in the opposite direction. That is to say, that the other car was driving straight towards them, but it seemed to be coming towards them *on their side of the road*. Often, when you are driving a long distance in open countryside in a hot climate, you do see things that aren't quite there. It's only when you get up close along an open road in a blazing forty-two degree summer's heat that you see that pool of water disappear, or the fleet of trucks become just one, or that the car that seemed to be driving straight towards you is in fact driving parallel to you and several metres to the side. Kate had thought that the car that *looked* as though it was on their side of the road and was driving straight towards them wasn't really on their side at all. It only looked like that. And so they kept on driving straight towards it.

"That car looks as though it's on our side of the road, but it isn't," she had said.

"It only looks like that," he said.

"It's going to pull over to the other side of the road now, isn't it?"

"It only looks as though it's on our side."

"It's going to pull right over, isn't it, Dave?"

"When we get nearer we'll see that it's on the other side."

And that was what they kept on saying all the way until seconds just before they hit the oncoming car head on, and the other car which was much smaller than Dave's heavy gas-guzzler took itself into a frenzied spin and whipped itself right off the road into a flurry of gum trees just in front of them and their heavier car wound down to a whining, crumpled-steel full-stop.

Miraculously, the only person who was visibly hurt by the accident had been the driver of the other car – and he had climbed drunkenly out of one of the windows of his now upside-down Mazda with his head actively bleeding, waved a bright "Gidday!" to Dave and Kate who sat motionless in the front of their now immobile car, and thumbed a ride from the very next vehicle that had come along.

Dave and Kate had given a shaking statement straight away to the police. But the driver of the other car had been found several hours later, happily drinking with his neighbours at a bar in a nearby town.

Even though the gas-guzzler had been a right-off they had not been hurt – apart from the pain that Dave had developed in his neck that was like a pliers being gripped around his spinal cord. But everybody in medicine knew that there was no such thing as whiplash after car crashes from head on: all those pains were only in the mind of seekers of big compensation claims.

Ever since that head-on collision, Kate hated the way Dave liked to drive with the car seat thrust back to its longest possible extension right away from the steering wheel. Every time Dave drove the car like this, she felt that every car on the opposite side of the road was going to drift inevitably across the white centre line and drive straight smack right into them. And so the more nervous she would get whenever Dave drove like this, the more she would clench her eyes shut and beg him to hold the steering wheel with both hands and the more brazen his one-finger steering-wheel-twirling became.

Perhaps it was because his wife hated it so much – or perhaps the accident that had terrified Kate had had the opposite effect on Dave and had therefore in some way convinced him that his driving habits were invincible. Either way, ever since the accident Dave had found an enormous pleasure in owning a car in which he could always plunge the driving seat back as far away as possible from the dashboard, leaving as wide as possible a space between his lap and the steering wheel.

But now they rarely drove anywhere together any more. Two separate cars made things much easier, when living two very separate lives.

Kate was fast asleep when Dave thudded into the bed beside her later on that night. She had read two chapters of *The Curious Incident of the Dog in the Night-time* before nodding off with her book in her hand. Dave creaked the bed noisily while he eased his heavy frame in beside her, and so he woke her up abruptly.

"You okay, Dave?" she whispered after a minute or two.

"Why are you whispering? There's no one here," he grumbled.

"I didn't want to wake you."

"You didn't want to wake me, so you ask me if I'm okay? Didn't you think that in order to get a reply you might have to find that I'm awake? What kind of logic is that?"

He was in a foul temper.

"I'm sorry."

He moved his heavy body away from her, although she reached out a small hand to touch his shoulder.

"Kate, I'm really trying now to go to sleep, if that's not too much trouble for you."

"I just wanted to say good night, Dave. I haven't seen you for two days."

"So you thought you'd wake me up to say that too, I suppose."

"I've had a *horrible* night on call last night too, Dave!" She was aware that her voice was rising. "I – well, I was hoping you might have come home earlier. I was hoping I could talk to you all about it."

She felt close to tears and at the same time furious with his dismissiveness. It seemed almost pathetic to have to *ask* him to listen to her. She closed her eyes tightly, in the dark, as if to keep out the negativity that she could almost palpate in the bed beside her, confronted as she was by Dave's large pyjama-clad back.

"Yeah, well, in the morning would be better. I'm wrecked too, you know."

"Dave, have you been drinking?"

"Jesus Christ almighty, what is this, the Spanish inquisition?" Dave yelled suddenly, and Kate jumped in fright.

"Shut *up*!" she barked at him. "Who the hell do you think you are, shouting at me like that?"

"Who do you think *you* are, nagging me like this when I've only just got into bed? I'm only five minutes in from the hospital and you're already treating me like shit! I'm getting up and going downstairs for another glass of wine! And yes, of course I've been drinking! Do you think I'd be able to get to sleep after the day I've had without a glass of wine?" He swung his legs heavily out of the bed and ruffled his hands through his thick blond hair.

"There's no need to shout," Kate growled.

She was getting pretty sick of the dark looks her next-door neighbour was regularly giving her in the mornings. She really wanted to slap Dave now, but she kept her voice measured, calm and even.

"I'm tired too. I just thought you sounded a bit slurred or something," she added in a quieter voice.

"Jesus, you *are* ridiculous! *This* is ridiculous. I'm going downstairs. Talk to me in the morning when you aren't going to be such a bitch."

She listened to his heavy footsteps on the staircase and the kitchen door downstairs creak miserably on its hinges. She heard the fridge door open. The time on the alarm clock said two o'clock. But she felt exhausted and she knew that she would fall asleep again quite quickly now.

Poor Dave though, she thought. He'll be in the horrors with a hangover in the morning.

The sky was still pitch black outside when Dave brought her in a cup of tea at seven in the morning and she turned the bedside light on and took the teacup from him cautiously. He kissed her on the nose.

"You're an angel when you're asleep," he told her, and he touched her nose with a finger where he had kissed her. The bad temper of night before wasn't even in his memory now.

"Thank you, Dave," she said. "That's lovely."

"I hope you slept all right?" he said, sitting at the end of the bed.

"Like a baby," she told him, easing herself up onto the pillows. "I was wrecked. I hope you got some rest too." She checked his face anxiously.

"Not a lot, but what's new?" he laughed without humour. He sat in silence on the edge of the bed, looking out of the window at the black street and the canal below.

Both of them loved the view of the canal and the long wide Georgian street from their bedroom window. Dave especially seemed to like to spend a lot of time sitting on the edge of the bed watching the world outside. She didn't speak to him now as he sat there watching it, and just sipped her tea, grateful for the small silence. The gentle morning intimacy before having to start work.

Dave spoke quietly now.

"I got a weird phone call yesterday."

"Is that why you were upset when I rang?"

"What?"

"When I rang you, on the way home from work. You seemed upset or something."

"What on earth are you talking about?"

Kate drew a breath. "Who was the weird phone call from?"

"It was from Jonathan Domville." He got up off the bed and walked over to the bathroom.

"Jonny Domville?" Her heart had almost stopped. She coughed. "Wow!"

Dave was brushing his teeth at the basin in the tiny en suite just off their big bedroom.

"Well," she carried on, nervously, "that's a surprise then, isn't it? Well, imagine that. After all these years. So, how is he? What did he want? Does he want to get in touch again? Is he still in Africa?"

Kate heard her voice come out of her head at a high squawkish pitch. It sounded shrill, as if it weren't her own. Her face suddenly began to prickle and she took a big gulp of her hot tea too quickly, scalding her tongue.

Dave was busy flossing and hadn't noticed her flushed alertness.

"He seems pretty upset, actually." Dave spoke through a mouthful of toothpaste. "About his wife it seems — they've just had their first baby and it's gone quite badly I gather. Premature I guess. He thought you might have heard something about it?"

Jonny Domville had a *wife*!

She swallowed before saying anything, not wanting to react too suddenly. Sucking on her burnt tongue for a moment. "Don't know any patients in called Domville," she called back to him in a flat, deliberately disinterested tone. But her heart was flapping like a tocograph. "Did he say what had gone wrong? Is the baby ... ?"

"No, I don't think it's the baby who's in trouble. I think it's the wife." She heard him gargle.

He spat. "But I didn't ask for details," he went on. "He was a bit upset, panicked, I think. He rang me from an airport somewhere, on my mobile would you believe – God knows how he got that number. The bloody hospital must have given it to him – they've no respect for privacy outside hours. Anyway he left a message saying that his wife was in Dublin and had gone into labour early so would I ask you to look out for her and that he would be a couple of days getting over to her from Geneva. That's all really." He came back into the room with the bottom half of his face covered in shaving foam. "I have to say though, Kate, I think he's got a cheek just ringing after all these years, looking for favours. It's not like he hasn't got family in Dublin who could help him . . ." Dave's voice became muffled again as he went back into the bathroom and began to shave.

"Perhaps he wanted to speak to me," she said in a cautious voice. "Because of the obstetrics side of things," she added.

Dave flushed the toilet and there was a pause before she heard him speak again.

"I felt sorry for him, actually," she heard him say above the noise of the water. "I just got the message and I wasn't going to reply." Dave came back in to the bedroom with one half of his chin shaved and the other in a beard of white. "But he seemed too distressed. So I rang him back and then he couldn't talk. He was busy organising a plane, I guess. He'll be in Dublin by tomorrow though, he said. He was hinting that we should meet up, of course, but I'm not going there. Not after all this time." He turned back to his toilet.

Kate nodded silently. Jonny Domville. She took a deep breath, and then put her teacup down.

"So, does this mean that you two are on speaking terms again, or not?" she asked him lightly when he came back into the room rubbing his face with a towel. He smelt gorgeous. Something very floral and citrussy and clean. She smiled at him. It was great to see him looking happy and awake and fresh, even if he was a bit put out over Jonny.

"Jesus, Kate! That was all Jonny's stuff — that was *never* anything to do with me!"

Kate said nothing. She had never spoken properly to Dave about what had happened in Kenya between him and Jonny. And she certainly wasn't going to start all of that up again now. Dave could become moody and depressed so easily nowadays and they were both so busy, she tended to cling on to every moment that they had together where neither of them were too tired or too cranky, and especially when Dave was feeling happy and relaxed — relatively speaking.

"Well, it would be very nice indeed to see him again, if he is coming over," she said instead. "And I'll have to try to find out about his wife. We didn't even know he'd got married, did we? Or did you know?" She looked at Dave who was pulling on underpants. He shook his head.

"You know, he did speak to me one more time after we got back from Africa," he said very quietly now. "It was the day we graduated. That was the last time I saw him of course, as he didn't come to our wedding. But I've only just remembered it now." He looked at her. "I've just remembered what he said. They were taking our photograph and he came over and said just this one thing. He said: 'Make sure you always look after Kate.' And then he went. Strange thing to say, for him. Wasn't it?" He smiled at her and reached out to ruffle her hair.

His hand felt awkward and suddenly unfamiliar on her head.

She swallowed. "I'll ring around and see what has happened to his wife, and go and see the baby," she said, thinking rapidly. And then she remembered something else. "Dave, is it their first?"

"Jesus, I haven't got a clue."

"What is her first name, Dave?" she asked him with false lightness.

"What?"

"What's Jonny's wife called? Do you know?"

"God, I've no idea. Mrs Domville, I suppose. He said that she was in ICU."

"ICU!" she said, echoing him.

It was too much to be a coincidence.

Madame Marianne Le Normand post-hysterectomy. Geneva. Switzerland. Oh, of course it was!

Kate's mouth went completely dry.

She swallowed carefully, trying to make it moist again but it was like swallowing razor blades.

"Dave, you said Geneva, didn't you?" Her voice sounded completely hollow. "Dave, was that where you said Jonny rang you from?" Prickles underneath her chest.

"Yes, that's where he lives. He works for the World Health Organisation, don't you remember? He left clinical medicine." He paused. "He's an epidemiologist, or some poncy thing like that," he muttered combing through his hair.

"Oh, dear God, Dave . . ." She put her face into her hands.

"What's wrong?" Dave turned around to face her. For a moment she wondered if he was annoyed. But his face was tender.

He sat down on the bed beside her and she curled her knees up underneath her face.

"Dave," Kate moaned into her knees, "this is what I've been trying to tell you about! If what I think is true, I delivered Jonny's wife last night. Jonny's wife has had an absolutely *disastrous* delivery! And it was one of mine!"

Kate and Caroline Gilmore grew up in Kildare. Their father, Commandant Charles Gilmore, was hardly ever there. For most of the eighties and nineties he chose overseas missions, in Lebanon, Western Sahara and Kosovo.

Charles Gilmore was the sort of man that in a different social or political circle might have been called a feminist. He tended to treat his two daughters with the same gravity other fathers hold for sons. Although Kate's mother Sadie had always been a beacon of femininity to him, Charles' influence over the upbringing and character development of their girls had outpaced his wife's at almost every step of the way, despite his frequent absences.

Kate and Caroline adored their father. They worshipped his military status. They respected deeply the prickly authority of his green uniform. Kate would pull his cap off and stroke her father's crew cut as if it were the fur of a pet cat, when she (at the age of nine) sat curled up on his lap. She loved to count his medals (he had two: one for Israel, and the second for the Lebanon). And she had always particularly enjoyed examining his guns.

"I want Captain Sarsfield to get a bravery medal too," Kate had solemnly told her father at the age of twelve, putting the glittery medals back in their box.

Captain Sarsfield was Kate's Action Man doll. Charles and Sadie had made a calculated lifestyle decision for the sisters when they were little, *against* Sindy and Barbie.

"You're too old to be playing with dolls – even soldier dolls!" Charles brushed her thick fringe out of her eyes. "And you need another haircut!"

"I know," Kate grinned at him.

At twelve, she clearly was too old for dolls but she still kept up the dialogue about the adventures of Captain Sarsfield for her father. Charles was off to Syria again, which made Kate want to sit up on his lap like a two-year-old despite herself, and rest her face against his rougher neck and smell the oily wool scent from his uniform.

"You'll get on very well at boarding school," Charles tucked her short dark hair behind her ears, "but keep a good and beady eye on Caroline. She's not half as sensible as you are."

"Neither of us is *sensible*, Daddy," Kate closed her eyes against her father's skin, smelling the sharp clean soap from him. "I'm mad and wild and completely out of control, you see – it's just that Caroline is a *lot lot* worse."

The Gilmores bought a townhouse just off Baggot Street in the 1980s which Charles had sensibly predicted would become a useful base in the city should his daughters become Dublin students. His prediction was correct in Kate's case and so the house in Percy Place became a den of student smoke-filled occupation in the 90s while Kate studied medicine at UCD.

And so it was in Number 92 Percy Place that Kate Gilmore spent her student days with Dave Hardiman and Jonny Domville, both med students who were at The Royal College of Surgeons.

Kate had known Dave before she started university. He was a neighbour in the Kildare countryside, although unlike Kate and Caroline he'd gone to Clongowes Wood for school. But in a neighbourhood of three houses along a country lane of two miles' hedgerow with acres of green fields, paddocks and stables in between, a neighbour of the same age group and the opposite gender may become very close indeed.

Perhaps it was due to Kate's tomboyishness and what she privately perceived as a rather undesirable lack of femininity, that Sadie Gilmore did not in any way appreciate the effect that her daughter Kate had on teenage boys and in particular on Dave Hardiman. Dave was a rugby-playing lad: the sort of man that Sadie admired for his straight back and large healthy appetite. Sadie was herself a picky, troubled eater who spent most of her time reading slimming magazines, but she was sufficiently aware of her own food issues to know that Caroline had problems. Nevertheless, although Kate seemed to eat whatever it was that she was given, Sadie was always greatly pleased to have one of the Hardimans around the house whenever they were home, to pile scones and sandwiches onto *his* plate and hand him fruit cakes, apple pie and biscuits.

Perhaps it was because Sadie enjoyed the masculine presence of Dave Hardiman while her husband was away – or perhaps she simply was too distracted by her own loneliness to notice that Kate was encouraging an obsessive flirtation with him – but either way Sadie did not seem to mind in the slightest that Kate spent long hours with him in seclusion. Meanwhile, Kate was busily making him feel that he loved her beyond belief.

Dave was not Kate's first lover. She had fallen in love at the age of fifteen with another boy after a school disco and had enjoyed a brief romance, discovering the taste of semen and the smell of condoms. But when she returned for the final year she discovered that the other boy had left for university, which left her with Dave Hardiman, the son of her mother's nearest friends, to continue her experiments in sex.

At the age of sixteen, Kate was aware of the effect that she'd had for many months on Dave. She knew that he could barely take his eyes off her, bewitched by her tiny bra-less breasts under a white tee-shirt and bare brown summer's neck and throat while they sat on the floor of her bedroom at the end of the long bungalow listening to REM and Simply Red. Dave's favourite band was

Simply Red, which Kate understood to be a symptom of his lovesickness.

She let him work himself into a frenzy of desire, lolling on the floor, her long slim brown legs outstretched in denim shorts, her polo shirt unbuttoned, enjoying his wide-eyed attempts at solemn conversation concerning guitar bands, while she lazily watched his pupils dilate.

Kate regarded Dave's lust as hugely rewarding. She smiled at him when his voice cracked with dryness.

But she did not want to rush *into* anything with Dave Hardiman.

In fact, she did not particularly find him to be attractive. Dave was big and over-burly as far as she was concerned. His thick and dark-blond hair was a boring colour, his skin too pale and freckled and his face was far too wide. Kate preferred darker boys who were slight in build. But for the moment, she was seriously flattered by Dave's obvious desire for her, and therefore spent several months enjoying her status as temptress.

One night after he had allowed himself to stay on in her bedroom long after his normal curfew of midnight, she finally reached up on tiptoe and kissed him slowly on the lips.

She was surprised at the sudden chasteness of the kiss that Dave had returned. She had in fact expected a *lot* more passion, given the serious efforts she had put into teasing him and playing with his emotions. But it was a kiss nonetheless and so she let him undress her and lose *his* virginity in a brisk ten seconds flat, and then make his own damp way on home. She was puzzled at his sudden underwhelmed desire, but not shaken by it.

And of course Dave would kiss her often enough again, she was to discover. Because at university she had always found that whenever she was alone and drunk at the end of a long night of partying, there was always Dave.

Kate's sister Caroline left Newbridge College with a modest Leaving Cert and, following an earlier flirtation with anorexia nervosa, became a photographic model in London, eventually moving to Los Angeles. She and Kate spoke infrequently by phone – about what exactly, Kate was becoming increasingly unsure. But she adored Caroline.

Although she would always find Dave to be a strange, dispassionate lover, who seemed to spend far more time *talking* about his feelings than putting them into action, given the circumstances in which she would eventually marry him Kate would tell herself that Dave's preference for polemic rather than passion was evidence of the solidity of his love for her, compared to that of Jonny.

Where Dave was cold and calculated in his lovemaking, Jonny was passionate – but ultimately rejecting.

Dave Hardiman and Jonny Domville were both from wealthy families.

"Rich kids who're thick," was what Kate mocked them, because they were studying at a more expensive university. But, of course, Dave and Jonny were very far from thick. They merely had the means and the background that Kate didn't have, to gain access into the more reliably lucrative world of establishment medicine. At some level Kate felt rather jealous of the two boys' superior prospects, compared to her own. Although Charles was adoring and supportive, he was not particularly *around*, and the Gilmores were not, compared to Jonnys' and Dave's families, well off. And although her mother Sadie was both helpful and uninterfering, she was quite useless to Kate from a career point of view.

Jonny Domville's father was a professor of psychiatry, which made him a career manager in a bag as far as Dave was concerned – although Jonny's Ballsbridge family were actually more *arty* than upper-class.

Dave's father, Paddy Hardiman, ran a stud farm.

At college, Dave and Jonny lived in rooms off Stephen's Green at the Mercer's building. But for six years of college all three of them spent most of their time at Number 92 Percy Place, smoking cigarettes and drinking tea in Kate Gilmore's kitchen.

Boarding-school education had given both Kate and Dave an interest in music and an instrument to play – in Kate's case it was piano and in Dave's a violin. But he didn't keep up much practice after college.

The lady who had owned Percy Place before them (whom they had nicknamed Mrs Mad Devine after they had discovered her vast collection of photographs of Padre Pio, the coal she kept underneath the bath tub, and the scratch marks she had left on the bedroom window, which she had tried to climb out of one night before being carted off to a nursing home), had left a piano in the house that Kate would sometimes still play. The piano was quite out of tune, but when Jonny Domville discovered it, and what he called its Tom Waits quality, he fell in love with it. And Jonny *was* a musician.

In fact, Kate began to fall in love with Jonathan Domville at the age of seventeen in first year of university more or less *because* he was a musician. He was known around the College of Surgeons as either Jonny D or Saxman. And although Kate had always thought that the saxophone was a bit of a cheesy eighties ska-band instrument, she soon learnt that between Jonny's lips it was a love affair.

"Not many trumpet players bother with the sax," he grinned at her. "They tend to despise it for some reason. Then again, for some reason I've always been bound to love something that somebody else despises."

Playing a duet on an out-of-tune piano, even with a musician as well-motivated as Jonny Domville, was a trial that required a lot of alcohol in order to produce forgiveness. And so forgive they did, simply retuning the expectation of the educated ear to allow for the one-and-a-half or almost two semi-tones that the piano had slipped out of key. Jonny was a good transposer anyway. You had to be, to be able to go from sax to trumpet to piano and then back again. Dave, of course, was too much out of practice to contemplate the jazz trio Jonathan had in mind. And in any case the tuning difficulties would have been impossible for him.

Kate, like most piano players, had only been classically trained. And so when she first met Jonny, she couldn't play by ear and needed music and a good bit of practice before she could hammer out any sort of tune.

The first time she met Jonny was on New Year's Eve in their first year. The weather was rapidly freezing. Dave turned up at Percy Place with his new best friend Jonathan at nine o'clock, saying that the two of them were on the prowl, looking for somewhere fun to go drinking. But then it had begun to snow, most unusually for Dublin on the first of January, and the house was icy cold. Kate lit a fire in the big front sitting-room for a change (normally they only lit a fire in the back room to watch TV in and the kitchen was always warm enough because it had an oily-smelling range). And as the snow thickened and became beautiful outside and the likelihood of an adventure up the road to Smyth's pub became more distant, Dave offered to run up to the off-licence to get a bottle of whiskey that the three of them could polish off by the fire and enjoy the sight of snow fall on the black canal outside.

At first sight, Kate was not particularly interested romantically in Dave's new best friend Jonny Domville. She'd had to listen to Dave talking non-stop about what she assumed would be the rather weedy son of a psychiatrist that he was now sharing rooms with, and getting to know him wasn't exactly the first of her resolutions that New Year's Eve.

And Jonny slipped quietly into the house that night

in Dave's bigger shadow. He sat silent, smoking a Marlboro by the window that overlooked the white-banked canal while Dave gabbed on and on about whether or not the lads would be over in The Swan tonight and whether or not it would be worth their while struggling all the way up Mount Street in the snow to get there. What she thought initially was that Jonny Domville seemed to be overly shy – quite sweet-natured, but that that was probably all there was to him – and so she happily let Dave do all the talking, and was even disappointed when Dave offered to go up to Smyth's on his own and get a bottle off-licence, leaving her with Jonny and the fire.

"Mind if I play the piano?" was the first thing Jonny said to her, to her great surprise. Maybe he wasn't so shy after all, she thought, watching him cross the room and slide onto the piano stool with what appeared to be relief. Not many people offer to play the piano before even starting up a conversation, but you had to admit it was pretty cool of him to get stuck in. And so while Dave struggled up to Ranelagh (Smyth's would not sell him anything off-licence on New Year's Eve and so the nearest still-open bottle shop was three bridges of the canal away that night), Kate sat in the small armchair by the fire and listened while Jonny Domville made her second-hand honky-tonk piano sound like heaven.

"How come you play so much jazz music?" she asked him quietly.

Jazz was a music that belonged to the beyond-middle-aged, Kate had previously thought. It belonged to her grandparents' generation. She was just astonished to hear the sort of tunes Jonny was interested in. "Autumn Leaves" – "Someone to Watch Over Me" – "All of Me" –"Fly Me to the Moon".

Cigarette clenched between his lips, neat thin long fingers spanning the keyboard.

"Well, I'm a sax and trumpet player, mostly," Jonny Domville said, squinting eyes creased up against the smoke, and he withdrew his cigarette and placed it on the piano's mahogany lid while continuing to play.

Kate's mother Sadie would have died if she could have seen a piano with a burning cigarette resting on it, in her daughter's sitting-room.

But Kate let the cigarette burn on while she watched him, gently wondering if it would leave a mark on the mahogany of the piano, and finding it almost agreeable that it did.

"Can you play *everything* by ear?" she asked him. She was green with envy. Jonny's music seemed to simply pour out of his fingers, whereas she would have to practise for weeks to be able to play something to performance standard.

"Playing by ear isn't difficult, you know – you just need to practise to get the hang of it," was what he told her. "You need to be familiar with the instrument, and just get to know what it sounds like. Then it's all a bit like learning any language. At first you need the grammar book and the dictionary – but if you only ever stick to that, you'll never learn to speak it fluently. You need to immerse yourself in it, just like children do. Like you do when you go to live abroad. After a while you just find yourself speaking it fluently. You start to think a different way."

"Show me, please?" she asked him, sliding onto the duet stool beside him.

"Show you now? How to play the piano?" he smiled at her.

"How to play by ear. I can read music. But show me how to improvise – how to play jazz music. I can play scales and exam stuff and all that. Show me how you know what chords to play."

"Jazz sounds are all in sevenths," Jonny told her, rescuing his cigarette from the top of the piano, trying to get one final drag of it and then flipping it into the fireplace. "I guess that it's all about getting the rhythm going and finding the right harmony and using the right sounds. Look, let's say for example, 'Jingle Bells'. I know it's almost January," he grinned at her, " but this is a good tune. Normally, you have 'Jingle Bells' like this," and he played a child–like version of the Christmas carol on her honky tonk piano, in a quick trot time. "Now, let's say we are going to write a jazz version, we'll use the seventh of the chord all the time, and mess with the rhythm, something like this."

Kate watched his long slender fingers meander through the song. She concentrated hard, trying to get the hang of the idea of the seventh chord, listening for the familiar tune in the music he was playing. It seemed somehow as if Jonny had turned her broken piano into a musical instrument.

"No pedal, also, that's the trick. That way you have to make the instrument *sing* for you." Jonny winked at her and changed the tune to "We Wish You A Merry Christmas", and after a few bars of that, to Gershwin's "Summertime". "Here, you have a go. Let's try 'Summertime'. It's an easy one, in A Minor." He put his arm around her, showing her the A minor seventh chord on the piano, and then the E major seventh. "Look how it goes from here. D minor seventh, F seventh, G seventh, B seventh, easy really. You can write it down if it helps. And then you start to get the hang of it, like this."

He played a few bars of "Summertime" in a fast New Orleans rhythm, and Kate slapped his arm.

"You big show off!" she squealed.

"Just kidding. Look, you have a go. A minor seventh, then E seventh, and go on."

In a very deep voice, he sang the words of "Summertime", while she played and picked out the chords.

"Now, let's pick up the rhythm a bit. It is jazz music after all, not a funeral march. You need to stick the chords in on the off-beats, make it seem a bit *unexpected*-sounding."

Kate followed his instruction, concentrating carefully on the ideas that were musically so new to her. On her previously almost unplayable piano, the jazz chords sounded almost beautiful.

"Tom Waits' piano," Jonny winked at her.

She fell in love with him there and then.

"Did you say you've got a trumpet too?" Kate felt her heart beat faster, in the firelight heat rising into her throat.

"And a sax. We'll have to start playing duets together," Jonny smiled, lighting up another fag.

The front door whined open and they heard footsteps stamping snow off in the hall.

His eyes were green, Kate noticed. Even though the room was only lit by firelight, she could see that they were green just like her own, although Jonny's were a browner green than hers, which people said looked sometimes almost blue.

"We've almost got the same colour eyes as each other – did you notice that?" she whispered to him and put her hand on his. His face was only inches away from hers.

"Dave's back now," he replied.

4

The corridor to the ICU had never seemed longer to her. Kate walked as slowly as she could, her mind carefully running through what she was going to say.

Kate decided that she would feel more in control in her theatre scrubs with her paper hat still on. There is a certain anonymity in uniform, she thought, as she stopped outside the big swing doors of the ICU to scrub up her hands and spray on antiseptic gel. She checked her appearance in the mirror at the sink and forced a tiny smile to reassure herself. It's going to be all right. You can do this.

Kate walked backwards through the double doors and into the ICU. The heat was more intense in here and she stood a moment taking in the hissing, humming stillness of the place.

Marianne, Jonny's wife, was right at the far end of the ward.

Nick Farrelly was standing at the end of her bed, writing up his notes. Marianne had just been extubated and Kate approached the bedside cautiously and nodded hello to Nick who had a stethoscope in his ears. He took it out and beamed at her.

"Hey there, Kate. Nice to see you. How are you?"

"Not too bad. How are things coming along here?" Kate worked hard to smile at Marianne.

"We are just finishing up now. Marianne's extubation has gone very well, so we are getting all geared up to transfer her to the ward tomorrow."

Kate nodded. "Good," she said.

"Is that throat feeling all right now, Marianne, since we took the tube out, or would you like more ice to suck?" he asked her.

Marianne Le Normand's honey-coloured hair had been tied back off her ghostly face and brushed into a neat pony tail. Her pale face was expressionless. Her huge brown eyes were dull. Kate decided that she'd wait to let her answer Nick's question about her sore throat before she introduced herself. Marianne brought up a hand that had an oxygen saturation clip on one finger like a clothes-peg, to stroke her throat and spoke in a hoarse, barely audible voice.

"*Ça pique*," she whispered.

"Yes, I'm sorry about that," Nick nodded at her. "It will settle down very soon. I'll get the nurses to bring you some more ice to suck."

He put down the clipboard on the bed-table and turned back to Kate.

"Give us a shout later on, Kate, and I'll come back down again tomorrow and see how she's doing."

Kate nodded. Then she turned to face Marianne Le Normand and said as gently as she could, "Marianne, there's something very important that I need to talk to you about. Do you mind if I sit here with you for a minute?" She pointed at a chair.

Marianne shook her head but her eyes did not engage. Kate stepped over a tangle of plugs and electric cables, almost kicking Marianne's catheter bag over as she moved towards the chair where she could sit down and speak quietly to her.

Most of the time obstetrics is good news. And most of the time, when Kate had bad news to give someone, she brought tissues with her. Most of the bad news wasn't about what happened during deliveries: it was about telling someone they had an inoperable and very painful cancer, or telling someone that they'd miscarried a baby they'd been desperate to conceive. And Kate more often than not needed the tissues for herself – she found that tears could be as contagious as laughter. The other staff would tease her about her easy waterworks, but the patients never seemed to mind. But as Kate searched Marianne's face now she wondered if Marianne *was* going to cry. The woman's expression, despite the discomfort she was clearly in, was removed and rather stoically cool. She wondered if she should try to hold Marianne's hand first, before she started telling her what had gone wrong. But Marianne had one hand strapped to an oxygen-saturation monitor and the other was tightly bound to a splint for a blood-filled IV line. She decided that she'd leave her hand nearby to be in easy reach, so she placed it on the bed beside Marianne's strapped-up wrist. But Marianne immediately moved her own hand away.

"Marianne," Kate heard her voice begin, but all of a sudden she couldn't see a patient in a bed with IV lines coming out of her and monitors and ECG electrodes on her chest; she could only see *Jonny's wife*. This wasn't any ordinary patient she was talking to. This situation wasn't something that affected a total stranger. *This is the woman that Jonny Domville loves.*

And I am the woman who's changed everything between them.

Kate's mouth dried up completely and she froze.

In the silence that had swollen now between them, Marianne turned her head slowly round on the pillow to face it towards Kate's. Her expression was still disengaged. Her pupils were pinholes. The ICU ward was intolerably hot. The sound of machines wheezing was becoming unbearable. Yet despite the noise Kate could hear her heart thumping wildly in her chest.

Then Marianne spoke. "Can you please bring for me some ice, nurse?"

Kate opened her mouth to speak, and closed it again. She swallowed. *Marianne thought she was a nurse.* Of course she wouldn't recognise her from the other night. And she was still quite sedated now. She would have to wait until she was stronger to talk about what had gone wrong. Maybe later on tonight, when Nick has moved her back down to the ward. When she was sitting up a bit. When she'd had some sips. She was exhausted now. It wasn't fair to expect her to want to talk about it yet.

Kate briefly touched Marianne's long white fingers, and stood up to go.

"Of course I'll get some ice for you. You poor thing, you must be very thirsty now."

She moved away from Marianne's bed, and walked down to the nurses' station as if in a dream. One of the charge nurses was busy with the roster.

"I think Madame Le Normand would like some ice," Kate heard her own voice saying.

"Well, she'll have to wait a minute so."

She walked through the doors and turned away from all the panic of the ICU. Her pager went off in her pocket like a burglar alarm.

"*Labour ward, Kate, labour ward.*"

In the empty corridor she quickened her steps. She turned sharply to go straight down the stairs.

Although Kate had fallen in love with Jonny while sitting at the piano in the firelight of Percy Place, they would spend four whole years of college together before she would let him know.

At the end of fourth med, everyone was going away for the summer.

Kate was going to California to see Caroline. And Dave and Jonny were going to Kenya. They had signed up for the medical students' Third World Medical Aid Mission and were busy getting vaccinated against Hepatitis B and taking malaria prophylaxis pills.

Caroline was going to Los Angeles, where she was hoping to get into a modelling agency. Kate had decided to go with her to keep an eye on her baby sister (and Caroline was, as far as Kate was concerned, at the age of twenty, still quite a baby).

The exams passed by uneventfully. Summer hit the streets of Dublin in a sudden blaze of light that swelled the park in Stephen's Green with bare arms and bronzed lunchtime limbs stretched out on the grass.

"We'll write to each other every week," Kate promised Dave and Jonny as the three of them lazed under a giant oak. She lay with her head resting on the top of Dave's thighs, closing her eyes to dream in the afternoon heat. Dave was sitting up with his back to the tree trunk, biro leaning on a folder to fill in a questionnaire. She moved a bit to nestle her head up further right into his lap and get even more comfortable, and the sudden development of firmness she felt underneath her neck made her want to wriggle into him even more. The fact that Jonny was there just beside him made it even more erotic.

"Kate, I'm trying to fill in this polio vaccine form, please stop wriggling your head so much," he grumbled.

Kate said, "Sorry, darling!" and wriggled even harder.

Dave was in research mode. While Jonny was being quite gung-ho about the Kenya trip, Dave had been spending time researching African politics and was concerned about the Sudanese civil war.

"I'll get my dad over to bail you out, if you come under gunfire," Kate had promised him.

Dave looked up, alarmed.

"I'm sure that humanitarian workers are always safe, even in conflict areas. They wouldn't send us out there if we weren't safe," Jonny said thoughtfully to him.

"You know they attacked a World Food Programme barge convoy operating in the Nile River basin earlier on this year?" Dave prodded Jonny with his foot. Kate frowned. "Although," he added, noticing her worried look, "everything is very safe in the village that we're going to."

"I'm more interested in where we're going tonight to celebrate the end of term," Jonny interrupted. "I fancy a night of triple therapy – Swan, Rio's, Leggs and then breakfast at Bewley's at two in the morning, if that's all right with you two."

They ended up in The Pod.

Kate had had a skinful in Hartigan's before she met the others in The Swan and was effervescent, but not uncontrollably so. She was desperately excited about Los Angeles, and was flying out the following evening to Heathrow to pick up Caroline at Terminal Four and get on a night flight directly to LA. In Percy Place her bags were packed and lined up in the hallway and so she wasn't even *trying* to prevent a hangover.

In The Swan, Jonny bought her several pints of

Guinness before she begged him to stop plying her with booze, and so he bought her a large gin and tonic. They were in fits of giggles by the time they got to The Pod, and Kate was having to get Jonny to hold her up.

At the nightclub she lost sight of Dave who had disappeared into a rugby crowd that he'd recognised as soon as they staggered in past the bouncers. But Kate didn't mind tonight. Usually she liked to keep Dave close at hand when she was out on the town with the boys because he would always see her safely home again, and also because if she were ever in between boyfriends, Dave would *always* be obliging.

But tonight, Jonny had been very attentive in the pub and all day long really since their lunchtime snoozing in the park. He seemed to be behaving somehow differently towards her, as if he were in some way emotionally responding to the fact that they were all saying goodbye for the summer and the next time that they would be together would be as final meds, on the way to internship. And now she and Jonny were alone together in the nightclub, pressed into a hot dark corner giggling drunkenly together for the last night of the term.

The band was playing a Bob Dylan song.

"My parents have this record," Jonny smiled at her. "My dad was an old hippy in the seventies. They bought this Dylan album the year I was born. 'Tangled Up In Blue', it's called."

She laughed at his attempt to sing along, mimicking

Dylan's raspy voice. And then she noticed that he was singing with real feeling. He knew all the words.

"What's this song about?" she asked him. He looked at her and the tenderness in his eyes made her want to hold her breath.

"It's about a love triangle."

Jonny bent his head towards her so that she could hear him and she shivered even though his breath was hot on her neck.

"It's about a guy who helps a girl he knows to run away from her husband – but he's really doing it because he's in love with her. And then after she gets divorced, he goes back to find her to see if she remembers him."

"And does she? Remember him? Do they end up together?" Her eyes implored his.

"It's hard to tell." Jonny ran a finger down her cheek. "But right now, I'd like to dance with you."

"We've never really done that before," she said. And it was true. She and Jonny had never danced together. Dave was always the one who'd be out on the floor.

He said, "Then it's time."

Jonny kissed her open neck while he danced with her. Despite her alcoholic blur, every caress his hands made on her body was electric. When she lifted her lips up to meet his she didn't have far to reach, unlike with Dave who was over a foot taller than she was.

Jonny's body was slimmer and smaller, but it seemed as though he had been physically made to fit with Kate's body completely. His mouth felt perfect. His tongue was just right in her mouth, it tasted her with just the right amount of tenderness.

She reached up to his head to caress his neck and hold his head while she kissed him desperately, almost forgetting that they were in a public place. At the end of the kiss she let him hold her face closely into his throat while he kissed the top of her head as if she were a child.

And by the time the lights came on at the end of the night, she'd almost forgotten that Dave had been there with them all along.

She would have gladly forgotten Dave forever. Except that he could not forget. And he *never* would forget the sight of Kate and Jonny, deep in one another's arms in the centre of a room surrounded by his friends, obviously in love.

"I need to talk to you, Kate." Dave's voice was broken.

She stood apart from Jonny miserably, knowing completely what it was that Dave was going to say.

It had suddenly become the most bewilderingly horrible night of her life.

She tried to hold on to Jonny's hand while he stumbled away from her, but he let go, his long slender fingers easily letting go of hers.

"Please, I need to talk to you, Kate," Dave had begged her. His voice was choked with tears.

"Dave, don't do this!" She felt tears begin to swell in her eyes. They had all had far too much to drink.

Dave would not be able to control his emotions so

full of drink and she would not be capable of rational discussion. She wanted Dave to go home without her. She wanted Jonny more than she had ever wanted any man before.

"Please go home, Dave," she told him, steadying her voice.

"I'm not going anywhere without you!" She felt humiliated for him. "Kate, please don't do this to me. I can't live without you. I'll die without you. Please! Please don't go to him."

He had raised his voice, embarrassing her. She knew that people were standing watching and she put her hand up to cover his mouth, to try to stop him making things worse.

"Please, Dave, not now. Please go home!" she said.

He backed away from her.

"I don't expect you to be faithful to me, Kate," he was sobbing now. "I've never asked you to go steady with me or marry me or anything like that, but please, please don't go to Jonny now! Not my friend! Not Jonny. Please, please don't do this to me, Kate! It would kill me completely."

"Dave, please go home, you're drunk and emotional," she begged him again.

She did love Dave very much, she knew. He was her best friend ever. He had always been there for her. He *had* always loved her. But she wanted Jonny now.

She wanted Jonny desperately, and if she didn't have a chance with him now, tonight, she might never have again.

But when she turned around to seek him, to take Jonny's hand and try to make him talk to Dave, to make him see some sense and bring the three of them back together again – Jonny had already gone.

The following morning she flew to Los Angeles, and Dave and Jonny left for Kenya.

5

The morning of the Perinatal Morbidity and Mortality Meeting, Kate woke up a full half-hour before her alarm went off. She lay in the dark, listening to the whizz of traffic just outside and the roar of the canal flowing over the lock. Normally she looked forward to these routine meetings when all the medical staff of the maternity wing met to discuss the birth-rate statistics for the month. She enjoyed the banter, the mild teasing that went on between surgeons and paediatricians, the hammering the doctors got from the midwives and the eager students vigorously taking notes. But today her stomach felt eaten up with nerves.

Dave, of course, had overslept and was furious.

"I can't believe you lay there dreaming away to yourself and didn't bother to wake me!" he whined at her, and thumped downstairs.

She shuddered in her bed as he barged out of the front door at half past seven instead of his usual time of ten to seven, and then the house went quiet again.

Kate sat bolt upright and switched on the radio to get the news, then switched it off again because it was all about the budget and she was depressed enough already.

Her head hurt and she felt almost nauseated.

She had a quick bath and pulled on a new grey silk jersey dress that was neat and came just to the knee and clung to her slim figure, fastening it with a wide clinch belt. Dave had told her she looked gorgeous in it. Kate didn't usually wear dresses or skirts either to work or on weekends, but she had bought this one recently with a view to having something serious enough to wear the next time she had to give a paper at a meeting. And although today's Perinatal Morbidity and Mortality didn't exactly count as giving a paper at a meeting, she felt she needed all the ammunition she could get.

Besides, she looked quite sexy in the dress, she thought, and if Jonny happened to be arriving in the hospital that morning, there was no harm in looking halfway decent for him.

And then she baulked at her reflection.

Jesus, what am I like!

Kate stared at her reflection in the bathroom mirror in horror. *What on earth am I thinking about looking sexy for a patient's husband who's going to have to deal with this kind of news?*

She frowned at herself and her cheeks burned in

shame. She brushed her teeth ferociously and decided against lipstick. The dress was enough of a statement.

Kate stood a moment in the kitchen not sure whether or not to try to eat something. She felt unable to stomach breakfast and so she made a pot of coffee with the little Moka that her father Charles had sent over to her from Italy last month for her birthday, and peeled a mandarin.

Outside the kitchen window on the canal bank people strode purposefully, swinging briefcases in their pinstriped pencil skirts with chunky-looking trainers underneath. Kate stood a moment while she munched her mandarin, watching the view that she loved to look at every morning: the incongruous combination of ducks, water reeds and business suits on their way to work.

She swallowed down two Paracetamol with half a cup of too-hot coffee and then grabbed her Italian leather briefcase from the landing, whirling out of the house without setting the burglar alarm.

She only just remembered the alarm as she revved the Mini towards a green traffic light across the Huband Bridge but decided she that wasn't going back now. To hell with flipping burglar alarms. Dave would kill her if he found out of course, but she'd deal with all that later. This Perinatal Morbidity and Mortality meeting had been looming up all day yesterday like an execution date. What she needed now was just to get out of the house, get into the hospital, and get it over with.

The worst thing was that everybody had been so nice to her at work all day yesterday. It was unnerving. Even the bitchiest midwives were being polite. The Prof had been subdued during his short debriefing with her, and he'd been very solemn with her ever since, which was a terrifyingly pleasant change from puerile.

Nick Farrelly was even cheekier than usual, trying hard to keep her giggling with ever more ridiculous puns.

"What's the difference between a nurse and a helicopter?" he had asked her yesterday over coffee.

She'd raised her eyebrows.

"Not everybody's been up in a helicopter!" Nick snorted, and she'd frowned because Sharon was there, but then both she and Sharon had creased up laughing.

To be fair, Kate thought, everyone was probably just a bit over-excited because it was almost Christmas and the "Res party" was on tomorrow night. Nick and Ronan had gone drinking without her after the theatre list on Wednesday night, but that was just their idea of gathering momentum in anticipation, Nick had said. She couldn't help worrying now that people were perhaps being too *obviously* nice to her. Even Natasha, the often lugubrious labour-ward midwife had been sweet-natured to her yesterday.

It was all a bit suspicious. She was bound to be in for a complete hockeying at the M and M today.

Ronan Clare was being an absolute angel, giving her solemn updates several times a day about how well Baby Le Normand was doing.

But she hadn't said a word to Ronan, or to anyone, about how well she knew the baby's father. She had just nodded and feigned vague polite interest in Ronan's reassuring remarks, as if Marianne Le Normand was just another tricky patient making a slow but steady recovery.

But the worst thing was that she hadn't got to talk to Marianne properly yesterday about the hysterectomy. The labour ward had been hopping all day long, and by the time she'd got to go back up to ICU, Marianne was fast asleep.

I'll talk to her first thing as soon as I get in today – I have to – and I will, Kate thought, swinging her Mini Cooper into the car park. At least, I'll talk to her as soon as the M and M is over, she re-decided. I'll be in a much better state by then.

Ronan had been impressed to find Kate hanging around the paediatric unit all day yesterday. He was amazed to find she was becoming so seriously interested in the work that he was doing on the baby and seemed almost touched by her attention to follow-up.

Kate went along with Ronan's assumption that she was just fascinated with his job. But the truth was that she had been to the SCBU an embarrassing four times since Marianne's delivery, and watched with panic, and then with some hope, and then joy when the tight corner seemed to have been finally turned. Ronan's pink and chubby face beamed whenever she popped into SCBU. Poor Ro was such a dote and she felt awful being less than honest with him. But at least he was chuffed by the attention she was paying to Jonny's tiny baby's determination to keep going.

Kate went straight down the stairs to the doctor's Res now as soon as she arrived at the hospital – she didn't want to go near the general wards until the M and M was over. She would go straight up to Marianne after the meeting, she decided, and have a proper long chat with her then – she could do the rest of her rounds after lunch, they were much less important.

She made a few phone calls to explain she'd be around later to the various wards and did a quick run through the labour ward before sitting back down alone in the kitchen of the Res again to drink a quiet cup of coffee and check through her PowerPoint.

Kate sat at the round table in the middle of the Res kitchen with her laptop, stroking the keys, scrolling through the data. She was well enough prepared, that wasn't the problem. She felt disarmed somehow, not knowing how the patient felt. The phone began to ring and Kate stared at it, wishing it to stop. She wasn't even on call today but she had her pager on her and the labour ward could use that if there was a real emergency.

She let the phone ring an irritating ten more times and then someone from down the corridor yelled at her, "Jesus, whoever is in the kitchen, will you pick that up? I'm trying to sleep!" and so she leaped up with guilty horror and snatched the receiver up.

It was Ronan.

"Ah, sorry, Kate, did I take you away from something?

But I heard you were in the Res and I didn't want to bleep you. Look, I just wanted to tell you you've got nothing to worry about any more," he told her with mild excitment. "I thought I'd let you know before the meeting."

"What do you mean?" she asked him with some caution.

"Baby *Lunnermond* is making great progress." Ro's French accent wasn't even bothered. "She's had a rough old start, but her oxygen sats and vitals are perfect this morning, and her X-ray has improved massively. So you can stop worrying now, Katie-cakes. You've done everything you can." He sounded as if he were announcing a mildly satisfactory sports result, not a life and death decision, she thought moodily to herself and then regretted the ingratitude. For Ronan it was just another patient. He wasn't personally involved.

"Thanks, Ronan, you're a star," she told him but her breath had caught in her chest. *And when are you going to get to talk to Marianne about the cock-up in theatre?* She heard again the horrible self-doubting voice that she'd begun to hear so often in the past few days, screaming at her inside her head. She took a breath.

"Ronan," she mumbled *sotto voce* into the phone, aware that the person who'd yelled at her to be quiet was probably still awake, "I feel as though I'm beginning to lose control over – things," she finished in a whisper.

"You are in my hat!" he yelped at her.

Then she heard his bleeper going off.

"You're a fucking hero, Gilmore!" she could hear him

say through the background rattle of the nasal electronic voice. She held the receiver away from her ear. "You saved two patients' lives that night, not one, and you should be proud of that. Come on in to the firing squad and we'll bring it on!"

He had made her laugh. She couldn't help it. But maybe he was right. She had saved Marianne's life. That was the bottom line. No matter what, Jonny at least would be able to see that when he arrived that day.

And it was still only ten o'clock. She would go straight to the post-natal ward to see Marianne, after the M and M.

"We are discussing your case with the rest of the team this morning," the *professeur* said to Marianne.

"Team?" She tried to speak a little louder and say it again, as he'd just ignored her and returned to his notes. "Team?" she said again. He was still ignoring her! Her voice was far too dry. She reached out with a shaking hand to take a glass of water from the little table beside her bed – oh, water at room temperature, in this place, it would be disgusting! – and knocked the glass of water on the floor.

"Whoops-a-daisy!" said the *professeur*.

Whoops-a-daisy? What on earth does that mean?

But now the nurse was beckoning someone over to clean up the mess. "Sorry," said Marianne, and waited for the cleaning woman to pour her out another glass. "Thank you. Do you have some ice?"

"No." The cleaning woman left.

"I'll get you ice." The nurse was smiling now and she winked at Marianne. Yes, winked. Astonishing. A nurse who winks. Am I seeing things again? Yesterday, when she looked out of the window she saw the tram covered in snakes as it crawled around the corner by the hospital. She'd told the nurse about it, and the nurse had said, "We'll ease up on the morphine so," and Marianne hadn't been quite sure what that had meant either – but things were definitely feeling more normal today. More discomfort, yes, but more normality too. And the baby – oh, if only she could see the baby too! She must ask to see the baby now.

She turned her attention to the professor again and swallowed very carefully, trying to think about what to say. He was busy reading notes, marking the chart with his pen. He looked up at her at last.

"Any questions so? Before I go?" he said.

She opened her mouth and tried to make the words come out. How to formulate the question. How long will I be disabled like this? I can't move – when will I be able to move again? Can you promise me that my baby will be perfect? Can I have more children? Is there any possibility? Will I ever be the same again?

"Can I – is the baby perfect to see?" she began. No! That wasn't even proper English. She tried to swallow again. The throat! It was so painful!

"She is doing very well. She needs a lot of help but she is in good hands."

"Good." *I love her! I love her so much!* He was looking impatient now.

She licked her lips. A whisper eventually came out. "Can I have more children?"

He was shaking his head. "No, Marianne. We did everything we could. I'm sorry about that."

Ask him to explain again.

"*Pas de tout? Euh* – not at all?"

He looked at the nurse.

"I am finished with this one?" she said, this time to the nurse. The nurse looked at him.

He looked back at Marianne. "Yes, I'm afraid you are," he said. "We had to remove your womb. We did everything we could, but in emergencies – things happen very quickly in obstetrics."

Things happen very quickly. Yes. The nurse was holding onto her hand now, but she wanted her to let it go. She did not want to be touched. She wanted to be alone. To think about herself. And yet – they were staying here to answer her questions. She felt abnormal in the bed, like an insect under scrutiny who has been discovered doing something disgusting underneath a stone. There were three of them standing all around her bed, all waiting for her to speak. It was as if she was being expected to perform – from this diminished place! This place where she did not even recognise herself.

Her body had become unrecognisable to her – the pregnancy had mushroomed it out of shape and given her breasts she didn't recognise, a belly that had life swimming around in it, poking hands and elbows and knees into her ribcage that had irritated and delighted her – and now her belly was another shape, swollen, bandaged with a giant pressure pad, a plastic tube drained blood-stained liquid from her side. Her feet had elastic, hot, horrid nylon stockings on them. Her face was porcelain pale and it itched. Her hand was streaked with blood from where someone had spilt some after puncturing her skin, and her throat had a giant pad over the collarbone covering a wound someone had pierced into her heart – the IV line, the doctor with the spectacles had said, pouring blood – Irish blood – straight into her heart! How ironic! She felt monstrous. And now this information – her womb had been removed.

She felt as though she had been refashioned as if by Frankenstein into a different creature, a creature that couldn't move, a creature that needed a wheelchair to be moved about the place, that needed nurses to lift her arms inside her nightdress, that needed nurses to lift a glass up to her lips, that needed soft pillows around her aching bones, and drugs to help her open her eyes, close her eyes. And yet . . . she was a mother now, wasn't she? Is this what motherhood is like?

No uterus. What was it like inside her female body, then? The place where she'd been a woman, the place where motherhood was designed. That ugly place – that place of pain that held women down with its cycles and its reproductive urge. That place that modelled babies, fed them, shaped them as they grew – her children.

Her uterus, her feeble, wretched uterus that had only been able to produce one child before it gave up on her completely. Only one ever.

And desperately, so overwhelmingly, she loved that precious baby now!

"I have to see the baby." She turned to the nurse. Her eyes filled with tears. Hot tears. They were going to spill out. In front of everyone. "I have to see the baby now!" What if the baby wasn't real? She had to see the baby! She had to see the baby now!

"We'll get you up as soon as possible," the nurse smiled back. "I'll come with you."

Marianne let hot tears fall and tried to lift a hand to wipe them but her hand was too weak, strapped down to the drip splint. "All right. Thank you."

The nurse nodded and they left.

Her lips were dry and painful but, oh, the sheer relief of being at long last understood! She would see the baby as soon as possible! Nothing else mattered now! Her body might be swollen, stretched and broken and all full of pain and betrayal but it had produced something – there was something out there that belonged to her. And she would see the daughter that was hers.

Kate stood quietly fiddling with her laptop at the podium of the lecture theatre, waiting for the meeting to begin. The medical students were beginning to slope in towards the higher-up seats at the back of the panelled lecture hall and Kate nodded to them with encouragement, glad that they were still coming even though the Christmas term officially finished up this week. The meeting was less likely to get nasty if there were students there, she decided firmly to herself.

Professor Crowe could be very sarcastic of course and difficult when they were alone, doctor-to-doctor, but he didn't always want people to know about it. And his desire to show himself to be a charming and paternalistic mentor normally overrode his desire to put any of the other medical staff in their place.

Ronan Clare slid back into the front benches now, carrying underneath his white coat a giant submarine sandwich that he'd popped out to buy while she was setting up. He beamed up at her as he pulled the plastic from the top of his snack.

Although she felt almost nauseated with nerves, Kate couldn't help smiling back at him. Ronan rarely went anywhere without something good to eat. Even though eating in the lecture hall was strictly forbidden, Ronan would always try to snaffle down a mouthful or two before secreting the rest of his sandwich about his solid person. Nice of him to sit at the front where he could get a word or two in, she thought, even if it meant not being able to sneak much more of his sandwich during the meeting.

Nick Farrelly came down to sit down at the front beside Ronan, and Kate felt immediately relieved to see that he'd been able to make it too. As an anaesthetist, Nick didn't usually get time to go to the M and M. She knew that he was there for her today, just to hold her hand so to speak, and she was beginning to feel a whole lot better now.

Ronan took another tiny nibble from his secret sandwich. Kate giggled and her stomach gurgled like a drain.

Nick winked at her and poked Ronan hard in the ribs. She wished now that she'd had something more than a mandarin orange to eat that morning.

The lecture theatre was a steep amphitheatre in the older part of the hospital with oak benches surrounding the podium where Kate had set up her laptop in front of the giant screen. The midwives were filing in now from the back of the lecture hall. From her position at the podium, Kate beckoned them to come down to the front of the hall so that the seats would fill up there. Ronan and Nick were the only two on the front bench and she felt as though the room was unbalanced with all the nurses yattering like a flock of birds at the back of the hall, ready to swoop on her if she came off her guard.

Sharon Guinness was sitting in the middle of the lecture hall, her halo of strawberry blonde curls bobbing animatedly, gabbling with a group of student midwives.

"Hi, Sharon!" Kate mouthed hopefully at her. She liked Sharon – she was sharp and sassy and didn't let the boys slag her off too much. She watched Sharon bossing the students for a moment and then caught her eye again, putting her head to one side and raising her eyebrows as if to ask, "Are you going to support me today?"

Sharon nodded at her, as if she knew exactly what Kate was thinking and Kate blinked at her in gratitude.

"Hhhherrrummmmm!"

Professor Crowe took his seat at the front of the hall, followed by the other obstetricians popping into their usual places behind him. Prof Crowe had only just been appointed this time last year but he was working hard on his reputation as a shit-shaker. Fresh from the Saint Mary's Hospital Paddington where he had contributed to two text-books on obstetrics, he liked to give the impression that here in Dublin he had come to put his feet up – and then have his boots licked by the rest of us, Kate would privately add.

Professor Dennis Crowe's chiselled face reminded her sometimes of her childhood Action Man doll, Captain Sarsfield. He had a cold, unsmiling face, a permanent suntan with deep brown eyes, and plenty of thick black hair flecked with steel, which Kate thought at the age of forty-two made him look fierce, rather than fiercely sexy. Ronan was convinced Prof dyed his hair and painted in the silver flecks, and spent all his free time sitting underneath a sunlamp at home. Kate was more inclined to think he spent every second weekend skiing in St Morritz, or golfing at his second home in Florida.

At any rate, the Prof was rarely ever *in* the hospital. He made his living from a giant private practice across town in a far, far leafier suburb. But he always showed up for meetings like this one and he liked to make his presence felt.

Kate glanced up at the clock. It was five past twelve.

She decided that she'd start the meeting even if they weren't all in their places. It would calm her nerves to get it going and would place her in a position of authority if she had to shut them all up.

"Good afternoon everyone! Now, let's get cracking, shall we, before we waste any more time? We have only got an hour and there are a lot of matters to present this morning. Great to see the students here." Kate smiled cautiously at the top row, gathering their attention.

They gradually stopped sniggering and gossiping and put their crisp packets away.

"No eating during the meeting of course," Kate pouted her mouth at Ronan who stuck the tip of his tongue out at her, "and make sure all mobile phones are off. Now." She dimmed the lights and switched on the slideshow on her laptop.

"Let's have a look at this first slide here." She flipped her PowerPoint on to light up the Perinatal statistics for the month. "I hope that the students can read all the way up there at the back because this is the important bit. I'll let you know as soon as you can go back to sleep." The audience murmured politely at the joke.

Ronan and Nick guffawed loudly. Jesus, lads, way too much! She cringed inside but they were trying to put her at her ease and she loved them for it.

Kate stood back and let the audience read the stats she had put up. Caesarean section rate thirty per cent this month, up by five per cent. She checked Prof Crowe's predictable frown at that one.

Total number of deliveries: two hundred and fifteen. Epidural anaesthetics: sixty-nine per cent of vaginal deliveries, Forty-two per cent of sections. Forceps deliveries: eighteen. Ventouse: thirty-two. Twin deliveries: eight. Breech vaginal deliveries: two. Neonatal deaths: one. Still births: two. First trimester miscarriages: twenty-four. Second trimester miscarriages: eight. Admissions for premature rupture of membranes: six.

Caesarean hysterectomies: one.

There it was, her big fat nightmare sitting all on its own.

Caesarean hysterectomies: one.

Only one.

All mine. No one else's. Not in this hospital. Nope. Just me.

"Do we think that the increase in Caesarean section rate is related to the increased epidural rate during first time labour?" Professor Crowe began in his smarmy drawl.

Kate sat down while the obstetricians bantered. She knew that Nick didn't really give a bollocks whether or not the Caesarean section rate was related to the epidural rate, but he was giving a lovely and polite impression of someone who thinks it's the most important thing in the world.

Jim Latham, a burly moustachioed obstetrician whom Kate liked, was wondering if the number of breech vaginal deliveries was rather low, and if the junior obstetricians weren't going to get enough training if they kept sectioning them all. A lively debate began, between the midwives and the medics: about the dangers of sitting on the tocograph too long (Professor Crowe), versus the dangers of junior obstetricians clinging to the tocograph as if it were a security blanket and not being trained to put their heads up to the Pinet stethoscope any more (Sharon), versus some of the doctors being very slow to get to the labour ward and too many cases ending up in theatre without a proper trial of labour (Natasha).

"Childbirth shouldn't have to be a trial – nobody's committed a crime – it should be a win-win situation," Ronan interrupted, and everybody laughed.

Nick Farrelly threw a provocative cat in among the pigeons by remarking that he felt that the Caesarean section rate was actually too low, considering the numbers of twins that they had successfully delivered vaginally last month – a bit risky when you think about it because the two biggest litigants in the last ten years were both twin deliveries that had cost the hospital insurers several millions in failure to move rapidly enough to section.

Ronan took the opportunity in the middle of the row to have a good chomp at his sandwich while he thought no one was looking. Kate caught Natasha furling up her lip in disgust at this, prodding the midwife next to her with her elbow.

Prof got sarcastic with Nick about the failure to go to section in the twin deliveries.

"It's very interesting, Doctor Farrelly, to examine the statistics with the *retrospectoscope*," he growled. "But seeing as the decision will always have to be made by someone other than yourself, which patients are for section and which will be delivered vaginally, you might remember that a Caesarean section rate is a mixture of elective sections, failed vaginal deliveries and traumatic labours with complicated outcomes. The twins are mostly all elective and of those that we choose to deliver vaginally, you will see that our outcome is in fact almost one hundred per cent."

Kate hadn't in fact prepared this particular statistic, so another row broke out as to how the maths were calculated to determine what percentage of the expected vaginal twins went to section, versus those who were planned for a section anyway, and whether or not this number was greater or less than it had been for the last two years.

It was a quarter to one already and they hadn't touched her patient yet.

She was barely listening to the clash of the giant egos across the lecture theatre, but she spotted Nick's anxious face at one point and knew that he was deliberately provoking the debate about the twin section rate to distract from her.

Dearest Nick, she thought. He means well. But we'd be better off if we grabbed the bull-shitters by the horns.

She raised her hand to Nick's open mouth.

"Thank you for that intervention, Nick. And I do agree with Professor Crowe that it will be a very interesting statistic to prepare for next month's M and M and I'll get someone to do a literature search in the meantime so we can have a think about what sort of comparisons are valid."

She looked up at the students with a questioning face.

"Any takers?"

There was a tittering and then a silence and so she smiled at the obstetricians on the front bench and carried on.

"Well, we'll remember your faces during the exams, won't we, Professor?" she said lightly and the tittering was replaced by grunts from the top row of students, and tittering from the obstetricians down below. "Meanwhile," she steadied herself, "we have had one very unusual outcome from a difficult unbooked section this month, which we do need to discuss."

She flicked on the slide.

Date, time, Bishop's score, time of transfer to theatre, blood-loss estimate, transfused units, fresh frozen plasma.

It was all there.

Kate began numbly to take the audience through that night, the night of hell on which Jonny's tiny daughter had been born. She was making a huge effort to steady her voice but it seemed almost artificial to her through the microphone, and she felt she sounded as robot-like as if she were reading from a catalogue of furniture at an auction. She gripped the edge of the podium so fiercely that her hands almost hurt.

She paused to flick on to another slide and licked her

stinging lips again. They were so dry she felt they were about to crack. There was a glass of water on the podium in front of her and it slopped about in her hand when she lifted it to her mouth.

With the next slide, she recited the history of the delivery. The date, the time, the unbooked patient, the length of time between the diagnosis of abruption to the time of delivery, the patient's blood pressure and oxygen saturation, the number of units of fresh frozen plasma; the condition of the baby, the Apgar score, the delivery of the placenta; the flaccidity of the empty uterus, the failure to contract, the numbers of units of oxytocin, the milligrams of rectal misoprostol, the dose of ergometrine, it was all there, every single "i" was dotted, and every "t" was crossed.

"Nick?" she asked him lightly, but her voice shook and she knew that it was noticeable. "Would you like to go through the anaesthetic notes with us now?"

Nick whipped briskly through the anaesthetic history in his rather high-pitched, meandering voice.

The presentation was faultless and professional, Kate told herself. Nick was always easygoing and good fun, but when it came to clinical accuracy, he was as tight as a whip. Nothing had been missed. Every single vital sign was accounted for.

They had made the right decision.

She looked around her at the faces of the midwives. They were listening carefully. The obstetricians were all looking down at their hands, but Kate knew what they were thinking.

She tried to remind herself of what she decided to repeat when in doubt, over and over like a broken record: at least the patient was still alive, and the baby was doing well, fair play to Ronan.

And thank Christ I wasn't the one who was on call that night, was what the others were all thinking.

Nick finished with the anaesthetics report. Kate nodded at him in thanks.

She raised her eyes carefully to study the faces in the room. There was a stiffened atmosphere in the theatre, as if people were holding onto their breaths. She noticed the unanimous looks of anguish on the faces of Sharon and the group of student midwives. Nobody was smiling. Nobody looked anything other than worried. But they weren't looking at her with criticism either, she felt.

Professor Crowe was sitting like a statue, his narrow hands clasped in front as if in prayer. Kate quickly checked Jim Latham's face to see what he was thinking. Jim was frowning and chewing on his moustache. He looked back at Kate, shaking his head as he chewed.

The case *was* awful. There was no way anyone was thinking otherwise.

But Jim's face *was* empathetic too.

"So," Kate's low-pitched voice was almost inaudible. The room was like a church of silence. "Let's begin with all the questions. And for the students at the back," she cleared her throat and tried to speak up louder, "this is a very difficult case for us to come to grips with because we had to make a tough decision with no history. It is difficult to have to manage an emergency for an unbooked patient who is a foreign national, and we did not have her husband there to give consent. There are therefore ethical as well as obstetric issues here that we need to discuss."

"And medico-legal ones," Professor Crowe chimed in.

"Yes." Kate spoke as strongly as she could manage but the voice that came out was just a very tiny croak. "Obviously. In these cases we are always worried about the risk of litigation."

The room fell silent again.

"Kate, the baby is doing very well now – I just thought you'd like to know," Ronan said.

She tried to smile at him. "Thank you, Ronan. That is very good news indeed."

Jim Latham was still frowning and chewing his moustache. Then he broke the awful silence.

"Tough call, Kate. Very tough. You did well. I don't envy you. How did the patient handle it when you talked to her?"

She cleared her throat again.

"Um. Prof is the only person who's got to speak to her yet. I went to speak to her about it yesterday, Jim. And thankfully she does speak perfect English. But she is only just out of ICU and quite sedated so I'm going to have to speak to her again properly this afternoon. She – she will need more counselling, obviously." Kate could feel her face burn up like a furnace. But she kept her voice steady and nodded carefully, watching the others nodding with her.

More silence. Kate glanced up at the clock again. It was a minute to one.

"Well," she began, "if that's all the questions for this month –"

"Just one thing," Professor Crowe whined in from the front row.

She looked solidly back at him. *What now?*

"Doctor Gilmore," he began, "I suppose that is what everybody will be most concerned about –" he looked around the hall, "– the fact that this is her first baby. And now, tragically, it is of course her last. But, according to the history you gave me that night on the phone after you had come out of surgery, you thought she'd had *two previous deliveries*. Where is that discrepancy coming from? I mean," he smiled a sardonic smile, "we don't make those kinds of mistakes here at Saint Xavier's, do we?"

Here we go, Kate thought. I should have known that this was coming.

"The parity," Kate coughed, "is something that I'm afraid I didn't check too carefully that night. You will remember, Natasha, that we were very rushed? We didn't have a chart made up yet?" She looked hopefully at the midwife, whose face was like a stone. "Mrs L was bleeding heavily in the labour ward," she continued and her tongue stuck to the roof of her mouth. She took another shaky sip of water. "And we knew that the placenta had separated. By the time I had been called, Natasha had made a very brisk diagnosis, and I'm very glad that she did."

Kate looked again at Natasha more hopefully, desperate for an ally. Natasha looked back at her with all the solidarity of Lot's wife.

"Natasha had got the patient already for theatre by the time I had arrived. The management by the labour-ward staff was superb." Even Kate knew her voice was beginning to sound vague now. She was sounding as though she didn't even believe herself, it was so over-sincere.

"Kate, I am not sure I quite understand what you are saying," Professor Crowe interrupted. "Did you or did you not tell me on the phone that night, that the patient was a Para II, whereas in fact this was her first?"

Kate took a deep breath. "I did tell you that she was a Para II," she replied. "And the reason that I did is . . . was . . . because that was what I thought she was."

She looked solidly at Natasha. Natasha sat like a statue.

Prof was clearly becoming impatient. "And the reason that you *thought* that she was a Para II was because . . . ?" He waved a sun-tanned hand around to encourage her to finish.

"When we are rushed into the labour ward for a crash section we might sometimes miss a minor detail," Kate breathed out.

"But parity is not a minor detail, doctor." Professor Crowe was frowning.

Kate's voice shook as she answered. "I may have misheard what the midwife said."

"*Mis-heard?*"

She drew a breath. "Yes."

The Prof whistled through his teeth. "Doctor Gilmore, you can't *mishear* what a midwife is saying to you in the middle of an emergency!" He turned around to face the medical students and the student midwives. "The truth is that she's a Para 0 plus II, isn't she? She'd miscarried her two previous pregnancies, isn't that correct?"

There was a silence.

"Clear and accurate communication is *essential* in a hospital, especially a maternity hospital," he began to lecture, "and there is no room for misunderstandings . . ."

Kate searched Ronan and Nick's eyes. They stared blankly back at her. There was nothing she could say – not in front of all these people. She couldn't start telling them that the reason she'd got so mixed up was that she had to do the most horrendous delivery of her life and she'd only had an hour's sleep. She couldn't tell them that she felt close to tears now, because she'd had to carry this anxiety around with her for the past two days and could no longer turn to her oldest friend – the man she'd married – for solace. And that he no longer wanted to be with her. She couldn't explain that for the past ten years as she and Dave had drifted solidly apart, her thoughts had returned time and time again to Jonny – *how would it have been different with Jonny?* – and that after wondering for years when they would meet again, instead of it being the tender reunion she'd imagined it would be, it was going to be in this hospital after this meeting and she was going to have to tell him and his beautiful wife that she had completely screwed up their chances of having any more children. That she had failed completely at the one thing that she was good at, the one thing of which she was most proud.

She wanted to lie down and just die in front of them on the spot.

"The midwives take the history when the patient presents, but if the obstetrician makes a mistake by misunderstanding what the midwife has said, or if she isn't properly listening to the midwife, well – serious mistakes can be made," Professor Crowe chimed on.

"Kate didn't make any mistakes!" Ronan butted in, his round face hot with loyalty.

But Prof raised his eyebrows at him. "Doctor Clare is the *paediatrician,*" he informed the students.

The bastard, Kate thought. Now he's trying to make Ronan look like an eejit.

Nick spoke up cautiously. "The delivery went as well as could have been expected and the section was much more complicated than anticipated. But the patient was in poor condition and we did well to deliver a live infant and avoid a maternal death."

"Yes, that is very true," the Prof agreed. "But

nevertheless the fact remains that your decision to do an emergency hysterectomy on a woman who had had no previous children was influenced by your mistaken belief that she already had two other children at home, isn't that the case?"

"No!" Kate whispered. There was a rumble of conversation beginning in the room.

Maybe it was just because people were complaining that Prof was keeping them on too long. She crossed her fingers and continued.

"That's *not* why I did the hysterectomy," she said quite firmly now. "We *had* to remove the uterus because the patient was dying, not because of the supposed parity. The parity was never what was in question."

Jim Latham was chewing his moustache ferociously and he was still frowning, but he was nodding at Kate.

Then he spoke up. "I'd say that Kate did the hysterectomy because the patient was in danger of dying on the table," he said thoughtfully. "Not because she had miscounted the kids she'd had."

Professor Crowe raised his eyebrows at him.

"Look," said Nick coolly, "whether this lady was on her first pregnancy or if she'd had ten other kids, she still needed a hysterectomy that night. The fact remains that we were losing her. We can't sit around worrying about future children when a patient is in theatre. We have to make a very serious decision about the present. And, on that occasion, we made the right one. For Mrs L and for the baby."

"Normally in these situations, when the patient is under general anaesthetic, the hospital protocol is that we get informed consent from the patient's partner if possible," Professor Crowe replied, more for the students than for the staff who knew the protocol almost off by heart. But it stung Kate to have to hear it spelt out like that in front of everyone.

Prof Crowe is being *so* patronising, she thought furiously.

I am *so* getting pissed tonight with Ronan and Nick.

"The patient's husband was unfortunately not in the country at the time of the delivery and he doesn't arrive until tonight," Kate told the room. "But I will speak to him as soon as we have finished here, as well as Mrs L." She felt her mouth go dry again.

She turned back around to face the Prof.

"I agree with you, Professor," she said evenly. "It *would* have been better if he could have given us consent for the hysterectomy that night. But he wasn't there. Sometimes we get all the time in the world to make all the right decisions. And sometimes we just have to do our best with whatever information we have. I'd like to thank my anaesthetic colleagues for a superb job that night, for all their support, and to thank the midwives in theatre for working so hard with me on a very difficult delivery, and to thank the paediatrics department for the very strong outcome that we have now."

"And if there were Oscars for obstetrics, I'm sure you would be nominated, Kate." Professor Crowe smiled graciously at her and the room murmured, full of nervous titters again.

I'm not getting pissed tonight, thought Kate.

I'm going to get absolutely rat-arsed.

6

Dave Hardiman's hands shook ridiculously as he opened up the plastic packaging of the mouth-piece set. The clear plastic wrapper crackled back at him. The noise was like a whip, ripping through his nerves, and he dropped the mouth-piece on the floor.

"Fuckit!" Dave breathed behind his paper mask, a fog of damp sweat thickening on his unshaved skin.

He opened up another pack and this time placed the mouthpiece carefully in between the patient's teeth and gently taped it into place before he tried again to tube the patient.

"You okay, Dave?"

It was a generic nurse's voice from somewhere in the theatre. Somewhere too close to his pounding head, Dave thought. But he wasn't going to look up to see who the hell was pestering him now in case he missed the intubation.

Dave bent his head closely over the anaesthetised face of the patient and passed the tube through the glistening larynx. Bright pink epiglottal folds gaped up like a wet hollow in the torchlight and he felt bile rise up into his own throat.

Dave gagged silently behind his theatre mask. Perhaps the sight of the patient's open throat with its gag reflex paralysed had brought about a sort of sympathetic reaction. Gag reflex by association. He taped the tube onto the patient's cheek as carefully as he could to stop his tremor from being noticed.

"Jesus, Dave, what's keeping you?" he heard the surgeon's voice behind him.

He swallowed hard. "Go ahead now – we're in," his muffled voice replied.

"Kate, there's something that we need to discuss further."

Professor Crowe was the only one left in the theatre, waiting while the staff and students filed out of the benches, yapping and gossiping their way back to work. She'd waved goodbye to Nick and Ronan and closed down her computer, watching Prof out of the corner of one eye, knowing that there was a reason he was staying back.

Kate fumbled with her laptop, waiting for him to speak:

"About the hysterectomy," he began.

"Yes, I know," she murmured.

"Do you want to come to my office where we can

chat properly?" he asked her and there was almost a kindness in his voice.

Kate steadied herself. She was surprised at the sudden change in tone, but at the same time wasn't quite sure if she could outrule sarcasm, or even pity, which was much, much worse.

She looked at him. She desperately wanted to go straight down to the ward to talk to Marianne but perhaps she'd better deal with the Prof first.

"Thanks," she said, keeping her voice bright and steady. "I'll just leave the laptop in my locker and meet you over there in ten. All right?"

Professor Dennis Crowe's office was on the top floor of St Xavier's, where he could bask in a spectacular view over the churches and rooftops of Dublin. He could see the Spire from here, and Liberty Hall and even further on across the bay, out all the way towards the hills.

"When I took up my post here," he told Kate now, standing with his back to her as he admired the skyline through a large wall of window, "I picked this office first, before I'd even signed the contract." He turned around to smile at her. "Every other office that I'd ever worked in had been a tiny poky study or a shared desk at the end of a ward somewhere. So I decided when I became a professor that I was going to have an office that I could really enjoy being in."

Kate nodded and made a polite noise. She felt almost dizzy after the steep climb of the stairs.

"Sit down here, Kate, please." Prof pulled a chair back at right angles to his own at the giant antique desk in the middle of the room. "I've got Mrs Le Normand's chart here with me – Sister sent it up – so we can go through this case bit by bit and see where it went wrong."

Kate felt her face pink up again but she was grateful, at least, to be sitting down.

"Where do you want to begin?" she heard her own voice say.

Prof breathed out heavily through his nose and opened up the notes, then closed them again. "Yellow chart." He looked at Kate with raised eyebrows.

"I know," Kate began. "I'm not colour blind. But we didn't have a chart made up when I spoke to you in theatre – we had gone straight from admission into crash . . ."

"Kate, there's no reason to be so defensive." Prof looked at her with steel in his eyes. "We need to approach this problem as a team. Now," he turned around and found his glasses, "you won't believe it," he looked at Kate again, this time from behind lenses, "but I need spectacles already!"

Kate tried to smile but she really didn't give a hoot about his spectacles.

He opened up the file again.

"Now. Mrs Marianne Le Normand, Para 0 plus II. So, to all intents and purposes, her *first* child. Both previous pregnancies were terminated, unfortunately." He examined her reaction from above his glasses again.

Kate's head was beginning to feel faint again. Prof

already knew more history about Marianne than she did. Oh, how stupid she had been to chicken out from talking to her yesterday!

She listened to him peel his way through the obstetric history while the facts were hitting her like bombs. Two abortions – but maybe they weren't both Jonny's? And then Marianne had got pregnant again, and this baby must be just so precious . . .

"Prof." She just had to stop him. "The history – we hadn't had a chance to clarify her past obstetrics history when –"

"Oh, Natasha has done all of that – don't worry, Kate – look, there's her writing in the chart," and he pointed at the notes she'd puzzled over that Tuesday evening when she'd sat with her head melting after her night on call. "Now, where were we?" he went on. "Yes. This pregnancy. And here's where we need to keep very careful records from now on." He looked over the rims of his spectacles at Kate. "Now: firstly, she knew her dates when she presented. And, according to the Paeds, the dates are accurate enough. So, if she knew that she was thirty-four weeks, well into the third trimester, then she must have known she should not have been travelling, or at least have known that her insurance company wouldn't cover her to travel. Which brings me to this."

Prof flipped through to the back of the chart again.

"Her insurance details. She is insured with an American company which will not now accept her charges but we have decided therefore to allow her private care as a hospital courtesy. It seems her father is involved in politics and she herself is a lawyer. So, naturally, we are now taking this situation very seriously indeed."

Kate looked up from the case notes they were both perusing and stared at him. Professor Crowe was meeting with her to discuss *risk assessment*, not clinical care. This was an exercise in damage control! He didn't give a fig about Jonny's baby, or about Jonny's wife, or about how hard it was going to be for her to talk to Marianne about the operation. He only cared about being sued!

"Prof," Kate began, shaking her head rapidly, "I know what you're thinking but I'm sure that you're wrong. Look, I know this couple. They are friends of – at least, I knew her husband. Her husband is a doctor too." Professor Crowe's scowl deepened. She drew breath and continued. "I've never met Mrs L before, of course, and I didn't know who she was until yesterday, but I've known her husband for years. I knew him at college. So they aren't going to sue us, I know they aren't. They'll be thrilled we saved the baby."

"You didn't save her womb, Kate." Prof said it like it was.

Kate sat there open-mouthed. "I saved her *life*!" she whispered. Her voice was barely audible.

"Look," Professor Crowe sighed, "my experience in these matters, which you will accept is far greater than yours, Kate, tells me that in these cases patients rarely count their blessings and thank us for the good things that we've done. They only see what they perceive to be a poor obstetric outcome, and they sue. They sue because they can. They pick the one tiny error, or in this case giant error, and they sue for that. And they are encouraged to do so, because they are led to believe that obstetrics is a miracle and that nothing will go wrong."

"Prof, with respect, this lady is married to a doctor!"

"Doesn't matter," Professor Crowe replied. "She wanted a perfect baby, a perfect recovery, and she would like to have perfect opportunity to do it all again. She didn't sign up for this –" he indicated *Procedure: Hysterectomy* on the theatre report in Kate's small handwriting, "and therefore it is our job to put some risk assessment in place for our lawyers so that if the inevitable legal letter comes, we can have all our ammunition in order."

"You make it sound like a war," she said miserably. *Childbirth is to women what war is to men.* This wasn't what she had expected from the Prof at all.

"Well," Prof replied, "unfortunately at the end of the day, a lot of things boil down to money. And so we need to look after the hospital, our investors, our patrons, and so on. Now, I've been through this case this morning, and I can see that if there were to be a case against us, then it would be this." He looked at Kate's pale face again, and pointed at her notes. "Here," he indicated the labour-ward Bishop's score, "this is where the case is weakest, Kate, and I know that this is not your writing but you have to take responsibility no matter what. In the end of the day, a midwife's mistake is still your liability."

"The Bishop's score?" Kate asked, bewildered. "But I thought the parity –"

"No," Prof cut in, "the parity isn't the main problem. Though I chose not to mention that fact at the M and M."

Kate stared, waiting for him to proceed.

"Well," he continued, "I see that you arrived at the labour ward at a minute past four, as soon as you were called, of course. And you made the decision to go to theatre for a section immediately. How did you know the dates?"

"The dates?"

"The gestation," he replied. "Of the foetus. Who told you that or did you scan her then?"

Kate shook her head. "There was no time to scan. The BP was low. We had to go to theatre –"

"Ah!" he replied.

"What do you mean?"

"You had to go to theatre. Who *said* you had to go?"

Kate shook her head. "I don't understand. It was quite obvious. There was foetal distress. Foetal heart was eighty by the time we opened and she had a concealed abruption. We didn't have a choice. She would have had a still-birth if we hadn't gone to theatre then."

"But," the Prof replied, "you didn't consult with any other doctor. And I was on call that night. You could have called me in."

Kate sat back in the chair and stared at him. "Professor," she began, and then stopped. The obvious reply was, of course, that if she *had* called him, he would have been absolutely furious and asked her why on earth she couldn't manage the case by herself. But it was difficult sometimes in medicine to speak the truth. Prof might be all enthusiastic *now,* about how keen he would have been to come on in that night and dig her out, but Kate knew the truth was that he wouldn't have come in if she'd asked. The reality was that if you rang to say you were in trouble, you'd be given short shrift and made to feel as though you were incompetent. It was a complete Catch 22.

"Prof," she said instead, "there really wasn't time to call you in, I'm afraid. And if I hadn't sectioned her, the baby – well, the baby could have died. Or been –" She shook her head with impatience.

"The patient might now have an intact womb."

"Yes. She might. But the baby would be –"

"Yes, I know. Cerebral Palsy, neonatal death, I know what you're thinking. You saved the mother and the child. Brave girl, and a happy ending. But *this* woman is going to be thinking of all the children that she couldn't have. People aren't always grateful to us, Kate, for the things we've done. They pick out the one thing that's gone wrong, and think only of what we *could* have done instead."

Kate put her hand out on the case notes and stopped him there.

"No. Prof, you are wrong." She suddenly felt much more confident now. "I'm sorry to have to speak so bluntly to you, but I don't believe for a minute that anyone would have judged it differently. Okay, I took a risk with the maternal side of things, taking her to theatre with a low BP and an unstable abruption. But my risk paid off. I saved the child. *And* the patient. That was my job to do that night, and that's what I did. She has one baby – one tiny, sick and premie baby I know – but the baby is alive and that's exactly what she wanted me to do that night. And today she is alive herself and that is everything. I don't believe for a moment she'll take issue with the hysterectomy once she knows what the alternatives were going to be."

"Oh, Kate, Kate!" Prof shook his head at her. He took his spectacles off and rubbed his eyes. "I wish I still had your naïve optimism," he smiled at her.

Patronising prick, Kate thought, and then she shook herself to remind herself to cop on. He is trying to be a help, she told herself. Why am I being so bloody defensive? But she knew the answer: it was because she still felt guilt. This wasn't an ordinary obstetric case. She was personally, deeply involved, and the patient herself didn't even know it. She sat on her hands instead, and let the Prof say what he had to say.

"Let's just put our case together carefully and anticipate all the odds," he told her calmly. "A professional medical litigant will easily find an expert witness who will say that you should *not* have gone to section, that you should have stabilised the patient before even *thinking* about theatre, that you should have got her BP up, made sure there was no risk of DIC and then delivered her vaginally if possible – and in that way, the patient would have saved her womb."

"And that so-called expert witness would have lost the baby and have a law-suit on *his* hands for failing to section!" Kate was swift in her reply.

"Yes, I know," he said. "But that is what an expert witness will say, if they are on the side of someone who wants to sue you for taking out her womb. In the courts, they are only interested in *evidence*, not in 'coulda, shoulda, woulda', if you can catch my drift. A law court is a question-and-answer session, not a scientific debating forum. Forget what you've seen on American TV with grand soliloquies in front of jurors. It's much more straightforward than that. 'Doctor, would the patient have had a better chance of avoiding hysterectomy without going to section with a blood pressure of a hundred over sixty and ten units of packed red cells?' 'Yes,' is the answer any witness would give. And *ch-ching*! They've won the jackpot. It's as simple as that."

Kate smiled weakly back at him. But he was completely wrong, she knew. There was no way that Jonny and Marianne were going to take it out on her. They would absolutely understand her point of view.

"All right," she told the Prof. "You are right. So let's arrange to go through the case notes bit by bit and see all the holes that your imaginary counsel for the prosecution is going to pick." She paused. "But first I need to talk to the couple and explain everything that went wrong that night. I'm sure after we've talked properly to them that things will look a lot less problematic from our point of view."

He frowned. "Kate," he said, "I've decided that I'm taking you off the management of this case altogether." He was looking at her shocked face very carefully now. "I'm going to manage this patient privately myself from now on. So I'd rather you left any further communication with the patient up to me."

Kate opened her mouth to speak but he stopped her with a well-placed talk-to-the-hand gesture.

"I want you to understand, Kate, that I think it's in everybody's best interest if you didn't have anything more to do with this patient from now on."

"So, what are we having?" In the Octagon bar of the Clarence Hotel, Ronan scrutinised the cocktail menu as if it were a lab report.

"I'm having a pint of Guinness," he added, before handing the red and gold Christmassy-designed menu to Kate and Nick.

Nick squinted at it and put on his glasses.

"Speaking of which, where is Sharon Guinness?" asked Kate.

"Busy riding the Prof," said Nick, buck teeth grinning like a rabbit, and handed the cocktail menu to Kate.

"No way!" Kate gasped but she couldn't help a snort of laughter. "You're joking?"

"No, I'm not."

"How do you know *that*?"

"Everybody knows *that*," Nick shrugged. "Hurry up and decide what you're having, Kate."

"Isn't Sharon Guinness married?" asked Kate, wide-eyed.

"Sharon Guinness is all right." Ronan snatched the menu back from her. "Not everybody's marriage can be as big a picnic as yours and Dave's is, you know, Katie-cakes. Jesus, you are so fucking slow, Kate, I don't know how you ever became an obstetrician. It's a cocktail menu not a cardiograph. Pick a drink for God's sake, woman!"

"You pick for me." Kate handed the menu back to him.

Reading the four-page cocktail menu seemed like a Herculean task in serious literature to her after the day she'd just had.

"I just need to be minded tonight, Ro," she told him. "And I need to get nicely pickled too, if you don't mind. I've had a hell of a day. Prof has wiped the floor with me. And to cap it all when I'm on call again tomorrow night, you lot are going to be at the hospital Res party, driving me cracked with the noise of it and I won't be able to drink a thing because I'll be up all night saving lives. So pick a nice big cocktail, Ronan, please, and pour it into me rapid."

"What about a shot of something absolutely lethal – say, a Slippery Nipple?" he suggested.

Kate shuddered and wrinkled her nose. "Too gynaecological. I want something that induces instant memory loss of everything that's got to do with work."

"Get her something fruity and full of vitamins," said

111

Nick. "She's on call tomorrow night and I don't want her crying all next week about some other delivery that's gone all wrong."

Kate stuck her tongue out at him.

Ronan tried to look helpful. "What about a Bloody Mary?"

"What about a bloody nose, for Nick?" Kate scowled. She snatched the menu back again. "Which cocktail has the most Serotonin Re-uptake Inhibitors in it?" she sighed. She eventually settled on a Cosmopolitan.

"Did you really think that the patient was a Para II when she was a Nullipara?" Nick asked her, three drinks later. "Or what's the real story there?"

"Oh, Nick, for God's sake!" Kate swirled around the orange peel in her third Cosmopolitan. "How can yous still be thinking about that schtuff? Para 0 plus II! I'll be saying it in my sleep. I need another Cosmopolitan!" She looked thunderously at Ronan.

"Like a hole in your head you do. Have a black coffee, lady – you might have to resuscitate me tomorrow night," Ronan grinned.

She ignored Ronan. "Nick. Buy me another drink. Now. Please."

Nick waved at the cocktail waiter, ignoring Ronan's frown.

"Katie, sweetheart, that's the bit I don't understand." Nick looked at her while they waited for the drinks to come over. "Didn't you check the notes?"

"The woman was unbooked," she moaned. "There

were no notes. The midwives took a quick history *while* they were admitting her – and then by the time I got to see her she was being prepped for theatre. I don't know, I was trying to speak French, I'd only had one hour's sleep. Parity wasn't an issue. A hysterectomy was the last thing I'd expected to be doing that night." She looked down.

"I mean, I know that in the end of the day, the clinical management would have been the same," Nick carried on. "But you *saw* the reaction of the Prof today. He's only got one thing on his mind: litigation, litigation, litigation. If she had already had a few kids, it would sort of take the sting out of all of that, wouldn't it?"

"Frendgh people don't sute doctors like the fucking Irish," Kate muttered.

"French people don't sue," Nick nodded. "Yeah. You're probably right – and French women don't get fat."

Kate gave him a dig.

"You won't be sued though, Kate." Ronan was clearly thinking it over more seriously. "They would only sue if there were clear-cut alternatives that you didn't pursue. And if they had evidence that you were medically negligent, which you weren't. Everyone agrees there. You did the right thing: okay, you didn't know about the parity because you misheard the midwife, but they will never know that."

"Who won't?" Nick asked.

"The patient won't," Ronan replied. "They won't get to know that Natasha gave Kate information that Kate misheard and that Kate acted on it –"

"I didn't act on *information*!" Kate felt suddenly very sober. "I acted on my clinical judgement!"

Her fourth Cosmopolitan arrived, and she sank it almost in one mouthful.

"I know. I know. I'm sorry. I didn't mean it to come out like that." Ronan took her tiny hand in his much larger one and kissed it better. "Hey! We've all had a rough time of it this week. And you've been very brave. Now please ease up on the binge drinking before I have to intubate you, all right?"

"All right." Kate held onto his chunky hand for a while, and then said, "They won't know that and you are right. But the worst thing is that now Prof won't let me talk to the patient and so now they might think I *had* made a misstate."

"Mistake," corrected Ronan, gently

"Yeah. Mistake. But I didn't make a mistake. I did the right think. *So* my hearing wasn't great. *So* Natasha might have said something that wasn't quite correct. It wasn't the substantial issue."

"Substantive," said Ronan quietly.

"Yeah, that too." Kate nodded, already reassured. "But I had a horrible session with the Prof today. And he thinks that there is a case for my not having gone to section at all that night. In other words, we could have stabilised the patient and delivered her without a section, even if it meant a still-born foetus. And avoided hysterectomy." She looked at them both glumly.

"But that's bonkers!" Nick replied. "Nobody would thank you for that."

"I know," Kate said. "That's what I said. But he's saying that an expert witness could argue that, and that people often think differently about what they would have wanted afterwards."

Ronan shook his head. "No way, Kate. Nobody sues because they would rather have had a still-birth than a hysterectomy."

"Oh, I know," she nodded. "But that isn't quite Prof's point of view. He just thinks in paranoia. He's thinking from the litigant's point of view: how can we make it look like she shouldn't have gone to theatre, rather than why she couldn't have possibly avoided theatre."

"A rock and a hard place, in other words?" Nick wondered, and Kate nodded. Ronan frowned and shook his head.

"You know," she said, "this job is supposed to be all about bringing new life into the world, not running around all day dodging legal bullets. This is all so wrong. What are we doing in this job, anyway?"

"Earning enough to pay for cocktails," Nick replied as the next round of drinks arrived.

Kate took a giant swig out of hers immediately, before turning to the others. "Well. All I can say now is cheers. And thanks for all your shippurt."

They clinked again.

"The most humiliating thing of all," she added, "is being told to stay away from her, as if I'm a complete liability. It's as though he's curtaining all my responsibilities."

Ronan opened his mouth to suggest "curtailing" – but

decided to say nothing. They sat in silence for a moment until Kate hiccoughed very loudly and they all laughed.

"Okay. Now, here's a good one," Nick began.

The other two looked at him, already smiling.

"What's Professor Crowe's favourite cocktail?" said Nick, his teeth breaking into a giant grin.

"I dunno. A Molotov cocktail, tossed from a great height right into the career of the nearest registrar?" grumbled Kate.

"No. A Sharon Guinness on the rocks with a twist," quipped Nick.

The three of them cracked up with laughter.

It was midnight by the time Kate stumbled in from the Clarence, and Dave was fast asleep. She had slammed the taxi door on the street outside, not noticing the row of curtains that twitched almost synchronously from the perfectly restored Georgian terrace where they lived. She slammed herself just as noisily into her own house, yelling "Dave?" and then suddenly realised that the house was completely dark inside and that the only sound she could hear was the creaking of the bed upstairs where Dave's heavy body had just been rudely woken up. Crap, she thought.

"Dave?" she said in a stage whisper, staggering up the stairs. "Dave? Are you awake?" she whispered louder, this time more hoarsely, and she banged her knee into the banister. "Shit!"

"I can't believe it. You've fucking woken me up again!" Dave thundered from the bedroom.

She heard him heave himself out of the bed. He was sitting on the edge of it when she entered the room.

"I'm really shorry," Kate giggled. "We went out for a few schoops."

"On a Thursday night?"

"We had the M and M today. It was all about Jonny's wife. I needed to unwind."

She sat down on the bed beside him, and began to stroke his large back. Her head swam. "Can't you sleep, Dave?"

"Well, I certainly can't now!" he scowled. He turned around and then suddenly smiled at her and ruffled her hair. "You're disgracefully drunk, you know." His voice was suddenly tender.

"Yeah, I know," she sighed. "But I'm going to have to miss the Res party tomorrow night, 'cos I'm on call, so I'm making up for it now instead."

"Wise move, getting hammered the night before you're on call," Dave said softly. He wrapped an arm around her and tucked her head underneath his neck. He kissed her on the top of her hair like a child, holding her there for a moment.

"Don't remind me. Come back to bed now, Dave. Please come. Please sleep with me."

But he was going to go downstairs again and then he'd never get back to sleep. And if he didn't get enough sleep then he would be in a foul temper again all day tomorrow.

And on Sunday Caroline was arriving. She couldn't

face into Christmas with Caroline if she and Dave were going to have another row.

"Come back to bed with me, Dave, please!" She pulled at his pyjama trousers.

"You're plastered, Kate! Get off! I'm not sleeping with a drunk woman!" He tickled her instead.

She kneeled up on the bed behind him, sliding her hand in between his legs and curled her fingers around his balls.

"But I'm great in bed when I'm plastered," she giggled, squeezing his balls hard, just the way he'd liked it once, stroking his thick penis with light fingers.

Dave stood up. "I can't, Kate. I'm exhausted. You need to get some sleep yourself too, sweetheart. It's too late already. I'm going down to get a drink, or something."

She rolled into a ball and fell into a sunken sleep.

The doses that he needed nowadays to ease the tension in his jaw had increased. Two hundred milligrams used to do it for a while. But that hardly seemed to have an effect any more, and so he'd upped the dose to three hundred for the last few times. And the pain in his neck was unbelievable now. Unbearable, really. Searing into his eardrums, marking his mind with its twisting intensity. Stress-related, that was what the ENT surgeon had said and he had pursed his mouth in sympathy at Dave, trying to look as though he completely understood what it was that he was going through. The common bond between doctors.

Stress-related.

"That's what surgeons tell you when they think the problem is all the patient's own fault," Dave had said.

"Well, of course it is. Isn't everything?"

Dave had laughed and the ENT surgeon had nodded his head, smiling back at him — but he couldn't have really thought that it was funny.

"Well, in that case, at least I know how to get rid of it," Dave had quipped and the Ear Nose and Throat specialist beamed at his good humour and showed him out the door.

How to get rid of it.

Dave smiled now to himself, all alone as he slid the needle comfortably to its home underneath his skin.

How does one get rid of *anything*?

He leaned back on the sofa and closed his eyes, letting the injection do its magic.

Stress-related. Hah!

7

Jonny Domville sat on a stiff-backed hospital chair and watched his wife's face while she slept. He felt like a spy. It was a hideous discomfort. Marianne, asleep, was not a sight that was in any way familiar to him any more. In fact, it had been over a year since they had actually *slept* together – that is to say, been asleep in the same place at the same time. But now this. Her face was deathly pale he thought, examining it in mild horror. Marianne's skin had always been a healthy golden bronze. Even in pregnancy she had enjoyed a long summer's vacation at Biarritz in August and although her usual skiing trip had been cancelled this year she generally kept a dark complexion all year round. But this ghostly white he didn't recognise. And her unwashed hair was dark and clinging to her skin. And this strange hospital nightgown – how suddenly vulnerable she was. Her eyes fluttered slightly and she woke.

"*Ciao*," he said. He could feel his face blush as if he had been seeking out a forbidden thing by stealth and was now caught, trapped in his indiscretion in a cave of wickedness.

"Jonny. What are you doing here?" Her voice was drowsy.

"Visiting," he said. "I am the next of kin," he added unnecessarily.

She began to struggle to sit up and he tried to help her but her body stiffened and he stepped back again.

"I can't sit up," she said.

"Let's call the nurse," he suggested, looking around helplessly.

She shook her head. "I'm too tired. I shall continue to lie down." She closed her eyes and opened them again.

"Are you feeling all right? How is the pain?" he asked.

She smiled a dry humourless smile. Her lips were parched and she tried to lick them. He picked up a glass of water at the bedside and she nodded. He lifted it to her lips and held it carefully while she sipped, watching his eyes all the time.

She swallowed. "*Merci*," she said. "There is no pain," she added. "Thankfully for that. A lot of morphine but no pain."

He nodded. "Then I'm very glad."

"Thank you for coming here," she said. "I'm sure it was inconvenient for you."

"I had to come when I heard you'd had the baby. I know we didn't plan it exactly like this —"

She interjected with a slight snort. "No! We certainly did not!"

"At least my mum and dad are in Dublin. So that's not too bad." He looked around at the calm hospital ward, as if to find something in it that would reassure him. "I'm going back to Sudan next week," he added, as if he hoped that this would relieve her of any possibility of the burden of having to endure further visits from him.

Ever since she had discovered that she was expecting a baby, Marianne had wanted to keep as far away as possible from him. Her pregnancy had been her own. A private, solitary relationship with a child still foetal, underwater, bound within her to her own body.

A child he hadn't wanted. After all they had been through and everything else she had forgiven, she had never forgiven him for that. And he had respected her. It was her dignity. That was the kind of woman she was and what she would always be.

"Yes, of course you are," she said. "And I am going back to Paris as soon as I possibly can. I must speak properly with the *professeur*."

He nodded. "My friend Kate Gilmore works here. I'll speak to her and make sure they do everything perfectly for you."

She pursed her lips slightly with false mirth. "There is no need." She moved slightly in the bed and then winced in discomfort. "I don't need your help or interference."

"All right," he said.

She closed her eyes. "I think I have to sleep again now, Jon," she said.

"All right. I'll go." He stood up. He paused a moment to see if there was anything else they ought to say to one another now.

"I don't need you – I am very capable myself," she said, opening her eyes again. She watched him as he stood there looking helpless. "You can go away now. Please," she added wearily.

"I'm going now. Don't worry. I am going to go. I am going to visit the baby though," he said.

She closed her eyes again. "*D'accord.*"

When you meet someone that you once loved, even after ten long years, you step inside a moment of intimacy that brings you crashing right back into the moment where you were ten years ago in one another's arms. You may have stumbled upon this person, or perhaps you have arranged to meet. Or perhaps you deliberately went to be in a place where you believed that you would find each other. Either way, when you first see the person that you once loved, for the first time in ten years, you'll see what inadvertently appears to be a forgotten part of yourself. You become a time-traveller. It is as if your lover has within him a perfect photograph, the perfect unwrapping of your subconscious memory, as if a sudden movie emerges from nowhere of the people that you used to be.

Kate knew that it was Jonny at the end of the ill-lit corridor from the moment that she reached the top of the staircase. Even in the late December dark of a midnight hospital ward, she knew the shape of his head from behind. She knew the posture that was his, the way he leaned against a wall.

He was leaning forward now with his back turned to the staircase, hands buried deep in the pockets of a bomber jacket, resting his forehead on the glass window into the SCBU. And although Kate's clogs tapped quietly on the lino corridor against the constant clatter of the hospital around her, the wheeze of the lift and the sharp chatter of nurses' voices, Jonny turned around and smiled. It was exactly as if he'd been expecting her.

She walked towards him slowly, and at that moment they were immediately the same people that they were ten years ago, as if they'd just picked up where they'd left off.

She didn't see the tired, worried father, the husband of Marianne Le Normand, her post-op patient who had just left ICU. She saw only Jonny, her Jonny who had graduated along with her and Dave and all the others ten years ago. Jonny, whose laconic smile had made her legs melt beneath her. Jonny, who had walked away from her and left her somehow dying on the inside, even after she had judiciously married Dave.

And so she walked more slowly now towards him, smiling to welcome him, not seeing at first the tiredness aching on his face, not noticing the anxiety there, not checking the few grey hairs he now had around his temples or the lines that creased his forehead.

"Kate," he said softly and he took her in his arms, almost as if it was to comfort *her*.

Did he know that it was she who'd delivered the baby? If so, he must just *know* how awful she felt about his wife. And so she pressed her face against his shirt, feeling the zip of his leather jacket scratch her cheek. *Poor Jonny*, and she felt herself melting for him again.

"I hope you're okay?" she said and he stroked her head and touched her nose. His smile was so sad when he smiled at her.

"I don't know what to feel," he replied.

"I know."

He turned her around in his arms so that she could look through the glass wall of the SCBU with him.

They stood together for a moment, his arm around her. It suddenly occurred to her that they might look like *they* were the parents, she and Jonny, standing watching the line-up of incubators. Tiny scraps of babies spread-eagled under lights, plugged into machinery like experimental plants. She raised her hand to touch her palm against the glass, as if to make a gesture of connection with the babies.

"Which one is yours, Jon?" she asked him softly.

"Number four," he smiled a wry smile. "The one who's having a nocturnal coiffure just there on the right."

Kate counted along the row of cots, and saw the baby

that was his. One of Ronan's colleagues working on it, shaving the tiny infant's scalp to put in an IV line.

"Oh, God, Jonny, I'm so sorry," she began.

"Don't be." He turned his face to her. "It's not your fault, Kate. These things just happen all the time."

She looked cautiously at him, and saw for the first time the deep lines that had folded into his forehead since she'd seen him last; the lines around the eyes, the greying tiredness in his cheeks.

"You look exhausted," she murmured, and touched the side of his face, feeling the bone beneath his cheek.

He shrugged. "It's all been a bit of a shock, that's all, all this happening so quickly." He turned away again to watch the baby and winced as the paediatrician inserted the IV line.

"Come away, Jonny," she tugged his arm. "You'll only get upset watching your own baby, you know. You don't have to watch."

"I know." He turned away and shoved his hands back into his pockets again.

He had never seemed more vulnerable.

"Let's go down and have a coffee or something," she suggested. "You probably need a break. When did you get here? Did you fly straight from Africa?"

"I had to stop in Geneva first. I couldn't get here till late last night."

They turned away to walk along the corridor together, but Jonny turned back for a moment before they reached the lift.

"I feel as though I ought to say goodnight, or something." He looked at her worriedly. "I mean, to the baby." He smiled at the irony of it. "I just feel sort of guilty about leaving her there, having her head shaved – I feel as though I ought to kiss her better or something. Only we can't go in."

"Let's come back afterwards when she's all settled down on her IV and you can kiss her then," she suggested.

"Yeah. Great." He smiled at her. "So, how are you?"

"Not too bad," Kate replied but rapidly changed the subject. "So, what have you decided to call the baby?"

"She's called Veronique," he solemnly replied.

She nodded. "Very grown-up. Elegant."

"I thought it seemed ridiculous for a teeny little thing like that," he said, "But Marianne liked it. It's a family name for her – they are very traditional. I didn't have any other name particularly in mind. It wasn't really my task, picking baby names," he said in a glum voice.

"How is she? Marianne?" Kate felt hollow. "Have you met Professor Crowe?"

"No, he's talked to her," Jonny replied. "She can barely even talk she's so knackered. I guess she'll be in better nick tomorrow."

Kate nodded. "Were you planning to have the baby in Geneva?" she asked him lightly.

"No, in Paris. That's where she lives actually. We had a holiday cottage here in Wicklow that we had to sell and she works in a big law firm that has offices in Dublin too, so she was over here to sign the papers for the cottage and hold a meeting with her Dublin office."

"Really? So near to her term?"

He smiled. "That's Marianne. She wasn't going to stop work until the week before the birth. She's like that. Tough, you know. A workaholic, I suppose. She *was* booked to have the baby in Paris to be near her job. I guess we hadn't thought that this might happen – the baby coming early. We were busy trying to get all the other things out of the way." He paused, then went on in a vaguer-sounding voice. "We've had some very serious decision-making to do and we were trying to just tie things up a bit. When all the domestic side of things are this difficult, you never think that other things might all go wrong."

Kate nodded, letting him talk on. *Paris –"that's where she lives actually"*. He'd said it as if they didn't actually live together. She checked his expression from the side as she walked beside him down the darkened corridor towards the night canteen. She hadn't expected him to be overjoyed about Marianne's operation, or about the premature delivery, or the fact that the baby was quite sick and in the Special Care Baby Unit; but there was more than just anxiety and disappointment in his face. There was no hope there, no joy for his newborn daughter. Jonny was *unhappy* now.

She looked carefully at every inch and corner of his face while they sat opposite each other in the canteen, she cradling a mug of coffee in her hands, he playing with a scone. Her eyes traced the contours of his eyebrows where she had once kissed the skin there. She inspected the angles of his cheek and jaw. The lines that had developed on his neck where she had once lain her own face and breathed in the scent of him.

It was as if she could feel his skin against her cheek again, just watching him there, and it felt as though she almost had to restrain herself from holding his hand just like she would have done years ago if he'd been upset, or taking it up to kiss it.

He looked so lost and in despair.

She was longing to ask him everything about his life since she'd last seen him over ten years ago, but that would be the wrong sort of thing to say. She was dressed in scrubs with a paper theatre hat still on, her bleeper parked in her breast pocket. He was waiting for his wife and baby to recover from near-death.

She had taken out his wife's womb.

Sitting drinking coffee with one of the patients' husbands in the middle of the night, she could feel the eyes of Natasha and the other midwives who weren't getting plastered at the Res party zooming in on her like snipers' sights, from where they sat muttering over midnight coffee in a corner. She took her paper hat off and stuffed it in a pocket, suddenly conscious of her appearance.

"That's better," Jonny smiled. His slightly crooked smile hadn't changed a bit. "Less theatrical. Do you want this scone? I'm just not hungry."

She shook her head. "Jonny, I wanted to talk to you

about – about Marianne's delivery, all the obstetric stuff. But first, can you tell me a bit about her?"

He sighed. "What do you want to know?"

"Where you met. How long you've been married. What's she like? Where you live. What she does. I mean, I've heard that she's a lawyer but –" She was itching to ask him why he'd said "*she lives in Paris*", rather than *we* live in Paris, but it sounded too nosey and inappropriate now. "Why didn't you tell us you were getting married?" she said instead. She lowered her eyes. "She doesn't use your name – in the hospital records, you know – so I would never have known she was your wife until Dave told me."

"She doesn't use my name because we are getting a divorce."

She stared at him.

"Perhaps I will eat this scone after all." He pulled it apart, and started spreading butter on it. "Kerrygold," he mumbled. "Lovely treat. French butter tastes like shite, you know."

"Jonny, is the baby –" She didn't want to finish the sentence, but she knew what she was hoping the answer to the question would be. *That it wouldn't be his.* That Marianne was just an ordinary patient who had nothing to do with her and Jonny now, and that the baby was someone else's, and that Marianne would recover from her hysterectomy and go away and live happily ever after and –

"Is the baby mine? Oh, God, yes! Of course!" He

smiled at her look of desperation. "Don't worry, Kate, we hadn't made that big a mess of it quite yet!"

Kate instantly felt ashamed. She felt her face buzz. And she certainly wasn't going to ask about the two terminations now.

"I didn't mean to imply —"

"No, you were all right to ask. People do have love affairs, all the time," he shrugged. "And it would have been a possibility, and in Marianne's case she is a beautiful and strong and wonderful woman and I don't know why she didn't have an affair, to be quite honest. But the truth is that I am the one who did. I'm the one who messed around. And the other truth is that I didn't want to have the baby. I didn't want us to have it at all, you see."

He looked so utterly miserable. Kate wanted to take his hand: but there was the question of an animated audience just across the room. She bit her lip instead.

"We were having a row the day I found out she was pregnant," he went on. "I had no right, of course, to tell her that I didn't want us to have it, after the way I had behaved." He looked down miserably at his buttered scone. "On the one hand I was furious with *myself* for getting into such a mess. And the worst thing was that I'd just told her I wanted a divorce. We were in the middle of a horrendous row with me telling her that our marriage wasn't working and that I needed a divorce, and in the middle of that, she told me. Well, you can imagine what that felt like. And then, of course, we didn't speak for days." He paused and picked away at his scone again. "The other woman was just the signal of the end, really. She knew that – both of us did. I wasn't going to be one of those caricature French guys who keep a series of mistresses on the side – she's very independent, you see. Anyway, after several days we decided that we needed to call a truce and so we both went out to dinner. It was one of those horrible fiddly ten-course meals in one of these tiny Left Bank bistros that she loves." He smiled. "So after the coffees and cheeses and God knows what, all the little cognacs and things, she told me that she'd got the divorce papers all drawn up. She's very efficient when she wants to get something done, of course." His voice stopped there. "And that she was going to have the baby all alone. I wasn't going to be a father, so to speak."

This was the last thing Kate could possibly have expected.

What she had thought she was going to be able to do when she met up with him was to sit down together as old friends and to talk to him, as a doctor, about how difficult the delivery had been. How sick Marianne had been. How wonderful it was that Veronique and Marianne were still alive and were doing well and that what she wanted more than anything was to be able to go down to the ward and talk to the two of them about it together but unfortunately the Prof had told her to stay away from Marianne from now on. But now, after hearing all of this. Her professional integrity was going to be the last thing he'd give a stuff about.

She watched him fiddle with the wrapper of a plastic packet of jam, saying nothing. He opened the jam, and put it down again. She took the buttered scone off his plate and bit into it. It tasted like cardboard.

"Jonny, that sounds absolutely awful. So what happened then?"

The nurses' voices from the other side of the room were hushed now, and Kate knew that they were dying to know what she was talking to this man about. But she didn't care any more. She just waited for Jonny to speak again. He leaned back in his chair and looked at her. He smiled briefly, and then frowned again.

"Marianne doesn't love me any more," he began unhappily.

Oh God, why is he telling me all this? she screamed inside herself. But she didn't try to stop him. If anything, she was quite desperate for him to tell her more.

"And the other woman?"

He shook his head. "That's all over now. It was very brief. It didn't really matter. That wasn't what the problem was. The problem was that I didn't ever really love Marianne properly."

Silence. In the clatter of the dishes, the nurses gossiping, the rattle of coffee cups and spoons, all that she could hear was their silence.

She lowered her voice to a mutter. "Then why did you marry her, Jon?" Jesus, she said to herself. Cop yourself on. Talk to him about the operation now instead – you're a doctor for God's sake, not his agony aunt!

"Because it seemed like a good idea at the time. Why did you marry Dave?" he glinted at her.

"I married Dave because I couldn't have you!"

She couldn't believe that she had said it, just like that. Her voice was a hoarse stage-whisper but it sounded like a roar. She felt the seven pairs of eyes snap on her again. She whipped her own sharp glare around to face their table, and checked the seven heads to make sure that they all turned briskly away from her and resumed their own conversations.

She turned to look back at Jonny.

He was saying nothing, just looking at her curiously.

"That was very unfair to Dave," he eventually said.

"Oh, Jonny, that's the worst thing you've ever said to me!" she snapped back at him. Suddenly she didn't give a sugar if the nurses heard her. "You married someone that you admit you never loved! But I did love you. And I did love Dave. I loved both of you – but that was what the problem was." She looked down again. She had crumbled the discarded scone into crumbs.

Jonny stared at her.

This conversation was pretty much going off the wall, she thought, but she couldn't stop herself now.

"But you didn't want me then," she hissed. "You walked away. You made love to me – Oh, God, Jonny, you slept with me when Dave was still in Kenya and I fell so badly in love with you. And in the morning you were bloody gone. I woke up and the room was empty, you had just walked out. I left messages with your mother, for God's sake! You ignored all of them. You *never* got in touch. But Dave came back and he was always there for me. He'd *always* loved me, unlike you. And you sit there telling me I was unfair to Dave? I married Dave because I knew that he *would* always be there when I needed him. Although the truth was," she looked down at her coffee miserably, "that in many ways he would have done anything to keep me away from you, and perhaps that's what I mistook for love. I guess that I mistook desperation for fidelity," she ended hollowly, and took her coffee cup in both her hands again.

It was stone cold. She peered into its gloomy contents. Always too hot when you want to drink it and gone too cold by the time you get around to it.

"And are you unhappy with Dave right now?" he asked her gently.

Kate felt the seven pairs on eyes on her again as he reached out to touch her forehead, tucking her hair back behind her ear. She didn't care. They could all go to hell.

She had said far too much to him already but there was no taking it all back now. She played with her spoon for a while, Jonny folding and unfolding a paper napkin.

"We all have our problems," she said in a softer voice, watching the napkin folding tightly and then springing back to life again. "Dave is permanently tired. He works very hard. And he gets quite depressed. His job is too demanding. And I'm never really there for him. I'm always on call, or he is too, so we never get to meet really." She smiled at Jonny, at the irony of it all. But she knew that he would understand.

"Medical marriages are notoriously tough," he told her.

It comforted her to hear it once again. The same truth that everybody told her. Everyone who had ever noticed the stony silences that erupted between herself and Dave. The late-night screaming. Her face when it was puffy in the mornings. The sheer joy she felt when they *could* be happy or relax together for a brief moment.

"Is that why you and Marianne don't get on, d'you think?" she asked him. "Is it the pressure of work? I never asked you what sort of law she does."

"She's a lawyer with a firm that does a lot of work for companies that deal with the EU. And is it pressure of work? No. It's nothing as exotic as that. We work hard and I go away a lot. We live in three different cities. And I'm not always there for her, nor is she for me. But I don't think that's it either. I just think that – Oh, I suppose she's just very French, really!" he ended with a smile.

Kate smiled weakly back. "You're so parochial!"

"No, I mean she's very beautiful and very elegant and very perfect. *Bon chic, bon genre* is what they call it in Paris. Very charming, very lady-like, highly organised, very bossy, rich family, very undermining – I'll stop now," he smiled. "But it wasn't working, Kate, and that's the long and the short of it. She would probably say that I'm too dreamy, too unmotivated, too Irish –" He took a sip of cold coffee and winced as it went down.

"So, what are you going to do now?" she asked him quietly.

He put his head into his hands and raked his hair back with his fingers. She watched the movement of long fingers that had once swept over her like a wave. Hands that had touched her and made her come like a lightning bolt in his arms. She watched him tug his hands through his black hair. She had once held him between her legs, and she felt herself stir down there again, wanting desperately to have those feelings back again. Feelings that she'd feared had only really belonged to her and Jonny.

Perhaps she had been right to fear that way.

"I have a daughter now. Even if I don't deserve one," he added miserably.

"Of course you do," she said. But her voice was dry. She swallowed hard again. "Everybody changes when a baby is born." But her voice wasn't her own one now. It was the voice of a neonatal parents' support-group manual, a calm and measured voice of reason and of a duty to care. Her own voice was the one that was still deep inside her head, screaming at her to seize him in her arms and cover his face with kisses, to take his mouth in hers and taste his breath again. Her own voice was telling him to forget all about this mess with Marianne, forget about bad marriages, forget about the guilt and sorrow and walk away, run away with me, forget about the babies and the hospital.

Her face burned hot with sudden shame.

"Do you want to go back up to the SCBU again and see if Veronique's ready for her goodnight kiss?" she asked him lightly.

He took her hand in his.

"Only if you'll come with me," he replied.

Kate did not believe in infidelity. She believed that people only sought affairs when they had been serially rejected by their lover. An affair is an attempt to console oneself and to repair the psychological damage of rejection, she decided, as she watched Jonny stroke his feeble baby's single wisp of damp black hair. That's the whole reason why I married Dave, she reminded herself.

I married Dave because of what happened between Jonathan Domville and me. What I started was an off-and-on *affair* with Dave Hardiman; perhaps it should never have *become* a marriage.

It was Jonny who rejected me.

One doesn't *want* to have simultaneous lovers, she remembered. One merely wants to heal the pain of sexual rejection.

Sometimes, affairs are pre-emptive strikes, Kate told herself, looking through the glass at Jonny now.

Professor Crowe decided to pop upstairs to see the French patient before leaving the hospital. Sharon had told him earlier that her husband would be arriving later on that night and so he hoped to have a quick word with him to make sure that nothing would go wrong, that they understood everything they needed to understand. But Marianne Le Normand was alone.

"I heard your husband was arriving tonight so I thought I'd just pop by. I was hoping to talk to him too."

"He has gone to take a break," she said in a cautious voice.

"Ah, well. I just wanted to see how you were doing. Much better I see today, although it'll be a while before you're back at work!" He beamed at her and then snapped the smile off when it was greeted with a stony face. "Although I'm sure you've got much better things to do now, than worrying about work – isn't that right?"

"Better things?"

He chuckled. "Motherhood is a full-time job!"

"Excuse me?" she replied. "I already have a job."

He smiled a very cheerful smile. "Ah, that's what every woman thinks. And a career is fun when you are young. But motherhood changes the way you feel about everything, doesn't it?" he beamed. He squeezed her toe reassuringly, where her foot was sticking up underneath the sparkling white hospital quilt.

She said nothing, staring back.

Probably she doesn't really understand, Professor Crowe thought impatiently, thinking that he'd probably just leave it at that. And then he thought of something else.

"You left it very late though, didn't you – travelling for work at thirty-four weeks gestation – that was very risky, wasn't it? I'm surprised the airline let you travel.

They are supposed to prevent women travelling in late pregnancy."

Again, she continued to stare. At this rate her eyes would cross over, she was staring at him so hard.

He raised his eyebrows and nodded, encouraging her to speak.

"I had business to attend to in Dublin. I don't drop everything," she said in a frosty voice. "I wasn't ill, till I came here."

"Yes, well, you're going to have to drop a lot of things now of course, you know," he replied. She was looking blankly back at him and so he carried on. "I suppose what I'm saying to you is that, obviously, until now you've always put your career first, but perhaps this is nature's way of telling you to slow down." He waved a hand to indicate the room with all its medical equipment, oxygen pipes, hand-sanitiser, taps, waste-bin, kidney dish gleaming by the sink.

"*Nature's* way?" she said.

"We need to listen to what nature is telling us more often," he replied. "Nature has been looking after women in childbirth for centuries and perhaps we should respect that, learn something from that." He smiled at her again. Oh, perhaps he wasn't getting through to her, but goddammit he was doing his best with the icy cow! She was just sitting there staring at him as if he had ten heads on him. Perhaps this had been a mistake. Talk to the husband later on instead. She was probably some sort of feminist Eurocrat anyway, spending years drawing up legislation for gay marriages or something. Two abortions – well, that said it all, didn't it?

"Get some rest now," he said warmly to her as he left the room. "I'll try to talk to your husband when he's in."

The Res party was in full swing when Kate arrived down to the on-call kitchen. Ronan was busy snogging one of the student midwives underneath the giant branch of mistletoe that someone had brought down from their dad's farm in County Leitrim. The branch of mistletoe looked ridiculous, like a witch's broom taped strategically onto the ceiling with hospital surgical tape. But it *was* getting some good feedback.

Kate smiled around her at the happy drunken faces and helped herself to a bowl of salt and vinegar crisps. Sharon Guinness was there too, squealing with laughter curled up in Jim Latham's lap, twirling his Tom Selleck moustache around in her pink manicured fingers. Jim was looking mortified but quite turned-on at the same time.

Kate made herself a cup of strong black coffee and rooted wearily around in one of the cupboards for the sugar.

Someone had set up an iPod with speakers and an interminable series of Christmas jingles were rocking the place. Bing Crosby, Louis Armstrong, Frank Sinatra – why does everything have to bloody remind me of Jonny? A familiar exhausted confusion of feelings welled up inside her again.

She stood with her back to the sink, drinking her coffee, and watched the others roar with laughter, and wondered for a moment if Jonny would like to be invited back down to join the party. There he was, spending every minute either sitting miserably beside Marianne, who was still too ill to speak, or sitting equally miserably in the SCBU with baby Veronique, his forehead creased up with guilt. He could probably do with a bit of a bash.

On the other hand, she thought, watching Jim Latham slide his hand up Sharon's Guinness's dress while Sharon writhed with glee before leaping away to dance around the room with Ronan, there are enough horny nurses down here to absolutely destroy Jonny. They'd eat him up for breakfast, she thought, as another nurse rapidly replaced Sharon Guinness on a grinning Jim's well-worn lap, and tried a Santa hat on his head, pressing her breasts into his purple face.

"Hi there, Ronan, having a good time?" Kate said a little later when Ronan swayed over to her, pouring himself another giant measure from the two-litre bottle of vodka that someone had brought back from a skiing holiday in Bulgaria.

"Whaddaya mistks with this, do you think?" Ronan asked her solemnly.

"Coke? Fruit juice? More vodka? Why don't you try to make Martinis?" She nodded at the side-board that was groaning with drink. "Look. Somebody's bound to have a bottle of dry vermouth over there."

Ronan kissed her on the lips.

"Kate, you're gorgeous," he mumbled boozily.

"Ronan, you're slaughtered."

"Kate, I ruv you!"

"Ronan, I so wish that that were true."

"Kate, I'm sorry to have to tell you this but I'm going to *have* to shag Sharon Guinness tonight. She is *so* up for it!"

"Jesus, Ronan, you are not!"

"I am. She promised me," he hiccoughed in her face.

"Ronan! She probably promised everyone. In any case, where's Professor Crowe? Isn't she supposed to be banging him, you said?"

"That's the whole fucking point." Ronan hissed alcoholic fumes at her. "He isn't *here*. He's wesh his wifelet."

"He's wet his Y-fronts?"

"No. He's with his wife. His missus. Her indoors. He's at home and Sharon's out. She's up for it. Definitely. I'm telling you!" He hiccoughed loudly again.

"Ronan!" Kate couldn't help laughing at him. "She's already wrapped herself around Jim Latham and look at what that's started. And in any case, she's married too. Oh, Ronan," she sighed and ruffled his thick, overgrown dark-brown hair, knocking it all sideways, "you should find yourself a nice sexy but reliable woman who isn't all complicated, you know."

"Yeah. But you're already married too, Katie-cakes. *And* you are far too complicated for me. You'd break my heart completely —"

"Stop it!" she punched him in the chest. "Go on. Get laid. Spread your love around, Ronan, while you still have it."

"Do you love your husband, Kate?" Ronan nuzzled his squidgy body up to her at the sink. She giggled and squirmed away while he smelled her neck.

"Get off me! You smell like a brothel! Of course I do!"

"So why isn't he here tonight? Why don't you ever go out with him? Why don't you bring him when you go out drinking with me and Nick and Sharon Guinness when she is in between lovers?" Ronan was kissing her neck, and she shrieked because it tickled.

"Speaking of Nick, where is Nick Farrelly tonight?" She pulled away from Ronan, whose body stumbled suddenly without her support.

He hiccoughed again and burped loudly.

"Fuck!" He burped again. "Sorry, Kate. Where's Nick? Oh, this party is far too *hettie* for him. He's gone to some big gay bash. The Anaesthetics Society Annual Christmas party. Something like that. Gay drug rep from Glaxo Smith Kline who looks like David Beckham coupled with free drinks at the Front Lounge – you couldn't see Nick Farrelly for dust!"

"Of course! The Anaesthetics Society. *That's* where my husband is tonight." She smiled happily to herself. Ronan burped again.

"See? It's not because I don't love him." She nudged Ronan's thickset waist.

"Hey up, there goes Sharon! Bye-bye Katie!"

And Ronan Clare fled into the corridor after Sharon Guinness.

At midnight that night, Kate Gilmore stood in theatre scrubs and gown performing a midnight Caesarean section for a drug-addicted nineteen-year-old in obstructed labour.

At midnight, Jonny Domville sat silently beside his estranged wife again, watching her heavily drugged sleep, thinking about the child still struggling on her ventilator. The child that they now shared.

Ronan Clare took Sharon Guinness from behind a disused theatre trolley with a wobbly leg that someone had left abandoned in an empty side room while the Res Christmas party rolled.

And Dave Hardiman slid his tall broad-shouldered body onto a purple barstool in The Front Lounge on Parliament Street.

There was nothing Dave loved more than to park himself on a good barstool to inspect the rows of bottles that were displayed behind the bar. To look at their colours. The depth of orange in a bottle of cognac. The lurid yellow of Chartreuse. Green vivid gin bottles like emeralds. Tight pouring spouts, erect like swan's beaks. Sitting looking at the row of spirits and liquors *was* like looking into the window of a jeweller's shop to Dave.

Nothing bad ever happens at Tiffany's.

Dave beckoned the Brazilian barman over and motioned for him to fill him up again.

Sometimes he longed to be a little bit more adventurous with the lesser-tried *apperitivos* and *digestivos*, as Charles Gilmore like to call them.

Frangelica. Grand Marnier. Pimms Number One. Blue Curacao.

But there was no real point in ordering a drink that one was not accustomed to.

There was a certain reassurance in wine, Dave thought, as he waved at the barman to serve him another quarter bottle of Wolf Blass. A dose dependency, Dave thought. You knew where you were with a miniature bottle of wine.

You knew the exact alcoholic hit from each glassful, each tiny bottleful. He could predict how many it would take before he got that wakefulness that he needed, when the spasm in his jaw released and his shoulders finally sank into place, and he could open up his eyes and look at people *right* there in the face. There was a point that he could reach after a certain number of glasses of red wine (it once was four – but that was a good while ago – nowadays it was several more – nine maybe – but that wasn't too much, really) when he could feel the longed-for numbness in his cheeks, as the tightness in the mandible released, as though his eyes at last were loose and free to roll almost independently in the sockets of his head.

Across the room, Nick Farrelly had just walked in.

8

The fact that a special order of extra-small-sized gloves had to be arranged regularly just for Doctor Kate Gilmore was a matter of endless mirth among the nurses.

"You'll never be able to deliver babies with those tiny hands!" the midwives used to tease her when she had started on the job.

"You'd fit your entire fist into that vagina, Kate, never mind two fingers," Nick had once said in theatre, to the huge titillation of the nurses. "Two fingers of one of your hands would be lost in there – you'll be right in up to your elbows like a vet examining a horse." Kate had thought his teasing her disgraceful.

But all the midwives now acknowledged that despite Kate's tiny hands and fingers, her sutures of the perineum were pretty neat, her section scars were impeccable, her wound infection rate was nil and she seemed to get in and out of wombs and abdomens with greater speed and accuracy than all her larger hairy-pawed male colleagues.

"Maybe obstetrics isn't all about brute strength," Kate had said when the men had teased her about the extra-small-sized gloves – splaying out her fingers with her two rings on the wedding finger, one ruby and one plain gold band. "Maybe it's about sensitivity too."

Kate worked briskly now, choosing metal clips to close the skin, happy with her neat result. She took enormous pride in her surgery. She tried to be as gentle as possible in tugging the abdomen apart, conscious of preserving the integrity of muscle, keeping the likelihood of ugly scarring to a minimum.

"That's a wrap then!" she smiled at the anaesthetist who had replaced Nick Farrelly that night, and snapped her extra-small-sized gloves into the bin.

"You going back down to the party?" one of the nurses asked her.

"Nah!" Kate wrinkled her nose, pulling off her mask. "That crowd are too unconscious to notice who's there and who isn't any more. I think I'll just hit the sack and get some sleep for as long as I can before we're up again."

She turned around in her clogs and walked briskly out of the theatre double doors, just noticing the clock, half-past midnight, on the wall above the Paeds station. In the recovery area, Kate stopped a moment to look briefly at the new-born she had just delivered. The baby would be jittery in an hour or so – it was scheduled to go straight to SCBU, leaving its mother from the moment it was born for observation in case drug-withdrawal symptoms began. The midwife was pottering around, and the baby lay alone for a moment, all wrapped like a fattened sausage roll in its clear box on high wheels. Pink cotton hospital blanket. Bright red face. Damp black hair peeking out from underneath the blanket like a tiny nun beneath her veil.

The door snapped open and a young, pimply shy face poked through the door.

"You're the baby's father?" Kate looked up with a smile.

He nodded, terrified-looking.

"Come on in!" she said, reaching out her hand to him, "and look at the beautiful daughter that you have!"

The youth stumbled through the door into the suffocating heat of the theatre suite and Kate stood back a little to let him get close to the cot. Across his shoulder, she saw the theatre nurse smile over at her. Kate tapped the young boy on the hand.

"Do you want to lift her up?" she asked.

"Would you be allowed?" he looked at Kate, anxiety on his face.

"Of course! She's your baby. Take her out and give her your first cuddle, Dad!" She lifted the small sausage up for him. "And think of it – for the rest of you life you will never forget this moment."

The boy took his little pink parcel out of Kate's hands and brought it closely to his chest.

"See?" Kate touched the baby's forehead and smiled

at the worried-looking youth. "She's so perfect, isn't she?"

"All her fingers and toes are there?" he asked in a hoarse voice.

"Everything," she nodded. "Have you got a name picked for her yet?"

He shook his head. "She's got one picked out." He nodded at the theatre, where nurses' voices and the clattering of metal could be heard.

Kate nodded. "She'll be out in just a minute. Look!" she said, and the double doors swung open and the trolley with her patient trundled through.

"There she is." Kate touched the young boy lightly on the back. "Congratulations, Mum and Dad."

"Can I put it back now?" the boy asked Kate.

"How long have you been waiting here?"

Kate couldn't believe it. There he was, sitting on the wooden bench outside theatre, waiting for her. Her face broke into a smile, and then she noticed his expression.

She sat down on the bench beside him in her scrubs, paper hat still on her head, and looked at him.

"What's happened, Jon? Have you been waiting for me out here all this time?"

"Kate," his face was a hollow of misery, "after I left you at the SCBU I talked to the professor on the phone. He told me Marianne can't have any more kids. He says he talked to her about it earlier."

She felt her face burst into flames. She grasped his

hand in hers, and squeezed it tight. So now he must know she'd done the delivery.

"Jonny, I'm so sorry. And I should have talked to you about it earlier too only we got caught up in so many other things. But, Jonny, I really wanted to tell you that I'm so, so sorry."

He said nothing to her, staring down at his brown shoes. Kate looked at his feet. Soft, beautiful Italian leather just like toffee. She squeezed his hand tighter.

"Jonny, the thing is that she didn't contract after the delivery. The uterus wouldn't close down. I did everything I could. We all did." To her horror she felt her eyes were filling up. "We tried so hard to stop the bleeding, but after fifteen units of fresh frozen plasma and six units of packed cells – well, you know the dangers of all that."

Jonny stared at her in bewilderment. "Kate," he said, "I haven't got a clue. I'm an epidemiologist. Don't talk surgery to me, please!"

"I'm sorry –" she began, but he squeezed her hand back.

"No, I'm sorry. Forget about it. Sorry, I just wasn't following. You'd had to transfuse her a lot. But, was there something wrong with her? Because – because of the abortions – is that why –?"

Kate stopped him right there before he had to ask her any more. "No, Jon. That wasn't it. The uterus was healthy, although we will have a pathology report soon on it. But the problems arose during the operation itself. We had to over-transfuse Marianne to keep Veronique alive. It was a tough decision, but I had to take out the one thing that was causing her to lose blood. She very nearly died, Jon, and that's the plain and simple truth of it. We saved Marianne and we saved the baby. Veronique. We saved Baby Veronique. That's why we went to section, and why we gave her so much blood. To save Veronique. And we took out Marianne's womb to save Marianne. And that's the beginning and the end of it."

He sat there silently, taking in what she had said.

There was one more thing that she knew she had to say next.

"Jonny, I did the operation and I'm the one who should have gone to speak to her. But Professor Crowe wants to look after her all himself now. And perhaps that's better, with you and I being friends, of course. And normally – I've been doing obstetrics now for seven years, and I can take responsibility for things. But I want you to please tell her that I am most terribly sorry about everything that went wrong."

Jonny lifted up his dark head wearily. "You think she'd care about anything I have to say?"

Kate looked at him. "Yes, she will. She'll need someone to be with her now."

"Thanks for telling me, anyway." Jonny squeezed her hand again.

But the truth was that she hadn't told him; she hadn't told him anything at all. He'd had to find out the hard way. She bit her lip again and then looked at him.

"Jonny, are you going to come around to the house,

while you are here? I mean, are you going to meet up with Dave again?"

"I did ring Dave, you know," he said.

"I know. But he —well, when I asked him, he said he thought that you didn't want to pick up the friendship any more. And so, I can't help wondering. Why not? Surely we're all over that stuff now. I mean, you've got Marianne — and Veronique now, haven't you? After everything that's happened now — can't we all be friends again?"

"What on *earth* are you talking about?" His voice was suddenly quite sharp.

Kate withdrew. "I didn't mean to upset you, Jon. I'm sorry."

"Upset *me*?"

"Jonny," she looked right into his eyes, "why *can't* we all be friends again? Please. We can put aside what happened between us — and Dave only knows that we kissed that time. I want to be there for you now. I just want us all to be there for one another. We all need each other now."

To her astonishment, Jonny laughed.

"What?" she smiled shamefacedly. At least he wasn't angry with her.

"Is that what you think the problem between me and Dave is? That we fell out over *you*?"

"Well —" She squirmed in her theatre clothes. She had never felt more foolish in her life. "I didn't have any other explanation for it. Dave is so, oh, *secretive* about it all. Oh, come on, Jonny, give me a break! There we were that summer, three of us, all the best of friends. And then you and I kissed each other and Dave caught us, and that was when it fell apart. That was when it all went wrong."

Jonny smiled quietly to himself and then shook his head. "Flattering and all as that version might be to you, you're not the reason Dave and I fell out."

"Then what is?" she said in a more prickly voice.

He sighed. "It was a complicated thing. But a lot of it is Dave's stuff really. Let him be the one to tell you. I don't want to speak for him."

"That's exactly what he says," she said.

"He admits that it was all his fault?"

"No! He says that it was all *your* stuff. I just don't understand the two of you. I just want us all to be friends again."

"So what *has* he told you then?"

"Nothing. Absolutely nothing. Just like you're doing now."

Jonny turned to look at her anxious face again and stroked her hair. "You look awfully cute in that theatre cap," he said.

"Oh. Crap. I forgot to take it off again," she grinned, pulling the paper hat away, and rubbed her short hair free again.

Jonny touched her hair lightly, and then her cheek. She bit her lip and lowered her eyes to where he had taken her hand again and held it, warm in both of his. She looked down at her tiny fingers in his long ones. At the tips of her short clean nails. There was powder stuck there from her theatre gloves.

"So what did you fight about in Kenya, really, Jonny?" she mumbled. "You can tell me anything, you know, no matter what it was."

She felt him stiffen again and grip her hand more firmly, but he shook his head.

He wasn't going to tell her, and that was the end of that.

Perhaps he thinks that all bad things are better off unsaid, she thought. Water under the bridge or something. Perhaps it's something that's just daft. She waited for him to say something but he said nothing now.

She wanted to ask him if he still played the piano, if he could play for her again, and the trumpet too, if he would play "Blue Mischief" with her again. But it would be completely out of context now. She wanted to return the firm grip of his fingers; to test him, see if their firm grip meant something. But that was not the thing to do.

Perhaps it was the flirtatious atmosphere downstairs at the Res party that was making her feel like this and it horrified her. But she kind of wanted him to stay here with her, just like this, for as long as they could.

Sitting on a hospital bench in damp theatre scrubs with stained clogs on, and hair like a hedgehog, there could hardly be a less romantic moment. And yet. Her breathing quickened. She closed her eyes to the silence. If she couldn't *see* that they were in a hospital, at her place of work, six feet away from where she had just been performing surgery, then perhaps it wouldn't feel so terrifyingly wrong. If she wasn't reminded by the pungent mixture of sour sweat and disinfectant and the rubber squeaks of heels on polished floors that she was sitting with this man just two hospital floors away from the high-dependency bed where his wife lay in her pale post-natal state with a haemoglobin of eight point four, she could almost believe that he still wanted to be with her too.

"Let's not keep going on about the past, Kate," was what she heard him say. And so she nodded, eyes still closed, saying nothing to him.

Then she heard him say. "And at least we two still love each other. Don't we?"

She opened up her eyes to see him twinkling at her. "I –"

He'd said it first. It was definitely him. *So it was true. He'd said he loved her.* She'd heard him say it.

"Well, I've always loved you, Jonny," she heard her own voice say and almost before the words had stumbled out the blood had rushed, ugly, into her face. He looked at her with eyebrows raised and her words seemed suddenly so ridiculous. It was as if they'd been written for her by someone else. Some twittering fool who was writing the sad script for this embarrassing conversation. De-realisation, Kate thought: that's what the psychiatrists call it. The feeling that you are not actually speaking from inside your own body, that you are watching yourself from outside your own body.

She felt as though she could see herself and Jonny from above, both sitting on the wooden bench, side by side holding hands, declaring love; it was like a dreadful hospital soap opera. Christ, if anybody walked by now. Doctor Gilmore sitting holding hands with one of her patients' husbands.

"I think I'm suffering from lack of sleep," she muttered.

He grinned. "Yeah, so am I. Let's go and get some rest. You're still at work, you poor thing. I'm terrible keeping you up all night. It's just kind of lonely, I guess, hanging around the hospital all the time. And I'm going to have to go back to Geneva soon and get back to work. We have so little time."

He seemed almost to be talking to himself now. Her head pounded. She suddenly realised that she was desperately tired. And it was definitely time to go. Time to move away again. Nothing lasts like this. It's just a moment. Nothing more.

She stood up slowly and released his hand. Her palms were damp, sticky with the talcum powder. She rubbed it off, smoothing the blue front of her theatre scrubs.

"Why don't you have dinner with me tomorrow night? Just us?" he said. "I could do with the company." He looked at her and his face was open.

She took a breath. Dinner.

How far away that all sounds at one o'clock in the morning while I'm still at work.

"You mean, you and me and Dave?" she said.

He said, "No, you and me."

In all her years of knowing Jonny, Kate realised that she had never actually been anywhere with him, to eat or drink *in public* when they were alone. They had *always* been a threesome: she, Dave and Jonny. She, Jonny and Dave. Jonny, Dave and Kate. Every restaurant, every café, every bar that they had ever been in, it had been the three of them. The only time she *had* spent on her own with Jonny had been in stealth. In secret love-filled places. A sudden stolen kiss on a piano stool. A single night of frantic sex.

But dinner – now that we are all grown up.

A date. Or just a catch-up between old friends? And when does a catch-up between old friends become a secret liaison between ex-lovers?

Perhaps when either one of their partners doesn't know.

In this case, she knew without having to ask him that neither Dave nor Marianne *would* know. It would automatically become another secret.

Jonny cocked his head sideways, waiting for her answer.

"I know a lovely restaurant here with jazz music," was what she heard her rather distant, breathless and unfamiliar voice tell him.

In their third year at university, Dave was playing rugby every week for Surgeons. Kate and Jonny spent their Tuesday nights and Saturday mornings screaming at the sidelines of one very muddy pitch after another, Kate jumping up and down with vigour whenever Dave scored a try, while Jonny whistled with his fingers in his mouth.

"Stop jumping so enthusiastically, you're making me feel sea-sick!" Jonny would laugh at her, and Kate would wind her scarf around his mouth to gag him quiet and then jump up and down and scream all the louder. The two of them would leap around an exuberant Dave when he came off the pitch when they'd won (Kate continually bouncing up and down like a frog, Jonny smoking a fag while he slapped Dave's mud-soaked back and told him, "Savage, man, savage!") and then they'd hole up in The Swan for the afternoon, or go to stuff their faces with pizza and red wine at Gotham Café on South Anne Street.

On a particularly rainy afternoon in late April, just before the exams were going to start, Dave had an important match in Blanchardstown, and so they all trucked up to watch him play, bringing supplies of sandwiches, a bottle of sherry and a pink Swiss Roll – just in case the famine was still going on in Blanch, Jonny said, watching Kate spread tuna paste thick on toasting bread.

"You'll be glad of this when you're a Starvin' Marvin," she said to Dave, "after scoring seventeen tries and the only places open out there are those scruffy little shops where the food is all out of date!"

And she was right. The only shop that was open near

the rugby pitch *was* a scruffy little shop and so she and Jonny munched their picnic happily while Dave thundered up and down the pitch with thirty other men, in his absolute element.

The score was pretty close and they were coming to the last five minutes of the match. Kate's heart was in her mouth, desperate that they shouldn't have to come away from a whole day out in windy, rainy Blanchardstown with a loss or even just a draw. She was starting her exams next week but Dave and Jonny were beginning theirs tomorrow in Pathology, so they all badly wanted the Surgeons team to win the last match of the season.

Dave scored a try just minutes before the final whistle blew and when he then converted it, the crowd of followers erupted into a hysterical choir of roaring. Kate jumped up into the air higher than she had ever jumped for joy before and then came down awkwardly, all on one ankle, twisting it sideways as she fell so that the whole of her weight came down on it – which wasn't very much, but it was enough to cause a knife of pain to shoot into her bone. She'd landed like a stone. She collapsed immediately into a ball on the side of the rugby pitch.

Dave, who was being carried around the pitch by his team, hadn't seen her fall and it was a good few minutes before he realised that the reason he couldn't make out Jonny's or her face in the throng was because Jonny was kneeling down beside Kate who was lying in a crumpled little heap, her face a small pale ghost, her body folded into a foetal pained position.

"Oh Jesus Christ! Oh, Kate!"

Dave ran to her and fell onto his knees, taking her up into his mud-soaked arms.

"She's twisted her ankle, jumping up and landing down on it," Jonny said.

Dave picked her up from the ground like a child. "Come on," he said, marching briskly to the physiotherapist who put an ice pack on the foot, gave her a Paracetamol and agreed with both Dave and Jonny that she needed to go right to the Casualty. And so they went.

Nine o'clock that night, as it was getting dark, she was still sitting in a cubicle in Casualty in Blanchardstown hospital waiting to be seen by yet another orthopaedic surgeon.

"I can't believe I'm here!" Kate moaned. "Rugby has got to be one of the most dangerous games in sport, and the only person who comes off that pitch injured is a spectator!"

"You'll be fine," Jonny reassured her but the truth was that she was in agony. There was a fracture in one of the small bones of the ankle and the soft tissue around the Achilles' tendon was quite badly inflamed. But they'd had to X-ray her four times to be sure they'd got it right.

By the time Dave and Jonny got Kate home to Percy Place it was midnight. They lifted her out of the taxi cab with her foot in a giant plaster of Paris and a sock, and Dave carried her across the street and up the stairs and put her into bed.

"Lads, you have to go home! You've got an exam

tomorrow!" she groaned when Dave and Jonny started fussing, bringing her up books and a tray of biscuits and tea and a bottle of Jameson.

"I'm not going anywhere," Dave said.

"Me neither," Jonny said.

"Thank you, Dave. You've been an angel. Both of you are angels. But you have to go. You've both got an exam tomorrow morning. I'm going to be all right," and she tried to move her leg stiffly just to show she could. "I can manoeuvre myself enough to get out of bed. I don't need you to be here as much as you both need to sit Pathology."

"I'm not going anywhere," Dave said.

"Me neither," said Jonny.

Eventually she fell asleep with Jonny on one side of her in bed and Dave on the other.

The next morning when she woke, Jonny had gone in to sit his exam. But Dave was still there, sleeping gently, his blond head beside her own.

"Jesus! Dave! It's ten o'clock! What about your exam? Oh, God, I'm dying to go to the loo!" she groaned.

"I told you. I'm not going anywhere," he had said.

He reached underneath her armpits, lifted her out of the bed, carried her in his arms and sat her on the loo.

"You've missed your pathology exam, Dave," she mumbled when he'd put her back to bed. "You're going to fail the entire year!" She looked at his face from under her eyelashes, in her guilt afraid to look properly at him.

"I told you. And I keep telling you. I'll never leave

you, Kate," he said, touching her hair with his fingers. "No matter what happens. I'm not going anywhere."

Dave sat his exams in the autumn with the repeat students who'd failed the first time round. Jonny said it wouldn't *really* affect his career prospects. Not much, that is. Kate sat her exams the next week as scheduled, hobbling in and out on a pair of crutches. Dave met her and got her a taxi home after each paper she sat.

Jonny got first class honours in pathology.

"Well done, man!" said Dave. "Savage! Absolutely savage stuff!"

"You brought me luck, that day on the pitch. The histology question was all about the re-ossification of bone tissue after fracture," Jonny grinned at Kate who was on crutches being propped up between the two of them while they read out their exam results from the notice board.

"Happy to oblige, Domville," she'd said to him. "Always happy to oblige."

She was linking Jonny's right arm with her left one to keep her balance, and with her right hand she reached out underneath the handle of her crutch and held Dave's hand.

"Thanks for staying with me," she said.

When Dave Hardiman and Nick Farrelly got into Dave's '07 Audi Cabriolet after the Anaesthetics Society pharmaceutical party in the Front Lounge, Nick was the one who climbed into the passenger seat – the one which would have been occupied by Kate, which meant that it was pulled into its flex-kneed position, quite near to the dashboard, where it would suit a person who was short-legged. Dave slid his larger body down into the driver's seat, which he had left in its accustomed position, leaving plenty of room between his lap and the rim of the steering wheel. The long and welcoming gap of space he left was exactly the amount of room that was needed that night to accommodate Nick's head.

Dave wouldn't exactly remember anything about his *driving* that particular night, once he and Nick Farrelly had left the night-club. He would remember pieces of the night: the roar of Christmas conversation round the bar, the shrieks of laughter, the flirting and the sudden holding of a glance from Nick Farrelly across a counter, entranced by his deep eyes. He would just about remember having left the night-club with Nick whose brown eyes, now minus their spectacles, had held his irresistibly from across the bar and whose wink had sent a growl down into his balls that automatically reflexed a quick impulse to down his glass of Wolf Blass in one mouthful and leave his bar-stool to approach the other man. Unfortunately, he wouldn't remember all of the lovely sexy conversation that he'd had with Nick (although he would so often try) and the sudden snap of frost that was in the air when they chased outside, or their fog of midnight breath, fumed with alcohol. Outside, he could just about remember where he had parked the car. That was somewhere round the back of Dublin Castle, and so he and Nick had had to browse the side streets, giggling and spluttering until they found it sitting gleaming for them just around the corner from the Iveagh Gym.

And although Dave would not remember that it was precisely *because* he always left the driver's seat at full extension that he was able to find that Nick's head fitted just perfectly inside the space between the steering wheel and the denim curve of his lap where his long legs pushed the chair right back to its furthest extension, what he definitely *would* remember was Nick's head having most certainly been there.

In all his dreams for the few remaining weeks that were to come, he would remember and relive Nick's mouth opening on his crotch, the slip of his tongue, velvety around the hard tip of his cock, the wet gasp of Nick's breath on his balls.

His cock would be forever in Nick's throat. That short and honeyed moment of the night would not, for the rest of his life, ever escape his memories, even if he would never really be sure *why* exactly it had happened.

There were some events that, even if Dave didn't quite remember them afterwards in the weeks that followed, he could piece together their *having happened* together as a result of having discovered evidence. He knew, for example, that afterwards he had driven away from there, because when he eventually discovered his 2007 Audi Cabriolet the next morning it was wrapped around a Kevin Street lamp-post in the freezing cold blue dawn, the airbag inflated. But the exact event of *how* it had all happened was a complete blank to him. He inspected the wreck of his silver Audi, shivering without his coat on *(How the fuck did I manage to go out without a coat last night? Or did I leave the coat somewhere? The Front Lounge? Oh Jesus Christ almighty! What a fucking nightmare!)* Someone had tried to smash a window, to rob the radio probably, but thanks to Vorsprung Durch Technik, their efforts had failed. The attempting burglar had merely left a futile scratch on the glass windscreen. It reminded Dave of the scratches that Mrs Mad Devine, who had owned the Percy Place house before Charles Gilmore, had made on the bedroom window. Mrs Mad Devine had gone demented one night and the neighbours called the fire brigade because they'd found her trying to scratch her way out of her bedroom through the glass.

Someone desperately trying to get out that time; this time, someone trying to get in.

At eight o'clock on a needle-cold, grey, dark December morning, Dave was not in any mood to walk home and sit down with his wife and chat about the car that he had in some way driven into a lamp-post, got out of, and managed to securely lock. He wasn't even sure whether or not he had spent the entire night with Nick. But he had spent it somewhere. And his head felt like it had been driven over. His eyes burnt. Nausea danced a jig around his stomach.

He would go back to the hospital. That was probably the safest place to be right now. He could find an empty on-call bed to lie on, get something into him to help him sleep. He would get something into him to take this fucking head away from him. To help him melt back into his dreams again.

In a trance, Dave raised his right hand to the taxi that was kerb-crawling by. Like a boxer emerging from the ring, he lifted himself into the back seat and let the taxi whirl him away. It was just as if he were being carried away from all the mess on somebody's strong shoulders: to a place where he knew he only had to try just a tiny little bit in order to feel right.

But he had been with Nick, and so many things about that had felt right.

9

"You look nice," said Marianne without affection.

She was looking much more herself now, Jonny noted. Her hair had obviously been washed and had resumed its honey glow, and although her face was still a deathly pale she had more energy about her. She'd put on a little lipstick too, he noticed, and felt relieved that she was coming back to being herself.

"And you look much better too," he said.

"Are you going somewhere?" she asked with suspicion.

He shook his head. "Just out to dinner with some friends. Dave and Kate Gilmore. You remember that I mentioned them."

"Yes — perhaps," she said in a disinterested voice. "How nice you have some friends to meet." She sighed heavily as if exhausted by his mere presence and then asked him impatiently, "Have you called Papa? I can't see *why* my cell-phone won't work in here."

"It can – but it's the hospital rules," he explained. "They won't let you use it in case it interferes with the machines."

Marianne rolled her eyes and muttered to herself in French.

"I did speak to Eric," Jonny said. "He's making sure everything is set up with Docteur Larocque in Paris. But the midwives are saying that you'll have to be more stable before they can transfer, and that Veronique isn't ready yet."

She sighed again. "They know absolutely nothing here. I can't get anyone to give me any sensible information. It's too frustrating. Thank God I have enough expertise myself to take matters further. I mean, what do other women do, being treated like imbeciles?" She looked at him. "They have made a horrible mess of the surgery and nobody seems to want to talk about it. I am sure that they have made a terrible mistake, done something negligent, done something very wrong. How can I be left without a womb? But nobody speaks about the operation! They have not shown me the case notes!"

Her face was very white. She looked exhausted and almost close to tears.

"No, I'm sure they did everything that they could do. This is a teaching hospital, after all."

"Pah!"

"Marianne, not everything is better in France, you

know. You are just missing home, that's all – you'll be able to leave in a few more days and we'll get you flown straight back to Paris. You'll feel much better then."

"I can't go anywhere without Veronique," she said in a suddenly more alarmed voice. "Do you think that they would try to send me back to France without her?"

"Don't worry. I'll make sure they don't."

"Jonny, I am not a child," she said, looking away from him towards the window where the black night was just a reflection of their own uncomfortable duet. "I am just a trapped animal in a cage. I can take care of my own medical arrangements."

"I know."

After a silence she spoke again. "Your parents both seem very proud of Veronique."

"Of course they are," he said.

She looked away towards the black window pane again.

"I'll go away," he said.

"Yes," she said to his reflection in the window pane. "That's a good idea. I need to rest again. Enjoy dinner. *Bon appétit*, Jonny."

"Marianne?"

"*Oui?*" she sighed heavily.

"I'm so sorry about the way the operation turned out. That Veronique is going to be your last. I wish – I hope that you don't mind too much about all that."

Her face hardened again. "I do mind. Of course I mind. I am in pain. I am furious. Everything hurts. I mind very much, you see. But I'll deal with it in my own way, Jonny."

The restaurant in a basement on Kildare Street that she'd been so sure was so lovely felt all wrong before Kate even descended the steps. It was all so obviously intimate, it was almost clichéd. But she was there and he was coming and it was too late to do anything about it now. The tinkly piano player was the sort of thing that she now realised Jonny would absolutely hate – cocktail lounge wallpaper, was what he used to call that sort of rhythm-less arpeggio-playing – "wandering through the tune as if you were trying to plaster the walls with it," he had once told her. She checked herself in the reflection of the glass doorway, took a lip-gloss out of her bag again for just one final stab and then went inside to where it was warm and smelt of garlic, fresh baked bread and charcoal meat being grilled.

To her relief, Jonny had already arrived. He was sitting at a tiny side table lit by a single candle, poking at a BlackBerry. She stood a moment while the maitre d' fussed about her coat and checked her reservation, wanting just to watch him. It gave her an unnerving thrill to see him waiting there for her, knowing that she hadn't had to be the one who sat playing with a napkin trying to look calm. So he was clearly early. Keen to see her. Happily, she walked over to him and touched his shoulder. He stood up and bent to kiss her. She offered her cheek but he kissed her lips instead.

"Mmm . . . sticky!" Jonny smiled. "Hey, you look lovely, Kate!" He inspected her outfit. "This is much nicer than that blue pyjama suit you usually wear."

She smiled and slid into the chair the maitre d' was pulling back for her. She had worn a black sleeveless wraparound cashmere evening top that Caroline had left behind after her last visit, over black satin pencil trousers and stiletto heels – the only pair of killer-heels that existed in her wardrobe, but nevertheless a pristine and shiny, beautifully unworn pair of bright red Christian Louboutin shoes that Caroline had insisted she buy in a sale last January.

"Investment shoes," Caro had called them, and Kate had bought them just to please her. So far, the shoes had remained in negative equity in their magnificent box on a perfectly tidy shelf all alone like a museum piece. But tonight Kate had felt that their time was due; their dividend was to be called in.

"You always look so lovely and natural."

He poured water into a glass for her and she checked his face to make sure that this was actually a compliment. If Dave had said "you always look so natural" to her, she could be sure that he was complaining that she hadn't shaved her armpits.

"You look better too, Jon, much much better tonight."

"Yeah. Veronique's off ventilation, and she's turned the corner completely."

Jonny was clearly quite at ease. But she still felt somehow as though they were being observed again, just like they'd been at the hospital, alone together in a public place, although there was no particular reason why they shouldn't be here. She glanced quickly around the restaurant, which was a fashionable place where it could be quite possible that consultants, or professors from Trinity or other about-town well-heeled diners might be out on a Saturday night before Christmas, but there was nobody there she recognised.

"My parents told me about this place too – they seem to like it. So, good choice, Kate." He hadn't noticed her anxiety about the over-romantic atmosphere at all. "Dad recommends the steak frites and the duck, of course. He's got very plain taste in food, I have to say. Although I have to admit, you do get sick eventually of all the neurotic dining that they do in France." He grinned, passing her the breadsticks.

"How is Dominic these days?" she asked him lightly, snapping one in two.

"Dad's great," he replied. "Still working in fact. He's very happy. Mum is too. They are thrilled about the baby, of course, and then at the same time they keep getting all upset about her being premature. And they think it's awful about Marianne, of course. But she seemed tons better tonight too when I left."

Kate nodded. It was like a slap in the face and a shoulder to cry on all at the same time. The tremendous tenderness she felt for Marianne that almost bordered on pity was like an ugly lump of something sour in her stomach. She desperately wanted Marianne's recovery. And she was desperately anxious about the pace of progress of Veronique. But it was in some awful, horribly shameful way a kind of pain to have to hear Jonny talk about his *family* like this. She looked hard at Jonny's face and tried to find a way to see the *father* in it that he'd now become. The husband to a beautiful woman. An important and now desperately vulnerable woman.

"I've always liked your dad," she said. "And Marcella, too," she added with a note of caution, although privately she had always thought that Jonny's mother was quite barmy.

"Yeah. They are over at the hospital tonight. Giving me a night off." He smiled, and she felt her body swim again. Veronique. Marianne. Even Dominic and Marcella didn't matter now as much to him as they did. It was inevitable. And yet he and Marianne had no relationship any more. She doesn't love him, he'd told her that quite clearly last night. And he had never loved her.

She hated herself for it, but she couldn't help feeling jealous of his sense of duty to Marianne and Veronique.

"It's good to get out of that place for the evening," he continued, munching on a breadstick. "Get the smell of hospital out of the air."

She nodded wordlessly again, hooking on his eyes. It was impossible for her to talk about Marianne to him; she felt it like a solid blockage in her throat. She could only listen to him silently. She hoped desperately that he could sense that what she was trying to convey was empathy.

"How do you put up with it all the time, Kate? You're there five days a week and several nights on call. Don't you ever feel the place sort of soaks into you and you can't get the smell –" he shuddered, "– that hot, oh, acid smell of disinfectant – out of your hair? You know?"

"I suppose I've got so used to it by now I hardly notice it," she said. "Surely it's not that long since you worked in a hospital that you don't remember what it's like?"

"Nope! Not at all." He shook his head emphatically. "I went straight into public health after my internship, which I have to admit went by in a sort of unconscious blur."

She looked down at the table, at the snow-whiteness of the linen. The pristine cutlery, like instruments. It was all so beautiful and calm, despite the tinkly wallpaper on the piano which Jonny didn't seem to mind in the slightest.

"I like my job, you know, Jonny," she said. "Most of the time it's really happy news. I love – well, babies, I suppose –" She couldn't help laughing at herself, feeling the remark sounded naïve, and he laughed at her. "I just love those tiny, wrinkly little newborn babies, and it's just really quite lovely and quite special to be around maternity wards all day, and hear the little cries, and know that you're a part of all that: all the – oh, the *parenthood* of it all."

He nodded at her. "I'm so glad it was you who delivered Veronique."

In the candlelight her face burned like a furnace. "I just wish, you know, that she hadn't had to –" her voice crumbled, "– that the delivery had been perfect."

Jonny nodded briskly. "Yeah. But it's all fine now. She's going to be all right. Isn't she?"

She checked his face – soft and innocent. His eyes were kind. She smiled at him. "Of course she is."

"So why no kids for you and Dave then?" he said gently.

She took a breath, suddenly disarmed by the question. "Because I'm only thirty-two!" she gasped. "Because we're both so busy. And because we've still got loads of time to think about that yet!"

She laughed, but he was looking seriously at her and now it didn't feel at all all right. A waiter arrived, making an enormous fuss, with a bottle of wine wrapped up in a linen napkin and a giant ice-bucket on a stand.

"I ordered wine for us already," he said. "I hope you don't mind me being so bossy. I was dying for a drink."

She beamed at him. "No. That sounds fantastic. You're wonderful to think ahead."

"You try it." He pointed at her glass and watched her taste the wine that was as crisp as winter.

"It's fabulous," she told the waiter, and glowed at Jonny, loving the fact that he had gone ahead and chosen beautiful wine for her, loving the thought that he had searched the wine list and thought hard about her, trying to anticipate her taste.

"It's from Marianne's father's vineyard," Jonny said.

"Although, this is ridiculously over-priced. But if you like it, I'll could get Marianne's father to send you over a crate or two."

She swallowed down her glassful almost in one go. "It's great," she said. The wine tasted acidic already. The restaurant wasn't hers to choose after all. Marianne's father was even on the wine list they were drinking.

She put the glass down again and looked up at him. "Jonny, what are you – and Marianne – going to do for Christmas now? Will you stay on in Dublin? Or –?"

"Sir, Madam, are you ready to order?"

"Have you decided, Kate? Do you need more time?"

She stared at the menu blankly, unable to read a thing. It was a list of over-complicated nonsense, food that meant nothing whatsoever. *Confit de* this, *coulis de* that, glazed with rosemary scented *jus*. All sorts of bundled-up conundrums of food that she already hated.

"Um."

"Take your time. I'll be back in a moment." The waiter swept away.

Jonny smiled at her. "It's all very French."

"I thought that was what you might like," she replied. She felt completely feeble. Unable to choose a meal in a restaurant she had recommended. She had wanted so badly to make him happy and instead she felt useless and quite impotent.

"Well, I'm going to have the duck," he said.

"Me too." She smiled in some relief. "And some pâté as a starter," she added much more confidently.

He snapped a breadstick in two and handed half to her, and then poured them both some more of Eric Le Normand's white Bourgogne. She stared at the glass, glistening yellow in the candlelight, full of empty promise.

"So, we were talking about Veronique," he said. "Marianne's father has suggested that we try to get the hospital to arrange some sort of a diplomatic escort back to Paris to the private hospital there, and for her mother too."

"Oh. Yes. Yes, of course he did. I – I'm sure that will please the Prof." Everything was out of her hands. And in the hands of people who were much more powerful, much more important than she was.

What on earth was I thinking? It grated on her slightly to hear him refer to Marianne as "her mother". It seemed so *middle-aged* all of a sudden. It was what middle-aged parents did. It was what her father had done, when he and Sadie had an argument about going back to the Middle East, about where the girls should stay – about why another foreign mission now, one coming straight after another –

"Your mother isn't keen to come, this time."

"Your mother doesn't quite agree."

"Your mother has some other plans, it seems."

"So, that will probably be shortly after Christmas then?" she nodded at Jonny.

He shrugged and then drained his glass of wine. "I have no idea. You'd know more about it than I would. I mean, how long does it usually take to go home from hospital after hysterectomy?"

"Well, usually less than a week, but after a delivery as well maybe up to two weeks or even more. It all just depends."

"And Veronique? When do you think she'll be able to come home?"

"Well, like you said, Ronan thinks she's really turned the corner and she's rallying now. As soon as she's feeding properly and off oxygen I'd say they'll let her go quite soon as well."

Jonny smiled. "That's wonderful. I can't believe how hard it's been for her. She's such a brave little thing." His eyes shone in the candlelight.

"Jonny, oh, God, are you crying?" She reached out to his face.

He shook his head. "I just want her to be all right. I feel so awful about all of it. She's such a tiny little thing and she doesn't deserve all of this."

"Premature babies are very brave."

"No. I mean she doesn't deserve all this – this nonsense between me and Marianne. This battle of wills, this stupid bourgeois marriage we've been having, always having to worry about what Papa will want, me wanting to just get on with my life and Marianne with her big job, and Papa always having to make sure that the politics of it all are – oh, look, it's all just so boring really. I'm sorry, Kate. You don't need to hear all that."

She was so tempted to say it: *oh yes I do*. I desperately

need to hear how awful other people's marriages are, especially yours! But she nodded solemnly instead.

The waiter arrived again and they gave their orders. Jonny asked him for another bottle of wine.

"Just a minute!" she called him back. She smiled at Jonny and then turned to the waiter. "I really liked the wine we've ordered but I'd like to see the list again, if you don't mind."

Jonny smiled at her and bit his lip. "Sorry for being bossy."

She touched his hand. "You're not. You're just married to the wine lake. And I just want to see the wine list in case I might like something different with the food. It's just as simple as all that."

He frowned at her. "I don't want to be married to the wine lake, Kate. I'm not into all the politics in France: you know, the election last year, the social expectations of it all. I know I become very wrapped up in my job but that's the nature of the work – it's very intense. International crises break out suddenly, epidemics happen almost overnight. When I get home from being abroad on a job I just want an easy time of it, playing music, drinking some wine, a little holiday here and there. Like other people have, I guess."

She looked at him cautiously. "What do you mean? Other people? Do you imagine that's what me and Dave have? Easy come easy go, lots of fun and and happy days?"

"Well, you must have something simpler than our lives." He shrugged again, and his dismissiveness irritated her.

"So what is Marianne's job like, then?" she asked instead, despite herself.

"I told you. She takes on work for multinationals doing business in the European economic area – using Swiss and French privacy laws, for example. Companies often like to hide their tracks."

"So, do you have a lot in common? Is she musical, for example?"

He took a sip of wine. "When I met Marianne," he said, "I thought that she was the most beautiful, elegant, perfect woman in the world. Problem is, it turns out that she is." He smiled ruefully. "Which means that I'll never be anything other than imperfect, I suppose. You and Dave *are* luckier."

She looked at him quizzically.

"You were friends since college," he went on, "so I suppose you know each other like a pair of old shoes or something maybe a bit less unglamorous than that. But, I suppose, at least you've got no other *expectations* of it all. That must make you happy, doesn't it?"

She lowered her head. "Dave –" she began, and then she stopped. "Jonny," she began again, "the thing is, Jonny, Dave and I haven't had sex in almost two years. Not proper sex. You know what I mean. And we fight all the time. About everything."

She stopped and sat in silence as her pâté arrived and Jonny's spinach salad. The waiter had brought her the wine list but she left it unopened.

"I'm sorry," he said quietly as soon as the waiter had gone. "I often wondered how it would all work out."

181

She looked at him again. "Why would you wonder?"

He shook his head. "Nothing. It's none of my business, Kate."

"Jonny —" she felt her neck begin to burn but carried on anyway. "I thought, when I married Dave, that it was the best thing to do because he would do anything for me. He — well, you remember what we were like. Like after that rugby match — he would do anything for me. He looked after me like a — a — you know, Jonny, I was going to say like I was his baby sister, and now I realise how crazy that sounds and how possibly telling it is too." She looked up at him.

He smiled at her, but his smile was tender. "Dave went crazy when he thought he might lose you, don't forget that," he said.

"That's because he knew that *you* were the only man that I would ever have actually wanted to be with. It wasn't all about me, it was about the three of us." She heard her voice becoming hoarse, and grasped her wineglass, draining it again. She put it down and poured herself a rather wobbly glass of water.

Jonny stared at her. Their starters lay untouched.

She took a fork and prodded at the lipstick-red cranberries lined up on the side of her pâté.

"I know he loves me, in his own way, Jonny. In his own way he always *has* loved me," she went on. "It's just that he doesn't really know *how*."

Jonny touched her cheek. "He should adore you."

She nodded, and smiled weakly at him.

"I always did," he said.

Her heart thumped in her chest.

"Want some spinach?" he said through a mouthful.

She shook her head. "No, thanks. What's it like?"

"Healthy," he grinned.

"Jonny, here's the thing. Dave drinks a lot, I think. He seems unhappy. I can't be there for him because I'm so busy myself with the hospital, but he seems to need something, somehow, that I can't give him."

"Yes, I know," he said.

She looked at him quite sharply.

"What do you mean – you know?" she said.

He was watching her face with caution. She stared back at him and he returned to his salad.

"I don't know," he eventually said.

"Meaning?"

"I'm sorry. I was trying to sound sympathetic. I mean, I hope that things work out and that you can be happier. Or something. But I think I know Dave pretty well too, Kate. And perhaps there's something in him that isn't quite – at symmetry, if that makes sense. It's hard to explain it, but I wish that – I just wish that things were different and that he knew what he wanted and he knew how to get it." He stopped, noticing her expression. "Find it. Oh, God, I'm sorry," he said rapidly. "I didn't mean to upset you. Look, let's swap starters. You obviously hate that thing you've ordered!"

She passed it over to him. "Not much of a swap, Domville, is it? You've eaten half your salad already!"

"I'm kind of hungry. Haven't eaten much this week, I guess. Hospital food was never my favourite cuisine. And poor old Mum invites me round for meals but then she forgets to cook anything!"

"So, what are you going to do for Christmas? If Veronique is still in hospital?"

"I'm going to the Sudan."

"You're *what*?" She dropped her fork.

He was studiously wiping his plate with a tiny piece of bread.

"The UNHCR are moving a hundred thousand refugees across the Chad boarder and it's a WHO thing. That's my job, Kate. That's what I do in my life, that *is* what my life is all about at the moment. I got a message here just tonight," he tapped his BlackBerry, "from the Red Cross via Geneva, about an outbreak of haemorrhagic fever in the refugee camps. So, I go out there and we respond. You deliver babies, I save lives. I go into the field where people are dying because of wars and crises. Stuff like that. That's just what I do."

It was as if she'd only just found him and now she was losing him again.

And then she suddenly felt ashamed. Desperately proud of him and yet slightly overwhelmed by the idea of it all. She watched him wolfing her pâté with a piece of bread. And then sitting there watching him, she felt herself begin to feel ever so slightly irritated with him, for some strange reason. Irritated with him for being so proud. For being, well, *smug* almost: pouring Eric Le

Normand's Château wine for her as if it mightn't grate on her palate like swallowing a razor blade and then talking about diving off into refugee crises all in the same breath. And yet. This was what he did. And the world survived because of people who would drop everything at Christmas time to deliver a baby or to fly out into an outbreak of haemorrhagic fever in the middle of the desert.

"What about Marianne, when you're in Sudan?" she asked him in a smaller voice.

"Well, as soon as she's discharged from your hospital she's going to go back to Paris and be there with her parents. If not by Christmas, well then at least my parents are here if she's still stuck here, although they aren't a lot of use to her, of course." He frowned again. "So have you decided what wine you want to drink next?"

The waiter was hovering nearby again.

Kate stared at the over-elaborate card he'd handed her. Italian. Australian. French. African. All the corners of the world that had pulled her life apart were laughing at her now from the contents of a wine list.

She suddenly recognised a light red wine from the Veneto that Charles had often had.

"We are going to have this one." She pointed at it for the waiter, then smiled at Jonny. "Because that's the part of the world where my dad lives. He mightn't have his own a vineyard but he's saved millions of lives all around the world too, you know."

"That sounds perfect." Jonny picked up his almost-empty glass of Château-Marianne's-father's-wine. "To Charles!" he toasted, and then he touched her fingers. "You could always come out to the Sudan with me, you know. They can always use skilled obstetricians in the field camps with the NGOs. Or in the WHO."

Kate coughed and almost choked on her wine. "Don't be ridiculous, Jonny. How on earth could I do that? You are joking, aren't you?"

"No," he simply replied. "I wish I were. But the NGOs would love to have you there. Why don't you think about it? Seriously? As a change from all this hospital stuff? What about working with the Red Cross? Or Médicins Sans Frontières? It's good to work abroad, you know. As an experience."

"I worked in Australia," she said.

"I meant in a challenging situation," he replied.

"I know what you meant."

"Well, look, think about it, that's all I'm saying. Let's eat our duck and be merry for tonight, anyway."

"Jonny, don't you think you've got enough challenges on your hands?"

He was still touching her fingers. "Look, I'll only be in the Sudan for a week or so," he said. "No longer than that. I'll come back to Dublin, or to Paris, or wherever Veronique and Marianne are going to be by then. I just want to make sure she's settled after everything before – you know. We have to arrange things. More things. Legal arrangements."

Her head was spinning with the thought of it all. It

sounded far too complicated to take in properly and the wine was making her mind fuzzy.

"I'll ring you and let you know when I'm back again," he continued. "I just thought that, well, because of what you were saying about Dave," his voice was lower, almost gruff, "I just thought that it would be nice for *us* to spend some time together over Christmas, on our own. I felt – I felt from listening to you that you seemed kind of lonely, I suppose. That you could do with an old friend. It helps, you know. I think it does, anyway. To be with someone who's known you all your life – well, a lot of your life. Life gets tough sometimes at our age. I don't know why it does. But being with you makes everything seem all right again. It's as if – oh, and this sounds pathetic but I've always felt as though I *belong* with you, Kate. It always feels so right to be with you."

She looked into his eyes: green flecked with brown, just a darker green than her own. She felt her cheeks buzz hotly in the candlelight. The light red wine she'd ordered was suddenly stronger than she'd thought, but then she hadn't eaten anything yet, and Jonny had polished off her starter. She suddenly didn't feel like eating anything ever again but she knew that if she didn't she'd be completely drunk and probably fall out of the door on all the wine they'd had. She took a piece of bread instead from the basket and dipped it in the gravy of her duck.

"I'd love –" she began.

"To come with me to Africa?" he asked her, beaming hopefully.

"To pick up where we left off, was what I was going to say." She felt her mouth fill with cotton wool. "But I can't come with you to Africa. Not just now, Jonny. Caroline's arriving tomorrow to spend Christmas with me. I've got work – I can't just drop everything and go to Africa! But I would love to *be* with you again. *You* know," she finished, looking back down at her food.

He nodded. "It was really lovely that one time – that one time we had." His voice was suddenly gruff, suddenly vulnerable again. She held her breath.

"I'd really like to kiss you now, too, actually," he said, smiling slightly, and he bit his lip.

She felt a million stars had come out in the sky. Suddenly all the things that had happened in her life had started to make sense to her at last.

There was a reason for the horrible events of the last few days, she thought, happily swallowing her wine. There was a reason Dave couldn't bear to be with her any more. Everything happens, eventually, for a reason.

10

The LA flight had definitely landed but there was still no sign of Caroline. Typically she was late. Over forty minutes late now, which was getting a bit much, Kate thought. She frowned at her watch again, and stretched on tiptoes again to try to see over the crowds hovering at the arrival gate. People came through the glass doors in a constant flow of ones and twos in business suits and then sudden gangs of men yelping in tee-shirts and stag reindeer horns, and then a crowd of chubby women in tight trousers all giggling in bunny ears.

She couldn't wait to see her sister again.

Even though she didn't have much in common with Caroline any more, Kate adored her. Being the elder of the two, she knew she tended to be over-protective of Caroline – a tendency that Caroline usually dismissed as bossiness. But Kate had always felt that Caroline needed looking out for. Caroline was the dreamy one, where she at least tried to be more practical. Practicality was one of the main reasons she'd decided to marry Dave.

Caroline could be very thick-skinned too, to an extent Kate found to be bordering on selfish. But then, Kate could become far too anxious about things that Caroline could just shrug off and let go. And now, with her whole life up in the air, she felt perhaps that she could have done with some of Caroline's breezy lack of insight to get her through everything that had happened in the last few days. Caroline was no stranger to heartbreak either. Many of the conversations that they'd had over the past few years, across the phone or whenever they'd meet up would be an attempt by Kate as an older (by a year) married woman to analyse all the agonies and ecstasies of Caroline's juvenile love-life and to try to make some sort of sense of it while Caroline crashed from one short-term fling to another. But now, for the first time in all their lives, Caroline seemed to be holding on to someone with more tenacity than she'd ever done before. Perhaps Kate should seek out her younger sister's more experienced judgement to sort out all the sudden turmoil that Jonny's parachuting back into her life had thrown up for her.

If Caroline ever gets off the plane that is, Kate thought, and checked the time again. Forty-five minutes and she still hadn't got out of the baggage hall. The airport was absolutely bursting with people and the crowds through the gliding doors seemed to be getting busier and noisier every time it opened. Kate suddenly realised that she might actually have missed Caroline already. The arrivals hall was so full you would easily miss her in the crowd. And Caroline was so dizzy she would have just walked out of the terminal building if she hadn't seen Kate waiting, and would have just got into a cab and gone home.

She tried to see through the crowds of people who were pushing and shoving trolleys and suitcases in and amongst one another, barging through the crowds to get to the doors, and tried to watch the gliding doors from the baggage hall and the crowds inside the arrival hall all at the same time.

And then she spotted her – so easily, of course – how could she ever have thought that she might for a moment have missed her? Caroline's long blonde hair was unmissable in the crowd and she sailed out of the baggage hall in a fur coat and giant sunglasses with no luggage whatsoever apart from a giant Gucci bag.

"What the hell are you doing with no luggage? And what in God's name are the sunglasses for, it's winter here! And you're indoors in case you haven't noticed and it's dark outside, you big thick plank!" Kate wrapped herself gratefully around her sister's bony body. Caroline towered above her older sister by almost seven inches, even in the battered pair of Converse she was wearing.

"Converse and a fur coat – I love it!" Kate shrieked at her happily.

"Fucking luggage lost in Heathrow, where else?" Caroline squeezed her sister and rested her head on the top of Kate's while they walked towards the exit with their arms around one another.

"And the shades?" Kate reached up to whip them off and winced at Caroline's puffy eyes beneath. "Darling, your pillar-box-red lipstick matches your eyes. You're all blood-shot! What happened?"

"Bloody jet lag." Caroline snatched her sunglasses back again. "Leave them on please, Kate – life is much much easier like this."

"Caroline, you aren't going to get papped in here!" Kate beamed at her, squeezing her waist as they walked through the exit of arrivals.

Caroline was paranoid about being papped in Los Angeles ever since she had got a reasonably successful role in a thriller in which she had been required to remove all her clothing. Being short on acting skills and experience, she had cashed in on the desirability of her body to make the bridge from modelling into acting and had landed the role, which she pragmatically regarded as a stepping-stone to loftier dramatic ambitions.

"No bother. Today's soft porn, tomorrow's Shakespeare," Kate had enthusiastically agreed with her, when Caroline had told her about the film. The prolonged nude scene in the thriller had certainly led to further offers: not much Shakespeare, it had to be admitted, but plenty more prolonged nudity in more thrillers. At the moment, however, having just finished a modelling contract for Victoria's Secret, Caroline was still resting.

"Didn't you get to fly first class?" Kate demanded as

they raced across the taxi rank to get inside the car park out of the furiously cold wind.

"No – I cashed the ticket in for two cheaper ones so that Luis could come over with me."

"And where is he, then?" Kate looked around them, rolling her eyes.

"Don't be such a jealous bitch! He's coming later. He's got caught up in something – something that might lead to an exhibition, we're hoping. He'll be over by next weekend at the latest."

Kate was rooting around in her handbag for coins for the machine. "Caro, he won't get a flight next week. It's Christmas Day on Tuesday, for God's sake!"

"He'll be over." Caroline yawned dramatically. "He's got loads of pictures ready for an exhibition and stuff."

"He's a kept man, Caroline."

Caroline pushed her. "You're just jealous because he's such a ride and your husband is a cranky bollocks!"

"I just want to see you happy." Kate force-fed coins into the machine. "Both of us deserve to be happy," she added.

"Fucking freezing!" Caroline grumbled, shivering beside her. "How do you survive the fucking weather here?"

"Get used to it, honey. It's Christmas time!" Kate tucked her arm under Caroline's fur-clad one and marched her towards the end of the carpark where she had parked the Mini.

She tugged at Caroline's fur while Caroline folded

herself into the passenger seat. "Sister, this coat is seriously politically incorrect."

Caroline grinned, showing a blaze of newly whitened teeth.

"Yeah, but I got it as a present when I did a photo shoot for Dolce&Gabbana."

Kate slammed the door of her driver's seat and stared at Caroline.

"Jesus, Caro, your teeth are gorgeous. Have you had them done again?"

Caroline winked at Kate. "*Now* you're jealous!" She lit a cigarette.

Kate didn't try to stop her. She hadn't seen Caro in over a year and she could spend the whole of January spraying Febreze around the car when Caroline was gone.

"Why can't Luis get his own plane tickets?" Kate asked her as she backed out of the parking space and then cringed inwardly as soon as she heard herself saying it. She knew Caroline would think she was being a picky little bitch but she worried all the time when she heard about another great boyfriend that was taking advantage of her sister. She still felt obliged in some way to protect her, even though she knew that at the same time Caroline was probably being spoilt rotten and loving every minute of it. And just at the back of her mind, in the tiniest place of all, was the niggling possibility that after all these years of feeling the need to protect Caroline, she might now envy her. "He could afford it, you know, if he did some real work and did the photographs for the big fashion shoots that you do, instead of farting around at art galleries," she continued. She could hear how spiteful it sounded and yet somehow she couldn't help herself. It was as if the thought of Caroline and Luis living on freebies and fresh air and wearing Dolce&Gabbana coats was the sharpest contrast imaginable to the workaholic, empty life she had with Dave.

Caro blew a ring of smoke at her in reply.

Kate nosed the Mini Cooper into thick traffic that was gathering towards the motorway. It was well past seven in the evening, but the traffic into town was just a snarl-up with Christmas shopping and people coming back in from the airport. She snapped the radio on, twirled the station rapidly away from the Christmas carol concert she'd been listening to and went for some fast-base techno stuff.

Caroline was sending a text message, studiously ignoring her.

"I just think that Luis seems to depend on you a lot, Caro, that's all." She glanced at Caroline again.

"Oh look, I don't mind giving him a dig-out when he's in-between jobs," Caroline yawned. "I can earn enough for both of us when I feel like it, and then some." She reached underneath her seat, found the lever for the reclining position and slammed her seat as far back as she could. "And Luis really wants to concentrate on more creative work now, not just commercial fashion stuff," she went on in a progressively sleepy voice. "And he deserves to have more exhibitions and that all takes time and money and networking."

Kate frowned to herself in the dark. "And how is Luis going to cope with the cold when he comes here? He's never been out of California."

"Katie, will you please shut up nagging me! You sound just like Mum used to when Dad was going abroad all the time!" Caroline snapped. "Luis will do fine. He'll put on a fucking jumper, or something. Haven't you got central heating in the house now, anyway? We can just drink hot whiskeys and have sex all day long to keep warm. Bloody hell, we've just been skiing in Colorado, you know. We aren't complete idiots. In any case, he's from Brazil. So he *has* been out of California already. He goes to Mexico loads nowadays for photographs."

"Hmmm. To somewhere even hotter?"

Caroline stuck her tongue out at her.

"How's husband Dave?" she said then, apparently to change the subject.

"Um. He's okay." Perhaps she'd leave it till later to talk about all that to Caroline.

"Liar."

"Pig!"

"Oh look, I know you, Katie," Caroline smiled. She took her sunglasses off to look at Kate properly. "You look tired, and I know when you're not happy."

"And I know me too," Kate replied evenly. "And I've got a lot on my plate and we'll talk all about it later on."

She reached out, took her sister's hand and squeezed it. "But I am very happy to see you. And *we* are going to have a fabulous time. I've just been having a stressful time at work, that's all."

"You work too hard." Caroline squeezed Kate's hand back, kissed it and then replaced it on the steering wheel. "I'm going to sleep." She yawned again and put her shades back on.

"Great. Fantastic company you're going to be over the Christmas."

"Fuck off. Wake me up when we hit Dame Street, will you? I love the fairy lights."

Kate switched the radio back to the Christmas carols while Caroline slept.

"So. Guess who's back in town again?" Kate handed her sister a foaming glass of Californian pink champagne.

She had decided to cook some dinner for the two of them. She didn't often get the time to cook and it was a worry trying to predict what Caroline would eat. But she and Caroline had eaten a spaghetti dish in Venice once at a trattoria that Charles and Caroline had loved, and so she hummed happily as she cooked the same dish for her now, poking strands of spaghetti into a pan of water while the overhead extractor whirred.

Dave still hadn't come home of course. She had tried to phone him twice, and had given up after Caroline had rolled her eyes and given her a told-you-so look that withered her completely. He wasn't on call tonight and she had already told Caroline that he'd be in by the time they got home. But that was Dave. And this is my sister, and we're going to have a fabulous Christmas.

"Cheers, babes!" Caroline downed her glass of champagne in one go. "Hate flying. My ankles are still like tree trunks. Guess who's back in town? Shit, I don't know. I don't know any of your so-called friends any more, Katie."

"Smart ass. You'll know this one, though. Jonny Domville."

Caroline whistled and rolled her lips into a pout to make a kiss.

"Don't start!" Kate shook her head, topping her glass up and poured Caroline another one. Caroline didn't even complain when the foam spilt over the top of the glass onto the beach-blonde fur of her coat.

"Caro, you can take the furs off now, you know. We are in the Winter Palace, and I've lit a fire," Kate said.

"The place really looks great now, sis. Mum would have been really proud of you."

Caroline began to prowl around, admiring Kate's neat display of Christmas cards on the piano in the dining-room, the overloaded tree, the polished dense antiques.

"Dave's taste in furnishing or yours?" She stroked a curly-legged console by the window. "You always liked grotty old things. Always holding onto the past."

"Dave likes going to auctions," Kate shouted from where she had started chopping chillies by the sink. "And some of the littler things are Dad's, of course. I love still having family things. Since Mum died, you know."

Buying her student-days house from Charles had given Kate a strong sense of settling down. Charles had been glad to offload Percy Place onto her hands after Sadie died and he'd retired, and she had let it out when they had spent the five years in Melbourne. But Dave had been very keen to modernise the house as soon as they moved back.

Dave had enthusiastically knocked the wall down in between the tiny rear parlour and the dining-room and made a giant open kitchen-living area. The front sitting-room where Kate and Jonny had once played duets was gone. Kate had been very reluctant to make the changes but it had been difficult to resist Dave's longing for more *space*. After the wall had come down she did find the light and the new views they gained were lovely. The tiny parlour was now a gleamingly black modern granite-layered kitchen with a broad view over the canal, opening into a long dining-sitting-room that still housed the piano which Kate regularly tuned – although she hardly ever played it any more.

"Why don't you play the piano any more, Katie?" Caroline swept her hand along the keys while she toured the room.

"No time any more, I guess, Caro."

Kate noticed quietly that Caroline couldn't keep still for a moment but decided that this was probably because of the cold more than anything. Caroline still hadn't taken her fur coat off.

Kate took some parsley out of the refrigerator and started chopping it evenly.

"Here —" she handed a bulb of garlic to Caroline, "peel that. Oh, no! Not in your good coat, Caro, you'll stink it up. Oh, here, chop this parsley instead. At least that won't smell up your fur."

"Luis and I are going to stay with Daddy after Christmas."

"No way! Oh. I mean, I thought you'd be here for over ten days, at least." Kate's face flared with sudden envy.

Caroline was chipping clumsily at the parsley as if she'd never handled a kitchen knife before. "Oh, I know," she was saying. "That would have been lovely. But Luis is dying to see Venice and I want to be in Italy good and early 'cos I've got a job for Milan fashion week in February anyway." She took a giant slug of the champagne.

Kate let her finish the awkward job, watching her impatiently out of the corner of her eye and then took the chopping board away from her as soon as she could while Caroline washed parsley off her manicured hands. She tossed the chilli and garlic in hot olive oil while Caroline wandered over from the sink sit to down again and pour herself another drink.

She didn't begrudge Caroline going to Venice to see Charles in the slightest. It was perfect really. She was thrilled really that he was going to have some company. She often worried that he must be quite lonely in Venice, even though there was never any real sign of it. He seemed to be extremely self-sufficient, actually, walking in the mountains in the summer time, sitting around piazzas drinking cappuccino in the foggy winter. But if only she and Dave weren't so bloody busy. If only they could get more time off work. If only – actually, there was nothing really stopping *her* going to Venice, not really. With Caroline, or on her own even. It was just that Dave had never wanted to go there. And at Christmas, everything was much more complicated. It was impossible to get off call. Stuff like that, Kate reminded herself while Caroline chattered on.

"I said: *so have you seen him?*" Caroline was mumbling with a cigarette between her teeth. She gave up shaking the redundant giant silver lighter she'd been flicking and came to light her cigarette off the cooker instead. Kate handed her a box of matches from the shelf.

"Who?"

"Jesus, Kate! Sax Man. Jonny D of course. What does he look like *now*?"

Kate took a long swig from her champagne glass and went back to the cooker to peer into the boiling pasta pan. She picked up a giant fork to stir the spaghetti around. She paused to think a bit about this one.

He looks beautiful of course, she thought. Crumpled. Elegant. Tired, but not in a bad way. Worried about his wife, of course. Worried about his child. And he still looks sexy.

He looks as sexy as hell, she thought.

"He looks very French, actually," she smiled at Caroline, fishing out a strand of spaghetti for her to taste.

"Deadly!" Carol blew a blue smoke ring.

Caroline was right. It was deadly. Last night's dinner with Jonny was still making her heart thump.

"How's the pasta?" she asked Caroline lightly.

"What? Oh, I don't know. I don't eat pasta." Caroline blew more smoke across the room at Kate.

Kate turned up the speed on the extractor fan. "Caro! You have to eat *some*thing," she pleaded. "And I've cooked. I never cook, you know that. I normally don't get the chance but I really wanted to cook for you. Eat a few strands. Please. For me."

Caroline tossed her head. "Not hungry. Sorry. But I'll watch you eat." She smiled at Kate.

Kate worried desperately when Caroline wasn't eating. She could get deeply moody and then overtired. And she was bound to have premature osteoporosis. And if her periods stopped she got maudlin about never having kids. That is, as if she ever would have wanted to have kids in the first place. But it generally wasn't a good thing when Caroline decided not to eat.

"What the fuck is Dave doing?" Caroline gave her a wicked look, and lit another fag.

"I don't know." Kate carried the pasta pan over to the Belfast sink that they'd had imported from Scotland. "He never tells me if he's coming home or not any more. He's very stressed at the moment, actually." She emptied the spaghetti into a colander and then turned to look cautiously at Caroline while it drained into the sink.

"Man, you two are mad." Caroline began to shiver.

"Why are you so cold, Caro? I've lit a fire and the heating's on. It's like an oven in here!" Kate stared at her sister in alarm. She was visibly shaking now. The cigarette was almost waving around in her fingers. And her whole body was shaking, in fact. It almost looked like rigors.

"Shut up!" said Caroline. "I'm just jet-lagged. And I feel the cold. I live in a country that has three hundred and ten days of sunshine a year. Tell me all about Jonny, please, sis." Caroline's eyes lit up, even though her lips were trembling and her hand shook as she stuck the cigarette between them.

Kate watched the spaghetti letting off clouds of steam that puffed into her face and condensed on the black shiny tiles. All about Jonny. It was hard to know where to begin. She tipped the garlic chilli mixture that she'd warmed up in olive oil onto the pasta and squished it around inside the pan, watching the oil gradually coat each strand until it shone. She scooped a careful plateful of the pasta out for herself and a tiny portion in a cereal bowl for Caroline, just in case she changed her mind, and sprinkled each with parsley.

"There you go. Have some, Caroline. It's delicious, honestly."

"Did you ever make Jonny Domville eat this?" Caroline twirled her fork around and started messing with her spaghetti.

At least she's playing with her food, Kate thought, even if she isn't going to eat much. She reached out her hand and stroked Caroline's bony fingers. Amazing that despite her totally inadequate diet Caro has such beautifully healthy nails, she thought. She must just live on vitamin pills.

"Caroline, Jonny's wife has just had a baby in my hospital," she began, and watched Caroline's eyes open up. Caro's eyes were just so beautiful. Kate smiled weakly at her. Everything about Caroline was beautiful. Eyes like Bambi, huge pools of blue liquid with lashes that seemed to sweep her cheeks, they were that long, and her cheekbones were that high.

Caroline's hair wasn't naturally blonde, of course. It had been the same dark brown that Kate's now was, but nine years in California had meant that nobody really remembered that Caroline wasn't a natural blonde and her colourist was a perfectionist. And despite the chain-smoking, Caro's skin was wonderful, even when she looked as tired and drawn as this. Caroline never sat in the sun ("I'm a smoker," she would rationalise, "I'm just not going there.") The backs of her hands looked wasted now, Kate thought. She was much too thin at the moment – her BMI was probably in single figures, although it was impossible to tell with that bloody fur coat on. Kate was melting in the kitchen heat, sitting in a tee-shirt.

"Wow! Jonny's married." Caroline's big Bambi eyes were growing bigger like a cartoon.

"And the baby is still sick," Kate said evenly. "She was quite premature. And his wife –" Kate stopped and took a deep breath, putting down her fork. "She's very sick now too."

"Aw, Kate!" Caroline's face was full of sympathy. "You can't go there. He's married now."

"I'm married too, you know. But you're right. That's the end of that, isn't it? He's married to this beautiful Frenchwoman, Marianne Le Normand, and she's a lawyer, and he's still gorgeous and I still love him, of course. Only here's the thing. They are splitting up. And she was going to have the baby on her own, only now they've got this sick baby so I think that they're kind of pulling together again. And I respect him for that, of course. And I did the section but things went very badly wrong. So now she can't have any more kids. She could have died. But thank goodness she's all right now. It's just that — well, I never thought that would be the way that I'd meet Jonny again." Her eyes felt crowded and she stared furiously at her plate. She twirled a forkful of spaghetti and forced it into her mouth while Caroline gazed on in amazement.

It was the cigarette smoke that was stinging her eyes, she decided.

The phone rang right beside Kate's elbow. They jumped. She looked at it ringing there.

Caroline looked at her. "Aren't you going to answer it? It's loud enough, I think you heard it." Kate picked the phone up, watching Caroline's face all the time.

"Hi, Dave. Yes, she's here. Are you — Oh shit, Dave! Oh Christ. Are you all right? Dave, I'm only asking because I'm worried about you. No, look I'm not giving out, I only want to know that you're not hurt. Shall I come out to you? Okay. I see. All right. Whatever you like, darling. I'm so sorry to hear about that. Are you sure you don't need anything?" She steadily avoided Caroline's eyes, knowing Caroline could hear the tone of Dave's voice at the other end. She prayed she couldn't hear what he was saying. "Shall I leave you some dinner out?" she ended feebly, looking at the plates of uneaten spaghetti, but Dave's drowsy voice, almost slurred it seemed, had hung up on her.

Caroline raised her eyebrows.

Kate put down the phone.

"Dave is going to be late," she said. "He pranged the Audi yesterday morning on the way to work."

"Jesus. Is he okay?"

"He says that he is. The car's a write-off though."

"Shit, I'm really sorry, Kate. But why's he only telling you about it now?"

She thought about this one for a moment. "We haven't seen each other all day. For several days, actually. He was out last night but so was I, and I was on call the night before. Then I was out Thursday night too – I guess I haven't seen him properly for days. So, I'm not sure what's happening for him really." She looked at Caroline, hoping somehow that she'd know exactly what to say.

Caroline took her hand. "I'm really sorry, Kate. You don't deserve all this."

"What do you mean?" She looked at her. "All what?"

Caroline shrugged. "This hassle," she said. "Me arriving. Dave's car crash. You're working tomorrow night too, aren't you? Look, I'll just go to bed early and stay out of trouble. I'm freezing cold, love. I'll get out of your way. Kate, can I have a hot-water bottle please?"

In the silence in the midnight kitchen Kate tidied up alone. She washed up slowly, contemplating the sparkling bubbles in the Belfast sink where she swirled a cotton cloth around the giant pasta pan. She felt dead tired now of course but didn't want to go to bed till Dave got in. Dave *had* been very tired all week. But he must have been out all night Friday night as well if the crash had happened in the morning. He had probably nodded off slightly at the wheel. He had rear-ended a taxi, he'd told her, some bastard that had been dithering at traffic lights. Of course, Dave had already decided that it was the other guy's fault. The Audi Cabriolet was now a crumpled mess, and poor Dave was in the horrors.

She stood still a moment listening to the traffic just outside, heard a car door slam, wondered if it were Dave, then listened to the car beep shut and realised that of course it wasn't – Dave would be coming in a taxi if the Audi was totalled. She suddenly wondered if he actually had bought proper fully comprehensive insurance for the Audi. It seemed ridiculous, but that might be the kind of thing that Dave would think was too much of a pain in the arse to pay for, after paying almost fifty grand for the car. Either way, he'll lose out on the no-claims bonus if he *has* rear-ended a taxi, she thought with a sudden swell of panic. It doesn't get much worse than that for culpability. But even if he was completely in the wrong Dave would in some way manage to believe that he was right, and that it was the taxi driver's fault for beckoning him to drive into him or something. Even if he was drunk. Oh Christ. What if he *was* drunk when he had the crash?

She stopped washing the pan again and stood very still, the hum of the dishwasher now the only sound. Outside, a police siren whined by, and then the silence fell again. She stared at the foaming bubbles of the washing up. If Dave *was* drunk-driving he'd be breathalysed. Especially if he hit a taxi: they always had to call the cops to have a witness. If he was found to be over the limit he'd lose his licence. What if he had to go to court? What if he'd hurt someone? *Jesus Christ Almighty!*

Kate pulled the rubber gloves off and sat down at the kitchen table again, leaning her head into her hands.

She wanted desperately to phone him again, to tell him that he was the stupidest prick that she had ever met and that he'd better not ever darken her door again, that he could just fuck off back to wherever he was last night and stay there. And then she also wanted desperately to find out where he was now, to beg him to come home, to tell him that she'd go anywhere to collect him because she loved him and she'd do anything to make sure he was okay. But something in his tone of voice had told her that another phone call was the last thing he wanted from her. Maybe he'd decide to spend the night in the hospital after having such a long day of it, she thought.

Maybe she'd get to see him tomorrow and she could kill him properly then. Except that she was on call again tomorrow night and so it wouldn't be till Tuesday that she'd see him. And Tuesday would be Christmas Day.

Tomorrow was Christmas Eve. She would have to find time tomorrow to call into Fallon and Byrne and collect the things she had ordered for Christmas dinner, and then maybe by Christmas Day Dave would cheer up a bit with Caroline being home.

She studied Caroline's discarded packet of Dunhill cigarettes, and wondered what it would be like to smoke one now. People who smoked always had something to *do* when they felt upset. She touched the jewel-red packet, so Christmassy and jolly-looking with beautifully crisp gold paper on the inside. She hadn't lit a cigarette in over ten or more years and then only for a second before she'd almost passed out in a fit of coughing and flung the thing away, much to the amusement of Jonny who was a chain-smoker in those days. From chain-smoker to public health physician in the twinkling of a decade. How we all have changed, changed utterly, she thought.

And then the front door slammed.

"Are you still up, Kate?" Dave was trembling with the cold and wasn't wearing any coat. "I thought you'd be in bed by now. It's absolutely Baltic weather out there." He looked horrendous.

"Where's your coat?" she gaped.

"Are you smoking?" He laughed over-merrily at her.

"They're Caroline's. Have you lost your coat somewhere?"

"Man!" He flopped down at the kitchen table, running his long hand through thick sandy unwashed hair.

"Whose is that spaghetti?" He looked up at her. His eyes were swollen, the whites bloodshot. "Can I have some, if it's leftover?"

"Here, I've saved you some. That's Caroline's. She's being anorexic again. She's got a job in Milan in February. Haven't you eaten? Where have you been? I've been so worried about you. What have you done with the car – I mean, do we have to collect it from anywhere? What are we going to do with it over Christmas? Did the Gardaí get involved?"

"Jesus, Kate, why are you fucking quizzing me up like this?" he said sharply and she jumped. "Do you spend all day trying to think of ways that you can make things even more difficult for me?" His voice sounded desperate. He looked as though he were about to cry.

She took a breath. "How's the car then, Dave?"

"I told you. Towed away by now."

"To where?"

"Fuck knows. I had to leave it on the street." He stuck a fork into his spaghetti and then left it there.

"What do you mean, you had to leave it on the street?" She stood up now to face him. At least standing she would be taller than he was sitting down. "Were the Gardaí called? Didn't they arrange to have it taken to a garage? How could you have just left it on the street?"

"Kate, please, please, *please* stop nagging me! I've had

a hell of a night and a hell of a day and I just can't take more questions now, tonight. Please." He turned away from her and leaned his forehead into his hands.

"Jesus!" she yelled at him. "Will you cop on to yourself for once in your life, Dave!" She started pulling plates out of the dishwasher. "We have to talk about this. This affects me too, you know! And it wasn't my idea that you should have gone out and got absolutely locked on Friday night and written your car off – ouch!"

The plates were far too hot to handle and she stood a moment watching the steam rise off them like a dragon's breath.

He looked up at her. "Kate will you please stop blaming me for everything that goes wrong!"

"Dave! I *know* you were at a party before you crashed the car. You don't expect me to believe that you sat sipping lemonade all night and that the taxi driver backed *his* car into *you* yesterday morning!" She stood with her back to the sink, facing him where he was sitting there, looking wretched at the table.

"And where did you *stay* the night before the crash?" she continued.

"At work," he replied hollowly.

"*What?* You were at the hospital drinking all night, *and* driving drunk into work in the morning? Do you expect me to think that makes sense? Are you *mad* or something?" Her voice had risen to a scream, she knew, but she couldn't help it. It was as if he was refusing to acknowledge her pain.

"Jesus, Kate! I've had a car crash and all you do is nag

me and complain that I'm not good enough for you. It's always been the same!" He thumped his hand on the table top. "You want everything to be perfect all the time! You complain if I'm drinking, if I go to a party, if I want to stay home, if I'm not there for you, if I'm around too much for you! I'm so bloody sick of being made to feel so *guilty* about everything!"

"*Me*, make *you* feel guilty?" she yelled. "I've never tried to make you feel guilty about anything in the whole of my life! You come and go as you please, you spend all of our money on whatever you want, you write off fifty-thousand euro cars as if they are dinkies – I work my *ass* off, Dave, to come home to have some sort of life with you and you – you – you're not *like* a husband any more! We hardly ever even see each other. You sleep all day and then you spend all night grumbling –"

"Oh, so now you want me to be around more for you, is that right? And then when I'm here, and I want to spend time with you, you start whining about where I've been when I *wasn't* with you?"

"Dave, look at me!" she roared. "Drinking yourself into a stupor every night and then sleeping all weekend isn't a relationship!" She banged the palm of her hand on the kitchen table.

"Kate, I'm so unhappy!" He put his head back into his hands. "Don't you see? Can't you – I don't want to hurt you, Kate! I love you, I'll always love you, and you know I will, but I'm so –" He stopped. "Kate, *I'm so fucked up*," he finished in a whisper. "And I'm sorry." He looked at her.

"Oh, it's always bloody about *you*, isn't it?" she yelled and she punched the top of his head sharply with the heel of her hand.

"Don't you dare hit me!" He stood up, pointing a finger into her face and she jumped back in shock.

But she shoved her hands into his chest, pushing him as hard as she could and he staggered backwards slightly. His pale grey face was purple now. He picked up the kitchen chair he'd been sitting on, and lifted it over his head.

"Oh, so you're going to hit *me* then!" she shouted.

"If you don't stop shouting at me then I will!" And he waved the kitchen chair at her.

"Why don't you go ahead then?" she yelled.

She *wanted* someone else to hear. Not Caroline – she didn't even think of her. She wanted someone from one of their perfect houses in the perfect terrace on the canal to wake up and see them in their perfectly open-planned living-dining *space* through the uncurtained window, and have to come and knock on their perfect duck-egg blue front door and ask Doctor Kate Gilmore and Doctor Dave Hardiman to please stop threatening one another in full view of the street. She wanted *someone* to see Dave Hardiman lifting up a chair over his head to smash it down on top of hers.

"Why *don't* you hit me?" she kept on yelling. "What are you afraid of, Dave?"

"I will – if you don't stop acting like a lunatic!" he yelled back, and she *did* want him to hit her – hurt her, kill her even – anything to get this over with. Anything to bring the tension of this marriage to its logical conclusion.

And so when Dave did bring the chair across her head, missing it by only millimetres and crashing it down onto the table-top, sending dishes and spoons and spaghetti flying across the floor, although he was momentarily stunned into complete submission by the shock of it, she was within seconds of it relieved.

"*Caroline!*"

Like a pale grey ghost in a fur coat, her sister stood in the doorway shaking hideously. Her mane of dark-blonde hair was dense with sweat. Long dark clumps of it sticking to her head like snakes. Her beautiful dewy skin was a horrendous green.

"Darling! I'm so sorry about this!" Kate began to sob.

"Kate, Dave, I'm so fucking ill," Caroline mumbled, and vomited yellow bile onto the kitchen floor.

"Do you think you've caught a bug? Or eaten something poisonous on the plane?" Kate wiped her sister's head with a damp towel again, perched on the edge of the roll-top bath, while Caroline sat on the toilet, emptying at both ends. "Dave will be back soon with some Stemetil for you. Oh, sweetheart, lean just your head onto my shoulder!"

"Kate!" Caroline dry-retched again and then leaned her head onto Kate's lap.

"Can you sip some more iced water? Please, Caro!"

"I can't! I'm too ill!"

"Can you get back into bed, do you think?"

"I can't move. It hurts everywhere." Caroline slid off the toilet and just about pulled her pants up before rolling down onto the floor.

"Darling, you can't lie there. You have to come back to bed. Here, let me help you."

She lifted Caroline up underneath the armpits, and even though she was much tinier Caroline seemed almost light to her. She must weigh less than seven stones again, Kate thought desperately. She'll dehydrate if we don't do something fast. The thought of having to bring her sister into St Xavier's A&E for the night had just struck her and the thought of it wasn't a good one.

"Caro." She said managed to get Caroline sitting up with her back to the wall and stroked her sticky hair out of her eyes. "When Dave gets back we'll give you an injection of some Stemetil and you'll be able to stop vomiting then, and then you'll have to drink some water."

They heard Dave's steps sounding on the landing. Jesus, had he not gone out to the chemist yet? But he came into the bathroom and had something with him that he began to unwrap at the sink.

"Thank you, Dave. God, you were very quick!" Kate smiled at him from where she was sitting holding Caroline on the floor.

He did not smile back.

She stroked Caroline's hair again and handed her the

mug of iced water from the floor. Caroline took a sip and gagged again.

"You'll be all right in a moment. I'll give you an injection and you'll feel much better soon," said Dave who was drawing up a syringe.

Kate turned to him. "Dave, where did you go? That was pretty quick. I thought you'd be at least twenty minutes or half an hour getting to a chemist open at this hour."

"Nowhere," he replied.

She opened her mouth and then shut it again. She had recognised the drug he was drawing up in an insulin syringe. It wasn't Stemetil.

"Dave," she asked him, and her voice shook. "Dave, what are you doing? Jesus, Dave? Where did you get that insulin syringe?"

"From a box of them," he replied, studiously ignoring her.

"Dave. That's not Stemetil. It's Cyclimorph! What the hell –"

"She's in pain." Dave knelt down beside Caroline, taking her scrawny arm in his hand. "You're all right – don't worry, this will sort you out, sweetheart," he mumbled tenderly to Caroline who was accepting him with open eyes.

"I'm so sorry, Kate," Caroline said in a quiet voice. All the panic had gone out of her. Kate stared at the two of them, her husband and her sister, sitting in a moment of mutual tenderness on her bathroom floor. She watched wordlessly as Dave fastened a pair of her own stockings that he must have brought in with him around Caroline's arm, and watched the blue vein in the front of her elbow bulge. She watched him slap Caroline's skinny grey goosepimpled arm, holding the syringe between his teeth, and then slip the needle into Caro's vein, letting the stocking go and pressing on the plunger. She watched in silence as Caroline's head relaxed and her pupils narrowed down to pins again and her mouth smiled gratefully at Dave who stroked her hair and stemmed the vein with a pad of Kate's own cotton wool.

She felt her legs become weak and had to sit down on the edge of the bath again. "I can't believe this," she whispered again, anger rising in her chest this time. "Caroline, what the hell – Jesus – Dave – how could you?"

"Just let her be, Kate, why don't you? Let her be. She just needs to get some sleep. She's going to be all right. Aren't you, sweetheart?" He touched Caroline's sticky hair, and smiled gently at her slackening face.

Kate felt tears spill over and she didn't try to stop them.

"You'll be all right, Caro. We'll sort you out. Don't worry," Dave was saying tenderly. "You'll be safe with us."

"I'm so sorry, Dave. I'm so sorry Kate. I didn't think that it would happen this time. I didn't realise how – I just thought I'd be all right this time."

"You will be, don't you worry," Dave kept saying. "I'll help you and you will be all right again."

"What about Italy? I can't let Daddy know. Not again." Caro's voice was drowsy but she seemed so relaxed that Kate felt, despite herself, deeply grateful.

"I'll sort you out before you go. Don't worry. You'll be grand. Just like before." Dave picked Caroline up off the floor and carried her out of the bathroom into her bedroom. The lovely sunny bedroom that Kate had decorated in Laura Ashley striped wallpaper with a beautiful pale green Chinese rug and a giant silk lampshade. She stood at the doorway now, watching her husband putting Caroline into bed.

They left the room, leaving the door only just ajar.

"Caro, I'll leave a bottle of Lucozade beside your bed. Please drink it all, you need the sugar now," Kate said in a dry, still shaky voice, turning off the light.

Caroline smiled at her and nodded. "I will. I promise, Katie. Honestly I will."

"So. Caroline is on drugs," Kate said.

They sat opposite each other now at the kitchen table. Plates broken everywhere, dishes and glasses smashed, an ashtray overturned, the smell of Caroline's puke still in the air, spaghetti sticking to the walls. Dave pulled the cork out of a bottle of whiskey and poured Kate out a good big glass.

"She's in opiate withdrawal, if that's what you meant by that. But it's all prescription stuff, if that's what you were wondering. A lot of models use it to come down off the coke, and she got a little strung, that's all," he said.

"Jesus, Dave, you make it sound so flip!"

He shrugged.

She glared at him. "What are we going to do?"

Dave sighed. "Well, after you've finished the headless-chicken dance, I suggest something for her to quickly detox off again. I don't think her habit is too bad at all. She's a pill-popper really. She's never really injected anything, you can tell. She'll be fine for a good few hours after the Cyclimorph and then we should get her some codeine or something to detox off for the next few days. She wants to be well by the time she gets to Venice, obviously." He poured himself a massive glass of whiskey.

"Dave. This is crazy stuff! Why don't you start telling me why *we* have hospital-controlled drugs in the house?"

"Because I'm an anaesthetist. Doh." He pushed the cork back into the whiskey bottle with a squeak.

She felt the same rage rising in her throat again. He was stonewalling her again – and the more desperate she felt, the more defensive and dismissive he'd become. "Dave, why can't our lives just be normal for once?"

And she burst into tears.

"Kate!" He reached a hand out across the table to take one of hers, and swallowed back his whiskey in the other. "I'm sorry about the car crash. I'm sorry about Caroline. We'll figure something out."

"We'd better." She sipped her drink and put it down. "At least we're all alive. For now." She looked around the kitchen in despair.

"We'd better tidy up the mess," he said.

By midnight on Christmas Eve Caroline was sitting up again, happily drinking gin and Slimline Tonic with Kate on the sofa while they watched *Titanic*. In the fluster of having to clean up the kitchen, throw out all the broken plates and care for Caroline before she left for work, she hadn't left herself enough time to pick up the lovely big game pie and the beautiful Christmas hamper that she'd ordered from Fallon and Byrne and so by the time she got home at ten o'clock on Christmas Eve night there was no turkey in the house, no ham, no sprouts, absolutely nothing that could remotely be cooked and put on the table to make it look Christmassy at all.

She and Caroline rummaged through the fridge and cupboards and found three tins of tuna, some baked beans, some mayonnaise, a brie, a stilton, a box of eggs, a cucumber, a packet of oatcakes, a loaf of rock-hard organic wholemeal bread in the freezer, a jar of olives, a tin of anchovy paste and a box of cocktail sticks. There were bananas, grapes and mandarins in the fruit bowl. And at least there was a wine-rack full of alcohol.

On Christmas Day, Kate and Caroline sat solemnly in front of one movie after another in their dressing-gowns and pyjamas and ate tuna and cucumber mashed with mayonnaise, followed by baked beans over anchovy paste on toast and then speared the cocktail sticks with the cheese and grapes and drank Prosecco wine. Dave was on call.

Caroline took the tablets Dave had given her, dutifully. On the day before New Year's Eve, armed with the remainder of Dave's prescription, she flew to Italy.

On New Year's Eve, Doctor Jonathan Domville flew into Chad with a delegation from the UNHCR, and set up a meeting in a refugee-camp tent in which to hold a long day of tense logistical planning with the International Committee of the Red Cross and a team from Médecins Sans Frontières.

On the night of New Year's Eve, Kate stood silently and alone, watching Marianne Le Normand through the glass wall of the SCBU, where she sat in a hospital wheelchair, holding her baby Veronique for the very first time in her arms, feeding her through a tube.

On New Year's Eve, Charles and Caroline Gilmore sat in St Mark's Square listening to the bells peal out over the lagoon, and cuddled up tightly together underneath her giant mink fur coat. They spent the night drinking Bellinis in Harry's Bar at sixty-five euros a glass and sent text messages to Kate, who wouldn't get to read them until morning, and to Luis who was delayed in Buenos Aires due to fog.

Dave Hardiman spent New Year's Eve with Nick Farrelly, getting very, *very* drunk in the jam-packed Odessa Club off Exchequer Street. While the bells from Christchurch rang out for the new year and the party all around them hopped and leaped up and down and danced and shrieked a tuneless "Auld Lang Syne", Nick took Dave's face in his hands and kissed him deeply on the mouth and told him that he loved him more than he'd ever loved anyone before.

At midnight on New Year's Eve, Ronan Clare put his

arm around Kate Gilmore, where he had found her standing all alone outside the SCBU, gave her a kiss on the forehead, and put a bar of chocolate in the pocket of her scrubs.

"Let's have a really, really happy new year, this year, Kate," he mumbled into her hair, and she let herself lean against him where she could feel the rapid movement of his chest.

"Thanks for looking after that baby so well for me, Ronan. You are such an angel," she told him, and he blushed so hard to the roots of his hair that he felt as though his head would probably explode. But he knew, at least, that Kate was far too small to actually see how red his face had gone.

On New Year's Eve, Connell Jones Cumberton, Barrister-at-Law and Counsel for St Xavier's hospital among other very lucrative clients, poured himself a glass of Veuve Clicquot, and toasted his beautiful, wonderful and magnificent wife, Sharon Guinness. Connell was overwhelmed with happiness that she was actually spending the evening with him, albeit with several dozen other guests, most of whom were other people's husbands that she was flirting outrageously with at their annual New Year's Eve party.

"To my wonderful wife Sharon, whom I absolutely adore!" he announced, to the general approval and raucous applause of the gathering. Sharon Guinness blew him a kiss from across their living-room, and he picked it out of the air and lifted his fingers to his heart, as if to try and keep it there.

Professor Dennis Crowe spent New Year's Eve playing golf in Florida.

11

On the morning of the first day of the new year, Marianne Le Normand watched the New Year's Day Concert from Vienna on a television that had been delivered to her private room in St Xavier's hospital, and cried.

She had never in her life felt more alone than this. Even though she enjoyed her independence and in her professional life she always preferred to work alone rather than in teams, here in this hospital in this dark and rainy city she felt more unable for life's challenges than she had ever felt.

Her breasts ached. Her entire body ached. The morphine they'd given her made her feel sick. She hated herself for crying now, over the stupid "Radetsky March" on the television with all those stupid Austrians clapping like performing seals. Their foolish joyfulness was making her misery all the worse. She blew her nose on a pink tissue paper, and then almost roared with pain.

"*Oh, merde!*" Marianne groaned out loud.

The door of her private room opened and the nurse put her head around it.

"Ready to come up and feed the baby, Marianne?" Sharon Guinness asked her in a gentle voice.

Sharon helped her to get out of bed, slowly, slowly, cautiously putting on slippers and nightgown, wiping her nose again and putting her glasses on for her.

"It's the hormones," Sharon reassured her, linking her by the arm as they walked down the corridor to the lift.

"I know, it's so stupid," admitted Marianne, smiling and wiping her nose again. "I have been perfectly all right until today. I can't understand what has hit me emotionally like this. These tears, just like a child."

"It's a lousy place to be at Christmas time," Sharon agreed, and they stepped slowly into the lift.

Sharon sat her down in the parenting room just off the end of the SCBU and made her comfortable on a triangle of pillows with another pillow on her lap to rest her arm on. She sat beside her on a little stool and patiently adjusted the breast pump to Marianne's engorged breast, easing the rubber seal into place, soothing her while she felt the first few painful tweaks.

Sharon winked at her. "Good girl, yourself!"

Marianne leaned back into the pillows. This extraordinary winking nurse! Good girl! It was astonishing behaviour. But she was exhausted with being insulted by it.

"Just relax," Sharon said to her. "Think about the baby and the milk will come. It's just a reflex." She smiled widely now at Marianne.

"It's becoming easier now," said Marianne, although it wasn't really. "Thank you for helping me with this, nurse."

"This is the hardest job you'll ever have to do – being a mum," said Sharon, indicating the blue-white milk that was forming a tiny trickle at the bottom of the jar. "You need to take all the time in the world to look after yourself. It isn't easy to remember to put everything else aside and just remember to be you."

"I am very comfortable now, I think."

Sharon said nothing. She watched the milk collect, millilitres only, a pathetic amount that the midwives would have to add to with a formula.

"Were you planning to have any other children after this one, Marianne?" Sharon asked her quietly, the only other sound the tiny spray of breast milk against a plastic bottle like a little spurt of rain. "After this baby? Did you and your husband want a larger family?"

Marianne looked up at her again. *This* is what she hated about the Irish. They never could stop talking. Always asking inappropriate questions. No idea of boundaries, of privacy. And yet they wouldn't actually tell you anything you really wanted to know. No manners in politics of course. The Irish delegates in the EU whom she'd met would make you cringe with shame to have once been married to an Irishman. Her father had once said that despite all the talk the Irish did, they never spoke directly to you about anything. They just made remarks and dropped hints and expected you to draw conclusions from all that. Marianne had had enough of it.

And the worst thing was that there didn't seem to be any way that she could persuade these doctors to discharge her back to her own doctor, Sophie Larocque, in Paris.

Nobody in this dreadful hospital seemed to be capable of giving her a straight answer about anything. First there was that idiotic professor who hadn't even been at the delivery but was taking what he called "personal responsibility" for her case – and was now in Florida. Florida! And nobody had been able to explain properly to her why the doctor who had delivered Veronique was no longer available to discuss the procedure with her.

Nobody had really explained why they had taken out her womb. That had clearly been a disaster. Nobody competent could have left her in a mess like this. But they just kept telling her that things go wrong, it was a complication – as if they were trying to disguise a bad attempt at surgery. The doctor was someone Jonny used to know, but how well-trained was she? Nobody had even introduced her yet to Marianne.

And yet her body was destroyed now! It was butchery. And now this nurse, asking her if she'd like to have more children – after what she'd been through? It was just insane. What kind of woman did they think she was? Did they think she would just want to sit here and accept something like this?

And yet for some reason she actually liked this round-faced, generous-bosomed strawberry-haired nurse with the huge blue eyes and freckles and the generously open and always pinked-up mouth. There was something about her confidence that she found to be attractive, in the same way in which she liked to work with female politicians who could show both empathy and strength. This nurse, Sharon, wasn't servile. And Marianne respected that.

She smiled at Sharon. "No," she said. "Actually, Sharon, I don't think I would ever have wanted to go through this again. Perhaps I am lucky even to have this," she said, indicating the breast pump at her side and laughed slightly. "Whoever expects it all to be like this, you know? Everything has been a disaster since I came here. The delivery was a disaster. The childbirth – to be honest, it couldn't have been worse."

Sharon Guinness said nothing, taking the tiny bottle of just under twenty millilitres of milk from her and fastening on the screw. Then she said, "Let's get her out of her cot now and get this into her with her little tube, shall we?" and she reached her arm out for Marianne to lean her weight upon.

Marianne sighed. "Sharon," she said as she got up slowly from her chair, "I have to get home to Paris as soon as possible. I can't stand being kept here." She paused to take a breath while the sudden discomfort passed. Then she looked at Sharon again. "I can't tolerate it here any longer. I need to be in France. I am fit to travel. And if Veronique is feeding then I think we should transfer to France. Can you please ask the hospital to just arrange that now, for me, please?"

Sharon smiled. "Yes, that would be lovely, wouldn't it? But that would have to be something that the Prof decides. I know he'll want to see you himself before you leave the hospital."

"Ugh!" said Marianne. "Have the nurses no authority? This *professeur* who is in Florida! Aren't there any other people in this hospital who can make decisions?"

Sharon was blushing furiously which irritated Marianne even more, but at the same time she didn't want to make the nurse feel it was her fault. Sharon had been very kind. And even if she seemed clumsy and intrusive, she did seem to want to help.

She put an arm out and touched Sharon's. "I'm sorry. It's just so horrible at the moment. For me, at least, it is."

"You know what, Marianne, maybe things work a bit slower round here than you're used to. I know it's hard being away from home at Christmas time. And you've been very sick and your hormones are all over the place. Your transfer back will take a bit of time to arrange. But I'm sure you'll be home within the next few weeks anyway."

Few weeks! Marianne felt frustrated tears begin to sting. Sharon the nurse was being very kind but she didn't really feel that she could tolerate that kind of attitude here any longer. She was not going to spend another week in this hospital waiting for someone who's on a golf course in Florida to make a decision. There must be something she could do herself get them moving on it. Jonny was useless to her, as always – he was in Africa and uncontactable most of the time, and of course she wasn't allowed to used her cell phone in the hospital. The mere thought of going to the pay-phone to argue with him that he must try to talk some sense into these people was more humiliating than it was worth. And in any case, he didn't seem to have any authority in this hospital at all. Nobody did!

Since she could walk, she could get into a plane. Since Veronique could feed, even if some of it had to go down a tube, and since she could manage without oxygen for several hours now, then surely she could fly a one-hour flight to Paris? Surely they could both be airlifted? If wounded soldiers could be airlifted out of battle without all the medical equipment they had here, then surely she and Veronique could be taken home? It was only Paris, my God, only a short flight! Hospital to hospital!

The sheer powerlessness of it made her want to cry with frustration and she clenched her hands into a fist. Walking arm in arm with Sharon along the lonely corridor down to Veronique's glass room she realised the anger she was feeling was something she'd seen so often before in clients who'd been wronged, whose sense of privacy and dignity had been robbed from them – all the pain of injustice. Nobody should have to feel like this. The doctor had clearly made a mistake, but nobody wanted to discuss it. It was horrible. It was insane.

But she'd have to do something about it. She had to find out what that doctor had done, see her notekeeping, see the description in her own words of the operation she'd performed. If she could find out what went throughout every step of the operation that night, what notes the doctor had written at the moment when she'd taken her to theatre – then she'd find out the truth. She would see every decision that she'd made, every step of the procedure that had led to hysterectomy, written down in black and white. And then she'd go through the case notes with Sophie Larocque who would be able to explain to her exactly where the mistake had been.

Marianne sniffed hard and forced her face to smile. At least Baby Veronique wouldn't see her angry or upset, no, never, no. And so she held her head up high while Sharon held the door of the SCBU open for her. And she made a decision. She was going to do exactly what she always told other people to do, when they felt like this.

"Sharon," she said. "Thank you." She sat down on the chair Sharon had arranged for her beside Veronique's cot.

"You're welcome," said Sharon. "I'll leave you up here for a while, then you just tell the nurses here when you're ready to come back down."

"Sharon," Marianne said, "can you do something for me please? Something important? I need to make a phone-call from your office first thing in the morning. A private phone-call. It's just a local call to a colleague in my firm's office in Dublin. But could I have the nurses' office to myself to do this? I need about one half an hour to make the call."

Sharon smiled. "'Course you can. The ward is very quiet today. It's no bother, Marianne. No bother at all. Just tell me when you're ready and I'll be back up to you. You just take your time."

12

When Kate arrived into work on the third of January, there was a card in her pigeon hole from Professor Crowe.

Kate. I've scheduled an appointment for you with Connell Jones Cumberton BL at the offices of Jones Cumberton and McCormick Solicitors who have instructed him in this matter on behalf of St Xavier's, in the second week of January. Please see the enclosed. All the best for a prosperous New Year. Dennis Crowe and family.

It was a photocopy of a letter with two address heads. One in Dublin and another in Paris – a company with offices in both towns. A long, over-complicated and obviously a legal letter. But there was one sentence that she most certainly understood. It was printed at the bottom of a long page that was peppered with Latin legal jargon, in a little paragraph of its own.

. . . undertaking to preserve all documents, notes, memoranda

*or data howsoever arising in relation to the treatment currently
being provided by you to our client Ms Marianne Le Normand.
Such documentary evidence to include, but not limited to, case-
notes, records, charts, x-rays and any and all prescriptions or
notices or requests of and concerning medication given to our
client during her stay at your hospital. Failure to provide the
above undertaking may result in an immediate application in
the High Court for appropriate Orders in respect of
contemplated legal proceedings on behalf of our client arising
from the standard of care being provided.*

And so there it was. The High Court. Kate let her
exhausted eyes swim over the words until they melted
into a blur and then slowly sank down to her knees,
letting her head fall heavily into her hands and sat for
what felt like hours on the floor of the Res corridor.

Her heart felt like a stone.

Connell Jones Cumberton, Barrister-at-Law, leaned back
in his dark-green leather swivel-chair with just enough
weight to make Kate jump at the possibility that he
might topple it over. The chair didn't topple. But Kate
was feeling pretty edgy anyway.

"Cigar?" he asked her abruptly, whipping open a
wooden box labelled *A Present From Havana*. Kate shook
her head, wide-eyed at the offer.

Connell frowned, and snapped the box shut again,
flipping it over to the far side of his giant littered desk.
"Yeah, horrible things aren't they? Christmas present.
One of my clients is the Cuban ambassador." He

beamed. "Hey, how do you fancy getting ourselves a really serious lunch, and we can talk all about this properly then? Eh?"

Kate opened her mouth, and then shut it again.

She hadn't been expecting Connell Jones Cumberton, Barrister-at-Law, Counsel for Jones Cumberton and McCormick Solicitors to invite her to lunch, never mind offer an illegal opportunity to laugh in the face of the smoking ban and light up a Havana.

On the other hand, lunch did sound like a reasonably decent proposal, now that she came to think of it. But shouldn't this meeting be a bit more *business-like?* The offices where Connell had arranged to meet her were on the light-filled top floor of a large modern building that overlooked the river. Kate couldn't help but feel relaxed in the warm atmosphere that Connell perpetuated, but she was also wondering about the winks he earlier gave fellow colleagues who sat at desks on phones. The way he tapped one of the lawyers on the head with his newspaper when he walked by his desk. The way he stopped halfway to the lift to take his shoe off and straighten the wrinkles in his sock which he said was giving him a fucking pain in the bollocks.

Professor Crowe had told her that the initial meeting with the hospital lawyers would be informal. And that was the understatement of the millennium.

"Oh, stop worrying about the letter about the patient from France," he said now, reading her worried face and waving a hand around. "I'll sort that stuff out. They write to us, snarl a bit, we send the notes on, bite our nails. They plot and hatch and scheme, and then, bingo, we settle out of court. Same old ding-dong every time, so don't worry about a thing. I've been doing this job for ten years now. I'm almost bored with it. So there's no point in boring the pair of us with it, is there? Now: how do you fancy Chez Claudine? I hear they do a really serious lunch there. And then we can take a walk and I'll be able to get back by half past, which suits me perfectly. If that's all right with you?"

Connell moved pretty quickly for such a large man and he was out of the green swivel-chair and into his pale grey Crombie before Kate could even begin to manufacture an answer.

"Come on!"

He flung the office door open wide in front of her, and stood there holding it open with one hand, winding a long navy-blue scarf around his slightly over-shaved neck with the other.

Kate rose slowly, not quite sure what to say. It was only eleven thirty in the morning, and the prospect of a lunch that was to go for another three hours with this rather distractible man seemed to be a bit too experimental.

On the other hand, there was something that she couldn't help liking about Connell Jones Cumberton, Barrister-at-Law. There was a slightly naïve fatherly soft look in his crumpled pale-blue eyes that gave the impression that he rarely ever got to bed before the small hours. But despite his obvious late nights, he didn't have the troubled, angry look of over-tiredness that Dave often did when his eyes were pinned with lack of sleep and his mood was a permanent scowl. Connell Jones Cumberton looked shattered all right, but he also looked slightly mischievous, as if his particular version of knackered was less as a result of working late at night and more as a result of having had far too much of a good time.

"So, how was your Christmas?" he began, as Kate walked towards the door he held open.

Kate was about to say, "Fine," – the automatic, brushing-under-the-carpet kind of response to the question of a happy Christmas, and yet something stopped her now. The real answer to the question of how her Christmas had been would need a three-hour lunch all to itself. Nobody really knew what a nightmare her personal life had become. But just how long can you keep these kinds of nightmares to yourself? And there was something about this man that made her think that on the question of a happy Christmas, he'd appreciate an honest reply.

She smiled back at him. "Mental."

"Well, thanks be to God for that!" he laughed. "I hate it when people tell you that they've had a quiet one!" Connell poked the button for the lift again. "I hear this place does a *very* serious lunch," he added, in a conspiratorial voice, examining Kate's expression with suddenly rather innocent-looking pale-blue eyes. She couldn't help smiling at the daft excitement he was showing.

"You like your grub, don't you?" she teased him.

"Shows, doesn't it?" Connell rubbed his tummy shame-facedly.

"Oh, I didn't mean *that!*" She bit her lip. "It's just that you're obviously really *really* looking forward to having lunch."

"Not much else to look forward to, in life, is there though?" Connell asked her, his face now solemn as they glided down in the lift.

He's right, thought Kate. Lousy Christmas, rotten cold weather, January. Back to work. And now this.

"Life's a pile of crap at the moment, isn't it?" he asked her softly.

She looked at his face. His expression half solemn, half merry, teasing her gently, and yet at the same time reading her thoughts aloud.

She swallowed. "I've had a very rough time at work lately," she replied. "And at home. And –" To her horror she felt that tears were suddenly cluttering at the back of her throat. Oh for Christ's sake, don't start crying in front of the bloody hospital lawyer! She blinked hard, staring at her shoes.

"New Year's Resolution: take everything less seriously from now on, except lunch," said Connell.

Kate looked fiercely at her toes. She let just one tear plop down, watching it stain the leather on the toe of her polished boot and then looked up again, forcing herself to smile instead.

Connell took her arm under his own cashmere coat-sleeve, and steered her briskly out of the building.

"Howaya, Eamonn – tickets for the rugby next month or I won't defend your divorce settlement next time!" he yelled at the desk porter as they swirled through the revolving door.

Despite herself, she was beginning to feel that she might be actually enjoying being whisked around by Connell. It made a change from having to be the one who was always making decisions for other people.

Chez Claudine was, of course, completely empty at a quarter to twelve on an ice-cold January Monday, but the maitre d' greeted Connell as if he were a movie star, sweeping them gracefully to a very private table in the corner.

Kate, who was feeling pretty cheerful now, decided that she was going to have a glass of wine after all. She didn't have to go back to work and Connell who was reading the wine list as if it were a love-letter looked as though he was going to have a drink despite the fact that he was due in court in the afternoon. And although there had been no mention as to who was paying the bill, she got the distinct feeling that it was pretty much covered. In any case, Connell could always bill it to the hospital afterwards she reassured herself. And the least the hospital bloody owed her was a good lunch.

"So, did you have a nice Christmas?" she asked him, sipping the Prosecco that he had insisted she order.

Connell sighed and fiddled with the ice-cubes in his Diet Coke. He'd handed the wine-list back to the waitress with a hang-dog expression.

"Too nice really. Desperate going back to work, isn't

it? I've got two kids – twins aged four. Our house is full of toys. Santy everywhere, recycling wrapping paper and cardboard boxes overflowing in the Green bin." He waved a large hand painting a picture of it in the air for her. "You just need another month in bed to get over it all, don't you?"

"We don't have any children yet."

"You've got enough on your hands," Connell nodded. "Big career, obstetrics is. Very time-consuming, stressful, and seriously rewarding. My wife is a midwife and a theatre nurse."

Kate swallowed. "Do I know her?" she asked politely.

He shrugged. "You probably know her better than I do, anyway," he smiled. "Sharon? Sharon Guinness?"

She choked on her Prosecco. "Mmm." She felt her face begin to flush. *Guinness on the rocks with a twist.* Oh, man. The world really was far too small. "We have met," she coughed. "Well, no, actually, I know her quite well really. Actually, Connell, I don't know if you know but Sharon was the theatre nurse on duty that night – the night that – well, you know. The night of the delivery that we are all in such a heap about." Kate checked him from behind her menu.

"Was she? Oh, well. Small world. Too bloody tiny. How about the fish?" He scoured the menu. "Or the roast pork is fantastic here. Actually," he leaned towards her, "the main reason I come here is that it's the one restaurant in Ireland where they don't have a Caesar Salad on the menu. Everything's a fucking Caesar Salad nowadays: Chicken Caesar Wrap, Tuna Caesar Sandwich,

Caesar fucking Cheesecake. We come to bury Caesars, not to serve them up on every bloody lunchtime menu!" He beamed at the waitress who looked alarmed as she topped up their water glasses.

"*Et tu, Brute*," Kate grinned back at him.

"And what's all the little slices of bacon about anyway?" he demanded of her over the wine list. "Why do they have to have this boiled bacon and cabbage version of a Caesar Salad everywhere? Is it that rashers are the fucking anchovies of Ireland?"

Kate didn't know whether to laugh or cry. She wondered if there was any way she could use the question of the Caesar Salad to get to the point of why she was meeting Connell Jones Cumberton in the first place. If it were left to him, they'd be sitting here at midnight still talking about food.

"Look, Connell, speaking of Caesar, about legal matters such as –" she began.

"More Prosecco?" he replied.

"No, thanks. Look, don't you think we need to talk about the solicitors' letter we've received from France?"

"Have you decided on your starter? I can't decide whether to go for the soup or the quail's eggs. What about you?"

"No. Er . . ."

"Well, I recommend the truffle soup, it's delicious." He watched her face solemnly.

Kate laughed in exasperation but she wasn't sure how to proceed. She looked around them to see if he was just being discreet in trying to avoid talking about the medico-legal situation. There were several other people dining in the restaurant now, but no one who would overhear them.

"Connell!" she barked at him suddenly.

"What? Now you have me terrified!" He turned his pale eyes to her in innocent alarm.

"Well, I hate to have to say it, but you've no business being terrified. I'm the one who should be terrified here!" She was half angry, half laughing at him. "I'm the one being sued, and you are the one who is supposed to be defending me, and you can't concentrate on anything for a moment!"

He was crumpling up his eyes in mock shame. "Okay. All right." He folded up his napkin. "I'm sorry, Kate. I'll fill you in. Okay: here's the skinny on the letter from the French lawyers."

He leaned closer to her as the waitress passed. Kate noticed that he had a nice clean soap-scrubbed smell. It reminded her of her father's smell when she was a child. Her head was beginning to feel the fuzzy effects of the Prosecco, and the sudden image of her father made her feel as though she were close to tears again. Poor Daddy, having to put up with Caroline and Luis, she thought, and the nightmare of Christmas came flooding back.

"Now you're not listening!" Connell pulled back from her.

"I was just thinking about my sister," Kate began and looked down at the table.

"Is something wrong?" he asked her gently.

"Lots of things are wrong," she smiled at him, "but Connell, really, let's just get down to brass tacks and deal with this legal situation that I'm in. I really don't want to have to talk about my family, if that's all right with you."

"Good idea. Families are a nightmare," he agreed. "I never talk about mine if I can help it. Ah, here we are!" He beamed happily at the waitress who had arrived to take their order. "Now, we'll start with the boiled bacon and cabbage salad . . ." He winked at the bewildered Czech waitress.

Kate gave up. He might be distractible, but at least he was kind. And he knows a good restaurant, she thought, looking around her at the tables filling up. And he has a very good track record. And I'll probably find out soon enough what's going to happen with the litigation. He's probably just trying to cheer me up and get me slightly tipsy before breaking the bad news. It's not a bad strategy, really.

She looked at Connell out of the corner of her eye while he discussed their orders with the waitress as if it were a banquet for a presidential summit. Perhaps Connell's idea for a New Year's resolution wasn't such a bad one, she thought, examining the dessert menu.

Her mobile phone suddenly rang in her bag, and she picked it out.

It was Dave. *Take nothing seriously except lunch*, she told herself. And for the first time in her life she switched her mobile off on Dave, and put it back into her bag, and turned to her new food-obsessed lawyer and said, " I've decided, Connell. Thank you. I've made a decision. I'm going to have to have the baked fish after all."

They walked along the boardwalk afterwards, Connell wrapped deeply in his pale grey Crombie, Kate hugging her short puffa jacket around her hips. He bought them each a paper cappuccino to drink while they walked, and the wind whipped in off the sea and up the Liffey estuary and slapped them in the face.

"It's like this, Kate," he told her, leaning on the barrier to admire the view of the south quays. "What you want is for this case – and I'm not saying that there is a case – all we have so far is a letter *threatening us* with legal action – what you want is for this case to settle quickly out of court. The media will turn it into an absolute circus otherwise. This lady is a well-known litigation lawyer in a company with offices in Dublin, New York and Paris." He held his hands out expansively. "She sues newspapers who have breached privacy laws. So if there's one person who'd know how to get a story that brings down a doctor spun in the newspapers, it would be her." He looked at her.

"Go on," she said.

"What I'm going to do is persuade the Prof that it's in his interest to do a rapid deal, even if it costs the hospital. But that means that if you *are* to be sued by them, you should admit liability."

Kate opened her mouth in horror.

He raised a hand to her to stop her from speaking. "Let me finish here, and then you'll understand." He drained his coffee, crushing the paper cup in his hand. "From the point of view of your career, you are this paper cup to the Irish media. Quite disposable. Useful as a vessel for a story – and then?" He tossed the cup into the bin across the boardwalk. "Good shot though, wasn't it?" He winked at her.

"I don't understand at all." She was horrified. "I can't admit liability for something that I didn't do. I handled the case really well, Connell. It was a very difficult decision to make and I made it with great caution and in the worst possible clinical circumstances. Everyone agrees about that. Even Sharon, your own wife." She implored him. "You wouldn't want her to be involved in a case where there was negligence, would you?"

This simply couldn't be happening, she told herself. He couldn't be serious about her admitting liability, just to save the skin of the hospital. He must have mis-understood something.

Connell Jones Cumberton shook his head. "This isn't about Sharon or any of the other staff. They aren't the ones whose careers are on the line. It's all about you I'm afraid, and I know you're scared. And I'm really sorry that this is going to be so awful for you. But if you try to fight the case, and it goes to court, you will have to get up in front of all those people and the jury and go through every single minute of that night on call, and trust me, your memory isn't that good – no one's memory is. They will try to make a fool of you. Your case notes will be trashed. Your past obstetric records will be ridiculed. They will produce expert witnesses who will argue that there is some other drug you could have given, or that you could have kept the patient alive some other way. Trust me, it's not just a case of doing a section or not doing a section."

She was shaking her head, trying to interrupt him at the same time.

He raised his hand up like a stop sign. "Let me finish."

She folded her arms and looked at him.

"Kate," he carried on, "this is not about a legal matter really. You and I both know that. This lady has been hurt and *I* know that you didn't mean to hurt her. But she is devastated. She wants somebody else to suffer for her pain. That's the basis of all litigation, Kate. It's not just about compensation. It's about —"

"Revenge?" Kate butted in sharply. She was furious. This was unjust crap he was spouting. The wind stung her eyes and they shone wildly at him with fresh tears. "You think she wants revenge?"

Connell sighed. "Oh, perhaps that's part of it. But who knows? People sue doctors for all kinds of reasons, but usually it's just because they want to understand what went wrong and they want the doctor to be sorry. That's all. And you can easily do all that without a fight." He wiped a tear from her cheek with a leather-gloved finger.

"I'm not crying." She rubbed her nose furiously. "It's the wind."

"I know. Are you too cold? Let's walk instead."

They crossed O'Connell Street and reached the end of the boardwalk, then continued past the Custom House along the quay, walking quickly in the bitter wind so that they were well past the financial district now, where a cabaret of cranes rose up to greet them like stiff-legged ballerinas from the Lego-land of dock developments. They passed Jury's hotel, the *Jeannie Johnston*, the CHQ and when they were nearly at the dockside's end they stopped walking and stood silently, hands in their pockets, facing the grimmest winter sea.

"You think I fucked up, don't you? That's what Prof's told you. And Sharon. You all think – or you want to blame me. To make it look like I'm to blame."

He shook his head. "People are only ever motivated by emotions." But he looked away from her as he spoke.

At some level Kate realised that he probably did know what he was talking about, and it would be foolish not to take his advice on board – even if she wasn't going to follow it completely. But it was killing her to have to listen to him now. Nobody seemed to care about how she felt. That night had been the worst night of her life – her whole career. Everything she cared about was being blown up in her face. And he wanted her to keep quiet and listen while he rubbed her nose in it.

But she listened. Shoved her hands into her pockets, tucked her chin into her chest against the wind and listened.

Inside she wanted to scream at him to stop.

"At this stage we only have a request for the patients' notes, with a threat of legal action," he said in a gentle voice. "That's the first stage that they go through. They will scrutinise the case notes and see if they have a case for compensation based on medical negligence. They may not – but they will try to find one. The lady can't have children now. She will want somebody to pay for the tragedy that has happened to her. And she and her lawyers will have no empathy for you. This is what you must understand, Kate." He looked at her. "It's not nice stuff. And the insurance company won't want to settle because they will want to prove her wrong and save some money. But the thing is that if you go to court, they will back away from you, and you will be on your own in the witness box, and it will be your name in all the papers, and your name that every woman in Dublin will remember when she's booking in for a delivery, and –"

"All right, all right, I get your drift." Kate put a small hand up to stop him.

He indicated her fingers. "I see you're married too."

She frowned and put her hands back into her pockets, hugging herself to keep the wind away.

Admitting liability seemed like a disaster too, though, she thought. How would that look on a CV? Admission of medical negligence for a procedure that she undertook to save a woman's life? It was unthinkable. It was grossly dishonest, hypocritical even.

"What would you do, Connell, if it were your wife?" she asked him.

"If my wife couldn't have more kids?"

"No, if your wife were being sued. If it was Sharon who had done a delivery and made a decision that resulted in something major like this happening. And saved a patient's life, but the patient was suing her anyway. Would you ask her to settle out of court to save her face?"

"If she were insured properly, yes," he said. "If she could hold her head up high and know in her heart that she had done the right thing, then yes. Because she wouldn't be agreeing that she'd done something wrong, she would only be exercising damage control. She would be allowing that patient the dignity to walk away without a media circus too. Nobody really wins or loses in these cases, Kate. It's all a Solomon's Choice."

"That's two women fighting over a baby that neither one can keep – it's a different metaphor," she snapped.

"Yeah, or in the case of lawyers, two dogs fighting over a bone," he grinned. "Look," he said in a gentler voice, "I'm in this job a good while now. I know what husbands and wives are like. I know that doctors make mistakes sometimes, and I know that sometimes they get away with it and they sometimes don't. And I know that sometimes patients are much more distressed about unfortunate deliveries than they need to be. We all have expectations for our future and when things turn out to be the complete opposite to what we expected, it's devastating. Childbirth *is* to women what war is to men. Women go into labour and can come out with their expectations of life shattered. So," he shrugged, "give her an olive branch."

Kate shook her head. "I can't just agree to something like that, Connell. It's like admitting something that I know isn't true, and that makes me also look like a bad doctor. I make mistakes sometimes, everybody does. But I didn't make any mistakes that night. I saved her life that night. She knows that. Or if she doesn't, then her legal team and expert witnesses should know that."

She paused a moment, watching the Stena Line ferry drift in towards Dun Laoghaire harbour. From that distance, the ship was like a serene giant. But you could tell from the white horses that the thick black January sea was as choppy as hell.

"They aren't going to see it that way," he told her softly. "The *lawyers* are only seeing dollar signs. The patient is only seeing pay-back for the kids she'll never have. And her husband is only trying to see a way out of his wife's pain."

"How can *you* know what her husband wants?" Kate asked him, hating the bitterness that she heard in her own voice.

Connell raised his eyebrows in surprise. "Because I'm a clever lawyer. And I'm a husband too. I know that if it were my wife, I'd want to support whatever she needed to do to make her feel better."

Kate's mind felt numb. *There's a lot about your wife that you don't know,* was what she was tempted to snap back at him, but she said nothing. In a sense, Connell was a victim in this crazy world as well. And as for Jonny – Jonny couldn't be supporting *this*. Could he?

"Her husband couldn't be involved in this. Her husband is away." Kate looked at Connell.

"Away? Where?"

"In the Sudan."

"Long-term?"

"No. Just for a few weeks."

"How do you know?"

"Oh. Perhaps she mentioned it to me *en passant*." Kate froze her eyes on his for a moment and then turned away again. *Goddamn you, Jonny, why can't you be here for any of us now?* "Can we go back the other way now?" she mumbled into her scarf.

"Sure thing." Connell wrapped a fraternal arm around her shoulders. "Sleep on it, Kate, why don't you? You don't have to do anything yet. This is very early stages. I'll keep in touch with you. And don't take things too seriously, whatever you decide to do."

"Take nothing seriously except lunch?" She smiled weakly at him.

He ruffled his gloved hand through her thick dark hair.

"Now you're talking sense, doctor."

251

13

Jonny Domville stood in the still of the January night and stretched his neck out to ease the tension caused by two long flights and then a long, long day of meetings and negotiations. He stretched his whole body out as far as it would go, arms outstretched, leaning backwards as he did, his gaze a prisoner to a desert-wide black sky that was a wash of stars. He would never get used to all the stars of Africa. No matter how often he came back. No matter how many times he'd stood beneath them. And in the frozen darkness of the desert, a silver blast of moonlight roamed the night. A collarbone-white moon that licked the night-time, as sharp as a blade. As evil as a devil's grin.

"Connell Jones Cumberton is possessed by the devil!" Nick Farrelly said to Kate, his face breaking with sardonic mirth.

"Meaning?" Kate sighed loudly at him.

"Actually no. I'm wrong. Forget that. The devil is possessed by Connell Jones Cumberton!" Nick giggled back at her.

Kate rolled her eyes at him and decided not to reply. She turned back instead to the task she was absorbed in, checking the giant pile of haemoglobin and virology results from the antenatal clinic. Nick could be irritatingly cryptic sometimes, she thought, and although normally she enjoyed his rather bitchy sense of humour she wasn't in the mood for any more banter tonight. She was in many ways beginning to regret having told Nick about what was now being generally referred to as the "French Letter". Nick didn't seem to be capable of taking it seriously enough to be supportive, but at the same time he was being flippant enough to be bordering on offensive. And she was also beginning to realise that Connell was absolutely right when he'd told her to be very discreet about who she spoke to in the hospital and if at all possible to keep matters completely to herself.

"I really wish I hadn't told you now," was what she eventually said to Nick, separating a positive hepatitis C result from the pile of negative ones. "You are being an absolute pig about the whole thing. What I need right now is a good friend, Nick, and you're being a pest."

"I'd have found out anyway – Sharon tells me everything," Nick replied with nonchalance.

"Do you think Sharon knows? Oh. Well, I suppose. Of course she knows." Kate stood still and thought a moment. Everything had changed. Even Nick, who could be bitchy at the best of times but who was generally so loyal to her, was being just plain bitchy now. Was it her – was she becoming touchy about everything? Was Dave right, when he said that she was pushing him away from her because she made too many demands? Perhaps she was pushing Nick away from her too. Nick was one of her best friends and yet ever since she'd come back after Christmas she couldn't help feeling that things had changed between them too. *Just because you're paranoid it doesn't mean they aren't out to get you,* she thought, remembering the joke Dave had cracked when he'd discovered the scratch marks poor Mrs Mad Devine had left.

She signed her initials *KG* in neat letters on the hepatitis-C-positive blood form that she'd just picked up, and stuck a yellow sticky note on it. Then she turned her attention back to Nick. Maybe she ought to try to be more honest with him, if she needed him as a friend.

"You know what I hate, Nick? I hate being the source of gossip in the hospital. People here can't mind their own business and it's doubly awkward with the patient still being on the ward. And then I feel as though I can't go near my other patients any more. I'm terrified that the other staff will start to feel like Prof does. And if I lose my confidence altogether then things will just get worse."

"They say that lack of communication is the primary cause of litigation," said Nick in a smooth voice, swinging backwards in his chair with his legs up on the outpatients reception desk, twirling his stethoscope around his neck.

"Nick, you are really being very unhelpful." Kate glared at him, and wrote *Phone in a.m., please, and ask to come in Monday* on a sticky note before sticking it neatly on another lab result.

"I'm only being frank with you, Kate. Oh, look, you'll figure something out. And if old JC can't save you, then you are unsalvageable."

"JC?"

"Jones Cumberton – not Jesus Christ, if that was what you were thinking. He defended that vascular surgeon last year who did an aortic aneurysm without checking the patient's platelet count and the guy exsanguinated on the table. If he can convince the family of that poor man to settle, he'd convince anybody."

"Yet again, Nick. Not reassuring me." Kate peeled another sticky note off and stuck it on a haemoglobin result. *Double this lady's iron, please,* she wrote on it.

"You know," she looked at him again, "I tried to make myself go to the patient and have a chat with her. I wanted to. I really did." She bit on her lip. "But that day, for the first time in my life I felt I couldn't communicate with a patient and I chickened out, leaving it till the next day to talk to her. And then the next thing I knew Prof was taking me off the case." She checked Nick's face. He was listening with a solemn expression. At least he's listening to me now, she thought. "And now," she continued, marking another lab result with *Scan and early review appointment, please,* "since the 'French Letter', as you keep calling it, Prof doesn't want me doing deliveries at all." She picked another bundle of lab results up from the outpatients clerk's desk, and started peeling through them carefully. "But the thing is, Nick," she said in a low voice, "I felt emotionally involved with her from the very start. You see, I haven't told you this yet, but her husband is a friend of mine. We were at college together."

"Shouldn't that make it easier then?" Nick took his glasses off and polished them with the corner of his scrub shirt.

"You'd think." She marked another urine culture with red biro.

"Polo mint?" Nick produced a tube from his overloaded white coat pocket.

She shook her head, and looked at him as she spoke. "Her husband was my husband's best friend and that was how I knew him in first med. The three of us were a sort of – a trio, I suppose."

Nick was open-mouthed. "You mean you had a threesome?"

"No! Although . . ." she said and she couldn't help smiling at him now.

"But then," she continued seriously, "they fell out. And then I married Dave. And now it's just all very awkward for me. Dave won't talk to me about what happened between them. It's like I feel I just can't go there."

"Hmmm." Nick crunched a Polo mint noisily. "He

was Dave's best friend, was that what you said?" He put his head on one side.

"Mmm." She carried on working in silence. It wasn't fair to talk about Dave's problems behind his back. Besides, there was too much to explain really, and too much about it that she didn't understand either. Dave's problems were terrifying – he was drinking way too much and didn't seem to realise it at all. He's written off his car and he wasn't even prepared to talk to her about it. But she wouldn't let him down by talking about him behind his back. "Nick," she turned to look at him, "did you ever think that you would want to have kids? You know. If you could."

Nick rolled his eyes. "I don't think kids would want to have me."

She thought a minute about this one.

"Feeling broody, Kate?" he said. "Re-circulated hormones in the air-conditioning affecting you?"

Kate's pager burst into sound in her breast pocket. "Sorry, Nick, I've got to go." She patted the last pile of lab results together and put her pen back in her pocket by the bleeper.

"I'll walk down that way with you. There's a lady whose epidural I want to top up anyway." Nick swung his legs off the desk and stood up to join her.

"Did you have a nice Christmas, Nick?" she asked him as they walked briskly together towards the labour ward.

"*Fabuloso*. Went home to Lahinch, ate for Ireland,

came back to Dublin and partied till my eyeballs almost popped out. How is Dave, by the way?"

She paused. "He's – um – back at work now, of course. But not great, actually, since you ask. He had a nasty accident just before Christmas, a car crash and his Audi's totalled."

"I know," he said quietly.

She groaned. "You do? You see, that's exactly what I'm talking about. That's exactly what I mean about this hospital. Nothing is private. Everyone knows everybody else's business."

"Well, actually, Dave told me himself, about the car crash."

"Oh. Of course." She carried on walking through the labour ward. "Dave hit a taxi. I'm terrified now that the taxi driver is going to sue us too, of course, but Dave doesn't seem to be that bothered. He's completely distracted nowadays. Where is your patient, Nick?" She turned to look at Nick and then realised that she was almost talking to herself. Nick had stopped behind her.

"I'm in here," he said, indicating. "You could always use your skills to help Dave, Kate. I believe you know a rather successful barrister in Dublin these days?" Nick's rabbit teeth broke into an uncontrollably mischievous smile.

She couldn't help smiling back at him. "You are being horrible and evil as usual, Nick Farrelly. You are laughing at my pain."

"I am attempting to anaesthetise it with good humour," he grinned at her.

She waved her hands, shooing him. "All right. Now go away. I'll see you later on for tea in the Res." She carried on walking to the nurses' station. Natasha was sitting at the phone like a sentry on duty. "Hi, Natasha. I'm in which room –?"

"Seven, Kate. It's just a tear for you to suture, please."

"Fine." She smiled warmly at Natasha. As warmly as she could.

"So, how was Florida, Dennis?" Kate asked him in as light a voice as she could manage.

She sat perched on the edge of the chair in front of his desk, knees clenched tight together. Her hands were clasped together on her knees.

"Very relaxing." Dennis Crowe turned around and beamed at her, his leather-deep-brown face incongruous in the January grey daylight. "Did you get a nice break over Christmas yourself?"

"Not really, no, I didn't actually." Kate looked down at the tight knot of her hands. "My sister was very ill. And my husband crashed the car." She looked up at him. "So, not great really. I was on call for New Year's which was kind of lonely too." She smiled a brave smile at him and cocked her head.

"Which is why you need a break now," he said.

"A break?"

"Because you look pale and exhausted. Your eyes are

– well, I'm not going to unflatter you by telling you how large the bags are underneath them."

"Please don't," Kate said in a gruff voice, looking at her hands again.

"And you are a bag of nerves," he continued, "which is not a good way to present yourself on the wards at the moment." He frowned at her, stroking his suntanned chiselled chin. "You used to be so competent and reliable, Kate. You've always been an excellent surgeon. What is going on that we don't know about? Is there something at home that is causing all of this deterioration in your work?"

She could smell the cloud of aftershave from where she sat on the other side of the room and it nauseated her. "I told you. Family problems. And you know, a threat of litigation isn't helping either." She raised her eyes to meet his.

"Yes." Dennis Crowe tapped his fountain-pen on the desk. "We'll just have to see what becomes of that. I know it isn't easy, though, having to write those enormous reports out for solicitors, going through every detail of a tough delivery."

"It's like rubbing salt into a wound! Nobody wants things to go wrong. We try so hard, all of us, to help women, to manage labour, to deliver healthy babies. We work really really hard to get good outcomes. Look at all the research I've done in this hospital. Look at all the audits we're doing. We spend every minute of the day trying to save babies and write birth plans, trying so hard to give people the kinds of delivery that they want. And then they sue us. All the time." She became aware that she was sounding shrill and stopped abruptly.

"Which is why this hospital pays out several million every year in insurance premia," Professor Crowe said evenly, meeting her eyes. He *was* trying to show her kindness, she realised, but it was actually making her feel worse.

"I'm suggesting that you take two weeks off, beginning now." He tapped his fountain pen more briskly. "Are you planning to visit family at any stage?"

She nodded. "My father lives in Venice."

"Well. Venice should be lovely and quiet at this time of year."

"Yes. Of course it should." She felt her heart sink. And yet. Perhaps this was the best thing to do right now. She was exhausted, Christmas had been horrible, and Venice – well, it was perfect, actually. She'd just hang out with Charles and get to see that Caro was all right – in fact, it would be a wonderful break.

Across the Professor's desk the view of the Dublin Mountains was like a perfect theatre set. A scattering of houses thinning out into dense green hills that were now topped with snow like icing on a perfect cake.

"You know, I think if I were you, Prof," she said, "with that view, I'd spend all day just hiding out up here." She looked at him with sudden consideration.

"Tempting, isn't it?" he said, raising his eyebrows in an attempt at humour but the resulting effect was only to make him look smug. "You'll get there, one day, Kate. You just need to be a bit more focused, you see."

She felt a sour taste in her mouth. "I'd better go on down again. I've got to finish up my rounds." She stood up.

"You'll be back at the end of January," he said. "That should be time enough."

"All right," she said. "I'll see you then. Thank you – I suppose."

"Yes. Well, have a good rest and come back full of energy." Dennis Crowe returned his attention to the paper he was marking at his desk.

She walked away.

She had never felt as small as this in all her life.

"Kate."

She caught her breath. His voice was the last thing she'd expected when the phone rang. "Jonny! Are you all right? Are you still in Africa?"

"Yes. I mean no. I've just got back. I'm just a bit jet-lagged."

"Are you in Dublin then?" she asked, sinking down to sit cross-legged on the floor beside the phone.

"No. I'm still in Paris."

"Oh. So. How was the Sudan?" She tried not to sound as if her heart was in her mouth.

"Busy. Full of celebrities trying to meet with the WHO. It's like a Hollywood red carpet in the middle of the desert at the moment."

She smiled. "That's really wicked, Jonny. So, what have you been doing since you got back?"

"I was just thinking about you, actually."

She held her breath. "What kind of thing were you thinking – about me in particular?" she said. This was it, she thought. This was the final pile of it, coming down on her like lava from a volcano. He was going to tell her that he and Marianne were going to sue.

She heard him utter a short happy laugh on the other end of the phone.

"Good things, mainly. I was just listening to '*Les Feuilles Mortes*', the Miles Davis version, and then I started listening to Chet Baker and playing it on the trumpet, well, trying to, so I put that away and started playing something else, and then I started thinking about you. In fact, I thought about you a lot during the past two weeks."

"Are you still playing the sax too?" She twirled the flex of the phone around her fingers like a tourniquet.

"Piano. I like the piano better these days for some reason."

"I think you always did."

"It's a very versatile instrument."

Kate paused a moment before replying. The conversation was bordering on the surreal. It was impossible to believe that he'd rung her just to talk about the versatility of musical instruments. She felt as though she might almost be sick with the anticipation of what she knew must be coming next if she didn't force him to address it.

He must be ringing her to talk to her about Marianne suing the hospital. So why didn't he just spit it out and get it over with? She felt a most unpleasant combination of absolute delight to be able to speak to him and what was almost anger at the blasé non-sequitur discourse.

"Kate. Are you still there?"

"Yes. I was waiting for you to speak," she said, forcing an evenness into her voice.

"Oh. Well, I was just thinking about you because of the song. Thinking about the way we used to sing it. On Tom Waits' piano."

She paused again before replying. This was beginning to seem almost ridiculous, really. And yet, there wasn't a note of anything covert in his voice at all.

"The way we used to sing it? You rang me up to tell me that? All the way from Paris?"

"Um. I was just thinking, how much you'd like it here in Paris too, I suppose."

He almost sounded coy, she felt. This was the silliest way to soften the blow that she'd ever imagined, and yet in some ways perhaps it was rather sweet of him. Perhaps he was trying to make it clear to her that even if Marianne was suing her, he and she would still be friends.

"I mean, there's lots of jazz in Paris, in the cafés," he continued. "I suppose that's mainly why I like it here. The music scene is very good." He paused. "What's the weather like in Dublin?"

Part of her wanted to yell at him to snap out of it and

just tell her what she already knew, and yet somehow she felt that there was a genuine innocence in the tone of his voice that he couldn't possibly be faking. It occurred to her that perhaps he *didn't* actually know about the litigation Marianne was planning.

"Have you talked to Marianne?" she finally asked, and she could feel the relief wash over her like a wave as soon as she had said it.

"She's still in Dublin. Of course, you know that. She's getting a lot better now, I think. I spoke to her earlier on the phone today. She is coming back to Paris next week."

"Next week. Yes." Kate felt her chest tighten again. "Jon, did – did she say anything else, though? About – something about the delivery? Or anything – further? About her plans. Or about me." And she bit her lip.

"We just talked about Veronique, I suppose. She said that her legal colleagues in Dublin were helping to organise getting her back here next week. So I've got a few days here on my own before they get here. Which is a bit lonely, really." He uttered a small laugh at his own humility.

He had missed the beat completely. "Her legal colleagues . . . helping to organise getting her back to Paris"– perhaps that's all Marianne had told him she was doing.

She had kept it from him that she was planning to sue.

So he didn't know. Or did he?

There was only one way to find out, really. She took a breath.

"I've just been asked to take two weeks off work." She could hear the echo of her own breathing on the phone coming back at her.

"Really? That sounds brilliant! Are you going to go away?"

There was no hint of anything. *She hasn't told him*, Kate thought. She hasn't told him anything. They aren't even *talking* to each other like a couple, she thought, without knowing how to feel. She's frozen him out completely, just like he says she does. He really, really doesn't know she's suing me.

Her voice was paper-dry. "Yes. I, well, I was thinking of going to Venice to see my dad. I really missed not seeing him this year."

"Wow! That sounds wonderful. Hey, I've just had an idea. Why don't you come to Paris on your way?" He sounded excited now.

"What?" She felt herself become light-headed.

"Well, it might be a nice way to arrive in Venice. You could fly to Charles de Gaulle and then take the overnight train to Venice. I just think, I've always thought, by the way, that arriving by train is the only way to arrive in Venice."

She laughed without humour. And then asked in sudden gravity, "Jonny, are you being serious?"

"Yes, of course. You just roll in across the lagoon, and the city rises up before you out of the fog and the sea, and it's absolutely beautiful . . ."

"No, I know all that. Of course it's beautiful. That's not what I meant at all, Jonny." She felt her heart thump in her chest, so loudly she felt that Jonny would hear it down the phone.

"Of course I'm being serious," he said. "So, will you come to Paris, Kate?"

"What would I do in Paris?" she asked cautiously. "With your – your wife in Dublin?"

"Well, I just thought that *we* could spend some time together," he replied, and she heard him swallow, and she couldn't but notice the anticipation he was trying to disguise. "It was just so nice, the other week, hanging out with you again. Alone with you. That's all that I was thinking. And I miss you. I really miss you, Kate. I – want to be with you." There was a pause. "I'm still in love with you, you see."

Outside, the canal lock roared as usual. The cars beeped and revved on Huband Bridge as usual. And the Dublin January rain pelted down like a clatter of knives onto the slate roof of number 92 Percy Place as usual. And inside, her heart sang as loudly as a nightingale.

"Will you meet me at the airport?" she eventually said.

It was the perfect outcome – it was more than she could have dreamed about. And the more she thought about it the more she knew that it was the right thing for her to do. Everything was over between her and Dave now, she could see that as clear as day. She belonged with Jonny. Perhaps she always had. Perhaps it had taken them both ten long years to realise it.

She had thought that Dave would always love her but he'd changed almost beyond recognition now. He was desperately unhappy, pill-popping and drinking like a fish, and she had tried to help – tried to be a wife, a friend, tried to make it work. But he'd only pushed her further and further away.

And what Dave's change in personality was making her realise was that, of the two men she had loved, she'd married the wrong one. And it had taken a crisis in Jonny's life too – the realisation he was in a marriage he couldn't work either – for him to see that Kate was really the one he should be with. Either way, there was nothing that would stop her from going to Paris now. She could go to Venice later in the week. But first she'd get to Paris – and she'd be with Jonny because it was the right thing for her to do. And from then on everything would fall into place.

She would think of something to tell Dave – she wouldn't tell him she was going to go to Jonny yet, of course. In his state, with his mood swings and the massive depression he'd been in ever since Christmas, she wasn't going to risk another row by even hinting at that. She'd tell him she was going to Venice to see her father, just like she'd told the Prof. It was easier not to tell anybody too much just yet – it was only the beginning. It was just the beginning of something that she should have done years ago.

And Marianne – well, what about her now? She had stamped her legal foot, and Professor Crowe had jumped. Jonny clearly didn't know that Marianne wanted to sue – and she wasn't going to complicate things further by telling him.

"Ronan!"

She was thrilled to see him. She'd been going around the hospital all day with more energy than she'd felt in weeks.

She had passed the SCBU earlier, where Marianne was sitting with Veronique in her arms, wearing a pair of glasses and examining some documents. Kate had briskly walked away. She was cautious about having to go near the SCBU again, not wanting to have to revisit the scene. And even though her heart sang every time she thought about being in Paris with Jonny by tomorrow night, the sight of Marianne was still unnerving her.

She couldn't help it. Despite what Jonny had told her about their marriage she couldn't help wanting the madonna-like presence of Marianne just to go away – or better still, to have never existed in the first place. She had tried to ask herself, in all honesty, if the fact that Marianne was suing her had some subtle influence over her decision to run away with Jonny – but the truth was that in many ways, despite her humiliation, she actually found it hard to think badly of Marianne at all.

In many ways, despite the disaster it had brought on her own career, she couldn't really blame Marianne for wanting to sue now. The sight of her sitting all alone in a Dublin hospital in January had made her realise that what Marianne looked like now was nothing like the tough lawyer Connell had described. She was a tough lawyer made powerless by events – and when Kate examined her feelings about Marianne she realised that they were very mixed.

There was her initial fear of confronting the woman. But at the same time there was a curious and contradictory, an almost welcome sense of empathy towards Jonny's wife. She found, when she examined the feelings that lay underneath, that she really felt no bitterness towards her at all.

Marianne and Jonny had clearly had just as many problems as she had with Dave – more perhaps, given that poor Marianne had been pregnant all the way through their break-up. But what unnerved her most of all was to think of how much she now had in common with Marianne.

But she couldn't *not* have been pleased to see Ronan Clare's chunky silhouette at the end of the corridor ambling along the ward between SCBU and theatre from where she had just emerged.

It had taken almost an hour to say goodbye to Sharon and the other nurses, and despite her exhilarated energy at getting away tomorrow, the day had seemed unusually long. She had spent hours battling with the nurses and the secretaries to make sure her work was all re-scheduled for the next two weeks. She really ought to just get out and go home now, pack and get an early night. But there was something always reassuring about hanging out for a while with Ronan Clare.

"You're exactly the very person that I'd like to spend the last hour of my last day with, having a nice long cup of coffee somewhere," she said to him. She jerked her thumb towards the glass walls of the SCBU. "Have you finished yet?"

"I'm finished – for today." His face was an absolutely radiant smile. "But guess what news *I've* got?" he beamed.

"What?" She linked his arm and turned him round to walk the other way.

"Guess who's going to France on Monday?" he said.

"*What?*" she whispered, stopping in horror in her tracks. "What do you know about going to France on Monday?"

"Guess who's airlifting Baby Lunnermond and her *maman* to Paris, in a *helicopter* with a diplomatic escort?" Ronan beamed, oblivious.

"*What?*"

Ronan whooped in delight. "Yup! Me and Nicko, off to Paris in the spring, first thing next week, Monday morning. Score!" He punched the air in delight.

She swallowed hard. "Well. Wow. I see." Her voice shook. "You know, it's not exactly spring – yet." She gave a short ill-humoured laugh and then cringed inside. Her reply had sounded almost sour and yet she didn't quite know what else to say. She feigned a brief, bright smile at Ronan who kept on walking and let him gabble on a bit longer until she couldn't help stopping him in mid-sentence, asking in an undisguisably horrified voice,

"Ronan, when did they decide all this? About you going to *Paris*?"

"Yesterday," Ronan happily replied. "Crowe and Sharon were in there all day long yesterday, sorting out the transfer."

"Well. I see. But how come *you're* going?"

"Because no one else wants to go! So me and Nick Farrelly are going to go with the two patients in the helicopter all the way, and then we make the transfer to the hospital in Paris and come back by helicopter too. Savage, Kate. Isn't it absolutely savage? Isn't it?"

"Yes – savage. Of course it is. But you won't be *staying* in Paris, will you?" she asked him in a doubtful voice.

"No. We can't. Wouldn't you know, they're sending us over on a Monday morning, so we're coming back straight away, that evening." He rolled his eyes and she couldn't disguise the magnitude of her relief. "But just imagine, Kate," he turned his over-excited face towards her once again, "imagine flying over Paris in a helicopter? All around the Eiffel Tower and stuff? It'll be amazing!"

She couldn't help grinning at his child-like expression now. "Oh, Ronan, it all sounds like brilliant fun. I'm really pleased for you. Hey, don't forget to keep the patient alive, though." She squeezed his arm. "I mean, patients," she said, emphasising the *s*.

"Hey," he turned to look at her, "what about going up the town? Just the two of us? And get a nicer cup of coffee? Somewhere posher than this place? Somewhere where we can have nice cakes and stuff?"

She turned her head sideways to look at him, still smiling at his uncontrollable bubbliness.

"All right," she said. "Let's go to Café Léon, and you can practise for all the *Viennoiserie* in Paris, and we can make absolute pigs of ourselves."

Dave Hardiman was exhausted. His brain felt swollen with over-tiredness, and he shuddered at the boggy greyness that was the texture of his skin. He was only thirty-two and yet he looked middle-aged tonight, he thought, miserably glaring at his expression. His eyes looked as though they had almost sunken into his face.

He turned the hot tap on full and splashed warm water on his face, trying to slap some life into it, and then took a striped towel off the rack and rubbed his head and neck briskly before inspecting his appearance once again. Not a whole lot better really.

Dave leaned against the sink, his head slumped forward onto the mirror and closed his eyes. The throbbing in his head was unbearable tonight.

The nausea that crawled up his throat seemed to be radiating along all of his skin as well, which felt almost as though there were insects *underneath* it. He scratched his arms again furiously and then tried to smooth out the red wheals that his fingernails had raised.

He was fucked. Completely fucked. Fucked-up completely.

He didn't know what he was doing any more. He couldn't talk to Kate. She seemed to be permanently angry with him. He didn't know where he could begin. He couldn't blame her most of the time. He was being an absolute bastard and he knew it and at the same time he couldn't stop himself and he couldn't tell her because if she was hurting now and angry with him she would absolutely *die* if she knew what kind of life he was really leading.

Jesus Christ!

Dave slapped his own face once again and glared at his reflection reddening in the mirror. He had never hated himself more than this. This moment now.

He loved Kate. He'd always loved her more than anyone. She'd been his closest friend – and yet now, thanks to his fucking around, it was almost impossible to *remember* a time when they had been friends, never mind lovers. He needed her to look after him. He always had needed her. And he couldn't bear the thought of losing her. He had wanted to protect her and to be with her forever and to always live with her. And yet sometimes the idea of touching her almost repulsed him.

Dave rubbed his face again and rinsed his rancid mouth with mouthwash, spitting furiously into the sink.

He had three units of Fentanyl left and if he took all three of them together that might do the job – but then what about later on tonight if the pain became worse and he still couldn't sleep? The swallowing pills just wasn't working any more and there was no point in wasting his last three units and then finding himself stuck again later. He'd be in bits trying to get out of bed again if he felt like this in the morning.

It would make a lot more sense to skin-pop it, one unit at a time and save on his supply because he wouldn't get back into the hospital till Monday – and that anaesthetics nurse who was a complete bitch was watching him like a hawk.

Nobody, not even Kate, would understand what he was going through, even if he told her. She was too caught up in her own world at the moment. And she would never forgive him if she knew everything.

Nick Farrelly was the only person who could understand him any more. Nick had said he loved him. Over and over again he'd said it. And it had been something that he'd been longing to hear.

They had good conversations too, he and Nick. No, they had brilliant conversations all the time. Nick was clever. Funny. Cultured without being a pretentious fart. If he hadn't met Nick, in fact, he couldn't imagine how crap his life might be now. Nick was like everything he'd ever known.

He turned more hopefully away from the bathroom mirror and went downstairs again, to the cupboard underneath the landing where his briefcase with the combination lock was kept.

"Bye, Nick!" Kate poked her head into the Res TV room where Nick was channel-surfing in between *America's Next Top Model* and *Grand Designs*. "I'll see you when I get back from Venice," she smiled fondly at him.

"Have a fabulous rest, Kate, and take your time

getting back," Nick drawled from where he lay languidly on the sofa.

"I'll see you on Monday, Nick." Ronan picked his denim jacket off the coat-rack and pulled it on tightly around his body.

Nick put his feet up on the coffee table. "Hey, Kate, what's the real difference between a nurse and a helicopter?" He grinned at her and Ronan.

"What?" she smiled.

"Ronan Clare's finally getting to go up in a helicopter." Nick winked at her. "Have fun in Venice, Katie." He turned back to the TV.

"Prick!" shouted Ronan over his shoulder as they left the building.

Kate found, after an hour and a half of giggling at the snootiness of the waitresses in Léon, followed by a glass of champagne in the Shelbourne, which Ronan insisted was the only way to end the evening, that she didn't really want to go home tonight. She didn't want to have to go home at all. It was pitch dark outside and the night was looking horribly gusty, with people floundering with umbrellas outside on Kildare Street. And here in the Shelbourne bar drinking champagne with Ronan it was warm and it was fun.

"You know what I often find myself wondering?" she asked him, peering at him over the rim of her glass.

"What?"

"Whether, if we'd known when we started out in

med school that this is what it would be like, we would have done it anyway?"

"What do you mean?" he asked.

"I mean, most doctors are miserable all the time. Aren't we?"

He shrugged. "I don't know. Some are, some aren't, I suppose."

"Well, we're overworked. Overstressed. And our lives are – Jesus, Ronan!" she laughed. "Our personal lives are either non-existent, if we're lucky, or else if we have a personal life then it's a complicated mess! Why does it have to be so hard?" She played with the stem of her glass, and then looked at him. "If you could be anything in the world except a doctor, Ronan, what would you want to be, if you could do it all again?" She picked a handful of peanuts out of a tiny china dish.

Ronan looked thoughtful for a moment and suddenly seemed rather sad.

"I think that what I really would have liked to be would be an astronaut, or something," he replied. "Or a deep-sea diver. Or an arctic explorer. Something kind of *tough* but with a sensitive edge."

Kate burst into howls of laughter.

"Hey!" He looked offended.

"Oh, Ronan, that's so cute!" She put a peanut into his mouth.

"Why? What do you mean, cute? Why can't I be tough but with a sensitive edge, and spend my time rescuing killer whales from certain death?" he grumbled.

"Because you *are* tough but with a sensitive edge, and you rescue tiny babies from certain death all day!" She smiled fondly at him.

"Yeah – but most of the time I don't think of it that way, I suppose." He wrinkled up his nose. "Paeds is nice but most of the time it's just standing up all night, crunching numbers and running up and down to the lab. In any case, I just thought that we were playing a game." He looked sheepish. "So I thought I was allowed to think up something where I could feel a bit more *heroic*."

She laughed loudly again.

"Well? What about you? What would you do if you could do it all again?" He put a peanut into her mouth.

She swirled her drink around while she chewed the peanut, and thought about it. "You know," she looked at him, "you know what I think the worst thing about me is? I think the worst thing about me is that if I got the chance to do it all again, I'd probably do the exact same thing. I'd probably do obstetrics *all* over again. Which is so boring of me, isn't it? So predictable. So clingy and security-seeking."

"No, it isn't, it's consistent," he said.

"Yes, but I've been so fed up with work for the past two weeks, and now I'm being sued –"

"You don't know that yet," he interrupted. "They've only asked for the case notes."

"Well, I'm under scrutiny and it isn't nice, I've been taken off my usual responsibilities and I've got a barrister appointed to me already so I'm not feeling too proud of myself at the moment." She looked at Ronan. "And if there were ever a moment in medicine that I felt like jacking it all in, it would be now." She put her glass down and picked up more peanuts. "You know, Ronan, I've always been the kind of person who needs to feel that nothing will go wrong in my life. I like to make safe decisions, to have a predictable outcome. Which is why, I suppose, I can be a bit bossy at work."

He smiled a gentle smile.

"It's just that I like to get things right," she went on. "It's important to me not to make mistakes. And I tend to do things that are safe, rather than take bravo risks. I married Dave because I thought that it would be safe."

Ronan raised his eyebrows at her.

She continued, nodding at him, "I think that because our family has always been so all over the place that I really needed some security so I married my best friend. But you know what? Doing the safe thing is often the most dangerous thing that you can do." She looked at him listening solemnly. "My dad used to always say that," she said and smiled slightly. "And now, it feels as though every safe decision I made in my life has just unravelled. And especially since that disastrous delivery before Christmas, I just feel as though I can't be sure of anything I do any more. I've lost all my confidence." Her voice dropped to a murmur.

"Shit. Is it really as bad as that?" He looked at her, deep in concern.

"So maybe that's why I feel like doing something risky now," she said. "Something dangerous. I feel like going to Paris and just not coming back."

"Venice," Ronan said.

"What?"

"You mean you feel like going to Venice and not coming back. It's me and Nick who are going to Paris, on Monday, Kate. *You're* going to Venice. Have another drink, Kate – it makes more sense the more you have of it." He waved across the length of the lounge room at a waiter who studiously ignored them.

Kate looked away to disguise her pinkening expression.

"Why do waiters always ignore me?" Ronan groaned.

"Because you are too nice and look too gentle, mild and kind," she replied. "Waiters only respond to people who are very badly behaved." She smiled at Ronan waving fruitlessly at the waiter and couldn't help remembering how rapidly Jonny had got attention that night with her on Kildare Street. Her skin prickled at the memory of that night – the candles, the way he'd told her that he wanted to kiss her, to be with her again. And she would actually be with him this time tomorrow! She shivered suddenly at the thought of it. She really ought to go home and pack – decide what to wear, try to negotiate with Dave. And yet. It was fun here. And fun was something she could certainly use a lot more of now.

Ronan's wild gesticulations eventually caught the waiter's attention. He pointed down at their empty drinks and the waiter nodded and turned wearily back to the bar.

"Well done," she said. "God, Ronan, I just don't seem to want to go home tonight at all!" She sighed with great drama, and then looked around her at the long comforting bar: the polished manes of hair being flicked about, the navy suits with crisp shirts under evening-loosened silk neck-ties. The glossy fingernails around cocktail glasses. She breathed in the blissful Friday-night-ness of it all. "And I've got to go home soon and pack and everything," she grumbled. "It's just so much nicer sitting here all night than in our house."

"It's nicer in here than in anybody's house," he said, leaning away from her to make room for the waiter who had just arrived.

"Okay. I've decided what I want to be when I grow up," she said while two more glasses of champagne were placed in front of them.

Ronan dropped a fifty on the waiter's tray. "Which is?" He handed her a glass.

"I want to be a pianist, or an opera singer, or something like that," she replied. "I want to be something wild and beautiful. In my next job. Not something that has to stay up all night, all smelly in stained theatre scrubs and over-tired all the time."

"You are already wildly beautiful, in your current job," Ronan told her solemnly.

"Oh, goody!" She clinked her glass against his. "Then we are both in our perfect professions already. You're tough but with a sensitive edge. Me, I'm wild and beautiful: paediatrician and obstetrician. We couldn't have done it better, Ro. We're geniuses."

And then she almost choked on her champagne.

"Jesus! Hide me, Ronan!" She shrank down underneath his arm, pressing herself into his chest, closing her eyes tightly shut.

"What the heck? Here, put your drink down at least!" He took it out of her fingers. "Which ghost have you just seen?"

"The bloody barrister! Connell Jones Cumberton! He's over there, by the bar, on a stool. That big kind-of-handsome-in-an-ugly-way guy with a big curly head of hair on him and a really posh grey suit! *Don't!*" she pulled Ronan's arm over her face again. "Don't let him see me here!"

"Why on earth not? He isn't suing you. He's defending you, Kate!" Ronan peered under his arm. "You look a little bit like a frightened animal under there. And, I'm sorry to have to say it, but you look a little bit crazy too. Are you all right?" He looked bemused and mildly troubled.

She looked up at him. "Um. Yes. I don't know why I'm hiding, really." She sat up properly again. "Of course he's defending me. I feel so stupid now. Only Nick told me that he's possessed by the devil – and it sort of put me off a bit. Don't know why really, because I actually quite liked him when I had lunch with him." She returned to her drink sheepishly, watching Connell with caution out of the corner of her eye.

"You shouldn't pay any attention to Nick," said Ronan. "He's too bitchy for words sometimes. That guy looks like any other barrister in here on a Friday night." He studied Connell carefully. "I mean, he doesn't look *particularly* any more satanic than any of the others. You look funny, though, Kate," he added with a grin, "with your hair sticking out all over the place. You look sort of like you've just come off your long-term neuroleptics and you're in reverse social drift or something."

"I'm making a complete fool of myself, aren't I?" She examined his face.

He maintained an expression of innocence. "I never said that."

"Jesus, Ronan! I've just remembered something that you don't know!" She stared at him open-mouthed. "Sharon!" she hissed, and then ducked her head down underneath his arm again.

"What about her?" Ronan whispered into his armpit.

"She's his husband."

"Kate – what the hell are you talking about now?"

She popped her head up again. "I mean *he's Sharon's* husband. Connell. He's married to Sharon Guinness. Sharon who's bonking the Professor? I thought that you might like to know." She checked his face for a reaction.

Sometimes, she thought, when you looked at Ronan and he was being thoughtful or excited about something, he was almost attractive, in an unintentional kind of way.

She watched him digest this information with polite but feigned surprise. Perhaps he wasn't chasing after Sharon Guinness after all, she thought. Perhaps he'd found another midwife who might be more available.

She opened up her mouth to ask, and then shut it again, not wanting to pry. There was nothing worse when you are chronically single than being quizzed constantly about your love-life, Caro had once told her. Especially by smug marrieds, she remembered, thinking then that it would be nice to actually meet Luis and to confirm that Caro's Bridget Jones days were over too – as if Caro could ever have been compared to Bridget Jones, she then reminded herself. Then the absurdity of her and Dave being thought of as smug marrieds came back to her in a horribly unwelcome memory of Dave injecting morphine into Caroline on the bathroom floor that night. She shivered again. At least by tomorrow night she'd be away from having to worry about all of that.

"Are you cold?" Ronan offered her his denim jacket. She shook her head.

"What are you thinking, Kate? You just keep staring at me. Have I got something on my teeth?" Ronan looked anxious, and then took his glasses off and tried to inspect his reflection in them. "What?" he asked her.

"You look nicer with your glasses on. You should wear them more often," she told him.

"I look blind," he grumbled. "But I can't wear my contacts after a night on call – they sting the shit out of my eyes."

She smiled at him. "I was just thinking about how thin my sister has become. She's a model, you know."

"All that size zero stuff?" he asked her.

She nodded. "Size triple zero now. And then we discovered that it's because she's using cocaine. She went into withdrawal when she was with us over Christmas. And then I thought about how difficult my husband has become. He's so distant, Ronan, so *incomplete*. And then I thought about how absolutely bizarre my life is at the moment because I think I'm still in love with someone who used to be Dave's best friend whom Dave won't talk to any more and I don't know why. And he's someone I can't have, and I never could have, and I'm going to be with him but I don't know why or what will ever become of it."

Ronan stared at her, and put his glasses on again. He said nothing.

"And that it's all too complicated with work to even begin to explain or sort it all out. But other than that, I wasn't thinking about anything special at all. I guess that it's all just the usual thirty-something stuff, isn't it really?" She downed the rest of her drink in one go.

Ronan smiled at her. "Shall we get a bottle then?"

Dave was very, very heavily asleep. She tip-toed around him making breakfast, then realised that it was going to be impossible without making some sort of noise, and that if Dave had decided to fall asleep on the kitchen sofa, he must have had it somewhere in mind that she might wake him up in the morning. The kitchen was bright and full of sunshine. But he did seem quite unrousable as she clattered a cup and saucer together, popped some toast and waited for the Moka pot to boil.

She stood calmly watching the little coffee pot gurgle and ooze out thick black espresso almost like blood oozing from a wound, while she boiled a small amount of milk in a little pan. She poured herself a large milky mug of coffee, watching Dave out of the corner of one eye for any signs of life. Dave was absolutely dead to the world.

She was suddenly tempted to pack and go without waking him. She could leave him a note, say she was going to Venice.

But no – she couldn't do that.

She took her coffee mug and toast over to the table and left it there sat on the edge of the sofa beside his long lean body and touched his hair, and then his eyes. He shuddered and then squinted up at her, and she got up again and returned quickly to the table, picking up a piece of toast.

"D'you want some breakfast?" she said with her mouth full, her back turned to him. "Some coffee, or will you fix it for yourself?"

"What time is it?" Dave's voice was thick with sleep.

"Eleven o'clock in the morning."

"*What?*" he sat up suddenly, and then groaned and rolled back down again.

"It's Saturday," she replied. "Where were *you* last night?"

"I was here. Where were *you*?"

She took a swig of her coffee. "Out."

He squinted at her out of one eye. "That's helpful. Out where?"

"In town," she replied in a clipped voice.

He sighed. "Do you have to be so sarcastic all the time, Kate?"

She stood up and picked her mug and plate of toast up off the table.

"Bye, Dave." She walked past the sofa and made her way towards the door. "I'm going to eat this in the bedroom." She turned around in the doorway of the kitchen and looked at him again. "If you're going out for the paper or anything there's a shopping list on the sideboard," she said. "I haven't got the time to go."

"Kate, why are you walking out on me like this?" He stared at her. "I've only just woken up."

"Me? Dave, I'm just walking out in the middle of a conversation because I don't want to get into an argument." She sipped her scalding coffee in the doorway, balancing her toast on one hand. The hot coffee felt almost like a defence weapon. He wouldn't dare lose his temper if she had a hot cup of coffee in her hand. "And," she carried on, trying not to let him hear the tremor in her voice, "I'm going away for a fortnight, today actually. And my flight's leaving at three. So, I guess I'd better get a move on now, if you don't mind. I've got a few things to do before I leave." She turned to go.

"You're going away *where* for a fortnight?" He had

stood up and was fixing the belt of his jeans. His hair was all over the place, dense sand-coloured tufts of it sticking out greasily at all angles and his feet were bare.

She turned again and stood very still now in the doorway waiting for him to finish fumbling with his trousers, noticing for the first time how much weight he seemed to have lost all of a sudden around his waist. Dave had always been very fat-less, but now his rugby-framed muscle mass seemed almost to have shrunk and he didn't seem to have the same broad-shouldered body that was so familiar to her. "You've changed, Dave. Everything about you has changed. You aren't eating properly either, are you?"

He shook his head briskly as if to try to wake himself up, like a wet dog does. "Kate, where are you – you're going away on a *holiday*? In January?" he said, bewildered.

"I have to, Dave. I've been put on leave from work. But I'm too unhappy here. I'm too unhappy now with you. I have to get away from Dublin for a while. I'm sorry." She walked out of the room.

It would be easiest to just get away as quickly as possible without too much of a fuss, she thought, heading up the stairs to the bathroom. Dave would be all right. The more she stayed around, trying to explain, the more the guilt would start to show in her face.

Kate was a terrible liar. She'd already let it slip to Ronan that she was going to Paris, and he'd noticed straight away and pulled her up on it. Dave would spot the flaw in her story a mile away if she tried to explain it any more. She'd known him for too long; he could read her mind. She'd just have to get her things out of the house and to the airport as quickly as possible and avoid talking anything else through with him. Holding back from him was only winding him up more, as he was obviously hung over to bits, but it was really going to be much, much easier this way.

On the other hand if he did lose his temper then perhaps a good row between them now would do a lot to deflate *her* guilt, she thought. But she rejected this thought rapidly, thinking about how horribly manipulative that would have been.

Is this what has become of us, she asked, staring at herself in the mirror of the bathroom – each of us, me, Dave, Jonny, each of us hiding secrets from one another, driving each other round the bend?

"Oh, great!" he shouted up at her. "You're going on holidays just like that! Waltzing off into the sunset – and don't bother telling me *where* you're going or anything!"

She heard him cursing to himself downstairs.

She locked the bedroom door while she packed her case.

Ten minutes later she heard the front door slam. She went to the window of their bedroom and watched Dave walk, hunch-shouldered in a short unsuitably light-weight coat in the January-cold morning, up the road towards Baggot Street Bridge. She wondered if he had remembered to take the shopping list – she wanted to take some Tampax away with her, just in case. She suddenly wondered if she should just phone a taxi and sneak away, or just go out and try to find one on the canal. But if he came back from the shops and found her outside on the canal getting into a taxi, they might end up having to have another row out on the street – and then she suddenly saw her Mini Cooper sitting on the street across the road, just sitting there waiting for her, like a welcoming little friend.

She touched the glass of her bedroom window. She felt almost as if she ought to say goodbye to the view she loved from up here, feeling with her fingertips for the scrapes that Mrs Mad Devine had left in the window-pane. Kate sometimes felt disturbed about the fact that Mrs Devine's scratch-marks were still on the window pane: it was like having the marks of a ghost in the house, but now for the first time she found herself wondering what sort of life Mrs Mad Devine had lived in the house up until that day. Perhaps she'd left these scratch marks deliberately. They were like message from the past, from one trapped-in woman to another.

She picked her suitcase up and turned to leave the room. She shut the bedroom door behind her and bumped down the stairs. The front door opened up in front of her abruptly.

Dave stamped his feet with the cold in the hallway, clutching the *Irish Times* under one arm.

"That was quick," she said.

He hadn't brought her stuff, but she wasn't going to bother with it now.

"You're really going on a holiday?" he asked.

He stood there looking grey and terrible, his face looked almost blue with cold.

She took a breath. "I've been asked to take two weeks' leave from work so I'm going to visit Dad and Caroline in Venice, Dave." She spoke in a quiet measured voice. "I decided it in the last few days and you haven't been around to talk to properly. So I hope that you don't mind, but perhaps you'll be happier on your own for a couple of weeks."

To her astonishment, he smiled.

"Of course that's all right," he said. "I'm all right, I really am. You don't have to worry about me. And that's a great idea, for you to have a little holiday now. I'm sorry I've been such a pig. I've been very hard to live with lately."

"Yes, you have," she said.

"Well, don't spare me any painful truths!" He laughed hollowly.

She smiled. "Don't worry. I won't." Her smile froze solid on her face.

"Life's so hard these days, isn't it? For both of us?" he asked her in a tender voice.

"But why is it? Dave?" she asked him in sudden despair. "Why does it have to be so hard? We've got everything we need. Why *can't* we be happy any more?"

"Nobody is happy any more, Kate," he told her with a gruff laugh. "Happiness is a myth. It's just about keeping your head above the water really. Have you got your passport?" He examined her small suitcase. "Does that case have a lock on it? Have you got enough money?" Even in the middle of all this, Dave looked after her, she thought, frustrated by the sudden tenderness she felt for him.

"*Have you packed this suitcase yourself?*" She looked at him. "Dave, I want you to be happy. But you're killing me."

"I don't mean it." He hung his head. "I don't know what I want any more, Kate. I'm so fucked-up."

She felt him tower over her. His height had once aroused her, she had felt protected by the breadth of his shoulders, excited by the way that he could pick her up and carry her, wrap her up almost in the whole of his body. Now, she left the suitcase on the floor in between them like a barrier.

"All I want, Dave, is a bit of peace. I want have a bit of fun for a change."

"I know," he nodded. "Everybody needs fun."

She indicated the front door. "I need to go, Dave. I'm going to drive myself to the airport. You look like you need to go back to bed."

He pushed his hand through his thatch of hair and stood aside to let her wheel her suitcase out the front door into the street.

"Oh," she turned to him, "I almost forgot." She opened her bag and rummaged in it for a moment before producing a businesss card.

"This is supposed to be a good lawer." She handed it to him.

"What?" he frowned at it. "Connell Jones Cumberton, Barrister-at-Law?"

"About the crash? The taxi you rear-ended? He's the lawyer for the hospital." She shrugged her shoulders. It was time to go.

"Safe trip!" he waved at her, and she turned to see him smiling. At least he had shoved the business card into the pocket of his jacket and was holding the front door open to watch her drive away. She felt, almost, that he seemed to be in some small way all of a sudden rather *happy*. Happier than she'd seen him look for months. She slammed the boot of her Mini shut and got into the car.

She started up the ignition, revving the engine to the immediate burst of "Mercy" from Duffy's angry voice. Inside her chest her heart felt lighter. We are splitting up. I can't believe it, she thought, driving past Dave waving, over Huband Bridge and down Mount Street into town. Our perfect marriage is actually splitting up, and both of us are finally feeling something that almost feels like happiness.

Dave sat down at his computer and flipped up the Aer Lingus website.

"Nick," he said breathlessly into Nick Farrelly's voicemail as he surfed, "Guess who's going to join you in Paris, babes?"

14

The flight to Paris was horrendous. Jonny's prediction of beautiful sunny crisp Parisian weather had turned into foul, wet, wintry turbulance that blew Kate's Air France carrier up and down in a series of sharp hiccoughs that made her gag, and she had to spend most of the journey with the sick-bag open to the palpable disgust of the smooth-suited businessman next to her. It took her over half an hour to find her suitcase because it had got mixed up with that of a very impatient German woman, and then she got quite lost in the concrete cave that was Charles de Gaulle airport – but she didn't care. She was going to be with him. She tugged her tiny case behind her, exhilarated by the maze of plastic corridors that criss-crossed Charles de Gaulle like a bizarre puzzle-tree.

And there he was, leaning up against a concrete pillar in the grey gloom of the arrivals hall, dressed in black jeans with a high-necked sweater under his leather jacket, looking unbearably handsome.

He leaped towards her, long limbs moving in excited strides, and he kissed her three times back and over on each cheek, a manoeuvre that was beginning to feel cumbersome and unnecessary until then he landed in the middle, where he lingered on her open mouth for just a heart-stopping second. She put her arms around his waist and hugged him, pressing her burning face into his chest. He rubbed her hair.

"It's wonderful to see you," he said and she heard his chest resonate. "How was the flight?"

"Ghastly!" she croaked. "Mega-sick." She looked up at him.

"You don't look too good," he replied.

"Do I smell of sick?" She covered her mouth with her hand.

He laughed, and said, "No, of course not, you just look a bit pale that's all," and reached his hand out for her bag which she let him wheel out of the airport.

"Did you drive?" she asked him.

"No. Never in Paris," he replied. "I don't keep a car here at all." He flung open the door of a taxi for her, swung her case into the boot and spoke in rapid French.

The driver looked disheartened and made a tutting and a hissing noise, and then a series of negative gestures before getting back into the driving seat. Kate and Jonny slid into the back.

"What's wrong?" she whispered.

"Nothing," he whispered back. "Why are we whispering?" he whispered again.

"I just thought," she spoke in a low voice, "that he seemed to be a bit cross with us." She indicated the taxi-driver. "As if you'd said something that had pissed him off?"

Jonny grinned at her. "A bit unmotivated, you thought?"

"Yes."

"Welcome to Paris." He kissed her on the mouth again.

She sat back in complete joy.

It was dark by the time they got to his apartment on the Left Bank.

There was a tiny street, ill-lit with tall elegant buildings on each side, long windows with pale shutters. There were little balconies, big double doorways and a little blue tile above each one with the building number on it. The street was very quiet but they could hear the roar of Boulevard Saint-Germain just a block away. She examined the list of apartments in the building while Jonny opened the long double outside door with a giant key – ten apartments altogether in this building. Number 10 was labelled *Le Normand*. A little round white marble button like a nipple on a copper plate.

They walked up the five flights of stairs, Jonny grumbling mildly that such a tiny suitcase must have been filled with stones for it to weigh so much, and she said very little, noticing only the cool dampness of the place, the tiles on walls, the echo of their steps on the old stone stairs, the small tables on landings with a plant, a newspaper and some mail, a child's tricycle outside one doorway, some boots beside another. A series of small mats placed neatly in front of each apartment, each mat different – masculine ones and feminine ones in front of different doors, Kate thought. And then they were breathlessly at the top, and he opened up another double, long heavy door with brass fittings and a definitely feminine-shaped mat on the floor in front of it and she stepped inside the Paris apartment with a little label on the wall outside that read, quite clearly, *Marianne Le Normand*.

He snapped on a light and she stood very still, taking in the warm smell of the place, the beautiful green and red and blue-checked tile floor, the umbrella stand, the painting in the hall of a roundly naked woman, the doors that led into a kitchen, and then further down to a salon. The other side of the corridor led to what must be the bathroom – she could just about see the bidet.

"Come on in," he told her, and she followed him into the salon, which turned out to be smaller than she had expected, but more beautiful. Sparsely furnished and book-lined, the baby grand piano took up most of the room. There was an empty fireplace, with another large painting over it (this time a giant abstract in blues and greens), and the only other significant piece of furniture was the rather spindly-looking and uncomfortably small sofa, underneath the long French windows. At the far end of the room was a highly polished table with a bowl of fruit on it.

"It's lovely, Jonny," she told him in a quiet voice, and he nodded, offering to take her coat.

"This is sort of the music room, I suppose – which is why there's nowhere to sit down. She'll keep this house, of course, after the divorce. I'm not here a lot actually anyway. We try not to be in the same house at the same time." He smiled cautiously at her. "But when I do have to be in Paris I tend to spend all my time in this room messing about on the piano. Let me show you the kitchen and we can have some wine or something."

She followed him out of the room again and into a small but very neatly arranged kitchen, with a tiny round table and two chairs placed café-style in front of long French windows that led onto a tiny balcony.

"Oh, this is so cosy!" she exclaimed, instantly comparing the masculine black granite kitchen that Dave had chosen for Percy Place with Jonny's dainty French one. A simple cooker. An under-counter fridge. Just two shelves that looked as though the wood had been smoothed and scrubbed-over for centuries. A basket of eggs by the window. A baguette, leaning sideways against a bowl of lemons. There was just enough about the little sink with its mini-dishwasher underneath and the one worktop to make sense; and the simplicity and at the same time lack of austerity about it stirred her.

"Let's have something nice to eat." Jonny started pulling pâté and jam and apples and a giant cheese out of the fridge and off shelves, plonking things on the table as if he were trying to throw a desperate and impromptu party.

"I should have bought some wine," she said feeling hopelessly shy all of a sudden, "only with Eric's vineyard and all that –"

She sat down at the window, suddenly noticing the view they had of a little courtyard down below. The flat was at the corner of the building and overlooked a roundabout of the meetings of four quiet side streets and a church.

"Oh, how gorgeous all this is!" she exclaimed.

"Isn't it? You can see why Marianne prefers this to Geneva. Or Dublin, for that matter. She lives here all the time now, of course."

"Of course." *Of course.* Kate looked about her, at the beautifully smooth wood of the table, the little blue-and-white kitchen implements. *This is another woman's house. But what about us now, Jonny?* She had to ask him. *What happens to all this now? What about Veronique? Are you really going to leave all of this?* But she said nothing.

He pulled the cork out of the wine with a loud pop that made her jump and they both laughed. He poured.

"Here." He handed her a glass and she took a grateful gulp. "To us, and the great weekend we're going to have! She'll be staying at the American hospital till Monday," he added.

She nodded back at him. It was as if he'd noticed the way she was feeling. Must have read her mind. She felt like a wicked and punishable mistress. Yet she had never wanted anything more than she now wanted this.

"And she'll be in hospital for another few days, so I've been told," he was saying. "Well, of course, you would know about all of that."

She didn't remind him that Prof had taken her off the case. She just nodded silently at him again.

"So," he waved a hand over the food he'd spread out for her, "eat something, Kate. You must be starving."

"I'm all right," she said, holding out her glass for more wine.

"Brie?" he said, slicing a glossy wodge of it. "Fruit? Some bread?"

She let him assemble a plate of things for her, enjoying the attention. After the first bottle of Eric Le Normand's finest she felt much better. She was starving, actually, having eaten nothing all day since the choppy flight, and the Burgundy *was* delicious. She munched happily while Jonny broke eggs to make an omelette that he cooked swiftly and then neatly split in two with a spatula and emptied onto two blue and white china plates.

He broke a piece off his omelette with a fork, and fed her with it. "Good?"

"Perfect."

He touched her cheek. "Let's have some sounds," he said.

She listened to him rummage in the other room for a CD while she took in the totality of the little kitchen. It struck her that for such a powerful woman, Marianne had such simple and uncluttered taste. The kitchen cupboards looked handmade, as if they might be a project from a woodwork class. There were stains on the wooden worktop but they didn't look unclean – rather the whole kitchen seemed to have a kind of lived-in, warm experience to narrate.

"How much time does she spend here?" she asked him when he came back in. He clicked his fingers at her. Oscar Peterson was playing "Ain't Misbehavin'" from the other room.

"She – oh, quite a lot really. Her parents live across town in the seventeenth, which is why she's going to the American Hospital. But Eric owned this flat before. It's been in the family, as they say."

"A bit like Percy Place?"

"Only longer. Grandparents and that sort of thing. More wine?"

He opened up another bottle. She felt blissfully relaxed at last, full of wonderful food, and the piano music from the other room was just enough to make her feel as though things could become something like they were always meant to be.

"Dance with me," he said, and she stood up to face him.

He took her hand and held her face to his chest while they danced together in the tiny kitchen, gently swaying to the rather hectic and unsuitable music. Kate giggled and he held her face back from him.

"The music's silly, isn't it?" he said.

"Why don't you play something then? Play for me,"

she said. He shrugged and took her by the hand and led her back to the salon.

"Turn that off." He indicated the CD.

She sat beside him at the piano. She closed her eyes while he began to play "The Way You Look Tonight", and then opened them again to watch him as he moved it into a series of sorrowful bluesey scales and riffs. He played a few more bars while she watched his hands and then he surprised her by turning to her suddenly. He grabbed her head with both his hands and pulled it towards his own and kissed her briskly on the lips. He pulled away and looked at her again, as if he was almost embarrassed by his own action. It was as if, she thought, he wanted to get it over with as quickly as possible.

He wasn't smiling at her any more. His face looked almost frightened. And then he reached out to her again and pulled her into him by her waist and so she let him lift her up into his lap where she could straddle him and where he kissed her more greedily now and she could hold herself into him with her legs wrapped around him, her buttocks spread across his thighs. He groaned and she let his face seek out her neck. Then he stood up, lifting her easily, and he walked towards the bedroom carrying her at his waist to which she clung tightly with her legs, nestling into his throat.

She lay very still on the bed for him while he undressed her, allowing her jeans to be removed from the bottoms of the legs, her shirt unbuttoned carefully. She watched his face while he cautiously removed her bra, listening to his breath thicken while he touched each part of her nakedness as it appeared. Her breasts. Her concave belly-button. When he drew white cotton underpants down along her thighs he sank his head in between them so that he could kiss her there.

She watched his face the whole time he was inside of her, never taking her eyes off his, only closing them when she could no longer keep them open. She screamed out loud when she came – it had been, oh, such a long time since she had felt this, she had almost forgotten – and he whispered, "Shhhh!" into her neck and kissed her face over and over. She felt tears beginning, and he laughed gently and told her not to be so silly, and slid out of her and made her come right in his mouth again. And then later on that night, he took her from behind.

She slept in a heap of him, breathing in as deeply as she could, deep inside the dark musk smell.

Kate had slept as though she never wanted to wake up, but the room was full of all the coffee scents of breakfast. The rather small double bed was suddenly quite empty too. She peered around the room, listening to Jonny rattling things in the kitchen to the background of Chet Baker singing "Let's Get Lost". This feels like a scene in a French film, she giggled to herself, sniffing at the heavy linen sheets for his scent. She hugged herself nakedly under the covers, feeling for the first time in *years* like someone who was loved.

The wallpaper in the room was rather interesting

though, she thought, examining the peculiar red and gold pattern of what looked to her like a silk fabric. Posh, she thought, and then glanced around at the other furnishings. A very large mahogany *armoire* with lovely curly mouldings on the doors which didn't seem to close properly as the wood had just warped too much with age. That would drive Dave crazy, she thought, the idea of buying an antique that wasn't properly restored, and then it struck her that most likely this particular piece of furniture hadn't actually been bought. Marianne's family had owned this apartment for generations.

She slid out of the bed and pulled her sweater off the floor and popped it on, then padded over to the big *armoire* to see why the two doors didn't actually close and took an irresistible peek inside. Jonny's breakfast-making sounds were comfortably preoccupied in the background and she opened the closet carefully, taking in the immediate smell of vague perfume – dry-cleaning fluid perhaps? And the row of plastic-wrapped outfits. Trouser suits by Max Mara. A single row of shoes – Yves Saint Laurant heels and Chanel pumps. A pair of very scratched but spotlessly clean ski boots. A Roland Mouret dress. Several light cashmere dresses in various beige colours with pleated skirts and A-line shapes. She took one out and held it up against her. It was a beautiful toffee-coloured light Italian wool, lined with silk and with a buckled leather belt. *Bon chic, bon genre*, she remembered Jonny say. This looked like the kind of outfit the Queen might wear to walk the corgis, Kate thought in amazement, looking at her crumpled jeans on the floor beside her bra and pants and knee-high flat-heeled boots.

She looked around the room and found a mirror in a corner, a long oval swivel one on four legs, and she inspected her reflection standing there naked, behind the shadow of a Prada dress of Marianne's.

You look like a little girl playing with her mother's wardrobe, she told herself.

"Kate, this is appalling."

He threw a newspaper on the bed.

She jumped a mile. "Jeez, you scared me! I was just – um. She's got some lovely clothes, hasn't she?"

"It's a disaster." He sat down on the bed. His face looked haggard with despair. "Look," he said, slapping the front page of *Le Monde*. "Yesterday's edition – I didn't see it until now. The election results in Kenya."

She stared at the newspaper. "My French isn't that good, Jonny."

"Well." He began to translate. "*Scores of people have been killed across Kenya in violence which they – blame on the disputed result of the presidential election. . .*"

She stood there silently.

" *. . . forty-three bodies with gunshot wounds in a mortuary in Kisumu . . .* that's where we were, Kate." He looked up to her with pained eyes. "That's near the place Dave and I stayed that year. You know."

"Oh," she said. "How awful."

"Er – '*there have been battles in Nairobi slums*' . . ." he continued. "*Police shot protesters* – er – then it says President

Mwai Kibaki has been declared the winner but Raila Odinga says he stole the victory from him by fraud – er – *Kenyan television reports one hundred and twenty-four people dead already* – violence, er, *violent battles in the seaside town of Mombasa . . . forty people killed in Nairobi . . . paramilitaries deployed by the government . . . people killing one another with machetes . . .*" He shook his head.

"Awful," she said again. She sat down on the bed beside him. "I'm – um – do you know anybody still there?"

He turned to her. "I'm going to go over."

"You? To Kenya? When?"

"There is a humanitarian crisis and the UNHCR will get involved with moving people. So I've got to go."

"But you're an epidemiologist. There isn't an epidemic yet. Is there?"

He took her hand. "It isn't just about that. This is the place where Dave and I lived, Kate. For months – we spent almost a year there, you remember. This place is in trouble now. The people there are very poor. The NGOs will need a lot of extra help."

"So. You are going to go out to Kenya to help them?"

He frowned. "Something like that. Sudden civil disruption leads to refugee crises. Which leads to disease. I'm going to get on to the UN later on today and see what they're planning. Don't worry. I'm not going anywhere without you." He kissed her mouth. "Come and have some breakfast." He stood up. "Then we can talk properly and decide what we can do."

From the salon she could hear Chet Baker's jolly

trumpet-playing. She rubbed her eyes and then her nose. The coffee smell and the suddenly sun-filled apartment. The idea of violence and machetes could not have felt further away.

She sat quietly at the little table where they'd dined last night, buttering a tartine, listening to Jonny while he described outbreaks and vaccination programmes and mass-evacuation plans. She sipped strong milky coffee from a beautiful blue and white china bowl and dunked her jammy bread in it, while he scrutinised a map of the Western Province of Kenya.

"You don't mind if I go into the office straight away?" he asked her, almost not waiting for her reply, while he scrolled his Blackberry.

But it's Sunday, she thought. And I'm here.

It was as if she'd ceased to exist for him, paled instantly into the background.

She shook her head meaninglessly. You don't mind if I don't exactly see what on earth I'm doing here, in your ex-wife's flat in Paris?

"Wouldn't you have to talk to Marianne before you go?" she eventually asked him in a careful voice, and he nodded.

"Yes." He looked up at the clock. "I'd better go as I have to go across town. The baby arrives back today too."

"Oh, yes. Of course." She couldn't disguise the flatness in her voice.

She sat and drank her coffee and watched him frowning at his emails.

He looked up at her suddenly.

"I want you to come with me, Kate," he said, and then he added, "Please."

She stared in surprise and then said, "I'm not sure that Marianne would understand exactly why I'm here."

"What? No. I mean to Africa. I want you to come on this mission with me."

"*What?* Are you crazy?"

"No," he said. "I really want you to be there with me. Please just come. We'll be well looked after. We'll be going over with the UN. But I really think that you should come with me. You would enjoy it, actually. It's so different –"

"Jonny," she interrupted him. She reached out and laid a hand on his arm. "Jon, I can't do that."

"Why not? Who's stopping you?"

"I – it's not a question of that. But are you sure you have to drop everything and go to Africa? I mean, what about the baby? Don't you – can't somebody else go instead, I mean?"

"Kate, this isn't just a *job*! I *need* to go there now. Don't you see? This isn't just another country with a war. This is where we *lived*. Think about *us*, Kate. We could go there. We could be together. Isn't that what you want too? Don't you want to be with me?"

"But Africa isn't our *home*, Jonny."

"Well, it was once mine. Once it was." He looked down at her hand gripping his sleeve.

She removed it again.

"I can't let you go again," he said.

She felt her cheeks begin to burn. "I do want us to be together. You know how much I do want that."

"But!" he said to the room, as if she weren't there.

"But everything! We haven't thought this through. And going off to Kenya now, in crisis – it just seems crazy! You've got to sort out things with Marianne. You've got Veronique. Why can't we just sit down and *organise* something? Something *possible*? Something that takes time?"

"Now you're being crass," he said and stood up abruptly, scraping his chair almost violently across the floor.

She started. "Jonny, I love you. Don't get cross with me."

"I'm not. I'm –" He smiled at last. "I'm sorry. Look." He took her hands and pulled her up towards him. "I guess I'm just upset about Kenya. And I'm going to have to go over there. I just can't do anything else right now. And now I'm going to have to go into the UN offices to do some things. A lot of things. Today. And I don't want you to get bored. Don't you have things you want to do in Paris?"

She stared at him. "You mean touristy things?"

"Well, I'm the one who dragged you over here, and now this has all blown up and so I'm going to have to get myself organised and see what the International Committee for Africa will want. And there's the baby. I mean, all of *that* will be a lot easier now that Marianne's home and near her parents. But this all would be so much easier for *us*, if you'd say you'll come to Africa with me." He was looking at her tenderly now. "We can just go and be somewhere. Just real life. Just you and me. And no one else. Your skills would be so important to people out there. So tell me please – why not?"

She took a breath. "Because," she said, "I just don't know."

"*What* don't you know?"

She looked down at her hands. It was so obvious and yet too difficult to say. *Because I don't know if you'll always love me.* The plain and honest truth was quite impossible to say, because there was no possible true answer to it. *Because I thought that Dave would always love me too and I was so, so wrong.* If she had spoken it out loud he would only have said, "Of course I will, I will always love you." And then what would she say? "Oh no, you won't?" "Oh yes, I will." As if they were both suddenly in some sort of pantomime farce?

"It's not about knowing. It's about much more than us," she said.

"Who – Dave?"

She shook her head. "I think he'd be all right. But then again," she looked at him, "I just don't know. He doesn't even know I'm here. I've always –"

"There is no such thing as always. People change."

She looked away.

"You don't trust me any more," he said.

She took his arm. "I need more time to think. I need to talk to people. To my dad."

Jonny rolled his eyes. "Father-fixated! Just like Marianne! Not everything has to be approved by Papa, you know!"

She blushed furiously. "Well, I need to talk to Caroline as well. And I need to talk to Dave. This is a big decision you want me to make. You need to talk to your family too. You know you do." She looked at him.

He took her hand and kissed it. "All right then. I know you're right. We'll be all right, I promise you. I'll talk to Marianne. I'll sort things out. Everything will work out properly – you'll see. Just remember that I love you and that there's a world out there where we can be together, in our work, making a real difference. You know?"

She nodded. "Yes. Yes. I do know. And I'll think about it all. Today." Then she added with a faint smile, "While I'm doing all those touristy things."

She watched him pull on his jacket. "When will I see you, then?" she asked.

"Later on today," he said. "I'll be in touch. You've got your phone. I'm going to have to go."

He gulped down his coffee and zipped the leather jacket. "This means an awful lot to me, Kate," he said.

"Jonny. I do want to be with you, you know I do."

"Then come to Africa," he said.

And he was gone.

15

Jonny walked very quickly down the street towards the Boulevard Saint-Michel with his two hands shoved deep into the pockets of his coat, frowning as he went. The same anxiety rising in his throat that he had first begun to feel those eleven, twelve years ago when it first began. The Nightmare, he sometimes called it, only to himself. Everybody talked about *Le Mal D'Afrique*. But nobody else spoke of the African Nightmare. People worked for Africa, studied Africa, made speeches about Africa, but nobody really talked about the overwhelming powerlessness and the guilt, and the sometimes sheer fury and injustice of it all. He could quite easily, nowadays, translate all of that emotion into *drive*. Into an irrepressible work-ethic, into the dogged appreciation for detail that had won him a PhD in Public Health and Epidemiology from the London School of Hygiene, and had led him to produce paper after paper on the medical effects of war, from Bosnia to Iraq to Chechnya and now to Kisumu.

Kisumu.

Until now, one of the most peaceful places that he'd ever been. And now. Another Mugabe? Who knows?

It wasn't fair to expect Kate to really understand what it all felt like to him. Africa is unpredictable, he thought, skipping precariously across the boulevard and just avoiding the front bumper of a screaming taxi-cab. In many ways it's still just like a dream, still like a dream to me. *Le Mal D'Afrique*. It never lets you go.

The Paris traffic charged doggedly all around him, bald trees along the boulevarde like ghosts, grey raincoats and umbrellas everywhere. He ducked into the Métro station at Sorbonne and descended it two steps at a time. Everyone knew that Africa was another world.

Inside the cavern of the underground he bought a ticket and another newspaper. He walked more slowly to his line and stood there staring at the same story on the front page while he waited for the train.

But no matter what happened to him now, he was going to be with Kate. Kate would always love him, no matter who he was. And he'd always been in love with her. Right from the moment he'd first seen her that snowy New Year's Eve when Dave Hardiman had brought him to Percy Place for the first time and she'd sat at the piano with him and he'd let her watch him play. Jonny didn't usually play the piano for other people – he hated being asked to perform. But for some reason he had always wanted to play something for Kate when she had asked. It was her child-like quality that he loved the most. Her easy innocence. "Why don't you play something?" she had asked. "Play for me." Kate had loved him as he was – unlike Marianne, who had loved him as she had intended to find him. And now he was going to be with Kate again.

She was the only person in the world he wanted to be with. She was uncomplicated and she was true. If there was one person that he knew would always love him no matter what he'd done, no matter how weak or stupid he had become, it would be Kate. And now with the way Marianne felt and this disaster in Kenya, he had never needed Kate more.

As the train clattered underneath the city of Paris, Jonny Domville closed his eyes. The train rattled like a machine gun out to the suburbs of the seventeenth district, and he mentally totted up the number of African countries that could be expected to be at war at any one time. Altogether, at this moment, he thought, until this election, there were at least ten. But not Kenya.

"The jewel of African democracy," its UN ambassador had once said to him, and at the time he had nodded his head politely in agreement. "Africa is cursed," the jolly Egyptian delegate had told him at the same meeting. And at that time he had laughed.

Jonny Domville, if he were not a scientist of international repute and a man who believed very deeply in logic and good sense, might well have started to believe that in many ways it might be *him* who was cursed.

Sometimes when he closed his eyes like this, all that he could see was Africa. But now there would be two of them, him and Kate, just them alone together and in Africa. It would be like a dream.

But dreams are unpredictable – the train lurched suddenly and he opened his eyes again, finding the face of a black man sitting solemnly opposite, his eyes yellow in the tunnel light.

The truth was, of course, that it was naïve to think that nothing could have ever gone wrong with Kenya. Almost as naïve as to think that nothing could go wrong with life, with marriage, with a love affair. The most painful thing of all when things go wrong is the unwelcome realisation of your true self.

It often came back to him in a dream.

The moon at night so bright that you could see colour.

Transport like a pick-up truck with a box on it. Chickens running in the street.

Kisumu.

And the flame trees. Flame trees, flame trees everywhere.

That was Africa.

And then.

A red earth, a river of terracotta mud. Rain every day at five o' clock. Ironed socks. Underwear. Fried peanuts.

Rozala. He woke up sometimes in the night-time, sick with memories.

The year was 1999 and they were twenty-two years old.

They were stationed at Rafiki hospital in Bungoma, Western Province. You had to fly into Nairobi, and then take a smaller charter to Kisumu. And then you travelled for four hours on a rattly bus, down into the plain and then up again into the mountains where the road climbed deep into the Kakamega rainforest. Rafiki hospital and the village was a thousand feet above sea level.

It was the altitude that caused that lovely, balmy weather all summer long, 100 km north of the equator. Hot bright sunshine, but the mountain air was clean and clear. Cooling down at night. And then every day at five o'clock, a sudden downpour of fresh mountain rain. You could time your watch by it. The first thing would be that the wind would pick up – it was like a tube train, Jonny thought. The way you'd be standing tight-throated in a hot windless tunnel and then suddenly, that whoosh of fresher air, that vivid gush of anticipation. And then the sky would open up like a magnificent blessing – a forgiveness. Lukewarm water pouring out as if a bucket had been emptied out onto the lushness, all the greenness, the vegatation that sprang up almost visibly along the roads, in gardens, behind flat-roofed buildings. The roads were red, a deep earth blood-like red, but in the sudden deluge they would turn into a paste of thickened mud until the hour of rain was up.

And that was it – one hour every evening, at exactly the same time. The perfect climate. Mud dried easily in the sudden comfortable heat of evening sun. Drenched roofs baked rapidly again.

"A bit different to Ireland," Jonny would smile, squinting his eyes up at the suddenly blue-again sky, blissful in the warmth of it. "Rain every day in the summer time, only much more predictable. Reliable wet weather."

They would work all day until the rain came down at five o'clock, and then after the rain had stopped they knew that it was time to go, and so they'd walk the half-hour home again to the little house among the flame trees.

The house had belonged to a Dutchwoman who had founded the charity hospital, but she had died and left behind a little dog called Simba.

"His name means Lion in Swahili," Pete the American student told them and they stared at the geriatric yellow dog, wondering where his once-feline majesty had disappeared to.

"He's fairly humble for a lion, isn't he?" Dave knelt down to ruffle Simba's throat. Simba whined appreciatively, and stretched out to have his tummy rubbed.

The American chuckled. "We used to think he was a racist dog. For a long time he only liked Kenyan people – he used to bark at all the white folks. He's mellowed down a lot now, since his mistress died."

They were the only three white people in the village.

"I can't believe you've got a flush toilet! And electricity!" The American inspected the Dutchwoman's little house, marvelling at the small neat tiled bathroom, the twin bedrooms, the book-lined living-room, the spotless scullery with taps and running water and a sink.

He shook his head and laughed at his own envy. "You'd wanna see the place they've put me in, the teacher's accommodation for the school. It's a barnyard compared to this place!"

Their house was perfect, they had to admit.

It was simply beautiful, a tiny cottage completely overgrown by vegetation. Rose bushes and honeysuckles and climbing vines twined and twirled around the doorway, smothering it with flowers and the warm damp scent of honey hummed with insects. The door opened in between two windows that were buried in the flowers. It was like waking into a rose bush. And in the background, like wild dancers completing a wonderful stage-set, were flame trees. Everywhere you looked. Their bright orange dazzling extravagance was everywhere.

Pete dropped by sometimes in the evening, bringing forbidden beers from the village, or sometimes the almost undrinkable local home-brew Chang'aa which they cooled in their tiny refrigerator ("You have a refrigerator! Why didn't I go to med school?" Pete moaned) and the three of them would spend the evening by the fire, burning logs that had been piled up outside the back door for them by Joshua who crept away, discreetly taking the twenty shillings that they left daily for him in a jam jar, tucking them carefully into his small leather side-pouch.

"Do you realise that twenty shillings is about thirty cents?" Pete laughed at them. He was an economics student with the Peace Corps.

"It seems a pathetic amount," Jonny nodded miserably.

"I *mean*, he doesn't expect half that amount, just for a leaving you a few logs from the forest! You guys!" He handed them another beer.

The money meant nothing to Jonny. There was very little to spend money on here anyway. A few illegal beers (the Christians who ran the hospital forbade drinking). Meat once every week when they could be bothered to go to the market at Kakamega. But their food was fruit, nuts, potatoes, yams – filling, and plenty of it, and their money could buy any amount of it they needed. There was no reason not to be generous with the Kenyans. The Kenyans were shit poor, as Pete explained.

Rozala had turned up almost as soon as they had opened the front door of the house, with a little boy by the hand. She spoke briefly to the boy, first in English so that the guys could understand, and then rapidly in Swahili. She told the little boy to wait aside until she had finished speaking to the gentlemen. The child nodded and immediately stood aside. He was only seven, but he had stood back graciously and with an almost military discipline when instructed by her, a quick nod of his head, his hands rigidly by his sides. Bare-footed in the dust.

Rozala bowed her head and asked in broken English with Swahili mixed, if she could please take up her position as housekeeper for the gentlemen, explaining that she was the given housekeeper who came with the cottage. She had worked there for the Dutch lady for the past seven years. The Dutch lady had told her that the job was hers, to work for everyone who would live there after she had died.

Dave looked down at his feet in their open-toed Doc-Marten sandals, and blushed at the idea that two medical students should be served by an African woman housekeeper. He began to rub his fingers through his sun-blond hair and scratched uncomfortably at his head. Jonny started to explain that the house was really very small and that they didn't really know how a housekeeper would fit in. There wasn't really much to clean, and they were quite happy to cook for themselves.

"No!" Rozala had barked, her eyes quickly ablaze with yellow despair. "I *am* your housekeeper. It *is* my job to keep the house! You will see. You need me. You need a woman to cook and wash and clean and iron clothes. You *see* my son," she pointed at the boy, standing to attention at the corner of the little house. "He needs to go to school. University I want for him. You *need* a housekeeper, *Wazungu*."

Dave nodded silently. There didn't seem to be much choice about it. Jonny scratched his sandal along the dirt. They smiled at her sheepishly, and they shrugged at one another.

Rozala tightened her kanga cloth around her shoulder and straightened her tall back.

"William!" She smiled and stretched her arm out to beckon the boy William towards her. "His father is died," she said in a slow deep voice, hugging the little boy around the shoulders, pressing him into her hip. "He will go to school in September. I will come to the house in the morning. Every morning. This you will be grateful for. I will thank you, sir." She smiled a wide, clean-toothed African smile, and bowed her head again. They watched her slowly walk away, her bottom swaying under the bright red cloth of the kanga.

"Massive!" Jonny was wide-eyed at the idea of house-keeping.

"Spoiled rotten, I guess," Dave said. "How much do you think we need to pay her?"

"Sixty shillings a day," Pete suggested when they asked him.

They decided that they'd give her a hundred and twenty.

Rozala did everything, and more. She cleaned the little house buried underneath the rose-bushes as if it were an operating theatre. She washed their clothes by hand, wringing each item out and hanging it in the bright midday heat to dry and then she ironed each single garment with the precision of a brain surgeon. She ironed their socks and underwear. Each day when they arrived home from the hospital she had left a small neat and crisply ironed fresh pile of clothing on a chair in each bedroom. The flush-toilet bowl they sat on shone with cleanliness. The mahogany dining-table sparkled. She left a bowl of fresh fruit for them daily on the sideboard near the cooker, and every evening draped a red and white striped tea-towel to keep flies away from the giant bowl of freshly fried peanuts. She fried peanuts for them every evening, cracking each nut herself by hand and carefully discarding the shells into a cotton bag which she took home with her for kindling. The fried peanuts were the food of the gods.

There was one doctor at Rafiki hospital, Doctor Sunday. He had trained in Nairobi medical school and spoke words of Luo and Luhya as well as fluent Swahili and English. Jonny and Dave had to simply rely on the nurses (and usually on other patients as well) to translate and take histories, which could take what seemed like hours translating from Luo to Luhya and then Swahili and then English. It was a challenge but it was exhilarating to them.

Doctor Sunday did everything until the medical students arrived and he then was in theatre almost all day long, which left Dave and Jonny to admit and treat the patients on the wards. One medical and one surgical, one paediatric and one maternity room, and that was all. Fifty beds for a population of a hundred thousand people. The simplicity of it both humbled and at the same time deeply bothered Jonny. People brought in their own food with them, families visiting daily with fresh-steamed marugu, plantain fried in oil, peanuts and hot chips from the chip vendors. There were chip vendors everywhere along the roads. The vendors cooked the chips at home and then displayed them outside in glass cases where they could stay warm in the sun. There was Fanta and Coke on sale in shops and roadside stalls wherever you went. Not enough water to drink or to waste, but Fanta and Coca-Cola were everywhere.

The hospital provided medicine and nursing but it did not provide the patients with their food.

At first they thought they understood malaria. A blood-borne parasite causing a diurnal fever, and they had expected to find lots of it in Kenya. Malaria was what they were there for and their task was to treat it. But the extent of the viciousness of the mosquito and the endemicity of the parasite horrified them.

Tiny children died in seizures from their fever. Blood transfusions had to be sought from family members or staff. There were no blood banks, no stores of plasma, no packed red cells in freezers in a lab. The lab was run by two nurses. The radiographer was a nurse. The midwife, Doctor Sister Jessie, was a nun. The blood transfusions were HIV positive; they knew all this, all of them knew it inside of them although they never spoke of it to one another. But what else was there to do? In an emergency of life and death, transfusions must be made. Several of the nurses from the hospital had already died of HIV, Pete had told them once. But the worst problem for the children was malaria.

"*Wazungu* – white people with malaria, they have no immunity so you get it really bad," Doctor Sister Jessie warned them.

"For Kenyans it's like getting flu – they get it every year," Pete explained.

Even so, Jonny Domville often forgot to take his malaria prophylaxis.

The evenings were blissful, playing chess and reading. They read everything – the Dutchwoman had left behind her, as well as a racist yellow dog, a house that was chock-full of books. It was almost like living in a library. Jonny read all of the long row of Charles Dickens one by one, riveted to every word in the evening glow of lamplight while Dave swished about trying to catch mosquitoes.

They didn't have a mosquito net ("Crazy, isn't it? Electricity and running water but no mosquito nets!" Pete would laugh at them) and so they took turns each evening to catch the whining insects that, no matter how firmly they remembered to close the screens, still crept into the little house to feast. They stuffed a towel under the door to stop them coming in. They lit a fire in the chimney every night. Dave swished and swatted with newspapers, tea-towels, whatever he could find to kill the beasts, but they bit him anyway.

Jonny discovered the Dutchwoman's collection of John Irving novels, and read *The Hotel New Hampshire* and *The World According To Garp*. Dave swished and swatted, cursing and laughing at the same time. They listened to the BBC World Service, singing along with the start-up tune for the news bulletins each time they began. They bought a little soapstone chess set from the market in Kakamega, and started up a league of nations: Ireland versus America.

America always seemed to win.

"Best of five," Dave demanded after another chess game with Pete.

"I've won the first three games already, man!" Pete groaned.

"Best of seven?"

"Jonny, why don't you get your lazy ass out of that armchair and rise to the challenge?"

"I'm crap at chess," Jonny shrugged. He was deep into *A Prayer For Owen Meany*, and wasn't going to put it down until he'd finished.

The only times they got to drag Jonny away from a book in the evening was if he'd bring his saxophone out. In the silence of the rain forest, the nasal jazz music rang out like a beautiful howling beast in the blackness of the night.

"Pity it does nothing to scare away the mosquitoes!" Dave slashed around the room again with a rolled-up tea-towel.

"At least it'll frighten all the snakes," Jonny grinned.

The fever came on him very suddenly – it was almost like a thunderbolt. So unexpectedly, it just completely crashed him out one evening. He found himself sweating and nauseated, and he'd got out of bed, stood up and then felt horrifyingly dizzy. Jonny staggered to the bathroom, swaying as he attempted to stand up to pee straight. The room was swimming round in front of him. Sweat pouring out of every pore, his skin was freezing. And the pain – pain in every bone and joint as if someone had actually set his body on fire and left him there to roast to death.

"You aren't dying, but you have malaria!" Peter told him, rolling up his eyes in exasperation. "How stupid were you for not taking your Proguanil? Are you crazy man?"

Dave insisted on dragging him into the hospital to be examined by Doctor Sunday.

"You will recover at home, not in the hospital," Doctor Sunday had told him, and he was relieved that he could lie down again in the cool shuttered bedroom where Rozala had left a basin of water beside his bed with a soft white towel to mop his brow, beside a bouquet of roses, their thick scent bathing him in sweetness while he groaned and rolled about, delirious.

Dave fed him Paracetamol and Chloroquin, bringing him into the toilet in the night when he was sick, helping him to eat and eventually the twice-daily fevers left him, and he stood up out of bed again, swaying only slightly this time, and made it to the living-room to eat some of the soup Rozala had left out with a towel wrapped around it to keep warm.

He lay on the sofa in the living-room during the days now, while Rozala swept and scrubbed and polished furniture around him, and he slept and woke and watched her graceful body move about the little house, enjoying the steady flow of her strong limbs around him. He had never in his life felt so weak. Her strength, her smooth ability amazed him.

He drifted in and out of sleep, always aware of her moving softly to and fro, the smell of her oiled skin, the shudder of her round bottom as she worked. She wore a green and yellow kanga, wrapped tightly around her waist and tied over one shoulder, and it draped down at the back where underneath the cloth her buttocks were both tight and mobile. Jonny closed his eyes again but it did not stop the stirring under his boxer shorts where he lay curled up with *The Cider House Rules,* and he tugged the crocheted blanked from the back of the sofa, to cover himself up.

The words of the novel blurred un-read while he held his breath, listening to her move about the kitchen. He felt his breathing quicken. Her legs were long and muscular from the long walk every day to and from her house on the other side of town. Her breasts sat high underneath the tee-shirt she wore beneath her kanga, held perfectly in place by her strong tall back, her long neck reached up to tight braids of hair kept in their neat place with a wide hairband. He felt his balls tighten again as the image of her smooth neck was visible to him.

She was kneeling down now on all fours, her back towards him, crouching down to polish the steps of the house, her long supple body swaying with the movement of her arms. From where he lay on the sofa, her back still turned to him, she leaned up balancing backwards on her heels now, her bottom spread towards him. He closed his eyes again.

There was more than enough money in the kitty to give some extra now to Rozala, Jonny thought. Now that I'm sick we're hardly going to the pub any more. That night he put an extra fifty shillings in the bowl by the front door for her.

"Why is William here today?" he asked her and she looked away ashamed. "I thought he was going back to school in September."

Jonny was sitting up at the table writing a letter to his parents, and it was pleasant to have William in the house. But surely he should have gone back to school this week with all the other kids? The school was quite near, halfway in between the little house and Rafiki hospital, and the kids had started back this week. Dave had told him how the playground was now full of tiny little kids running in cheap cotton uniforms, and how they'd come running over shrieking in a pack of excitement when he'd walked by – a *Wazungu* with pale spots on both his arms! There was one other white Scottish nurse who'd worked at the hospital last year, red-haired with freckles, and the children knew what freckles looked like, but they couldn't help coming over to stare at them again, and giggle and wave and smile before they ran away.

Rozala met Jonny's eyes and hung her head.

"William started school last week," she explained slowly. "But I have no money for books until next week. So, he must stay home and help me work. He cannot be the only boy in school with no school books. That would not be right for him."

"Jesus!" Jonny sighed. He reached out to her, taking her smooth arm in his hand. "Why didn't you ask us for more money, Rozala? We can give it to you." He touched her long smooth arm higher up, reaching her above the elbow.

She flinched slightly and he withdrew it, wondering if he'd offended her. African men touched each other all the time; the male nurses would hold hands with you if you walked down the street with them (Dave had found this to be deeply alarming at first, but Jonny got used to it). But between men and women things were much more modest. He put his hand back on the table and she looked at it.

"I'd like to help you with some money," he said, this time avoiding her eyes.

"There is something more you want from me, sir?" she said in a gentle voice.

"No," he shook his head. "You work hard enough. Here." He rummaged in his pockets and pulled out two hundred shillings. "Will this be a good start?"

Rozala's eyes filled with tears. She knelt down on the floor in front of him, her eyes never leaving his face for a second. She took his hand back from the table, holding it in both of hers.

"You are a good man, *Daktari Wazungu*," she whispered. He could not take his gaze off her beautiful round, open-mouthed face. The lips that were deep deep black and teeth like pearls. She closed her eyes and placed his hand on her chest, so that he could feel the beating of her heart. "I am very very thankful for you," she murmured, and then she lay her face on his lap.

He felt ashamed, and yet overwhelmed. Horror mixed with lust. From where he sat above her he could see beneath her throat the soft swell of her breasts, dark black beneath her kanga, smell her skin, the thick scent of her hair.

The scritch-scratching sound behind them reminded him that William was raking leaves off the little path in the garden behind them. She raised her liquid eyes to meet his.

"He will return to school tomorrow. You will be blessed by God." She closed her eyes again.

Jonny rose. "Stand up, Rozala," he said in a hoarse voice. He pulled her gently, up off the floor with him still watching her. They smiled at one another. They were no longer embarrassed, but the intimacy was there now in between them. And it would not just go away.

"You look so thin, man!" Pete whistled at him when he saw him walk along the road towards the school.

Jonny smiled. "I feel great," he said. "I've never felt better. The rest was excellent. I'm completely fit for work again."

Daily life at the hospital went on. Tiny children came and went, some lived and some died in their mother's arms, their wails of misery beat into Jonny's heart. He steeled himself against the worst indignities of poverty, he shielded himself from the pain of knowing that children would die because their mothers couldn't afford medicines.

He often came into work in the evenings now when Dave had gone home or was sitting in a bar with the American in Kakamega. He still felt tired in the long hot afternoons, he said. He took long naps at the little house inside the rose bush. He took Rozala into his arms and breathed deeply into her sharp-scented skin. He spread her legs and leaned her body across the backrest of the sofa, where he'd lain for weeks longing for her. He fell heavily into her neck and cupped her breasts in his grateful two hands from where he stood behind her, while she allowed him to love her there. He loved her over and over, and over and over again.

Her son William studied hard at school. Rozala met the increases in her daily stipend with a graceful dignity.

It was an evening when there was very little happening at Rafiki hospital. Dave had gone home long before the rain and Jonny had planned to leave shortly too, spending just a few more minutes to try to persuade the grandmother of a small child to let her cool down again in fever.

"No more blankets, please!" he begged her. "Please, mama, let the child sleep naked. *Hatari!*" he explained, tugging at the cotton blanket. "*Moto mbaya! Baridi harara!* Take away the blanket! Please."

The grandmother rescinded the blanket, allowing Jonny to walk away before she tucked it back again around her sweating grandchild.

He stepped outside onto the porch of the outpatients

room, squinting lazily into the evening sun, wondering if it might be a nice idea to go on into town and meet the lads for a lukewarm beer. And then a shout from back inside again.

"*Daktari! Ita, Daktari!*"

Jonny sighed, and wondered briefly if Doctor Sunday was out of theatre, and then checking the sun sliding in the sky remembered that he could not be as he'd gone in only half an hour ago to remove a burst appendix. Turning around again, he walked towards the admitting room, only to be met by Doctor Sister Jessie who was hurrying along the corridor towards the maternity suite.

"Come along, Jonny!" she barked at him. "We have a sick, sick lady, very sick in pregnancy. She has been to a very bad witchdoctor. Come along quickly now, please. We need to take a blood transfusion for her now." She looked at Jonny sideways as they walked rapidly together. "She has *been* at the witch doctor," she said underneath her breath, shuddering dramatically as she spoke.

"All right." Jonny followed her into the suite. There was a woman already on the labour bed, behind the nurses where they worked and he checked himself slightly before entering the commotion that was already in place. Three nurses and red-soaked sheeting, the oxygen tank hissing furiously.

"Blood transfusion, *Daktari. Hapa, Daktari!*" one of the nurses pointed at the lab technician who was setting up a trolley for him. And he began to roll up his sleeve, accustomed to the idea that at some stage he was going to have to give blood. His malaria was gone, the lab technician had assured him. He was healthy and had gained weight again. He winced slightly as Jojo the technician inserted the canula into the crook of his elbow, siphoning off the dark transfusion for the woman on the labour bed.

"What happened to her?" he asked the midwife casually, his eyes closed trying to ignore the blood that left his arm rapidly into a giving set.

Doctor Sister Jessie sucked her teeth and rolled her eyes and sighed. "This witchdoctor makes a lot of mistakes. This is very sad for this poor woman," and she stroked the woman's forehead. "Very low blood pressure. Septic shock, Jonny." Doctor Sister Jessie looked at Jonny sadly and he nodded as the midwife moved away from the woman's head and went towards the storing area to take some more sheeting down. And then he saw the woman's face.

"Oh Jesus Christ!" he cried out, and everybody in the labour room jumped in fright.

"Ah, she is his housekeeper," Sister Jessie explained to the technician, and they both looked at Jonny in sympathy.

"*What happened to her?*" Jonny whispered, the blood-soaked sheet was now one of horror to him. The greyness of the black woman's pallor was like the blue skin of a steely ghost.

"*Mimba*, you know," the technician mimed a woman with a pregnant belly, "and she tried to get rid of it. But this is illegal in Kenya. This witchdoctor makes far too many mistakes." He connected the giving set with the woman's IV line.

"My blood, is it crossmatched?" Jonny was shaking now and he touched Rozala's motionless face. His hands trembled as he placed his stethoscope on her chest. He listened to her fluttering heart. Her breaths were shallower. "She's in deep shock, Sister!" He stared at the nun.

"We'll give her this transfusion and we'll see," Sister Jessie replied.

"Get Doctor Sunday!" Jonny almost screamed at her.

Sister Jessie looked taken aback. "Jonny," she retorted, "you will speak to me with manners, please."

"I'm so sorry, Sister." His voice was choking up. "But I know her. She works for us. She is a friend. We have to get Doctor Sunday out of theatre. Please!"

"Jonny, you are the doctor on duty. Doctor Sunday is in theatre still. He can't come down till he is finished there."

"I'm not a doctor! I'm a fucking medical student! She needs to go to theatre. Can't you see that?" He felt like slapping the smooth face of the nun.

She looked away from him indignantly. "You speak to me with very bad manners, Jonny."

"Get him! Just get him! We have to save her!" He pumped the blood pressure cuff again around Rozala's slender arm, but the pressure was unrecordable.

"Witchdoctors cause a lot of harm," Doctor Sister Jessie spoke sternly to him. "Septic abortions lead to maternal fever and to shock. She may not survive but it happens often in Kenya. Let's just see what happens. We will do our best for her."

"We can't *just* see! Jesus!" He tore his hands through his hair. "Sister Jessie! She's got no pressure. She's dying! You have to get Doctor Sunday out of theatre!"

"Jonny, Jonny, you must understand!" Sister Jessie placed a warm dark hand on his shoulder. "This abortion is illegal here in Kenya. Here, give the antibiotics to her again, please." She handed him a glass syringe.

He had never felt so useless in all of his life.

Dave went out and bought beer. At lot of it. And when they'd run out of beer they drank Chang'aa. Dave sat at the table with Jonny as they drank, sat for hours with him, feeling helpless beyond belief. They were both completely drunk on Chang'aa, the revolting Kenyan home-brew known as "kill-me-quick" that you could buy illegally from two local women – anything to try to kill the pain. Any alcohol would do. And the more of it they drank, the more Jonny wept. Great heaving sobs of tears into his folded arms where he sat at the table while Dave sat there not knowing what to say. Jesus, nothing should be this terrible, not even the death of a patient. Even a patient that they knew. Even a patient who was a friend. A lover even. Now he knew.

But Dave could *feel* the guilt and shame that Jonny felt. With every sob, he felt Jon's pain and shared his nightmare. The horror of it was breaking him too. This wasn't just some colleague whose patient had died, this was happening to his best, best ever friend. He wanted to tell Jonny that it was all right. That these things happen.

He desperately wanted to say something soothing like that. *These things happen sometimes, Jon.*

But it would sound ridiculous. What kinds of things are *these?* Illegal abortions, maternal deaths, prostitution? These things do happen: *this is Africa.* But in our house – our beloved Rozala? Our cook, our cleaner, our friend? *Our whore?* Was it really possible that this evil could have come to us? That we could be responsible for this?

Dave opened up his mouth to speak, but his words were stuck somewhere deeper in his throat. Nothing he could say would make it go away. Jonny bawled and Dave listened to the snot gurgling in his nose, watched his shoulders heave with misery and there was nothing to be said.

You didn't mean for her to die. You loved her, that was why you screwed her. You wanted to have sex – that's not a crime. She was a beautiful woman. She wanted to be with you too, she asked you for it didn't she? She needed money and she wanted to provide. She thought that you preferred to pay. White people always feel guilty over Africa. She didn't mean to die. You didn't mean for her to die. You've saved so many people's lives. Look at all the good things that you've done here.

But none of that made sense. It was all true, but he could not bring himself to say it. Rozala was dead. That was the simple fact. And it was because of Jonny: there was no one else. Her beautiful black body that had opened itself in love to him because he'd given her a few school-books for her son was lying now in rigor mortis. Her satin skin stiffened in the morgue, while Jonny wept thick tears onto the table she had polished.

"I wish that I was dead."

The words came out slurred with drunkenness and muffled with mucus and hoarse breathing, but Dave heard what he'd said quite clearly.

"Jonny, please. Don't say things like that. She – you –" and then he felt his own tears sting.

"I swear to God, Dave." Jonny looked at him. Eyes tiny with despair, face puffy with drink. "I wish that I could fucking kill myself!"

Dave moved at last. He stood up, swaying slightly and he grabbed the tabletop to steady himself. Jonny was still sitting at the table, a glass of Chang'aa in one outstretched hand, his head on the other arm on the table top, his breathing clogged.

Dave stood in front of him. He took the glass of Chang'aa out of Jonny's hand and put it down away from him, where it wouldn't spill.

Jonny looked up at him, eyes droopy with drunkenness. "Hey, that's my drink!" He smiled weakly at Dave and then sat up and pushed his chair away from the table, leaning back to sprawl his legs outstretched.

Dave swept Jonny's hair out of his eyes and ran his fingers down his cheek. Then he took Jonny's hot red swollen face in his two hands gently and then held it close into his own throat. Jonny's face was wet with tears and snot against his skin. Dave didn't care. He loved him. He loved everything about him now. All he wanted was to take away his pain. He lifted Jonny's face up to his mouth, breathing in the fumes of alcohol off Jonny's drunken breath. Jonny Domville was his soul mate. He was the closest friend that he would ever have. Jonny had done nothing wrong, nothing that was meant to hurt Rozala. It was all a terrible accident. He would do anything to protect him now.

"I love you," he told him, "I'll always love you, Jon," and kissed his open mouth, tasting salty tears. His tongue tasted Jonny's tongue. He locked his lips with his, taking his face in his hands. And Jonny stood up very suddenly, swaying as he did and Dave felt a sudden clang of despair.

He felt Jonny's body lose its balance, felt his shoulders swing drunkenly away from him and for a dreadful split second of a moment he thought Jonny would pull away from him altogether.

But he did not. His lips softened. And parted. His mouth opened and for the first time he tasted what he'd so often dreamed about – what he'd so often longed to do but never, ever planned it! No! He tasted Jonny's kiss.

Never in his most secret dreams could he have imagined what Jonny's body would eventually feel like in his arms. What his body would do in Jonny's arms, in between his legs, what parts of him Jonny would let him kiss, suck, fuck. What his face would feel like when he held it in his hands, how firm his neck, what his cock would feel like, hard, swollen and pressed against his own. He wanted him. He wanted him. He wanted him so bad! He pulled off Jonny's shirt, and then his own. And as their faces parted and in the split second before he grasped his face again to take his mouth back so that he could – Oh! He would *eat* him! – he locked eyes with him again. And in that split second, for the first time ever in his life, everything made sense. This was what love felt like.

In the morning, everything had changed. The room was hot and new and damp with sweat, and outside there was a burst of sunshine in the trees and birdsong, but in his heart – oh, in his heart there was nothing but an empty taste of horrible. He didn't even need to open his eyes. He didn't want what he knew he'd see. He reached out a hand instead and felt the creases in the sheets, felt the cold, the emptiness beside him.

Jonny was dressing quickly in the corner. Bending down, his shirt already on, pulling up his underpants.

"Are you okay?" Dave's voice was hoarse with drink and he tried to clear his throat again. "Jon? Are you okay?"

But Jonny said nothing. He was buttoning his shirt as quickly as he could, pulling trousers on. His back was turned.

"Would you like a coffee?"

"No."

"Come back to bed?"

"No! I just want to get out of here."

"Jonny, it's all right. It's going to be all right."

But it wasn't. It would never be all right again.

There was only one thing to do and that was to get the hell out of there and never go back. Dave was a bastard.

It was Dave who bought the Chang'aa, Dave who got him drunk, and he knew the crazy effects it would have. He knew what he was doing – he must have known. *He took advantage of me! He fucking well took advantage of me on the worst day of my fucking life! I trusted him. I told him everything! I thought he was my friend! But he was just using me. He couldn't pour the drink into me fast enough last night! Jesus, he took advantage of me! He only had one thing on his mind.*

"Jonny, talk to me!"

"I've got to go."

"Wait – at least let's talk about it!"

But Jonny didn't reply. He couldn't get out of there fast enough. His shirt buttons were done up arseways but he didn't give a shit. He slammed the door as he left and it banged on its hinges and swung back open again but he didn't give a shit.

He walked a few meters as quickly as he could away from the little house, then ran, ran faster, ran as fast as he possibly could because all he wanted to do was get away from that house and never, ever speak to Dave Hardiman again.

He hated Dave now. Hated everything about him. Hated everything he'd ever done with him. But most of all he hated himself for allowing it to happen.

16

"So. This is it."

Marianne looked away from him out of the window at the view of the Paris street that she had craved for weeks.

"I hope you'll be all right," he said.

"Of course. I am at home in Paris now. This will not take long. I can leave the hospital after a few days."

He opened his mouth to say something else and then thought the better of it. The awkwardness between them had become as solid as wax. Everything seemed to sound all wrong. He tried speaking French to her instead but that didn't help. She despised his accent far too much.

"We'll have to speak when you are back from Kenya," she told him in a weary voice. "And we can make further arrangements then."

"All right," he said. "If that's what you would like."

She looked relieved to see him going now, he felt, pulling on his leather jacket. There was nothing more to say to her. And yet – why does this have to be so hard? Is she right, when she says that I am always chasing dreams, he asked himself in despair, and then he looked at her again. But there was nothing left.

He zipped his jacket up and the noise of the zip filled the silent room like a machine-gun rip.

"I'm sure you will find someone quite rapidly who will take over where I've left off."

"No one will *replace* you," he said.

"Don't be tedious," she replied. "You'll find someone who amuses you. I have no doubt."

He said nothing.

"And I have Veronique," she said.

"You are very strong, Marianne."

She reached her hand out to the cot. "You will have left the apartment by the time I come home?"

"Yes," he said. "Don't worry. Everything as planned."

At the Café Danton on Boulevard Saint-Germain, Kate ordered an entrecôte with salade frites and waited on a knife edge for Jonny. It was Tuesday and they were leaving for Africa the following night. A steak seemed like a good decision after desperately examining the menu for almost half an hour, which seemed to be a toss-up between the benign (Croque Monsieur), and the ridiculous (a salad made with pieces of lamb's pancreas, her little pocket dictionary implied – how could that be possible?). She waited for her steak to be brought to her in some trepidation. You never really knew where you were with a French steak, she thought anxiously. French meat could be revoltingly raw. In Ireland, although waitresses did offer you a choice of done-ness it was almost as an afterthought and it made absolutely no difference whatsoever to the end product.

Kate was very pleasantly surprised when it arrived, slapped down onto her tiny table by an extremely distracted waiter, to find the steak a perfect medium rare. Her *entrecôte* came with a rather slippery salad (of raw spinach perhaps – it was nice) and some very crispy fries – the shoe-string kind that she liked best. She surveyed the success of her meal as it lay beautifully on the tiny round table in front of her. Her French might be pretty scratch, but her lunch was looking optimistic thus far. And she had drunk two glasses of a really nice chablis already, and listened to a London male voice behind her with his (she presumed) date. Paris was full of English visitors.

"You've never been to New York? New York is the best city in the world . . . Woody Allen . . . they shag each other senseless and end up in each other's magazines . . . huge neo-con . . ."

She strained to listen to the entire plot of their conversation while she fiddled with her steak, but it was impossible.

"The social scientist guy? He wrote *The End of Ideology* . . . I read about him . . . I can't remember his surname."

The man's voice was one of those squawky London high-pitched male voices that sound as though he were speaking with his neck in a stranglehold. She bought another glass of wine – which was a mistake, she knew it, as soon as it arrived. But what does one do, when one has bought a glass of wine by mistake?

One could just leave it there. One could send it back. Or one could drink it. In Kate's case she drank it quickly, more quickly than she really needed to, so that it would disappear.

Her stomach was an ugly bag of nerves. She put down her knife and turned away from the English conversation she'd been ear-wigging and decided that she'd people-watch *parisiens* instead. So much more interesting. And then she saw something quite astonishing just across the street.

Because surely that was Nick Farrelly, strolling casually along the pavement towards the Boulevard Saint-Germain? But this was Tuesday. And they were supposed to have come over and gone back to Dublin all in the same day yesterday. Unless something terrible had happened to Veronique during the transfer and now they had to stay on in Paris – oh Jesus!

Kate stood up abruptly, and was about to rush out of the café and onto the street, and then she suddenly remembered that nobody actually *knew* that she was in Paris. And most of all, *Dave* thought that she was not. And if Nick knew she was in Paris – well, she would have to tell him not to tell Dave. And that would mean having to force Nick to collude with her. To get him to lie for her — or at least withhold the truth. And so she stopped and stood there with her mouth open, watching Nick walk across the street, halt in front of a fruit and sweets and newspaper vendor, and watched him buy a bag of sweets right in front of the café where she sat with her half-eaten lunch. And then she asked herself, would it be so terrible if Nick did know that she'd lied to Dave? Would it be so terrible if Dave *did* know that she was in Paris with Jonny? — but the more she thought about it, the more she knew that she did not want him to know — not now, anyway. "*Not with him!*" She could still hear the words Dave had said ten years ago when she'd first kissed Jonny. "*Please don't go to Jonny now! Not my friend! Not Jonny. Please, please don't do this to me, Kate! It would kill me completely!*"

And then she realised that even though the last thing she wanted was for Nick to know that she was only meters away from *him* on a pavement in Paris, that she couldn't *not* find out why *he* was still here. Something must have gone wrong, if Nick and Ronan were still in Paris. And so with much trepidation and discretion, she took her mobile phone out of her handbag and dialled Nick Farrelly's number.

"Hello?"

"Er, Nick? Is that you?"

"Hi, Kate! Nice surprise. How's Venice?" Nick's voice breezed against the background of the boulevard.

"Fine. Um, foggy," Kate replied, remembering what

Caroline had said the last time that they'd spoken. "How is everything in Paris?" she asked him.

"It was fine. The transfer went well and the French people were charming. The French doctors all speak very good English. Ro and I were put to shame."

"So you're still over there then? Is there a problem then? With Veronique – I mean Baby Le Normand?" she asked.

"No, she's doing fine. I'm back in Dublin now."

"You are?" She strained her neck and watched him, in incredulity, standing just outside her café with his mobile phone.

"Yes. I'm in Grafton Street."

"*Grafton Street?*"

"Yes. At the corner of the Green. You're breaking up a bit though. The line's not great. Say hello to Caroline for me, won't you, Kate?"

"Yes. Of course." She didn't know what to say to him. It was too bizarre.

"Look, I've got to go, I'm meeting someone in the Shelbourne. Have a fab holiday, you, and I'll see you when you're back in February."

"All right," she said. "I'll hang up so." And she watched him hang up his own phone and put it back in his breast pocket. She watched him skip across the street until he disappeared through the crowds and down a lane.

She stared at her uneaten food. What the *hell* was Nick playing at now? It hurt to think he'd lied to her. And yet he must be covering-up something pretty major to have gone to such an elaborate effort to make up all that. And there was no way of finding out either – no amount of searching in the hospital gossip machine when she got back would solve this one, because she wasn't supposed to be here in Paris either, having an affair with her patient's husband.

What a very, very tangled web we weave.

"You've had a very complicated birth," Docteur Sophie Larocque said to Marianne as she read the case notes from Ireland.

Marianne waited patiently. She watched the doctor's face while she read the handwritten text but Docteur Larocque was obviously going to take her time. Marianne looked up, out of the window of the spotlessly clean private room in the American Hospital in Paris and watched the trees blow almost sideways in the wintry wind. It looked to be so cold outside. It was raining heavily and blackly now and she had been in hospital altogether for a month. It was an appalling waste of time. She watched the dancing trees to pass the time while she waited for Sophie Larocoque to finish scrutinising the case file.

"I am desperate to get home," she said, trying very hard to smile. "You must understand that, Docteur. Or even to my parents in the seventeenth, if you prefer."

Docteur Larocque gave a cautious nod.

She would rather have been absolutely anywhere, truly, that wasn't a hospital bed with a bell to call a nurse and smelt of disinfectant, sweat, and boiling vegetables.

The American hospital in Paris was better – much better, of course – than the one in Ireland had been. And at least – thank God! – in a Paris hospital she could eat the food. But although she had felt immediate relief as soon as they had landed at the hospital in Paris, that at *least* she wasn't in Ireland any more, now she didn't think she'd *survive* another day in hospital.

"Let me just finish reading all your file. Then I'll examine you again. Then we'll make a plan for your discharge. Agreed?"

"I am very grateful, Docteur," she told Sophie Larocque while she returned to watching the tops of the wintery trees at their dance.

Of course, Jonny seemed to be slightly less relaxed in Paris than he'd been in Dublin visiting her. But overall, since Veronique's birth his overall tendency to bleak moodiness had lifted in some way. She sensed now, seeing him in Paris, a new contentment that she hadn't seen in – well, it was probably in almost nine months. Exactly nine. Since she'd come home to the Geneva apartment to surprise him with what she had decided was going to be wonderful news and found him in their house with that *woman* – Marianne still shuddered still at the memory of *that* particular afternoon.

Even so, despite her fury and dishonour on the day she'd decided that they would divorce, she'd wanted to tell him that she was pregnant. And as soon as she had done so she had felt as though she had suddenly assumed a new power over him that had signalled the end of any hold he had ever had on her. No matter what he had, no matter how much he had humiliated her, she had Veronique. There is no love that can compare with that of a mother for her child, is what Eric had told her in a rather pat way, and she was in many ways beginning to see how this cliché, like all clichés, have their ground in truth.

Today Jonny had been very silent of course – quite preoccupied no doubt. He was off to Kenya tomorrow night – naturally. But that was probably what was making him feel strong again, responsible and important – much more so than fatherhood would ever have done. Thank God that sorry tale was at an end.

"We will be planning to discharge Veronique," Docteur Sophie was saying, "in perhaps a fortnight, perhaps even less."

Marianne watched Sophie Larocque's face while she took her blood pressure once again.

"You *were* very lucky, Marianne," Docteur Larocque was saying now. "They worked very hard on her in Ireland." She sat down beside the bed checking how the blood pressure had been in Dublin from the nurses' notes that were clipped together in the massive case file that had come over in the helicopter. "So no more children, now. Just this little one," she said in a more cautious voice, writing in today's blood pressure, temperature and pulse.

Marianne nodded slowly back at her. No more children now. Definitely not. Never again. Although she'd only ever imagined having one it was suddenly painful to realise that she no longer had the choice. Would she ever have changed her mind? To go through something like this childbirth again – no, certainly, never. But to be left without any alternative than the decision that she'd already made . . . despite her rationalisation of it, she couldn't help feeling at once relieved and yet at the same time infuriated and bereaved.

Knowing that she would never have another child was as if somewhere, someone whom she'd never even known, had died. It was as if her body had betrayed her. It had betrayed her right to be a mother again.

But this baby was a miracle! As her father Eric had announced as soon as he had heard the news and ordered a special selection of wine to be put down to commemorate the birth. Jonny and Marianne had laughed together briefly at the idea – but not too much.

Jonny was relieved at least that the baby had survived and seemed to be developing perfectly. Veronique was starting to swallow now and suck and would be feeding fully from the bottle in a day or so, the paediatrician had told her already.

She pictured Jonny again now and the stilted conversation that he'd had with her today. At least he seemed to be absorbed in work again. That was better than having to put up with him wasting all that time on that music. And without a doubt there would be quite soon another woman. Wherever there was music, there were women. But *music* is an unfaithful lover, as she'd often said.

Jonny was incapable of knowing what he wanted when it came to women until it was far too late for him to find out.

Jonny would always hurt the people whom he loved the most. How strange that they had ever even been drawn together in the first place, she thought, examining Veronique again sleeping blissfully in her little Perspex cot.

Her own days were absorbed now with watching Veronique at every possible moment – she watched her sleep, or tried to feed her with the droplets of milk. She felt passive and powerless and sometimes during that horrendous time in Dublin she had felt so vulnerable and so exposed to the command of others that it had made her feel out of control. These were grossly unfamiliar feelings. It was at times like this that she hardly recognised herself – the strong woman that she'd formally been, now weak and pale and haggard in a dressing-gown, crying in pain, unable to pass urine without help. Every moment of her day dictated by a baby's heartbeat, her breasts answerable only to its diminutive cry, her emotions overwhelmed. At least the legal inquiry she'd initiated into the conduct of the Dublin hospital would give her back some of her sense of who she was.

"Everything changes when you have a child," the doctor was saying, writing something in her chart. "Your body will not be the same again. The post-natal exercises are very important to regain muscular control."

Nothing is the same again. Everything changes.

How many times had people told her that since

Veronique had been born? In the past year her entire *life* had been turned upside-down! But no matter how much chaos had erupted between herself and Jonny, no matter how vulnerable she had felt for those two weeks in Dublin where every modicum of power had been taken away from her, she would do whatever it took now to regain control.

She was a lawyer. She had access to authority and she would not lie down and let others run her life.

"So, tell me, Docteur. What do you think about the surgery notes? How did the doctor conduct the procedure?"

Sophie Larocque raised her eyebrows and pursed her lips. "There is nothing untoward," she said. Docteur Larocque ran her finger through the chart. "She has made very extensive notes. And it all makes perfect sense, the decision to go to hysterectomy. She has performed the operation correctly. The indication for hysterectomy was there. There was nothing else she could have done, according to these notes." She looked at Marianne with a reassuring smile. "Perhaps that makes you feel a bit better, knowing that there was in fact no actual mistake?"

Marianne blinked. Did it make her feel better? To know that no one was to blame? To know that her own body had let her down – had been incapable of normal childbirth? To know that the pain and deformity she now felt – the unrecognisable form her female body now took – was nobody else's fault? "In fact," Docteur Larocque was saying cheerfully, "I feel that the standard of care you received was probably excellent."

Marianne said nothing. She watched the doctor write a few more sentences in the notes. Perhaps there was nothing more to say.

There is something wonderfully private about a hotel room, Dave Hardiman thought to himself, puttting his tee-shirt in the trouser press. It is a *sanctuary*. You can watch terrible television almost with your back turned.

Living in Paris, Nick had told him, is like staying at a five-star hotel and not even being allowed to leave the room. Nick had spent a whole year living in Paris, working at the American Hospital. Nick told him that if you actually live and work in Paris you don't get time to touch, to feel, to own it most of the time. It becomes a theatre backdrop to the misery of your life. The French are miserable fuckers too, Nick had told him.

Dave couldn't imagine anyone being unhappy in Paris. He had been unhappy in Dublin, unhappy leaving Melbourne, he had been desperately unhappy after the Jonny disaster in Kenya. But now here he was, in Paris, and in a very good five-star hotel room. He had a bottle of champagne and a full mini-bar to play with. He had plenty of cocaine. And he had Nick. Or would have, soon.

Everything had changed since he'd met Nick. He wasn't sure *why* Nick liked him so much, or whether or not what he felt for Nick *was* love – he'd been so wrong about being in love before. And Nick was so intense; he was romantic, really. He liked poetry, classical music, countertenors and Renaissance art. Dave liked rugby, going to pubs, crime novels and film noir. But he and Nick were going to have a brilliant time in Paris, there was no bloody doubt about that.

Dave cut up a second line of coke on the top of the glass desk-top, and marvelled happily at a hotel that provided both glass desk-tops and mini-bars. He leaned back, naked, onto the padded cover of the bed, and let his body melt into the mattress. Through floor-length windows from where he lay he watched upside-down a flock of birds flap briskly through the Paris sky, sailing above the rooftops towards heaven. In between bleak clouds he watched the sky open up and saw the flock of birds turn into a crucifix and then disappear like magic. He thought of Nick.

His penis stirred at the thought of Nick, and it alarmed him. Was he naked? Yes he was. He giggled to himself at his baldy nakedness lying on a Paris hotel bed.

He couldn't wait to see Nick again. It had been a big disappointment to find he couldn't get the time off work until that afternoon.

Nick was bound to be here within an hour. Dave visualised Nick's white buttocks like the shells of two boiled eggs, and then stared out of the window at the view again – the birds had gone. The view was crowded with the roofs of buildings, balconies, French windows, rows and rows of them but he couldn't get the previous image out of his head no matter how he tried. He stroked his hard-on rapidly, then sat up, furious with himself.

Fuck it.

He leaped up off the bed and flung open the mini-bar again. Two miniature bottles of gin, one vodka, two whiskeys, a bottle of champagne, the usual wines, minerals, tonics, boring, boring – oh, a darling little bottle of cognac. Dave liked cognac.

He padded into the marbled bathroom and collected a large tooth mug (fuck those piddly little wineglasses on the top of the mini-bar!) and padded back to the suite again. He cracked the seals open on two miniature bottles of gin, one vodka, two whiskeys, and the mini bottle of cognac, and tipped each evenly into his beaker without spilling a drop. He dug into the ice bucket, scooping out three cubes of ice.

He prised the cork out of the champagne and hit a light fitting, breaking into giggles as he did.

He topped his cocktail up with champagne, and took a long and generous swig. Absolutely delicious. Why don't they put this one on the cocktail menus? One mini-bar delight.

Dave sat down, naked on the Louis XIV armchair beside the glass-topped table, and contemplated just another line of coke. There were only four or five more lines left in the stash he'd brought over with him, and he wanted to save something for Nick. But he was feeling nervous again now, and despite the drink that he swallowed back in three mouthfuls, he couldn't relax at all. He stood up again, rummaging in the chest of drawers for the room-service menu, and contemplated ordering more booze. But his

French was atrocious and he wasn't sure if the amount of drink he felt he needed was going to be something that he could explain properly on the phone to the downstairs staff.

He poured another tall glassful of the champagne and drank it down, and then regretted that he now had nothing left from the entire mini-bar to offer Nick.

And then he remembered he'd bought a bottle of whiskey in the Duty Free. Nick had told him everyone in France loved Irish whiskey for some reason and so he'd bought over with him a bottle of Tullamore Dew. It wasn't as if they were going to be meeting anyone now that the hospital stuff was over. Nick had been at the hospital all day transferring his maternity patient over to the French team, whereas he had had all day to get the hotel ready for the two of them. So now what?

Nick would probably be tired after having to transfer a patient by helicopter all the way from Dublin to Paris the day before. And there was a baby, too, although Nick had said something about the paediatrician coming with the baby, a guy called Ronan that Kate had mentioned to him sometimes.

Kate.

He felt the giant wave of guilt wash over him again, as if it was trying to drown him in it. He quickly slugged down the rest of the champagne. What the fuck was he doing to Kate? She was already suffering and she didn't know anything yet about him and Nick. *Jesus.* Poor little Kate – he loved her, but she was so bloody unhappy with him too. She was so caught up in her own little world of *hospital* – all the stupid one-upmanship and the bitching and the gossiping. She thought that she was always so on top of things, and yet she hadn't got a clue about what was really going on most of the time. All that stuff Nick had said about the hospital being sued – she was probably taking all of that far too seriously. That was just Domville acting the bollocks, of course. And then that desperate look of shock over her, the Caroline night at Christmas. But then he wondered just how much of Kate's naïveté was for real. She must have known about Caroline, he thought. Nobody is that stupid. Kate is naïve, but she probably just hides whatever she doesn't want to see from herself, almost lying to herself a lot of the time. He might have a bad temper in some ways, Dave thought, but Kate was *passive aggressive*. In a weird way, he might have almost got a kick out of her finding out about Caro in that way. But the truth was that he didn't really relish the thought. It was just another round of guilt.

She had looked so tiny and quite helpless all that night, he remembered. Crying over Caroline like a baby. Old Caroline was all right, of course, he thought with a hollow laugh. That cookie would sail through anything. Probably getting good and stoned again in Italy by now.

Christ, he wished that he was stoned properly right now.

He went to his toilet bag that he'd left beside the TV and took out the tiny plastic screwed-up package of cocaine again, and contemplated it. Just one more line, perhaps? And then he remembered that he also had

Fentanyl. And needles. Which could be good. Mix them both together – that'd work if you crush the coke into the Fentanyl and inject it right into a bigger vein. Screw the little veins. He'd inject into the femoral and get a decent turn-on and then there'd be plenty of coke left for when Nick got here and he'd save his skin. Only an idiot would inject into his skin again.

And so Dave drew up five hundred micrograms of Fentanyl into his blue IM syringe and, thanking Christ that he was an anaesthetist and knew exactly how to inject into the femoral vein without any problem whatsoever, took the last turn-on that he would ever take.

Jonny was very late.

Although the rain outside was pelting down icicles, the café was still cosy and full of steam and rattling kitchen noises. Kate sipped her second glass of wine and chewed her thoughts over until she felt her brain would melt.

First there was the way Nick had lied to her about being in Paris – and the more she thought about it the more she realised that Nick had been behaving differently towards her for quite some time now. Ever since Christmas.

They had been friends – yes, she had no doubt about that, and she flipped through the events of the past few weeks to remind herself of when exactly it was that Nick had changed. She thought about the last time she had worked with him – at the delivery of Veronique. He had been a rock of support. The way he'd tried to make sure she was supported at the M and M. The night he'd taken her out with Ronan and cheered her up and made a party out of a horrible occasion. And then there was the Res Christmas party – except he wasn't there of course. And then she'd come back to work after the Christmas and he'd been a bit funny with her, after the letter had come from Marianne's law firm. The French Letter.

It was because she was being sued – that was why he might be pulling back from her. He was trying to protect himself from being sullied by her reputation, just like Prof was too! Everybody thought she was useless now. She watched the agitated smokers outside sitting underneath an awning that was full of rain, shivering under heating lamps, puffing furiously against the wind that chased up the boulevard from the Seine.

But still, that didn't fully explain why he'd lied to her about being in Paris. And in any case, Nick could hardly be Machiavellian enough to be her friend all along, to support her all the time at work, to stand by her and cheer her up and crack jokes with her about the way the Prof behaved and the kind of bullying that goes on in the hospital – and then turn on her at the moment when she was most vulnerable. But no matter how much she tried to puzzle out where things had gone wrong, what exactly had changed Nick's mind about her, what had happened that had made him think he had to lie to her about being in Paris, the less sense it all made. And the longer she sat alone with just her thoughts to torture her, the more time she had to remind herself that by lying to Dave, by hiding the truth about her lifelong love for Jonny, that she too was hurting Dave.

If only Jonny would come. It was awful sitting here alone in a big, busy, strange city and the longer she sat and watched other people eat and smoke and laugh the more complicated the reality of what she and Jonny were planning seemed.

All her life she had wanted most of all to feel at home. Having grown up with a father who couldn't seem to sit still in the same house for more than two or three months, she had imagined a life with Dave which would be solid and reliable. Both doctors, both friends, both absorbed in each other's lives. They were supposed to have had a marriage that was without nasty surprises, one that was based on life-long friendship. It was perhaps not the most exciting love affair, but it was supposed to be a certain, a predictable and unchangeable kind of love. And where had all that gone now?

It was in many ways impossible to believe that Dave had ever loved her now. At least, what he'd called love had obviously been something completely different. Friendship – yes. Commonality, certainly. But compared to what she felt for Jonny now, it was nothing.

And yet there was something about Jonny's desperate passion for her that almost disturbed her now. It was as if he expected that their lives together were now a given – as if he assumed that she *belonged* to him. And although, on many levels, there was nothing she wanted more than to belong to him, for him to possess her completely, there was something in that possession that filled her with trepidation.

The whole reason she had married Dave, the entire reason she had chosen him in the first place was because he was familiar. They had both sought marriage, both sought reassurance in the familiar, both mistrusting adventure as a journey filled with danger.

And now Jonny. She was embarking on an adventure with him. She was leaving the familiar, leaving everything she'd built around her – her marriage, her friends, her job, the family home she'd bought from her own father – in order to try to change her life. And the unfamiliarity of it at once both exhilarated and discomforted her.

At the heart of this conflict *was* her fundamental desire to find protection in the familiar. But what happens when the familiar changes too? Dave had changed – her marriage with him had changed utterly. And her career, the most important expression of who she was and what she was there for – that had been snatched away from her and turned into something else because of a series of unpredictable events. Perhaps we *can't* insulate ourselves against change, she thought, gazing through the steamy windows, watching the unfamiliar city at its beat. Perhaps we need to change to force us to seek out adventure, to become the people whom we are meant to be.

The truth was that despite themselves, they *had* all changed – all three of them. They had been close, so close once, but that was years ago. Life's events had *made* all of them different. Dave, the man she'd married, was the complete opposite of the boy she'd known. And Jonny – Jonny was even more complicated now. It was as if the closeness of medical school life had just crumbled after graduation and they had all been scattered in different directions. Even her marrying Dave had not kept their friendship close. And although she still adored Jonny, perhaps more than she had ever done, and she did most desperately want her life to change, she wasn't sure *how* to do this thing he wanted her to do. She wasn't sure if she could put aside the entirety of *her* life that had grown around her.

There was the question of Caroline – she still wasn't sure that Caroline would be all right at all. What if Caroline became ill again? What if she needed to come back and stay with her? And when would she get to see Charles? He'd been expecting her – and she hadn't had a chance to ring him yet to talk to him. What she would have loved more than anything would have been to talk to Charles, to talk through all of this with him and then she'd know what was the right thing to do – but that wasn't going to be an option in a café on a mobile phone. She needed to talk to Charles properly. Face to face. She needed to see him.

Jonny *had* said it might take ages at the hospital, and it did seem to be quite acceptable to sit alone and dine in Paris – but this was not how she had envisaged the weekend at all. And although she loved flicking through the *Paris Match* she'd bought, she could barely understand a word of it.

One thought that she couldn't get out of the back of

her brain was that Dave had been almost *pleased* that she had wanted to get away. She'd expected him to be sad, upset, angry even. But he'd actually almost looked relieved.

And so now there was Jonny. For the hundredth time that day, she tried to picture what it might be like to be in Africa working together. She imagined them laughing at a joke in the hospital together just like she might laugh at something with Nick or Ronan, only they'd be all colonial-looking and sun-tanned she supposed, which did seem very attractive now as she gazed out of the café windows at the foul, grey Paris night. But on the other hand, perhaps it wouldn't be funny at all in Kenya in the middle of a political crisis. They would just be busy all the time at meetings and in clinics and refugee centres. Some things never change – the constancy of work, the constancy of human need. She dipped one of her frites into the mayonnaise and tried again not to think about Marianne, but that was quite impossible.

Marianne.

In hospital, still convalescing, but nevertheless in the dangerous position of being in the very same city as she, Kate, who was about to spend another night in Marianne's bed. With her ex-husband.

There was a part of Kate that was really quite furious with Jonny for having brought her to Marianne's apartment. On the one hand, it was convenient, yes. And beautiful. And it was to all intents and purposes still his Paris home. But still. In a secret place that she didn't really want to acknowledge, she wished that he had brought her to an hotel. And then from that same secret place, the question begged her – *so why didn't he then?*

Why did he have to bring me to her house?

She put the next frite down again without biting into it. She would love another glass of wine right now, but three was really more than enough. If only he would bloody well arrive. She took her phone out of her handbag and examined it again for missed calls. It was very tempting to ring Nick again, but she didn't know what to say to him and it would sound stupid if she rang him for a second time, pretending to be in Venice. And yet it hurt her more than she could have predicted to think he'd lied to her for absolutely no reason whatsoever. It seemed, all of a sudden, as though everyone she thought that she could ever trust – even Dave whom she'd trusted to be with her all her life – had turned into someone that she didn't know.

There was one missed call from Ronan. She stared at the screen and wished for the first time since she'd left Dublin that she could talk to him now. The one thing about Ronan was that he could accept change quite readily and he didn't react – he absorbed the information when something went wrong, and then he dealt with it. She thought about the night when Veronique was born – how calm and gentle Ronan had been despite the life and death situation which she had placed him in by having to deliver the baby in such poor condition. He'd worked at it as if it was quite routine – and at the same time he'd managed to treat the baby with such devotion, working all night to manage her on the ventilator, and it made her eyes prick now just to think about it. Ronan never blamed people for things that went wrong – he just got on with making sure that they could be sorted out again. And of all her friends in the hospital, Ronan was the one friend she could always turn to who would make sure that no matter what kinds of awful things happened they would always have something fun to look forward to afterwards.

Nick had always been all smart remarks and jokes and was always happy to get everybody laughing – but it was always, Kate now realised, at someone else's expense. Ronan, she now thought wistfully looking at his name on her mobile screen, had been a far, far truer friend – only she had never seen it until now. And now that she was going to Africa, perhaps she'd never see him again. The thought of it brought a sudden pang into her chest and she tried to ring her message server just to see what he had said, just to hear his voice again. But it wasn't working here in Paris.

Would that mean that if Jonny rang, she'd miss his message too if he left one? She bit her lip, and wondered whether or not to send *him* a text message and then remembered that he couldn't have his phone on anyway because he was in the hospital with Marianne. And so she bought herself another glass of wine.

And then suddenly, there he was.

"Hey, gorgeous!"

His black hair was wild with wind and rain and his face rain-soaked when he kissed her cheek. And she stood up to hug him, and they embraced rather clumsily over the little round café table, almost knocking her cold steak dinner on the floor.

"You ordered without me! I told you I'd be coming! I'm so sorry I'm so late. It took ages signing forms and making sure the baby was all right."

He took a frite from her plate and beckoned the waiter, who flew to his side in an instant. Kate watched him rattle off his order in brisk confident French, without even looking at the menu, and she thought about Ronan Clare waving madly at the waiter and making her giggle and all the champagne and chocolate cake she'd had on Friday night; so recently and yet so long ago.

But that had been the most fun she'd had in ages. And she'd spent the whole night out with Ronan talking about herself, and how her job had gone pear-shaped, and how her marriage was in crisis – and poor Ronan had just listened, and bought her champagne and chocolate cake and made her feel as though her dilemma was important, but not insurmountable. He'd allowed her to let off steam and at the same time get on with the job of making sure she had a great night out.

"How's the steak? You've hardly touched it?" Jonny beamed, pinching another frite from her plate. "You weren't waiting for me to start, were you?"

"Yes, sort of," she replied. "How was the International Committee for Africa?"

"Very busy. Difficult and tragic, but there is a lot of work that we can do. But it'll make a huge difference that you're coming with me. What time did you arrive? I'm so sorry I left you waiting, but you can imagine – trying to sort out the flights and paperwork for Kenya as well as the paperwork at the hospital –" He waved his hand.

"How did Veronique get on?" she asked. "I mean, I know the paediatrician who brought her over very well – he is very good." She felt almost as if she needed to *contribute something* to the passage of Veronique across the seas: feeling as though she might be otherwise rather left out of all the *drama* that was going on in Jonny's life. And she also wondered if poor Ronan had had to go back to Dublin on his own, seeing as Nick had now taken this mysterious side-trip.

"Veronique is superb," Jonny replied, and she nodded at the seriousness in his voice. "She has settled down well into the unit, and her feeding is going well and she is nearly on to bottles. I got to give her a little tube feed too, today, so that was nice even though it's all a bit technical rather than cuddly. But I enjoyed it." He smiled, and she smiled back, wanting his happiness, and at the same time feeling almost defeated by it.

"And Marianne?" she asked lightly.

"Good," he nodded, and then began to speak again in rapid French to the waiter who had brought him a large salad and a plate of bread with a bottle of red wine.

"You're so lucky, Jonny, you always get to eat such lovely food!" She watched him examining the wine.

"I'll eat your cold steak though, won't I?" he grinned

at her. "I can see you aren't going to manage all of that. You know, it's so nice to be here with you, sitting eating ordinary café food like this, not having to fuss about some *menu dégustation*, or something. The French have this habit of spending an entire meal *talking* about nothing but the food. And Marianne is so neurotic about meals – she won't contemplate a restaurant unless there's a waiting list. It's lovely being just with you."

She smiled a grateful smile. "It sounds like what Caroline calls 'The Tyranny of Meals'," she said, and he laughed with her. She wanted to touch him then, just to touch his hand which seemed so beautiful forking through his *salade composée* – a smooth, gentle, almost delicate brown hand; even though she'd touched him all weekend she wanted just to see what his hand felt like again.

"Kate, there's one thing I didn't ask you," he said, pouring himself a big glass of Bourgogne. "Did you tell Dave you're here?"

She felt her face becoming hot. "No. He doesn't know," she replied. "He thinks I'm in Venice."

He nodded and smiled briefly, looking quite relieved again, and forked into his salad, pushing pieces of chicken onto his fork with a piece of bread. He was so at home in Paris where she felt so foreign, even if he did say that he felt out of place here. And she wondered if in Africa she would feel at home with him or if she'd never stop feeling foreign, feeling like the odd one out. She wondered then if this was how *he'd* felt at her hospital, sitting around with her in the night-canteen, spilling out his heart to her. Had he felt like she did now, as if he didn't fit in at all, as if he had been beamed onto a planet where there was a completely different species? She looked around her. A restaurant full of strangers, talking to each other. And she with this one man.

She watched him prong some cheese on his fork and wondered just how well exactly did she know this man? This man that she had felt, had so often felt, was meant to be her *soul mate*?

And when she had felt this incredible, this impossible closeness to Jonny Domville, despite the fact that she had *loved* Dave for being always fun and chatty and adoring (once – how odd it was to think that now), she had found with Jonny that it was almost as if they had breathed the same breath: it was as if they had *thought* in unison. She checked his face again to see if he was sensitive to what she might be thinking. But his face was blank.

She smiled a cautious smile at him. "I was just thinking that it's funny how we've been thrown together like this again after all these years and we're sitting here now in Paris, eating dinner in this – this ordinary way. I can't help feeling very strange about it now."

He leaned back in his chair, and looked steadily at her. "I don't feel strange at all. I feel very good, actually, being here with you."

"I'm very happy. Don't get me wrong, Jonny."

"I've always thought you were so beautiful, Kate. Not just on the outside. I mean on the inside. You really are a very beautiful person."

She wasn't sure whether or not to roar with laughter, or just look pleased and make a witty remark, or smile demurely which she was afraid might look a bit like a simper. It was such a ridiculously over-extravagant compliment. But yet there he was, looking at her with such defined sincerity that she felt she was going to have to respond appropriately. She tried the demure smile, which she felt was probably the only possible response, and then felt faintly ludicrous.

"I think I've probably had too much to drink – again!" She gasped a short laugh and wiped her mouth.

"Shall we go home?" he asked her in a low voice, staring at her eyes.

"Home," she echoed back at him.

"I mean to our place. My place. My apartment."

"It's Marianne's apartment." She kept her voice very calm. She felt quite proud of the mature tone she had assumed, but the constant reminder of Marianne made her feel as though she was being electrocuted.

"She isn't there," he said. "She'll never know about this. I'm not trying to hurt her, Kate, but it's completely over between me and her, and you *know* how I feel about you." His voice was like gravel. "I can't help it. It's always been you. You've always been the one." He reached out and took her hands in both of his, and she felt an enormous sense of relief that she could actually reach out and touch him at last.

She examined the long, slim fingers that held hers, relishing the smoothness of him, the way he played with her fingertips again, remembering the talcum powder on her fingernails that night, just outside the operating theatre.

She looked into his eyes. "Let's go, Jonny," she said quickly. "Let's get out of here."

Nick Farrelly pushed open the glass door of the hotel on Rue des Beaux Arts and stepped into the hallway out of the thickening Paris rain. He glanced about him, taking in the trying-to-look-preoccupied concierge and then passed a tiny cocktail counter and walked a little further into the next little hallway of the hotel. He stood still for a moment contemplating what to say to the concierge. Shaking the rainwater out of his hair he looked up, and then almost gasped at the suddenness of the narrow dome that rose out of the central lobby of the hotel, reaching up into the heavens like a magnificent phallic tower above him. He almost fell backwards trying to take in the extraordinary height. It reminded him of what it might be like to stand inside the middle of the leaning tower of Pisa. He shivered slightly from the rain (who would have thought that Paris could be as wet and miserable as Dublin? Hah!) and then slightly dizzy from gazing upward, went back to the reception desk again.

"*La chambre du Monsieur Hardiman,*" he began.

"Good evening, sir. We were expecting you," the concierge said in his perfect Oxford English, giving him a beautifully elegant but at the same time rather cheeky smile. "Docteur Hardiman has left a key for you so you can reach him there. Do you have luggage?"

Nick was momentarily embarrassed. Who would expect anyone to check into a five-star hotel in the middle of Paris on a wet Monday night with no luggage? He drew a breath. *Fuck 'em!* Who cares what they think or believe? This is just routine for hotel people. I could be just going for a business meeting. We could be business colleagues meeting for a dinner or something. Not that the hotel looked in the slightest way business-like. It was the campest-looking place that Nick Farrelly had ever seen.

Jesus, Dave Hardiman is as mad as a flea to have booked us into this joint!

"Er, no, no luggage, *merci*. Just my briefcase!" Nick lifted his man-bag, smiling but, he felt, rather foolishly.

The smooth concierge smiled another sexy smile. "You are welcome to the Hotel. Please let me know if I can be of any more assistance." He handed Nick an envelope with the key.

"Thank you. *Merci. Au revoir.*"

Nick could have sworn the concierge had winked.

He turned about and contemplated the incredible, leopard-skin-carpeted staircase, winding like a magical thing, sharply into the mysterious tower-like dome of the hotel. And then he checked his room number on the envelope: fifth floor. Bollocks.

The hotel was a palace though, Nick thought. Plush drapes everywhere, velvet and tassels and intricate French furniture with lions' feet, and marble, gold, and silk. It was like staying at Liberace's Winter Palace, he giggled to himself as he arrived at his floor. He stepped out onto the landing and looked around him for the room. Beautiful silk wallpaper on the walls, he noticed. Dim lighting from silk lampshades on polished tables in corners, mad-looking carpets. He found Dave's room and slid his key quickly into the door. Red light. He slid it in again. Green and then red again. Bloody things never work properly, Nick grumbled to himself, and slid it in a third time more carefully, swiping it out slowly. Third time lucky. He pushed the door open and cheerfully called Dave's name.

"Hardiman? You there? I'm fucking soaked. It's lashing outside now —"

The silence from within the room hit him like a grave. And then the smell. The unmistakable smell. In the darkness of the unlit room, the mini-bar fridge was the only illumination: but it was enough. A large and heavily furnished, over-luxurious suite with magnificent flowing velvet drapes surrounding delicate French windows through which the beauty of night-time Paris glowed. A giant, silk-covered bed complete with an array of cushions and pillows and a stunning headboard upholstered in gold and red and blue. And in the middle of the bed, stiff and unmoving in the way in which Nick knew was the way that only dead people can lie, was Dave.

He felt that his heart was going to stop.

Dave was lying there naked. Nick crept forward to him, inch by inch, dreading every move that he was about to make.

"Dave," he whispered. And then he sobbed out loud.

He reached out very cautiously and touched his skin. He was cold. Quite cold, really. Not ice cold, but cooler, much much cooler than body temperature would be in this luxuriously heated room. Nick felt rapid nausea rising in his throat and he gagged and coughed. He touched Dave's leg more firmly now. He touched his thigh. The skin was still quite soft. And then he saw it, in the darkness and the lonely little light of the open mini-bar fridge: the syringe that was still clasped redundantly in Dave's left hand, and the ooze of dark black blood that trailed along his groin and into the darker place between his legs where Nick had once sucked him, had so longed to kiss and taste him there and breathe the scent of him again. He felt his stomach lurch and looked round desperately about the room to see what else might have just happened. The mini-bar was emptied, and a dustbin just near it explained how. There was a smell of vomitus in the room? Or was it – Nick shuddered and uttered a small sob again. He really didn't want to know.

Stumbling to find his way back out to the door again, he tripped over Dave's discarded shoes. He gave a brief gasp, and then almost cried. Wrapping his sleeve around the fist of his right hand, he opened out the door again, carefully rubbing the knob of it with his wool-covered hand, his sobs now uncontrollably in his chest. He gulped back the tears and briskly rubbed the outside of the doorknob again, asking himself what the fuck he was doing this for – and yet at the same time feeling that it might possibly be the only sensible thing to do. And then he turned and walked away as quickly as he could, this time taking the steep narrow staircase two steps at a time. He left the building and ran as hard as he could along the narrow dark wet Paris streets to God knows where – anywhere, just to get away from this.

17

At Paris Charles de Gaulle Kate tugged her little suitcase behind her while Jonny checked gates and satellites, *niveau embarquement* and gate numbers. There was a complicated system through glass-corridored flat escalators that criss-crossed and climbed over one another up, up, up into a giant dome: the wobbly corridors were like a cross between a tacky fun-fair and the glass dome of *2001: A Space Odyssey*, and she giggled and told Jonny this, who looked in a puzzled but kindly way at her.

In the bewildering corridors of duty-free stores that stank of cheese and perfume shops she waited for him to finish exploring every international newspaper while she examined cigarettes and liquor, purchasing neither (although Jonny bought a large bottle of whiskey) and she messed around with sprays of Chanel and Gaultier until the shop assistant's prowling pressured her to go away.

They sat very still now, waiting for the flight to Zurich on hard white plastic seating in a large and almost empty departure lounge. She read American *Vogue,* thinking only of Caroline. He read *Le Monde,* scouring every detail of the Kenyan uprising. Outside in the night-time the giant aeroplanes taxied and refuelled and parked their noses up against the glass building, and with every flight that flipped by, *boarded, last call* and *departed* on the screen above her, she felt inside the growing dread – the dread that she had known would have to come eventually.

"I need to ring my father, Jonny. He's expecting me to arrive in Venice and I still haven't told him that I'm going with you," she said suddenly to him, and when he gave his mobile phone to her she knew with just one breath what he was thinking. She had left it far too late for it to be realistic to be phoning Charles now. The truth was, of course, that somewhere deep inside her she knew exactly why she had lÂft it all till this ridiculous last moment. She wanted somehow, wanted desperately in a perhaps perverse and yet at the same time completely unintentional way, for Charles to tell her not to go.

She waited now for the phone answer and there was no reply. Caroline didn't have a mobile phone that worked in Italy. Kate hung the phone up one more time and stared blankly at its useless little screen.

Jonny's screensaver was a photograph of Veronique.

She knew that she could try to ring them both again

when they got to Zurich, or even the next day from Tanzania, but that would be leaving it very late. And it was (she looked for the clock on the phone again, pressing Veronique's little face away) already seven o'clock in Venice.

"They should be home by now." She looked miserably at Jonny. "Unless they've been out all day and then gone straight out for dinner somewhere." The sudden picture that came to her mind of Caroline and Charles happily drinking wine together in a trattoria made her throat tighten. Jonny had been so vague about the amount of time he wanted to spend in Kenya: it was quite ludicrous really.

She didn't care about her job any more – they weren't expecting her back for at least a fortnight, and then who knows? She felt like quitting anyway. There were plenty of other places she could go. Jonny was so full of ideas. He was excited about the prospect of working in Africa, in the middle of what was suddenly becoming civil war. She was worried about the fact that they hadn't had time to get her vaccinated but Jonny had said not to worry about it; he'd give her vaccines when they got to Tanzania, and the NGO had plenty. But they had to get malaria prophylaxis organised as well. She shivered suddenly.

Charles Gilmore had gone to Africa and the Middle East, over there and back again for what seemed like every single year of his working life for as long as she could remember, and yet she couldn't remember him ever worrying about vaccinations or resources in the camps. He had lit up with a new energy every time he had been posted on a foreign mission. The trepidation that she felt now, sitting beside Jonny reading *Vogue* in Charles de Gaulle airport – Charles had never experienced that. It was different for Charles, she knew, travelling in a large group of officers with several other armies. But this was only her and Jonny now.

The little piece of text on the departures screen that she was dreading turned from white to orange. So their flight was boarding.

"Let's get on last, so we don't have to queue," she said desperately, and he nodded patiently.

"Fine," he said, and they waited for the queue of all the other people who were boarding the night flight to Zurich to clear and he smiled at her and touched her nose.

The flight attendants were beckoning them. He stood up. "Come on," he urged, and he reached out for her hand.

She looked at him. "Does Marianne know I'm going with you?"

He stared at her. "Of course not. Why?"

She looked away. "Because."

"Because what, Kate? Because what? She's still in hospital. She doesn't *know*. This is just another foreign field mission to me."

"What?"

"To her. Just another foreign field mission to *her*."

She shook her head. "Jonny, I don't want her to think that I'm just another – you promised me you'd talk to her about it. I don't want to – what about Veronique? You can't leave Veronique!"

"Kate, this isn't the time –"

"Yes, it is! You spent ages with the baby, you spent ages at the hospital. You shouldn't be leaving your baby like this. You should have sorted it out with her."

"She knows I'm going to Africa."

"She doesn't know you're going with *me*!"

"Kate," he sighed. "I can't tell her about you, not just yet. She – she's thrilled about the baby, Kate. That was what she wanted. Our marriage isn't working – she knows that and so do I. But let's not complicate this further. Let's just go. Let's just get away together. Please. Kate, we have to get on that flight now. This is not the time to go through all of this again."

"Jonny, I need to know the answer to this question – what happens after Africa? What happens to us then? I need to be able to speak to Dave about all this. I need to know what to tell people – what to say. Or are you just going to pretend that this all just fell into place – that you didn't mean for it to happen?"

This is just another foreign field mission to me.

"Is it really about me, Jonny? I need to know –" She paused. But she had to say it now or she would never say it. "Jonny, what I need to know is this: are we going somewhere we both want to be, or are you running off on another field mission and I'm being dragged along because I've nowhere else to go?"

He sighed and rubbed his fingers briskly through his hair. "Marianne knows I'm going to Africa. That's exactly where I *am* going so it just happens that she knows the truth. Surely we don't need to make things even more complicated?"

"But it already is too complicated, Jonny!" she cried out loud, and the flight attendants looked at one another. "Everything *about* you is too complicated!"

He was taken aback. "What on earth are you talking about?"

A loud *bong*. The loudspeaker made rapid announcements in English, German, then in French. She heard the number of their flight. Zurich.

But then it would be Tanzania in the morning – and then by UN convoy to somewhere whose name she couldn't even remember now. Kanga-something. And then –

It wasn't going to happen. She knew that by now. If she'd ever been unsure of anything before, she was sure of this. She knew what was the right decision now to make.

She took a breath. "I can't go with you," she said in a suddenly over-confident voice. "And I'm so so sorry that it had to be like this, Jonny."

He stood back to look at her, quite solidly. It was the first time that she'd ever seen a flick of anger in his eyes.

"I'm so very, very sorry," she said one more time but he was saying nothing and she knew that he wasn't going to speak, and she felt grateful for that because if she'd heard his words she would have melted into tears. She stood up from the hard white seat to face him properly, to reach up, touching the side of his face, to let him know that she understood that he was clenching his jaw, and she traced her finger over his tight cheekbone, as if to trace the path of a teardrop, had it only fallen. He let her touch him, steel-eyed, and then he smiled just slightly as the words came out again.

"I just can't go with you, Jonny. I'm so sorry. I really, really am."

There was nothing left to say.

"*Madame Gilmore et Monsieur Domville…*"

"Well. *I* have to go," he said.

"I know," she said. "You go. Just go without me. You'll be better off that way."

"I have to go. There's nothing else to do. I just can't stay away. Not now."

She said again, "I know. I'll see you soon. Whenever you get back. Just phone me soon. Or I'll phone you."

"I have to go," he said.

He took her into his arms and pressed her face against him, kissing fiercely at the top of her head and she smelt the sharp leather of his jacket and felt the metal zipper scratch her raw cheek there. He lifted up her face in both his hands, and for the last time kissed her face before he turned away.

She watched him walk into the corridor that was Gate 19, and the airport roared around her, gloating at her now.

"*Passengers Gilmore and Domville . . .*"

She felt her knees crumble underneath her and then she let her body fall so that she knelt down on the cold tiled airport floor with her head covered in her arms until she couldn't hear it any more.

18

Jonny was right about one thing, she thought, as she awoke to a clear cloudless blue morning in the sparkling snow of the Alps. This is the most beautiful way to get to Venice. A porter knocked loudly on the door of her *wagon-lit* and she heard "*Teekets, teekets! Biglietti! Billets! Fahrkarten bitte!*" in four languages being shouted up and down the train. She tried to read a station sign that they flew through at breakneck speed, unable to see anything but a blur and an empty morning platform, but then she noticed factories in the distance and the familiar logo of a pharmaceutical company sign. They had just entered Switzerland.

The train slid over the black water of the lagoon towards Venice, which was kissed with an early morning mist that would lift much later on that day. Kate felt her heart begin to race as she gathered her things together from her night on the train. The thought of Charles being at the platform to take her in his arms – the thought of seeing Caroline again and seeing that fur coat put to some proper use – she looked out of the window at the sudden maritime landscape that she'd seen so often before, but it never lost its magic no matter how often you came here. The snowy Dolomites had reminded her that it was much, much colder here than in Ireland. And the thought that, even if it was another foreign city, coming to Venice now was the nearest thing to coming home. And really, when you thought about it, that was the only thing that she had ever really wanted to do.

Charles had booked her favourite trattoria on the Fondamente Misericordiae and the staff made a nice fuss of Charles and her and gave them each an amaretto.

"You look so pale!" Charles had exclaimed, and compared his own nut-brown complexion fresh from a week's skiing at Sesto with her own wan cheeks. "You've been working far too hard."

She smiled and let him flap around for her, finding her a pudding from the kitchen that wasn't on the menu, getting the waiter to pick out a special bottle of wine that they kept aside only for him, or so he thought. Kate suspected that the whole finding-a-special-bottle-of-wine venture was a con, but she loved him for it anyway. Caroline left them alone in the restaurant after they had finished eating, to spend the rest of the evening at the

Casino with Luis. Luis, as it had turned out, was a rather shy, gentle, and excessively handsome man who clearly adored her. Kate couldn't have been more astonished. But she was relieved for Caroline.

"I'm so sorry I didn't bring presents," she explained, "but I clean forgot."

Luis, rather charmingly, offered to buy them all presents instead and had taken them on the vaporetto to the market at Rialto where he bought Caroline a glass necklace, a giant cocktail ring for Kate and a huge salami for Charles. They had eaten the salami for lunch with a bottle of wine and a huge minestrone that Luis had prepared the night before. The dampness made Venice seem so much colder than she'd anticipated and the trench coat that had seemed so smart in Paris was useless in the wind that swept up from the sea. Caroline had lent her a neat waist-length Armani fur-cuffed woollen jacket that covered Kate down to her hips, with a little stripey hat that looked like the sort of thing a Christmas gnome might wear, and Kate suspected, glancing at the label, had cost an absolute mint.

After dinner they decided to take a walk through the empty narrow alleyways, to take *una passagiatta* as Charles called it, an evening stroll through the damp back streets to the Piazza San Marco. In the cold damp darkness Charles tucked her woollen-coated arm underneath his own and she clung tightly to him, making him grumble that he was losing his footing on the cobblestones because of her meandering three-legged-race, she grumbling affectionately that a military goose-step wasn't a relaxing evening pace. They walked for over an hour until they got to the very edge of the island, to the mouth of the Canale Grande at Calle di Dio where the lagoon opened out into the sea, into a twinkle of a thousand lights from boats and buoys and guiding lines and the fairytale of Venice surrounded them on all sides with perfect magic.

She gasped and shivered, partly from the foggy coldness and partly from the almost unbearable beauty of it all.

"Let's sit over there." He pointed at a little bench beside the water.

"We'll freeze," she grumbled, and he scoffed at her.

"Nonsense, we'll cuddle tightly. You've got a hat and gloves, haven't you? Come on. Just listen to the silence and the boats and the lapping of the sea against the walls. It's the most beautiful sound in all the world." He tugged her over to the bench and wrapped his arm around her shoulders. He stretched out his legs. "Where *are* your gloves, Katie?"

She grinned. "It's not that cold, really, is it?" she said, cuddling in to him.

Over on Lido, the low-set spread of buildings were like a scatter of fairy dust and the domes and churches on Giudecca and the palaces of the Canale Grande with their subdued lighting were the stage-set for a ghost story. The three islands of Giudecca, Lido and Venice encircling them in a perfect embrace. Sometimes it was hard in Venice to believe that it was all quite *real,* she thought. This is why people come here, people like Charles, to be somewhere that actually was a fairytale, but at the same time, almost unbelievably a real part of the human world – the world of noise and horror and of wars. Kate thought about the people who had lived and worked here for centuries, calmly and meaningfully. The clamour and corruption of it all. It's like a picture for the story of the world, Kate thought, breathing in the damp sea air.

"Daddy, I think that Dave and I are splitting up," she said, very quietly, and she felt Charles stiffen slightly. There was a pause. She tried to imagine what he might be thinking. What did it feel like, suddenly becoming the father of a divorcée? She wondered if he felt ashamed. Or shocked. Or bereaved, even? And then to her surprise, he chuckled.

She looked at him sideways. Charles was smiling an ironic smile.

"So is that why you're in Venice?" He looked at her.

She felt almost affronted by his lack of distress. "I missed you, Dad. And Caroline. I needed somewhere to come home to."

She didn't know whether to feel relieved that he wasn't expressing alarm, or to feel rejected by his ambivalence.

"You're your father's daughter all right," he said looking out to sea again, dreamily.

She said nothing. It was most bizarre, this rather off-beat reaction. She had expected Charles to be at least slightly *emotional*. Perhaps he might have been upset for her – or even embarrassed by her failure. But he seemed to be *unphased*, which she found almost hurtful.

And then he asked more cautiously, "Is there someone else?"

"No. I mean – yes. Sort of." She sighed. "I mean, there was. There is. There still might be – oh, I don't know. But I don't know if that's the real reason. I don't know why Dave and I haven't worked it out. It's been happening long before I started . . ." She looked down at her hands that were clasped into a tight knot on her lap.

"You can tell me," he replied, and then added with a conspiratorial hint in his voice, "It won't be anything I haven't thought of or heard about before."

She drew a breath. "I've been having an affair with Jonny Domville," she said, staring fixedly at her hands.

They sat a moment. She stared down at her hands. She couldn't help but be almost mesmerised now, by the little row of diamonds on her finger, the gold wedding ring underneath, glaring back at her like a clutter of foreign jewels on a thief. She twisted the rings around the base of her ice-cold finger with the tip of her thumb, almost willing them to be too loose for her.

And then Charles chuckled at her again and uttered a long low whistle underneath his breath. He tugged her head in its woolly hat towards his shoulder, nestling it into the crook of his neck. He kissed the top of her head and then lifted her face up in his hand.

"I always knew you two would get up to some sort of mischief, one day," he said, putting a weary sound into his voice, but she could see that there was merriment in his eyes.

"I didn't start the affair to hurt Dave," she began defensively. "The truth is Dave doesn't love me any more." She had admitted it, and it still felt like agony to say it, even now. How horrible to admit the end to something one had been so sure would be forever. She looked carefully again at Charles. "And he drinks a lot. I mean, who doesn't? But he drinks a lot, Dad, all of the time. And drugs. I mean, loads of people party with drugs nowadays – but this is different. He's become secretive."

"How do you know then, that he doesn't love you?" he asked, raising one eyebrow.

"Because he hates me," she replied.

Charles frowned and tucked a few stray hairs back under her hat. "Marriages don't usually end in hate," he said. "They end in indifference."

"I don't find that comforting. I'm sorry, Dad," she said.

"I know. I don't want anything to be painful for you," he replied. "But Kate, you can't just run away when things get tough, you know."

"Why not? What else would I do? Go back in for six more rounds?"

"Doesn't Dave know that you're leaving him?"

"Not as such."

"And have you discussed your feelings, what you've just said to me, with *him*?"

"No," she said. "I can't talk to him any more. He can't listen."

"I mean," he said, "have you told *him* what you have just told me?"

"About Jonny Domville? Oh God no! He's fallen out with Jonny. They fell out years ago!"

"And why haven't you told him that you now want to leave him?"

"I –" she began, and then stopped. She took Charles by the hand. "Because I don't know how."

"And you say you think he hates you? So wouldn't he be pleased then, if someone that he hated went away?"

She frowned at this. Logically he was right. But it was impossible to explain it all to him, really. Not when she didn't even understand it all herself.

He chuckled at her again and squeezed her hand. "Kate, you are much stronger than I was a your age – but I can see you and Jonny and Dave making the same mistakes I made too."

She glared at him. "Meaning?"

Charles sighed. "Meaning running away when things get difficult at home. Not talking about things that hurt, just losing yourself in your work, making your job your life. Hopping on the next plane out of the country and burying your head in the sand. Literally."

"That's not what you did! Is it?"

"Yes it is. And there's plenty of sand to bury yourself in the Lebanon, and Cyprus, and in Bosnia, Somalia, you name it." He looked away from her again, out towards the sea. "I love living here, you know. I miss you and Caroline of course, but I love it here. Looking at the sea, the ships and boats, all the little islands and the water and just thinking. All the ships that sailed from here – bringing riches back to Europe. It was like a great big cultural hub here in the past – it was our connection with Africa, the Far East, the Near East, everywhere. A bit like Charles De Gaulle Airport is today." He smiled at her.

Kate leaned against his shoulder again.

"I left your mother on her own to cope with everything," he said gruffly. "Every single time we had to work something out together, no matter what it was, I walked away. I'd just lose myself in another foreign mission. I didn't want to share responsibilities. And so I didn't face up to the problems she knew we were having. I thought that I was doing the right thing just to let her stew it out." He huffed a short little humourless laugh. "That's what men did in those days. Most men, anyway. But I was leaving her, really, over and over again you know, and forcing her to come running after me – or deal with it." He looked away. "Anyway, in those days, people married and their wives put up with it. But I doubt an army wife would tolerate being walked out on over and over again nowadays – she'd get on with her own career and find another chap who'd stand by her properly." He laughed a short huff-like laugh again and lowered his head, pursing his lips.

Kate she sat up and looked at Charles. "I think that's just what Jonny's doing now," she said. "He's running away because he can't face up to the mistakes he's made in his life either. And that's why I couldn't go with him, in the end. But what does that say about me? That I can't cope with complicated lives?"

"Which of us can?" He looked at her. "All of us run away from complications in our own way. None of us want to deal with things. Caroline – well, she's in good form now but you never know what she's running from either."

"But I need to be able to sort out the complications. I don't *want* to be someone who just runs and hides." She frowned. "I wouldn't go with Jonny because I didn't want to be a part of his hiding from Marianne. But I've done just the same thing, hiding my stuff from Dave."

He turned to search her face again. "Anyone can be tough and brave in their job, Kate, but at home that tough stuff is much harder. You don't walk out on your patients when you can't solve a problem at work. So, don't just run away from things at home when they are tricky either. It will only end in tears. Your mother *died* alone at home and I have never stopped regretting that I wasn't there to hold her, or phone an ambulance, or something. . ."

She squeezed his hand.

He smiled and touched her cheek. "But the point is that I wasn't there because I didn't *want* to be," he replied. "And she didn't need to be alone. She shouldn't have *had* to be alone. She should have had a husband who would *cope* with things. Family life. The ups and downs of it."

They sat in silence for a moment.

"*You're* a coper, Kate," he continued. "You get that combination of resilience and gentleness from your mother. And you get your tougher side from me." He looked at her, twinkling. "Oh yes, you do. Your bossy side. Your arrogance." Kate pushed him and he swayed against her. "Just don't be a fool like I was and think that you can run away from other people's struggles and think that they will disappear when you do. Go home and sort things out with Dave. Dave needs you to be very strong for him. You don't have to agree with him, you don't have to even see his point of view. But you should tell him how you feel. Tell him what you told me here tonight. He needs to hear it, so he does. Maybe then you can give him a chance to fix whatever it is you think he's broken."

"What if it's my heart he's broken?" she asked bitterly. "What if he can't fix that?"

Charles looked solemn. "Then at least go home and *tell* him that. Just communicate. He deserves a conversation at the very least and so do you. Anything can be sorted out eventually."

She nodded, saying nothing. He was right. Of course he was.

She and Dave had solved nothing, and she had two weeks now – well, more like one week really seeing as she'd spent all that time in Paris and now coming here – but she had another week off work before all the chaos would start up again. And she had let Jonny go because she couldn't face deceiving Marianne. She needed to face up to Dave. Maybe she should go back to Dublin now and they should take some time off work together. She should insist on sitting down with him to work out what they were going to do. Even if they *were* going to do it all without each other from now on.

"You're right, Dad," she said eventually.

"There's a flight to Dublin the day after tomorrow," he said. "By this time next week you'll be so much happier than you are now. You will have faced the music and you'll know exactly where you stand. Both of you. And if it doesn't work out for you at least you'll always know that you did the right thing because you tried. And that's the best that any of us can do."

The flight back to Dublin was so beautiful that Kate spent almost the entire time with her nose pinned to the glass, across the snow-peaked Alps in perfect sunshine and then over mainland France, where clouds gathered densely like a cushion underneath. And then the plane flew into Dublin Bay over a sea of steel, a thick blue cloudy desert underneath. The world always looks so perfect when you fly above it, Kate thought. And still below her lay the earth, as full of turmoil as it ever was.

19

Mints, Yoghurt, Newspaper, Soya Milk, Tampax, Raisins, Batteries, Cod Liver Oil.

"As suicide notes go, it's a pretty short one, isn't it?" Connell Jones Cumberton knew he was being smart-arsed but this was all becoming a bit unbearable now.

The policeman gave him a curious look.

"Have you touched it?" the policeman asked Connell.

Connell shook his head wearily. "I hadn't even read it until now."

"This, as well as your business card is all they found on him. He has been identified as a Doctor David Hardiman of Number 92, Percy Place, Dublin 4, and they believe that his wife is also a doctor. We assumed you'd know them both."

Connell shrugged. "I know a lot of doctors."

Connell Jones Cumberton was hardly in the mood

to solve a murder-mystery-stroke-suicide-stroke-drug-overdose. But at the same time the guy, whoever he was, was dead. And he had died with *his* business card in the pocket of his jeans.

The note was just a pretty unappetising-looking shopping list but it didn't ring any bells for Connell Jones Cumberton that morning other than the clanging of a giant hangover behind his temples that reminded him that he had drunk a vat of wine the night before, had concluded his disastrous marriage with his wife, and was now sitting in his office at ten o'clock in the morning of a very unseasonably warm January morning being hounded by two lumpen Garda Siochána. Life didn't get much worse than this.

The heating was turned off in the office building but Connell still felt unbearably sticky, sitting there with the two puce-faced Gardaí. All of us are over-dressed, Connell thought, fingering the fountain pen on his desk while he let his mind crash out.

David Hardiman. Who the fuck? Dead doctor in a Paris posh hotel. Big fucking deal. My head is hopping. My wife has just left me. Am I supposed to care about this stuff?

"Christ on a bike, anybody could have had my business card," he told them, knowing he was being irascible but not really quite caring enough to disguise it. "It could have been passed onto him by a friend."

The cop nodded patiently. "We thought of that."

Connell tried to look contrite.

"The problem we have is that we have to go around and tell his wife," the cop explained more cautiously. "We have driven by the house and she doesn't seem to be there right now. We are going to leave it a few more hours and try again. But we hoped that if you knew him, or her, that you would come with us and help us break the news. It is always better for the family of a deceased in a sudden death like this to have a person that they know with them."

"Better for you lot, you mean," Connell grumbled, and then felt ashamed of his foul mood. He smiled a mildly embarrassed smile at the two stone-faced Gardaí.

"Yeah, I know," he said then, stretching his fingers out and shoving his hands back through his grey flecked hair again. "Breaking bad news to a stranger. It's a pig's life – sorry, dog's life, dog's life it is. Sorry, lads." He blushed.

Stony faces. Deeper shade of puce.

"All right. It's no bother, lads. I'll come with you. But look, honestly, I'm telling you I don't know the guy from Adam!"

"Try your client records," the younger, smoother cop suggested. "It's unlikely that you'd remember everyone who passes through a busy office like this one." He twirled his eyes around to take in as much of the world of Connell Jones Cumberton as he could.

Connell sighed and gathered himself up from his large leather swivel-chair. Try the client records. Piece of cake.

Not.

Of course, this smooth pie-eyed copper wouldn't necessarily know that Connell didn't *quite* know his way around the office computer system yet. (Not that he'd actually bothered trying to learn – Bilijana, his enthusiastic secretary was a complete whizz with computers, so why *would* you bother?) But he thought he'd better make some sort of an effort to appear to be obliging.

"All right then, let's have a look and see what we can find." He sloped off over towards Bilijana's large and barren desk and switched her terminal on. The screen blinked and flickered into life.

Christ, Connell thought, that screen is really far too bright.

He could really do with a coffee.

"Fancy a coffee? Or something stronger, lads?" he asked the cops hopefully.

They brewed up a giant pot of Lavazza Espresso and sucked down thick sweet mugs of it while Bilijana's impeccable filing system revealed absolutely nothing.

"*Nada.*" Connell shrugged his big shoulders, relieved that the task appeared to be resolved.

The cops looked despondent. Connell was actually beginning to pity them by now.

"Looks like you're going to have to visit the wife on her own – I mean, no point in three of us all turning up and her not knowing any of us, now is there?" he ventured hopefully. "Who's his wife, anyway?"

The smoother cop flicked through his paper file one more time.

"A doctor Katherine Gilmore. Same address. Her name was in his passport. I mean, we could just ring her but the protocol is a home visit."

Connell shrugged. Katherine . . . Gilmore . . . didn't ring a . . . *Oh Jesus! I know who that is!* "Oh for fuck's sake!" He slapped a large hand down on the desk top. "I do know her! *She* is a client of mine, not him, you eejits! Oh, God. Poor Katie! Oh my poor poor poor little Kate! Oh, God, this is truly awful." He covered his eyes with his two hands. The cops were sitting up very straight now. "Oh God help her. Oh, poor Kate."

He shoved his hands through his hair again, and this time the cops looked on almost in pity.

Dave wasn't in the house when she got home from the airport and the house was freezing cold. The least thing he could have done would be to have left the heating on! She tugged her case upstairs. Couldn't wait to get a jumper on. Of course, Dave would never have left the heating on when he was out of the house anyway.

But the house felt kind of funny in other ways. She stood a moment in the doorway of the bedroom, just surveying the scene. There were signs about the room that were just not like Dave. Like the clothes that were tossed about all over the place. Underpants spilling out of drawers, tee-shirts dropped unfolded on the chaise longue, a belt dropped on the floor.

That was definitely not like Dave would leave the place.

The thought suddenly occurred to her that perhaps they had been *robbed*. But no. The room wasn't exactly *ransacked*. It was just — well, it was just not like Dave would leave it. In the bathroom his toothbrush and his shaving stuff was gone.

He must have taken it into work with him and have stayed out all last night again.

She sat down on the unmade bed — unmade? That was not like Dave, either. He had always been meticulously neat. It was as if he'd been just rifling through his stuff, not caring about the way he left the place at all, dressing himself in a hurry to be somewhere else.

She picked her mobile phone out of her pocket and tried his number — but just like always nowadays, his phone was switched off.

And then from downstairs she realised that someone was tapping softly at the door. A timid little knock, an apologetic sort of knock on the big brass lion's face of a doorknocker. Well, that couldn't be him, she thought glumly, getting up off the bed to go to look out at the street. He'd have banged the door much harder if he'd known that she was there, and in any case he'd have his keys.

She tried to see if she could spot whoever it was at the front door and noticed that there was a Garda car parked just across the road beside her Mini with two policemen standing by it at the canal. They appeared to be looking at her house. And then it became obvious to her. They were looking for Dave!

The accident. She caught her breath.

Oh, the stupid eejit, he must be in trouble with the cops! He had been drunk out of his skull that night and the cops must have breathalysed him! That was why he had been out all night after the crash and that was why he had been so secretive about where he'd been. He'd been arrested and spent the night in custody!

And then something much, much worse occurred to her.

Perhaps the guards were something to do with drugs.

The gentle little knock again. The cops were watching her at the window and they were waiting for whoever it was who was tapping at her door. She felt her heart thump and a cold prickle spread across her face. She couldn't hide. They knew that she was there. There was nothing else to do but go downstairs and let them in. She walked very slowly down the stairs to answer the front door, dread growing like a lump within her throat.

She opened the front door.

"*Connell?*"

She couldn't have been more surprised. And, well, quite pleased really. Relieved. But Connell looked terrible. Pale, exhausted and worried. And he didn't return her smile. In fact, he looked distraught.

"Kate, I've got some really bad news for you."

She looked past his shoulder at the police car. At the bright sunshine on the canal, at the bald trees and ducks and the blueness of the air outside and all of a sudden she felt as though she were in a film, as though this weren't happening to her at all.

"What happened?" Her voice wasn't even her own.

Afterwards, Kate would replay the words that Connell had said to her as soon as he stepped into the hall, over and over again in her mind, during the nights and sleepless weeks that followed. The bright sunshine outside, the police car, the two uniformed policemen, the duck-egg blue front door, the navy carpet in the hall, every element of that scene would be there in her memory like a frozen frame that she could not move forward or backwards or delete. Connell's rough skin as he put his arms around her and his cheek scraped hers. The wool smell from his coat. And most of all, those words that he'd said to her. The thing he'd come to tell her. The thing that for hours, days even, she found so incomprehensible, so unbelievable, so other-worldish that it was not until after she would see and touch Dave's body that she could actually accept that it had happened.

"It seems that David has been found dead."

Connell put a teacup down in front of her.

"Three sugars," he said nervously. "I think it's always good for situations of shock, isn't it?"

Kate looked up into his anxious face and said nothing. She didn't even feel awake. She felt as though she'd simply stepped into a dream. She had been put inside some completely different version of her life and was waiting to be let back out. It was like being forced to see what it would be like to have to become this other person, a person whose husband had just been found dead in Paris, and so all she wanted was to scream, to tell them that she'd had enough, that they could stop it now. Stop! Stop playing this tape, turn it off, I don't like this world! Turn it off and we can go back to the old one now. And the growing realisation that she couldn't turn it off, that the new world was beginning to settle in and become real, brought a sudden horror to her forehead, creasing it up as if her brain were being crumpled into a vortex. And yet despite that she was sitting here acting as though it was all going quite well for her and looking rather glad that Connell Jones Cumberton was there in her kitchen making tea.

Tea with three sugars sounded absolutely horrible but its horribleness at this moment almost consoled her.

"The paper is relatively glossy." The garda sucked his teeth. He picked the shopping list note up again with tweezers and popped it into another plastic bag. Zip seal. Farewell and goodbye. She felt a sudden rage boil up in her throat.

"Please don't take it away!" she snapped.

The garda breathed out heavily.

Connell sat down at the table beside her and took her hand in his. Kate felt her eyes becoming very heavy now. She felt suddenly very, very tired. She knew that she was not in any shape to argue with the police, but for God's sake, it was only a bloody shopping list she'd written, not a smoking gun.

Dave, who had hardly ever done the shopping, had gone to bloody Paris – Paris! – with a shopping list she'd written in his pocket. It was the only way that she could identify him from here, her glossy pharmaceutical give-away notepaper in her glossy black granite kitchen in Percy Place. Dave, who had ignored every single list she had ever left him, pretending that he hadn't seen them, had kept a stupid shopping list that she had left out on the kitchen worktop on that last morning that she had ever seen him. Dave had left the house, to go to Paris, obviously to look for her and Jonny and then to die, and in his pocket as he had died, as his heart had stopped, as his last breath had drifted out of his body and into nothingness, was her shoping list. And even though she had written it herself, it was the last communication she would ever receive from him.

"Please, *please* let me keep it," she whispered desperately. And then suddenly, she didn't even try to stop the hidden tears from emptying out onto the table. She let her shoulders throw themselves into a howling hunch of roars. Nothing mattered now, except holding on to that stupid note that Dave had kept for her.

How much worse can life become when you end up sitting in your kitchen one night fighting with a policeman over a bloody shopping list?

She looked up at Connell in despair.

Connell coughed.

"Do you really need the fucking shopping list?" Connell growled, and pulled a face the garda.

"We can give it back to you if you like after it's been finger-printed." The policeman looked ashamed. "I'm very sorry for your troubles," he muttered at Kate.

She sniffed and rubbed her face briskly with a tea towel. "You know, I'd really really love for you to go now," she told the policeman in a sharper voice.

"We'll just have a quick look around one more time and then we'll let you be."

Kate took a long hot sip from her over-sweetened tea. She and Connell sat at the table in silence waiting for the gardaí to leave the house. She half-wondered for a moment what Connell must be thinking, sitting there in her kitchen, having only met her just a fortnight ago, but realistically she didn't really care. He was just sitting there cradling his teacup, gazing sorrowfully out the window onto the canal. She rested her head for a few minutes in her hands and then looked up. A pair of ducks sailed by. She looked at Connell's face. He looked as though he'd been up all night.

"Thanks for coming with them, Connell. It's really very kind of you. I don't know what I'd have done if I'd been here alone and only the gardaí called."

He looked miserable. "I just wish there was something more that I could do. You must be – let me know what I can do to help."

She shook her head. "I wish I could ask you to do something but I don't even know where to begin. I can't really believe that this is actually happening. I keep waiting for you to tell me that it's all a huge mistake or something." She looked at him and he lowered his head. "I'll have to phone people, won't I?" she mumbled, and loudly blew her nose.

"I can help with that," he said.

"Perhaps you could phone work for me. Phone Dave's job. I . . ." she looked around the kitchen. "I don't know where to begin with all of this," she whispered.

"I'm here." He took her hand and held it very tight.

The two gardaí came back in to the kitchen.

"We'll be in touch," the smoother cop said to Kate. "And the Department of Foreign Affairs will need to contact you, and the Irish Embassy. Mr Cumberton will probably be able to help you with some of the procedures?" He looked hopefully at him. Connell nodded.

She looked away, new tears spilling over now, sobs heaving in her chest. The gardaí mumbled their final goodbyes and clicked carefully away out of the heavy big front door. Connell took her in his giant arms.

The sugary tea that he'd made actually tasted quite good though. She shrugged him off and turned back to drink some more, rubbing her dripping nose with the back of her hand. Her head felt weak and incapable of making decisions. She wanted silence and she wanted noise. She wanted to be alone and yet she didn't want to be on her own. The house without Dave – forever without Dave now – felt already like a stranger all around her.

She hadn't been here all week.

Dave had been here all alone. The food that was in the fridge wasn't even hers. Dave had bought it. Dave's socks were sitting moulding in the washing machine. Dave's pens and biros and notebooks were spread out on the kitchen table. Dave's sweat would be still smelling in the sheets upstairs. And Dave's awful bloated body was lying stiff and frozen in the Paris mortuary.

"Are you going anywhere, Connell?" she heard herself ask him with a voice that sounded as if it had come from a long way off far away outside her head. The last thing she could possibly have borne, was the possibility of having to be alone again.

He shook his head. "No. I'm taking you out for dinner. And then we are going back to Paris. As soon as you're ready to go out, of course."

Kate stared at him, taking in the many-creased anxiety of his brow, his large and rather flattened nose, his wide and floppy over-talkative lips, the thick curls of his once-black now streaked-with-silver hair, and she almost smiled. Jesus Christ Almighty, where does this guy get off with all the dinners? It felt even more like a completely ridiculous and unreal dream.

"That's crazy, Connell. You don't have to do that."

"Yeah, I know. But I just like having meals with you," he said bashfully. "And we do need to talk, properly you know, about what you are going to have to do first thing in the morning. About going to Paris. To identify your husband, Kate."

"I have to ring my father," she said in a frail voice. "And Dave's parents."

"Well, let's do that now," he said.

"And I have to ring Jonny." She stood up very suddenly. "He's the first person that I want to ring."

"Okay. Take your time. Shall I make more tea?"

She shook her head. And then changed her mind. "Actually, do. Please do." She picked up the telephone from the window ledge. She knew his mobile number off by heart.

Kate bit her thumbnail while she listened to the single French dial-tone, urging it to be picked up. Connell's bustling in the background was inaudible to her – she might as well have been alone. The phone rang out completely after seventeen rings and she re-dialled it, not noticing the large mug of fresh tea he'd placed in front of her. She began to bite the skin around her thumbnail. And then:

"*Allô?*"

It was a woman's voice. High-pitched and sharp-toned. She hung up immediately, and stared at the phone in sudden shock as if it had burnt her.

"Nobody home?" Connell asked.

"He's in Kenya," she mumbled. "Perhaps the phones don't work . . . or perhaps I've got the number wrong." She picked her handbag off the chair and began to rummage for her diary.

She dialled again.

"*Allô?*" It was the same sharp voice.

Kate coughed. "Er, Hello. I – do you speak English? I'm looking for Doctor Jonathan Domville. *Parlez-vous anglais? Je cherche le Docteur Domville.*"

"I am sorry but Docteur Domville is in Africa," the woman's voice replied. "But he has the international phone. This is the Paris address. I can perhaps help you?"

Kate took a breath. Her head felt full of fuzz. The American pronunciation of *ad*-dress.

"Marianne?" she said.

"Yes, this is Marianne Le Normand. Can I help you, Madame?"

Her mouth had gone completely dry. She licked her lips and tried to speak again, but had to cough instead. "Excuse me," she growled, and with a shaking hand picked up the mug of tea Connell pushed towards her. The tea slopped. He touched her wrist lightly but she barely noticed. "I wasn't sure," she said. She stopped herself.

Wasn't sure of what? Of Jonny? Of herself? Of life itself?

"My husband has just died," she said to Marianne at last.

Silence.

"I'm sorry, I didn't quite catch your name? Are you phoning from the UN?" Marianne's voice was softer now.

Kate took a breath. "My name is Kate Gilmore, Marianne. I am a friend of Jonny's. And – I delivered Veronique, actually. I was your doctor in Dublin when you had the baby."

There was a pause.

"Kate. Yes. Gilmore. Yes, I know who you are," Marianne said. "Jonny spoke of you, in fact."

Kate swallowed, trying to make herself audible again.

"Is he still in Kenya then?" she asked Marianne in a clotted voice. It was stupid, of course he was still in Kenya, but she didn't know what else to say.

"Yes, he is. Jonny is in Kenya. But perhaps I misheard you – did you say that your husband had just *died*?"

"Yes. He was Jonny's best friend." There was a longer pause. Then she said through a blocked nose, "Dave has died in Paris, Marianne."

"Oh, my God," she heard Marianne say. "That is just appalling. I am so sorry for you, Kate. What – *euh* – do you know what happened to him? How did he die?"

"I don't know the full story yet," she said, and for some strange reason she was beginning almost to feel comforted by the rather odd conversation she was now having with Marianne. The distress in the other woman's voice was for some reason oddly consoling. Kate suddenly realised that it was now Marianne who was *receiving* the bad news, and that she was the one giving it – and that it was the only relationship with bad news that she was in any way familiar with. How much easier it is to console than to be consoled, she thought.

"I've only just come back from Venice myself, Marianne. I was visiting my dad." She heard Marianne sigh on the end of the line. "And then when I got home the police were here, saying that Dave has been found dead in Paris. In a hotel. And I don't understand it. I just don't understand what could have happened to him. He was booked into this hotel in Paris all on his own. But why, Marianne? Why would he do that? Book into a hotel in Paris, near your flat where – where Jonny was staying – all on his own?"

"He was near my flat?"

"Yes. I think so. A hotel that's on the Left Bank. I thought perhaps – I wondered if he might have been there in some way – something to do with Jonny? It's just that Jonny is the only person Dave knew in Paris, Jonny was there during the past few days, and it's too much of a coincidence for there to be no connection. Only Jonny didn't say anything to me and they haven't spoken to each other properly for years now, and I just don't understand it. I don't understand any of it at all." She was almost talking to herself. *Something to do with Jonny.*

But I was the only thing to do with Jonny that weekend.

There was a pause.

"I haven't spoken to Jonny since he left for Kenya," Marianne said.

Kate felt her face begin to flush. "I spoke to him while you were in hospital, Marianne. In fact we talked a lot – about you, of course." She suddenly realised what she had said, and quickly added, "I'm sorry, I didn't mean that the way it sounded. I mean, we talked when you were very ill."

There was another pause.

"I will phone Jonny to tell him that Dave has just died," Marianne said. "But what do you want me to say to him? About the death?"

"The French police say it's drug overdose," Kate mumbled.

"Oh, mon dieu," Marianne said quietly. "Jonny will be

very shocked." She paused again. "I am very sorry for you, Kate."

"Marianne, I have to go to Paris in the morning to identify him."

"In that case, I am going to help you."

"What?"

"You will need help. With French. With the police. With the newspapers."

"*What?*"

Marianne's voice was low-toned now and business-like. "I suspect you will want to keep the story of this out of the Irish newspapers? And the French ones too, although I don't think it would be of much interest to them. But you will want to make sure there is no scandal in the newspapers back home. That would be very horrible for you, I think."

Kate felt her mouth fill with nausea. "I had never thought of that," she said. She turned to look at Connell who was quietly stirring tea. "Jesus, Marianne," she said as she watched him, "how would the Irish newspapers find out about this?"

Marianne sighed. "Oh, it would be very easy and it would be no surprise if they already know. But don't worry about it. Let me make a few phone calls and we will stop it before it happens. I know just the people to phone in this case. This is the kind of work I am familiar with. Don't worry, Kate. Just come to Paris. Come to my apartment if you like as soon as you get here. I can help you to the mortuary. I can help you with the French."

It was the word mortuary that made her cry.

"I'm so sorry for you, Kate," she heard Marianne say once again.

"I'm going to have to go now, Marianne. Thank you for talking to me. And for telling Jonny about all this."

"He will be devastated to hear," Marianne replied. "Again, I am so sorry for you. But come to Rue Cujas in the morning, Kate, as soon as you get to Paris and we can sort things out."

"How is Veronique?" Kate asked.

"She is wonderful!" said Marianne, her voice suddenly warm again. "Really wonderful since coming back to France. Thank you for asking about her."

"Thank you for talking to me," Kate said. "I'll see you tomorrow." And she hung up the phone.

Connell's eyes looked as though they were itching with inquisitiveness.

"That was the woman who is suing us," said Kate.

Connell's eyes looked as though they were about to pop right out of his head.

"Don't ask," said Kate. "It's all a bit complicated."

Connell coughed loudly. "Drink your tea," he said.

"I've been having an affair with her husband," Kate continued.

Connell choked and began another fit of coughing. Kate slapped him gently on the back. He loosened his tie and then looked at her with his thick eyebrows raised.

"But it's over now," she said, and poured herself more tea, adding three more sugars. She offered the sugar bowl to Connell. "Here," she said. "We'll both be diabetics if we get any more bad news."

"Thanks," he wheezed, still winded after the coughing fit. "Well. That's good to know. From the point of view of the defence."

Kate gave him a judgemental look.

"I'm sorry," he looked down again. "But you've got to admit that this does thicken the plot, just slightly."

"The whole world has just gone crazy, Connell," she said in an empty voice. "Do you think I care any more about being sued?" She sat back down beside him, staring into space. "All my life I thought that doing the safe thing was the right thing to do. I just wanted things to be ordinary and predictable. And now look. How could Dave do this to me?" She turned to face him angrily now. "How could he go to Paris without telling me where he was, and leave me with this *mess*?" She began to cry again and didn't try to stop it now. "We had everything!" She thumped her hand down on the table. "We had it all. This house, great jobs, good friends – and we both had one very good lifelong friend. Jonny. And I loved them both. And that's how it got all screwed up somehow, and I don't know why, but nobody tells the truth to anyone any more. And now Dave is dead. How the hell do these nightmares happen to just ordinary people?" Her hot red tear-stained face searched his.

"Nobody is just ordinary," Connell replied. "Everthing is chaos, really. My wife's just left me. Out of the blue. Gone off with your boss, actually."

Kate bit her lip and then began to blow her nose loudly again. "I'm really so sorry to hear that, Connell," she said in a quieter voice.

"When you think about it," he said gloomily, "all the personal crises that you have to deal with in life, it's a wonder anything ordinary ever gets done by anyone." He stared at his teacup. "I think we are being absolutely bloody marvellous in the circumstances. Both of us."

She smiled slightly. "Thanks for being so understanding," she said.

"Do you want me to make the rest of the phone calls?" he asked.

She shook her head. "No, I can manage those. There are no more weird surprises. Just stay with me, Connell, while I talk to Dave's parents, please. If you don't mind, that is. They can be a bit funny."

"No problem," he replied. "I said I'd make the phone calls for you. And I'll book us some flights to Paris in the morning and organise a hotel. I take it you're not *staying* in Paris with Madame Le Normand, are you?"

"No, of course I can't." She looked at him and saw that he was joking. "But are you really going to come to Paris with me? You don't have to do that, Connell," she added quietly. "You've been far too kind already."

"Well, I can't let you go over on your own. I don't know what you'd get up to – sorry," he added quickly.

She smiled again. "Perhaps we should have something stronger than just tea to drink."

She looked helplessly around the kitchen as if it was

all at once quite unfamiliar to her. She realised that she had no idea if there was any alcohol left in the house. You never knew with Dave. You could buy a case of wine in for New Year's Eve and find that it was full of empties by Christmas. Whole litres of duty free that people brought from holidays mysteriously disappeared. Caroline had brought champagne, but they had already drunk all of that. She stood up to inspect the contents of the cupboards above the glistening granite counter tops, noticing for the first time how cold they felt to touch now, how like marble gravestones all her kitchen fittings were.

At the back of a neglected cupboard of tinned things she found a half-full bottle of sweet sherry, probably something she'd bought once to make a trifle for Charles who loved that sort of thing. She pulled the cork out and sniffed it cautiously: nothing undrinkable about that, she decided.

"Cheers?" She waved the bottle at Connell.

"Why not?" He lifted his teacup up to her and let her splash some in. She emptied the rest of the bottle into her own cup. Sitting down wearily again, she opened up the desk diary that they kept beside the phone, and checked the first phone number that she had to ring, for Paddy and Annette Hardiman, Dave's mum and dad.

20

Bizarrely, Paris was full of the most gloriously unseasonable sunshine. Connell had, despite a crushing hangover, been able to pull together business class flights on Air France and a four-star hotel in the 6th *Arrondissement* that was near enough to the Institut Médico-légal which they had been informed by the Irish Embassy was exactly on the right bank of the Seine just opposite Gare d'Austerlitz.

But the cold wintry morning sunshine made the place seem somehow even sadder now to Kate than last weekend's freezing rain had done.

She wanted first thing in the morning to visit the hotel where Dave had died. Connell's secretary was a genius, Kate thought, to have found a hotel for them at zero notice that was just a ten-minute walk from both Marianne's apartment and Dave's hotel, which at the same time did not appear on first inspection to be too close to either. The Boulevards Saint-Germain and Saint-Michel acted as a sort of duo of barriers against both, which satisfied her greatly, making her feel cocooned and relatively safe.

She and Connell walked slowly now in pale morning sun towards the Rue des Beaux Arts and she barely noticed the cafés and tiny shops and markets that buzzed merrily with life on a warm January morning. She felt numb with tiredness after a sleepless night and very early flight. They almost missed the hotel. It was such a strangely *discreet* building, with an extraordinary ram's head mounted on the doorway. The ram's head was absolutely hideous, Kate thought. And then she saw the plaque to Oscar Wilde.

"Are you sure this is the place?" she said. "He normally goes for bigger, much more comfortable places."

"I think that this is very posh inside," Connell explained softly.

A very rock-and-roll-looking young American couple emerged from the hotel, squinting in the daylight. They reminded her of what Caroline and Luis might look like after a good night out.

"It's that hideous ram's head." Kate suddenly shivered in the narrow cobbled street out of the sunlight. "Let's just go, Connell. Let's just go to the mortuary. Please."

He took her by the arm and they walked quickly back up the tiny street towards Boulevard Saint-Germain to get a taxi to the *Institut*. Kate wanted to pop back to their hotel briefly to take some headache tablets that she'd left in her toilet bag, and so they crossed the boulevard and Connell waited for her on the main road near the taxi rank, and when she came back down with her sunglasses, she found herself standing looking at Connell who was waiting for her at exactly the same spot in front of the Café Danton where she had seen Nick Farrelly only days before.

Nick.

Nick had been in Paris on that horrid wet, rainy night that Dave had died.

Oh, God! Nick was visiting him when he died! That was why he'd lied to her about being in Paris! He knew that Dave was dead! And although the sudden realisation of what that meant was beating a rhythm into her head that felt like a hammer (*Nick was with him when he died!*) she had to ring him now. She had to speak to Nick. She had to find out what had happened. And then she suddenly realised that perhaps Nick didn't *know* that Dave was dead. Perhaps they'd been together at first but then Nick had gone home – or what if Dave had still been alive when Nick phoned? Or if Nick had been killed too? She scrolled her phone desperately, searching for him, unable to say anything to Connell who was waiting patiently at her side, unphased by her sudden panic. Nick's phone rang out. And rang out. And rang out again.

"He was here!" she said desperately to Connell. "He was in this very spot last week!" And she began to cry with the sheer frustration of it all.

"Dave was?" Connell asked.

She shook her head, frantically dialling Nick again.

"No!" she said. "But his friend was! Nick Farrelly. He's a friend of mine. And he was here!" she sobbed. "I saw him here! I was sitting in that café, I was waiting here for Jon. And now Dave is dead. They were in Paris together, I just know it, Connell! That's who was with Dave!" She looked up at him in anguish. "I have to speak to Nick and find out what happened. Why he died! What was happening when he died!"

But no matter how often she dialled Nick's number, there was never a reply. Nor would there ever be.

The Institut Médico-Légal was, just as the people at the embassy had said, a small low brown-brick building nestling down between bridges and flyovers and the railway line. It sat there humbly behind a crop of trees that enclosed a small public garden in which, curiously, a number of children played. But there was no atmosphere of peace.

Trains rattled by. Traffic screamed across the bridge. The river spread out underneath and boats patrolled like surveillants. They stood a moment at the entrance, in the roar of traffic, just taking in the meaning of the building until an icy blast of wind from the Seine forced them shivering to make a move. She walked slowly up the path that led to the stone steps, Connell almost as a reflex took her arm. Together they ascended the stone steps to the very grand doors of the *Institut,* like a rather odd macabre duo of robots.

Inside there was a large hall that reminded her instantly of Baggot Street Hospital. And then more doors, glass this time, with a sign saying *Accueil Des Familles*. Inside the building there was a great attempt to create an atmosphere of reverence, solemnity and peace – but all the grandeur led inadvertently to austerity. A small internal courtyard garden had been created as a feature for mourners, which could have been beautiful had it not been overlooked by a row of busts on pedestals that only reminded Kate of decapitations.

"I'm so frightened," she whispered to Connell. "I can't believe I'm actually really here. Doing this."

He tucked his arm around her shoulders.

"*Madame.*" The desk clerk addressed her. She stepped forward and began explaining who they were, and the clerk stood up very gracefully and extended her hand to Kate, holding it warmly in both of hers. It was an extraordinary gesture of compassion and the last thing she had expected from a civil servant, but Kate felt overwhelmingly touched. A man appeared from what was clearly the laboratory area. The desk clerk spoke briefly to him and he clasped her hand as well, speaking softly and her eyes filled up at the sheer decency of the effort they were making to be reverent. And then she heard them speak to one another, and to Connell, and she heard them say *la veuve*.

I am a widow, Kate thought. *La veuve.*

Connell steered her towards the view of the little garden while they gathered paperwork for her, and then they called her over again to join them, and Kate followed the direction that they took, towards the mortuary.

She was reminded suddenly of Emily Dickinson – whom Dave had loved. "*Because I could not stop for death, he kindly stopped for me.*"

Dave had gone away somewhere and his body was quite empty now. The eyes closed, the skin rough with a slight growth of a beard that Dave would never have allowed in life. His hair seemed strangely fake to touch, stiffened perhaps with the embalming chemical. And the coldness of the waxy skin strangely consoled her.

He was most definitely gone.

"*C'est lui*? *Votre mari, Madame*?" she heard the voice.

"Yes – *oui. C'est lui*," she said. "It is my husband. And he's gone away somewhere."

She could easily see that now. The nothingness of everything. And then suddenly she couldn't see anything at all.

"You will feel better after a cup of tea," Marianne said from the front seat of the taxicab. "The police will do the rest of the work to find your friend Nick. There's nothing more that you need to do."

Connell's big paw of a hand touched Kate's fingers lightly and she was tempted to play with his giant Claddagh ring for some reason, wanting to feel the micro interdents between the two hands clasped around the heart there.

"Why do they make the hands so tiny and the heart

so big?" she asked him and he kissed her on the top of her forehead.

He wrapped an arm around her shoulders and let her rest her head onto his chest. His coat smelled of spiced aftershave and of cold.

"You have been to Paris before?" Marianne said to Kate as she stood in the hallway.

Kate looked up at her. "Yes." She looked down again.

"Recently?"

"Yes. I visited Jonny here," Kate said in a humble voice.

Marianne raised her eyebrows and said, "Ah."

Kate felt thirsty and weak again and her headache was pounding harder now but she said nothing else.

Marianne took her coat and led them both into the kitchen. Kate tried to avoid Connell's curious face, but couldn't. She looked at him. His face held a mixture of surprise and bewilderment.

The apartment was so cosy though, after the cold staircase, and she and Connell sat down in the elegant little kitchen at the table where only days ago she'd sat with Jonny and drank wine and made love.

Marianne filled a large whistling kettle from the tap.

"You seemed to recognise this street. Connell on the other hand did not. I notice things," she said, placing the kettle on the gas cooker.

"Yes," said Kate.

They fell silent again and she and Connell watched Marianne take down china cups from shelves, the dainty blue and white china that was painfully familiar to her now. The familiarity of it all was unbearable. She wanted to be able to say, I've been here before! I know this place! She wanted to be able to tell Marianne the truth about them all. It made her feel sick to know what a hypocrite she was being. She was doing to Marianne just what Nick had done to her, hiding her intentions, manipulating a friend.

Marianne was absorbed in arranging tea things in a business-like fashion. Kate watched her, her discomfort growing as she watched the banal ritual of tea being arranged and then she shook herself. She was here for a reason.

"Marianne," she began, "I can't remember much about what happened at the Institut. I mean, after I fainted and so on, I just – what happens now, I mean? With the post-mortem and the funeral and all that stuff?"

"There is a *code de procédure pénale*," Marianne said carefully, sitting down beside her at the table.

"Oh my God!" Kate looked at Connell. "This sounds so awful already."

The kettle shrieked.

"Don't worry, it will be explained." Marianne got up and put one tea-bag into a glass teapot and poured boiled water over it and set it down in the middle of the table. "I thought you would prefer tea? Than coffee?" she said sweetly to the pair of them.

"I'd murder a cappuccino," Connell said. Marianne looked astonished.

"Coffee?" he repeated.

"Yes," she said. "I know what cappuccino is," she said in a rather stiff voice. "But I can't make it here. Will a plain French café crème be all right for you?"

"*Parfait!*" Connell clapped his hands together.

She smiled gently and got up again.

"No, don't to that. Here!" He stood up quickly and put his arm around her shoulder. "You're just out of hospital. Tell me where the coffee is and I'll get everything."

She looked slightly prickled, but sat down again and pointed at the shelves. "It's all over there. And thank you for that. Now I can talk properly to Kate."

Connell had already started pottering around the little kitchen.

Marianne turned back to Kate. "So," she began, "there is a complicated procedure for the death now, but we will figure it out, no?" She poured herself and Kate cups of very weak unappetising-looking tea.

"So," Marianne cupped delicately long hands around her drink, "what will have happened is that an officer of the *police judiciaire* goes to inspect the scene and check that the person is dead."

Kate nodded. "Yes. I know that," she said in a thick voice.

"The purpose of this is to establish the cause of the death – whether or not it was a suicide, accident or foul play."

"Foul play." Kate echoed the words. *Foul. Play.* As if it were a game, she thought.

"Yes. I think you understand what that means?"

"It means murder," Kate replied. The picture that came suddenly to her mind was Nick, standing at the corner of the Boulevard Saint-Germain with his phone in his hand, and she made a desperate attempt to drive it rapidly away.

"Yes," said Marianne. "But this visit has to be carried out in the presence of witnesses – ideally in the presence of the *chef de maison,* or two other witnesses."

"Nobody would murder Dave," Kate said.

"The police said that he had a visitor, it seems," Marianne replied. "But, the initial examination seems to conclude that the visit happened after Dave had died."

"But how could Nick have visited Dave *after* he died?" She stared at Connell.

Marianne put a hand on top of hers. "The investigation is a two-fold thing," she said. "The office of the *police judiciaire* is acting on behalf of the *Procureur de la Republique.* The *Procureur de la Republique* must be immediately informed if there is a suspicion of foul play, and she has to *authorise* the police to remove evidence or anything pertaining to the enquiry."

"The shopping list," Kate said in an empty voice.

"Yes. They removed that to send to Ireland to help identify you, it seems. But here is where they have fumbled." Marianne looked at Connell who was busy watching coffee boil. "The *Procureur* did not authorise the removal of the shopping list. When I telephoned today, there was no record of its judicial removal. This means that there was an irregular act of investigation. And the police don't have the authority to search the premises until the *Procureur de la Republique* gives them the authority. They can't make the – the er, *saisies*? Er, it means to confiscate, to grab, remove . . ." She waved a hand at Connell. "Seizures," he supplied. He added milk to his coffee and sat down again.

"The seizures," she continued, "have to be carried out in the presence of a witness. They can remove a weapon, a suicide note, a rope, et cetera . . ."

Kate buried her head in both her hands.

"They may remove the *saisies* only after the *Procureur* directs them to do so," Marianne continued. "When he has considered what the police find, the *Procureur* may decide to instigate an enquiry to find out if it was foul play or suicide, et cetera."

"An inquest," added Connell.

"But," said Marianne, "there is a possible witness to the death, and they cannot really outrule foul play if there is another person who is yet unknown."

Kate's head felt as though it was about to burst. It was all way too much. Marianne was being very patient, but the legalese, and then the French version of the legalese – *Jesus!* She wanted to just scream. She felt her throat constrict again.

"Nobody would murder Dave!" she said roughly to the two of them.

Marianne nodded. "But, in my mind there needs to be an *inquête*, Kate. So," she looked at Connell, "this will take a lot of time. And time causes problems with newspapers, stories, rumours, et cetera." She waved a hand around again. "This is where my office helps. If we telephone the right people we can swiftly have a judgement on the newspapers which will block the story pending investigation. At this point, various things still have to be checked. If the door was locked from the inside, for instance. If there was a break-in. If the room was untidy. Or if there was a struggle. So, the *Procureur* may instruct the judge to open again the case – it becomes a criminal investigation. The Institut Médico-Légal will probably help with more things like the funeral," she ended cautiously.

There was a very long silence. Outside, the traffic and the river and the cafés of Paris carried on. In here, time was standing still.

"Marianne, you are being so kind to me," Kate said flatly.

Marianne lifted her teacup. "Jonny loved him," she replied.

"You knew that they were friends?" Kate asked.

"Yes. I knew. I knew that they were, long ago. Jonny called him when I had Veronique. We hoped that he might have visited the hospital but . . ." She shrugged her shoulders, shook her head and sighed. "I am so sorry for you, Kate."

"I know." She looked at Marianne. "I loved him so much, you know."

"Of course," Marianne said politely.

"But," Kate said very softly now, "there's something

else I haven't told you yet. It's just that when we were students, long ago, I was in love with Jonny too. Before he met you, of course. Long before."

Connell who had been sitting silently sipping his café crème spluttered loudly and choked on a mouthful. "Pardon me," he coughed in between wheezy gasps.

Marianne's face had become very pale. Connell looked around the room in desperation.

Kate couldn't look at Marianne again. She put her face into her hands instead.

Then she heard Marianne loudly putting a teacup down. In her ridiculously childish hiding place behind her hands she felt small and foolish. She could hear Connell breathing heavily through his nose. And then she took her hands away again and clasped them both together in front of her face in a prayer position. Marianne's expression was almost Botox-blank. Connell coughed, eyes resolutely down.

"I've known Jonny forever, you see," Kate pushed on. "I loved him and I thought I'd always love him. And he had feelings for me too. But the thing is, now that I know what's happened between you two, I can see he loved you more. I know what he is like, you see." But it was going from bad to worse.

Marianne stood up rapidly, her chair scraping on the tiles like a sudden scream.

"You asked me to help you –" Marianne began.

Connell's eyes were popping open.

"I . . ." Kate looked around her helplessly. "Actually,

you offered to help me, when I rang you," she said, realising the abysmal inappropriateness of it all.

"Would you like us to leave?" Connell mumbled.

Marianne stood back from the kitchen table slightly. She appeared to be unsteady on her feet and having difficulty swallowing. Kate leaped up, reaching her hands out for her, and the table wobbled, slopping tea onto the tablecloth.

"I'm sorry!" Kate began to make a feeble attempt to wipe it off, and the tea stain spread, until Connell placed a large hand over her wrist and hooked her with his eyes.

Kate sat down again. "Okay."

Marianne had turned her back to Kate and was possibly crying, Kate thought – in the very long silence she was sure she could hear something, very heavy breaths being taken, and she watched her helplessly. Marianne was leaning forward, balancing herself with both hands heavily on the edge of the sink. Kate closed her eyes again. She didn't want to look at Connell.

But despite the atmosphere of horror that she had just cracked open in the kitchen, she was determined to be able to fix things between herself and Marianne. Closure, Kate thought to herself. This is what we all need – closure now.

"Marianne, I discovered something today about my husband, Dave, and that's why I decided I should be more honest with you about what happened between me and Jon."

But Connell was cringing visibly.

Marianne turned around to stare at her. "And what marvellous decision have you made now, that you speak about?" she barked.

Kate drew a breath. "I decided to tell you, Marianne, about Jonny and me because I hated myself for hiding something about my feelings about you, from you. You are a good, kind, clever woman –"

Marianne harrumphed.

Kate jumped. She swallowed hard and took a breath. "But I was – oh, jealous, I suppose. Threatened by you. I thought I still loved Jonny, you see – it had lasted inside me for years and years even though I hadn't even seen him since before I married Dave. But the truth is that Dave and I had a terrible marriage because I couldn't let Jonny go. And both of us made huge mistakes. I would give anything if Dave could still be alive, and I could –" and she stopped, her voice smothered with a sudden flood of tears.

Connell produced a large white cotton handkerchief and Kate took it from him with some suspicion. It was, as she had predicted, a napkin from an upmarket Dublin restaurant.

Marianne sat down again. "Have you spoken to Jonny about David's death?" she asked in a very cold voice.

"No. I came here to Paris just before Jonny left for Kenya. I left him at the airport actually. Then I went to Venice to see my dad and when I came back to Dublin to try to sort things out with Dave I found that he was dead. Jonny was the first person that I tried to ring. But then – well, you answered." She looked down again. "So I haven't spoken to him about Dave." She looked up suddenly. "Have you?"

Marianne nodded. "He cried," she said more softly. "He wept when I told him on the phone. He is in Kenya – of course, you knew that – and he is emotional about the elections and the violence, of course. And then he –" Marianne shrugged her shoulders.

Kate saw her huge liquid brown eyes had just filled up and she reached out to Marianne's hand again. The Frenchwoman flinched underneath her touch, but she didn't withdraw.

Then she said, "You know all about our marriage," and she pulled away her hand, glaring at Kate with new coldness.

There was a very long pause. Kate rubbed her nose and tried hard to think how best to answer this. "The only thing I know is that you are divorcing and that he feels that it's his fault," she eventually said, holding Marianne with her eyes. "I think, ultimately, Marianne, that for him being with me again was a way of trying to get over losing you. Which isn't easy for me to admit, either."

Marianne straightened back her shoulders again. "He brought you to Paris," she said to Kate, "like a dog proudly brings home a rat that he has caught."

"Oh, that's too harsh, Marianne!" Kate said.

"I know," said Marianne. "It hurts, doesn't it, to be treated like a prize?" She stiffened again and then said in a gentler voice, "But Jonny was always cruellest to those who love him most."

Kate said nothing. There was another very long pause. Connell breathed out noisily.

Had he been holding in his breath all this time? Kate wondered.

"You have to go to the Irish Embassy in the morning?" Marianne asked her. Kate nodded.

"Well. So. We are going make a phone call now to the *procureur*, and the *ministre*, and we'll put a stop to the newspapers for the morning, and the Irish ones, too, of course. That's why we need to phone the *ministre*. Let's see," Marianne picked a pencil up and tapped it impatiently on the table, "what else? Oh, the autopsy. You have made a request for that examination to take place after the identification, so we should write immediately to the *procureur* to request the report – presumably tomorrow."

Marianne curled her bottom lip inwards, and the two women looked at one another.

"You are very efficient. And you have a lot of dignity," said Kate.

"I have what the Americans call a very *legal* mind."

Connell stirred slightly.

Marianne carried on, pointedly. "Logical, evidence-based, conclusive. You are a scientist. You can relate to that, surely?" she said coldly.

"Why are you suing me, Marianne?" Kate asked her, still holding her eyes.

Marianne started. There was a pause. Then she said,

"Legal action is sometimes the only way to find out what we need to know, isn't it?"

"Sometimes, but actually, most of the time, it isn't," Kate replied.

Connell covered his eyes with both his hands this time.

"I really really wish that Veronique's delivery had gone better for you, Marianne," she said in a quieter voice. "If there was anything I could do in my life that I could do better, it would be that one thing. If there was just one night I could re-live and make it different it would be to make that delivery easier for you. But I need you to know I did my very best for you that night. I really did. I want you to believe that."

Marianne stared at her. "I am sure that you did," she said eventually. "But I needed to examine my own case file, naturally. And I needed to understand it. I merely sought my own expert opinion."

"And?" Kate said.

Connell peeked through his thick fingers at her face.

"My physician here in Paris feels that I was very lucky to survive that night," Marianne said in a lower voice. "I hadn't realised until she examined the evidence I received from your hospital how very close to death I was. And the baby," she looked suddenly at Kate, "you managed to save the baby. At that gestation, and so small and sick. The physician whom I have in Paris was impressed by that," she ended very quietly.

Kate said, "Thank you for saying that."

Marianne nodded.

"You had a wonderful paediatrician, too, by the way. You were very lucky there," Kate reminded her, thinking how hard Ronan had worked night after night on Veronique.

"I needed to see the evidence myself, you understand," Marianne said. She looked carefully at her. "And I needed to get back some control over my life. Everything had gone wrong, for me. You understand? Everything. I needed to take charge again. It's what I'm used to. I am used to being in charge. Surely you can understand all of that?"

"I understand," said Kate. "I understand completely."

Marianne tucked a stray rib of her heavy frame of hair behind her ear and seemed for a slight moment to be lost for words. Kate said nothing, wanting now to let her speak. Connell was still sitting, eyes behind his hands, terrified to look at either of them.

"I know I really am very lucky," Marianne said eventually. "I have something most women long for. I have Veronique. And I know now that she was all I ever wanted, really."

"You have Jonny too," Kate said to her.

"Not so much," Marianne replied. "Jonny was right when he told me that I wanted the baby more than I wanted him. I knew he did not want children, but I did." She smiled ruefully. "Jonny wants desperately to be loved – but he can never bear the consequences. He is always living in the ideal rather than the real." She looked carefully at Kate. "You can't ever really know Jonny," she said, "because he doesn't want to have to know himself."

435

"Why aren't you more angry with me, for trying to take him away from you?" Kate asked her, and she could feel Connell wince again beside her.

Marianne appeared to think about this for a moment, and then she said, "The thing about Jonny is that he's always leaving – he's left all of us – at one time or another, I suppose." She looked knowingly at Kate. "And I suppose the only thing that you can do is to leave him first before he can leave you." She looked at Connell who was sitting very still, and then at Kate again. "Jonny wants nothing more than intimacy," she said, "but he fears nothing more."

Kate nodded. "Poor Jonny. Poor Dave. Poor us!" She looked at Connell. The three of them sat, eyes glued to one another.

"Has anybody thought about having dinner?" Connell suggested in a rather cautious voice.

Kate almost laughed. "I couldn't possibly think about it if you paid me," she replied. "What time is it anyway?" She looked about her for a clock, "I have to meet Caroline and Dad at the *Gare de Lyon* at nine."

"I would like to have dinner with you, Connell," said Marianne.

Connell's pale blue eyes lit up like stars. He twinkled merrily at Marianne. "I've got a reservation at Le Comptoir, at the Carrefour de L'Odeon," he said with an unmistakable air of mischief.

Marianne's eyebrows shot up and she opened her liquid-brown eyes at him like a Disney cartoon.

"*Oh, la la!* You know Paris dining, Connell! How did

you get such reservations? They are all booked up for six or eighteen months!"

Jesus, she's actually flirting with him! Kate thought to herself in amazement.

"I'm a regular." Connell winked slowly at her.

I've seen it all, Kate decided, staring at them both. The only person who could possibly be as neurotic as Marianne was about food, if what Jonny said was true, was definitely going to be Connell Jones Cumberton.

She stood up, the chair scraping loudly on the tiled floor again, and pulled her coat up with her. "Does anybody mind if I go to the station? I don't want to miss their train. I'll go back up to that taxi rank where we were earlier and get a cab."

Connell looked at her guiltily. "Would you mind if I didn't come with you?"

She shook her head. "Of course not. You've done enough for me today. *Bon appétit!*" She smiled at both of them.

"Telephone me tomorrow after you have spoken to the *Institut*," Marianne said, averting her eyes. "Actually, I'll be at the hospital, then I'll be at my parents. Telephone me there on Jonny's cell-phone. Like you did before."

Kate nodded. "I'll let myself out, Marianne." She turned to leave the room. "Thank you both for being so wonderful." She stood a moment in the doorway, searching Marianne's face for absolution.

The Frenchwoman nodded. And then she smiled just very briefly, a small but not too sad a smile, at Kate.

21

Ronan Clare didn't know what to think any more. First Nick, and now Kate, had gone away on what ostensibly had been declared to be short winter city breaks to get out of Dublin and now neither had come back. And there was a rumour going around the hospital that Kate's husband had disappeared too – and although Ronan didn't know him very well, he knew all too well that Kate and he had been having – well, the truth was, of course, that Kate had never *really* told him the full story. But he'd always known from the way that she spoke about Dave, that they were having what Nick would have termed *issues*. But where the hell *was* Nick, anyway?

Ronan hadn't really paid attention to what Nick was going on about after they'd left the American hospital and gone to have a *croque* and a couple of beers with someone in a bar nearby. Ronan was furious of course that they had to go back to Dublin the same night they'd gone over, but Nick was full of giddiness and he wasn't listening to a word that Ronan was saying either. He had flirted unashamedly with the waiter who had looked like thunder (which had only amused Nick more) and then had slapped twenty euros down on the counter, checked his text messages and said to Ronan that he was going to have to leave him now, that Ronan was to fly safely home again but that he was going to hang around Paris for a few more days. Sorry just to spring this on you, Ro, but there's something here that I'd much rather be doing now so cheerio! And then he'd whisked off towards the Métro.

And he, Ronan, had gone back out to Charles de Gaulle airport feeling more than just a little bit put out. And now, here he was back in Dublin and there was still no sign of Nick. And, even though he'd expected her back from Venice by now too, there was no sign of Kate either. His two best friends had suddenly vanished in a puff of smoke.

He'd tried to ring her several times when Nick had disappeared so strangely that night, but she hadn't even picked up. Ronan scrutinised the dialled numbers list in his log on his mobile, and counted twenty-three calls that he'd made to Nick, and three to Kate today already – and still nobody home.

Kate had been hinting to him that she was up to something that night he'd taken her for champagne in the Shelbourne, the last night he'd seen her. The Friday before he and Nick had flown to Paris. She'd even made a Freudian slip about going to Paris herself, and had tried to backtrack – he could still see her gorgeous heart-shaped face, blushing like a child when she'd let slip she was going away to have an affair, and he'd been too thick and slow and too goddamned crucified with shyness to intervene, to ask her not to go, to tell her that she was making a terrible mistake. He'd tried to be gentlemanly and discreet. He had refrained from judgement and comment and instead just behaved like every other stupid Irishman and just sat there and got her pissed, instead of telling her exactly what he felt – what a fucking eejit he was to have said nothing to her then! Letting her go like that – and now he didn't know if he'd ever even see her again.

She'd told him then that she'd been in love with one of Dave's best friends and that she was in the middle of a passionate affair and was all in turmoil over it. There was only one thing he could conclude from all that had since happened. Nick had gone to Paris and had run away with Kate. All that crap about being gay – horse-shit, Ronan thought, putting his mobile back into his pocket.

"Nick's as gay as Christmas, Ro," Sharon Guinness tried to reassure him over coffee in the Obs theatre. "And Kate would *never* leave her husband – she's completely bonkers about Dave. You're overreacting. Lighten up, Ronan, there's a good lad."

"Lots of people leave their husbands when we never expect them to," Ronan told her pointedly.

Sharon glared at him. Then she said, "Well, if Kate

were going to leave her husband, she would leave him for someone much better-looking than Nick Farrelly. And she'd leave him for someone straight. Cop on, for fuck's sake!" She handed him the biscuit tin.

Ronan frowned. He'd try to ring Kate later on again, he decided. Maybe after work tonight. "I'm just worried about Kate, that's all," he said.

Sharon Guinness sipped her coffee and lowered her eyes. She was saying nothing more.

"So that's the report of the post-mortem," explained Marianne. "That is all it says. Death due to overdose of drugs, and the police still cannot identify the man who visited after he died."

"If I know who he was, do I have to tell the police?"

Marianne pursed her lips. "They may want to know. Do you have concerns for this individual?" she asked.

"He was my friend."

"A friend of Dave?"

Kate swallowed hard. "Yes. I think he was his lover." There was a pause. Marianne did not react. Kate continued, "I think he must have panicked when Dave overdosed and ran away. That fits with the description of the scene that the police have reconstructed, doesn't it?"

"Yes. That's what the police have said." Marianne looked up from the report that she was holding in her hand. "I'm just so sorry, Kate."

Kate scrubbed away a tear. "I just wish he'd told me!" she mumbled. "You know, about the men. I just wish, oh,

God! If there was one thing that I wish for, it would be that he could have told me before now!"

"I know." There was a very long pause. And then Marianne said, "I'm sure Jonny would have told you if he could."

"Jonny knew, didn't he, Marianne? I mean, do you think that's why they fought? Because Dave slept with men?"

Marianne nodded. "I think so. A little bit. He felt so bad about it all. He thought —" She paused, as if trying to think of what to say.

Then Kate said, "Were you going to say, 'he thought Dave would want to sleep with him?'"

Marianne nodded. "Yes. I guess that's it. That's pretty much what Jonny said. They were great friends at first, but Dave had always wanted something more. It caused them both great pain." She looked at Kate. "It was a long, long time ago."

Kate said nothing for a while. And then she said, "You know what, Marianne? I told you a few days ago that I knew your husband better than you did. And now, it seems, you knew my husband better than I did too."

Dave's body was cremated in Paris, and Kate flew the ashes home. She didn't want a funeral in Dublin.

The Paris ceremony was tiny and discreet. Just her and Connell, Charles and Caroline, Luis, and Marianne. Jonny send a giant bouquet of flowers by Interflora, and she put them with a rugby shirt on top of the coffin where they went into the furnace with Dave. They had lunch at the something or other hotel, which Connell had recommended as a suitable venue.

They would have a proper memorial service at home in Dublin after everything had settled down.

Kate, Caroline, Luis and Charles stood in a solemn line waiting for their baggage to arrive from Paris, in an unhelpfully crowded baggage hall at Dublin airport. Luis, Kate had decided, was actually really very nice. She eyed him cautiously now standing next to Caroline like a sort of sentinel, and she had to admit that she liked him very much. Really liked him a lot. Good for Caro, Kate thought, thank goodness one of us has found somebody to love, and she watched Luis leap forward and spring their first bag off the carousel as if it were a feather. Luis had muscles like Popeye, Kate had noticed, but she didn't even want to think about whether or not his were steroid-induced or just plain overworked from the gym.

Caroline was happy with him, Kate could see that now. Charles was enjoying practising Portuguese with Luis, mispronouncing everything, and Luis patiently corrected his appalling accent.

"Did you switch your phone back on?" Caroline asked her, and she stared at her.

"What for?" she asked.

"In case somebody tries to call you."

"Like who?" Kate said heavily.

Caroline opened her mouth, and shut it again.

"Last bag!" Luis was arranging them carefully like a Jenga game onto the trolley, and so they walked, all four of them through the big glass doors into the arrivals hall, where amid the crowds of signs and hopeful faces, there was nobody to greet them.

In the taxi, she squashed in the back seat next to Luis and felt something hard poke her in her hip. She pulled it out – her mobile phone. Caroline, Luis and Charles were all talking about the memorial service. Who they should invite, what date they should have it on, who would know to come anyway, and she suddenly couldn't bear it any more. Everything was unbearable now.

Dave. Dead. Jonny. Gone forever as far as she was concerned. Nick – one of her best friends in Dublin, or so she thought, had clearly been in Paris with Dave when he had died and was now uncontactable and there was going to have to be a horrid inquest if he didn't make contact with the Paris police. Dave and Nick, lying to her all the time – she couldn't bear to think about it and yet, like a scab that she was dying to pick, she kept turning the image over and over again in her mind. Dave and Nick.

In many ways of course, it all made perfect sense to her.

Caroline had told her over and over again since Dave had died that she shouldn't be all hurt that Dave had been sometimes into men – it was very trendy nowadays in LA to have a gay husband and the female models boasted all the time about the odd lesbian fling. That hadn't helped her in the *slightest*, but she knew that Caroline had meant well.

What she felt most of all was humiliation.

Overwhelmed with grief that Dave had died, despair at the way in which he'd died, and at the same time, so angry, so engulfed with anger that he'd died in such a way, in someone else's life, belonging all the time to someone else! As if he couldn't have *told* her. How could he have thought he'd have to hide all that from her? Surely he could have told her something as important as that?

That was the worst of all — the realisation that to Dave she had not been trustworthy. As if she'd never loved him all along. And the pain of realising that was what Dave had died thinking, that she hadn't loved him enough to accept who he was, was too much to bear.

And what did other people know? At the hospital? She wondered now, staring at the brick-brown buildings and the shops on Dorset Street as their taxi crawled through town. It had obviously been going on for quite a time, this thing with Nick — and were there other men? There were so many things she felt exhausted with curiosity to know, and yet there was no one left to ask. Nick had gone AWOL. Jonny was engulfed in grief. And Dave had gone forever.

Her whole life had been a lie. She felt abused and at the same time overcome with her own self-hatred and guilt.

Whatever rejection she had felt in the past from Jonny

that had led her steadfastly into a marriage with Dave was compounded cruelly with this. Her every sense of what it meant to be a woman who attracts a man, to be sexual, to make love, to orgasm – everything she'd ever felt in bed with Jonny just two *weeks* ago! Now, all of that very brief moment of what it felt like to be truly loved had been wiped out in a single flood, like a tsunami of realisation.

She had fallen down a rabbit hole. And there was no way out of this. And yet, somewhere in the darkest corner of her mind she knew the truth was all about the long-ago love triangle that she had quite deliberately nurtured between herself and Dave and Jonny, long, long ago. It all went back as far as that. She and Dave were two people who should never have got married in the first place – there was no way she could avoid seeing that now. But they had married one another in good faith to try to solve a problem that they shared – and in doing so they'd just created an even bigger one.

In the grey Dublin drizzle, the movement of the taxi was making her feel sick and so she switched her phone back on, thinking yes perhaps she should see if someone was trying to call her as Caroline had suggested. And as the screen lit up she saw the calls log in – all the seventeen calls she'd missed, all from Ronan. Oh, poor Ronan! She'd never even told him what had happened.

And suddenly she realised how much she missed him. And that he was the one person who hadn't gone anywhere.

He would be still here in Dublin if she called. And

there was no one in the whole world that she would rather talk to now.

"Where the hell are you?" Ronan roared on the phone, sounding delighted. And then the sound of her empty, unfamiliar, nasal voice saying, "I am in hell," made him hold his breath.

"What's happened, Kate?" he murmured.

"I'm coming from the airport."

"You sound – what happened to you, Kate? And Kate, have you seen Nick? He's gone AWOL somewhere too."

"Dave has died in Paris," she replied.

"Dave. *What?*"

"He's dead, Ronan. He died in a hotel in Paris. Last weekend. I've been over there organising a cremation, actually."

"Jesus!" Ronan whispered. "Where are you now though, Kate?"

"In a taxi. I'm on my way home to Percy Place," she replied.

"I'm leaving now." And he'd hung up.

Connell Jones Cumberton sat alone in his large empty kitchen with the double doors that overlooked the decking and the garden and opened up the bottle of cognac that he'd bought at Charles de Gaulle. This would be, Connell thought, a good time to take up smoking again. He listened to the thunder of a toddler running down the landing just above his head, and the scamper of another trying to escape Anja the au pair who was chasing them both back into bed.

His wife Sharon, he presumed, was busy chasing Professor Dennis Crowe into his bed.

Connell sighed heavily again, and wondered for the hundred-and- somethingth time that day, whether or not it would be weird, or seem a bit foolish, or stalkerish even, if he were to phone Marianne Le Normand again, just to see how she was getting along?

Kate stepped out of the taxi, holding the door open for Luis and Caroline while Charles paid the driver and they watched him lift their cases out of the boot, lining them up along the pathway in a little row.

"Well?" Caroline asked her gently. "Aren't you going to let us in?"

She looked at her. "I –" she began.

Charles took her handbag from her and his face was full of understanding.

"Tell me where your keys are, Kate, and I'll open up the door. There can't be any more ghosts inside now, can there, sweetheart?"

She shook her head. But she let Caroline and Luis enter the house before her anyway. She stood there very still on the step for just a moment, almost not going in – but where else was there for her to go? This was her house – she had lived here for six years of college and for most of her married life with Dave, and yet it had never felt less like a home to her. And then.

"Kate!"

She turned. And it was Ronan.

He ran across the road to her, and she ran towards him, and she let herself at long last be buried in the comfort of his big, friendly body. Underneath his armpit she buried her face, into the corner of his chest that was where, when she pressed very close to him, she could almost hear his heart.

22

The memorial service was in March. Kate chose the Unitarian church in Stephen's Green (neither she nor Dave were church-goers, and she had decided that a simple service with music would be more appropriate than a Mass, despite what Dave's rather dictatorial parents might think). The tiny church was absolutely packed – there was standing room only, and people on the stairs outside.

Jonny Domville played a trumpet solo by Purcell, and "A Whiter Shade of Pale" on the church organ. They all sang "Somewhere Over the Rainbow", which Dave's mother suggested as his favourite song when he was a child, although Kate would probably have picked something else. But it had everybody singing heartily in absolute floods of tears, which she felt was probably quite the right thing to happen, Dave might have felt.

And Caroline and Luis looked wonderful: both

dressed head to toe in black Armani straight from Milan, looking very solemn behind Dolce&Gabanna shades in a cold, inadequate sun.

Kate wore her grey dress, the one that she'd bought to present Marianne's delivery at the Morbidity and Mortality meeting – Dave had once told her she looked gorgeous in it. And Sharon Guinness wore a tight navy-blue suit and killer heels. She sat with Dennis Crowe who fumbled with his collar and looked even more orange-tanned than Kate had ever remembered.

Kate smiled through her tears at Sharon as she walked past them to leave the church, and she felt for the first time in a long while a tiny spot of something quite like empathy for Sharon. Sharon had simply fallen into the trap that anyone can fall in – that of thinking an affair can solve a problem with a marriage that's all wrong.

"Thanks for coming today, Sharon," she told her, letting Sharon clasp her arms tightly around her.

"I'm sorry for your troubles," Dennis Crowe murmured.

Outside she spotted Connell.

"Connell." She let him hug her into him and she breathed the familiar smell of his cashmere once again, that reminded her of Paris and of sadness and of rain.

"Marianne would have come but it's a bit too soon to be travelling after the baby," Connell said in a hopeful tone.

"Connell?" Kate looked at him.

"I told her all about the service," he explained.

451

"You look rather coy," she said.

"Well, at least Jonny came for you," he went on. "He played so beautifully. And it's been nice for me to meet him, after –" He gesticulated with his head.

She gave him a small grateful smile. "I know. I'm going over there to talk to him now," she said.

He was standing alone by a pillar looking almost lost, and she reached out her arms to hug him close to her. "You played beautifully," she said, and she let him hold her for a minute. "How is Marianne?"

"Not sure," he said, letting her pull away from him. "But I think she's met someone." She couldn't help a smile. "We fucked up royally, didn't we, Kate?" he began, but she shook her head.

"I'm all out of blame and self-loathing, I'm afraid," she said. "Look – we can beat ourselves up forever about what happened to Dave, or we can do something else, do the best to love the people who still need us. That's what I want to do now. Don't you?"

"Good for you," he said, but his eyes were full of misery.

"I've got to talk to people. Got to go. We'll catch up later." She squeezed his hand before he let her go.

It felt so very different seeing Jonny now – now that everything had changed. And yet she felt stronger around him than she'd ever done. Knowing that he had rejected Dave much more than he had ever rejected her, put everything in a new light.

She went to stand for a few moments listening to

Dave's mother accept condolences, and then saw Ronan approach Jonny on the pavement just outside the church, and she watched the two of them, thinking how odd the world was that *this* was what had brought all of them together. She pretended to listen to Dave's mother while she gazed around her at the mourners, the sharp suits, the nurses all dressed up and out of uniform, the friends of Dave's family in their fur coats. And then, suddenly, standing on the corner of St Stephen's Green just in front of the Luas track, watching them (just how long *had* he been there watching them?) she saw him.

Unmistakably, it was *him*.

"Nick!" she shrieked, and with a quick apology to Dave's mother who had leaped in shock at having her ear pierced, Kate ran across the pavement and the empty tracks of the Luas and flung herself at Nick. She landed her two hands palms outstretched in the middle of his chest and gave him an almighty thump. Then she grabbed him by the shoulders and began to shake him. Furiously.

"Jesus Christ!" Nick gaped, winded by her punch.

"*Where have you been, you bastard?*" she roared, and punched him in the chest again. "Ronan's been out of his mind worrying about you. And the police are after you in Paris! How could you have left Dave all alone?"

"*What?*" Nick stared at her.

"Oh, for God's sake!" she snapped. "It's all right. They aren't going to have an inquest. They know exactly why Dave died, it was obvious from the autopsy. But Jesus,

Nick!" She grabbed him by the shoulders again, glaring into his eyes, and howled at him in absolute fury. "Why didn't you *tell* me you were *with him*? How could you have left him all alone that way? You were my *friend*! How *could* you have put me through all this? The police, the embassy – even if you didn't want the police to know you were with him, you could have phoned *me* as soon as you knew! You bastard!" She punched him again much harder in the chest, sending him reeling. "You absolute bastard! You left him all alone!" She shoved him hard again and he fell over on the ground.

There were people staring at them from across the street. The mourners tried to make polite conversation, but it was quite clear that the widow had just started an almighty punch-up with somebody just across the road. Connell stepped off the pavement to go over to her, but Ronan pulled him back.

"Don't go there," he said in a very firm voice.

Charles looked at him.

"She *needs* to talk to him," Ronan said. "That's the guy who was with Dave." Charles stood very still.

Connell nodded and stepped back, but he kept his eyes pinned on the two of them.

Nick was trying to get up off the ground, shaking like a leaf. "I couldn't, Kate, I just couldn't talk to anyone about it!" he was saying. "I got there after he had died. I couldn't have told anybody. It was too awful."

"So where did you go?" she roared.

"Mont Saint-Michel," he said.

"Mont? What the hell!" She kicked his shin.

Connell and Charles started to move across the road again then looked at one another and stood still.

"Kate." Nick managed to get upright once again, and grabbed her by the arms. "I am really very very sorry. I was just so terrified. We weren't supposed to be in Paris. We –"

"I don't even *want* to know!"

"I know. And I'm not going to tell you either. But we didn't want to hurt you. Please," he took her shoulders and stared into her eyes, "you've got to believe me when I say Dave loved you and he hated himself for hurting you. He loved you, Kate. He always did. It's just that he wanted to be with me too. We loved one another. It just happens to people." And his voice finally broke into tears.

"Why did you have to come here today then, above all days?" she sobbed, thumping him weakly on the chest again. "And why did you leave him all alone?"

"Because I was so scared. Because I was a fool. Because I was a complete idiot and a coward, that's why. And I hate myself for it."

She said nothing. Then she said very quietly, "I hate you for it too, Nick."

"I'll go away now," he said, and his face creased up. "I just wanted to say goodbye to Dave." And then the tears that he'd been trying to disguise fell from underneath his glasses and she let him lean his head against her for a moment.

"Where are you going now?" she said to him gruffly then.

"I'm going back home again tonight, and then I'm flying out of Shannon in the morning. I'm going to America."

"Running away from all of this?" she said sarcastically and pulled away from him.

"No, Kate. I'm just leaving Dublin while I can – I know that I'm not wanted here. The thing is, Kate," he looked at her, "I did love him. I shouldn't have left him there in that hotel that night – it was the worst thing in my life that I've ever done, or that I'll ever do. But I was so scared. There were drugs – I was on my own in Paris – I just got scared to death."

"Hah! You are pathetic!"

"I know. I can't live with myself now after what's happened to Dave, so there's no reason why I'd expect to carry on living in the same town as you do. And so I *am* running away I suppose, but there really isn't anything else that I can do. Who would want me here?" he ended miserably.

"I really hate you, Nick."

"I know."

They stood a moment, each avoiding the other's face, looking at the ground. Her tears continuing to fall. His fogging his glasses. And then she reached her hand out and touched his arm. He put his arms around her and she let him hold her there.

"Wait," she said. She put a hand out, touching his lightly. "Come and have a drink with us, at least."

He looked puzzled. "Won't – do you really want me around you, your family? I don't want –"

"I know," she said. "I don't want either. I'll never speak to you again. I still hate you. And I always will. I'll never forgive you for leaving Dave alone like that. Never. But I want you to say hello to Ronan, please, before you leave us all forever. He's missed you too, Nick. He's missed you very much. He deserves an explanation too."

He looked doubtful. "All right," he said. "And thanks."

"Don't thank me. Thank Ro. He might be able to forgive you. But I never will."

He hung his head again.

"I'm not angry with you for loving Dave," she said very softly. "I don't blame you at all for that. I just wish *he* could have told me that before he died. But I'm angry with you for not loving him enough. You left him all alone. You left him for the police to find! I don't want to waste my life being angry with you. You're not worth being angry with. But I've said what I had to say to you and I'm going to forget you ever existed. I'm not going to let your cowardice ruin my life."

He nodded and looked down again.

She looked across the street again. Charles was walking back towards the crowd of mourners now, who were beginning to make their way along the pavement towards the Grafton Street end of the Green. All except Connell who was still watching her, pretending to be looking at his shoes.

"The opposite of love isn't hate," she said. "The opposite of love is indifference. So I refuse to hate you, Nick. I am going to indifference you."

He nodded, almost smiling at the joke. "Where are you going anyway, for the drinks?"

She looked at him. "Café En Seine," she said. "If you can believe that. Come on. I'll introduce you to my sister. She's just flown in from the Milan fashion week. You're going to love *her* boyfriend."

"Don't, Kate."

"Let's get a corner where we can sit down with Ro. And no more lies," she said. "No more secrets between friends."

She was with a group, just standing listlessly on the edge of a few people from the hospital not listening to them, trying to pretend to be in the conversation when he came across to talk to her, and she knew even before she'd turned around that it was his hand on her shoulder.

"Kate," he said and she took in the familiar face, the face that she'd once loved, once felt was all she'd ever want to see.

"Jonny."

"How are you? Are you doing okay?" he said.

She shook her head. "It's over now," she said and she touched his cheek. "But thanks for being here. I really appreciate you being here. And I know it was so hard for you but you played more beautifully than I'd ever heard you play."

"He would have liked it. Wouldn't he?" He looked quite pained, still.

She nodded. "'Course he would."

They took their drinks over to a quiet corner by the window where they could watch the street and sat down.

"We had dinner just over there that night," he said, indicating with a nod.

"Seems like years ago now, doesn't it?" she said.

"No. It seems like yesterday." He hooked her with his eyes. "I know this isn't the right time to say this, but I need to know. What happens now for us? We – we never really said what we would do."

She looked down at her hands. "It's over for us now, Jonny. It has to be. I want things to be different now. I want to do different things at work. I'm going to sell the house. I've got a lot of changes that I need to make. But your life – I just don't think I can fit in with all of that. I need to be more independent now. But we should stay in touch." She looked up at him. "You should keep coming back to Dublin and we can talk on the phone. Still be friends. You know what I mean."

He looked in pain for just a moment and she sat very still and waited for him to speak.

"All right," he said. "Whatever you like. We'll stay in touch."

"Everything changes," she said. "Life changes everything. We just have to make it work. What other choices to we have?"

He shook his head. "I don't know. I don't know what to think any more. You, Dave, Marianne – everything is all over the place!" He smiled sadly. "You know I'll always love you, Kate."

She looked carefully at his face. "I know," she said. "And I'll always stay in touch."

But she knew that she could live the rest of her life without him now.

23

One Year Later

Connell Jones Cumberton drove at breakneck speed along the motorway, and Kate had to slam her fist into her mouth to keep herself from squealing at him every time he tried to overtake.

"Jesus!" she gasped as he swung around a lorry, and then stuffed her fist into her mouth again.

"What?" he looked at her innocently, and she giggled.

"I'm a terrible passenger," she squealed.

"Well, I'm a terrible driver, so we're well matched, aren't we?" he grinned at her, and she almost grabbed the steering wheel out of his hands to avoid a truck.

"*Please* keep your eyes on the road," she begged him, half terrified, half laughing, and he crouched lower in the seat, squinting over the steering wheel mimicking a little old lady driving.

"Stop it!" She slapped his arm gently.

"Jeez, there ain't no pleasing you," he muttered, and she smiled contentedly.

"I can't believe you're leaving me forever, Katie-kins," he said.

"Liar!" She grinned happily. "In any case, I'm not leaving you forever. I've only signed a one-year contract with this South African project and then I'll see how I feel next. In any case, you've got my fabulous house to live in for the rest of your life and you got it at a bargain price – you're over the moon, and you know it, Jonesie, so you do."

He turned to look at her happily.

"Watch the road!" she shrieked again.

"Yeah, yeah, yeah," he said. "But do you think that Marianne will ever settle in Dublin for me, Kate?"

Kate laughed. "She wouldn't settle in Geneva for Jonny, so why on earth would she settle back in Dublin for you?"

"Hey!" He looked hurt. "No need to ridicule. My ego's not that robust, Gilmore. Veronique has grandparents here, you know. It wouldn't be too bad a thing at all. With them being just around the corner from your, I mean *my* new house," he said.

"And have you asked her to?" she said.

He bit his lip. "Not yet," he replied. "I'm still a bit too scared."

"Of rejection?" she raised one eyebrow.

"Well, let's say, the long distance thing is working well – but."

"But?"

"Is it?"

"Can't you just not fix what isn't yet broken?" she asked him.

"Wise words," he nodded. "But at least she likes the house."

Kate laughed. "Mad, isn't it? I can't think of a single house in all the world that might be less to Marianne's taste. And all the weird memories." She shook her head. "But I'm very glad for her."

He smiled at her.

"One thing at a time, so?" She looked at him.

He nodded. "But I still can't *believe* that you're leaving Dublin for good, you know. You'll be back after six months. I know you will."

He swung the car off the roundabout and they sailed past the big yellow *Welcome To Dublin Airport* sign.

"I've always loved this town," she said. "I've always loved coming home to this airport. But now I just don't belong here any more, Connell," she said. "Too many horrid things have happened – too many memories now. I want to go to where the sun will always shine. And you can come and visit. And the girls. All of them," she added.

"Here we are," he said.

He stopped the car abruptly in the middle of a stream of taxis that beeped aggressively at him, and he turned to look at her, reaching out to tuck a strand of hair off her forehead.

"Lovely since you grew your hair," he said.

She shook it out like a fan around her shoulders. "Will you miss me?" she asked, checking his face carefully.

"Desperately," he said.

"I'll write. Email. Come and visit." She kissed him on the cheek.

"Kate," he said. "Won't you be lonely in South Africa all on your own? I mean, I know you've got a big medical project going on, but what if you miss people? Me, for example?" He grinned sheepishly.

She suddenly felt so touched by his concern.

"Nah," she kissed his lips. "Surprise surprise. I've got someone coming with me."

The flight from Dublin to Johannesburg via Zurich wasn't going to be very full – just a shortish queue of mostly business passengers, and one or two families in economy. Kate looked around her sharply, thinking for one awful moment that he was going to be late, or that he might have mistaken the time, and so she began to rummage in her bag for her mobile phone to call and see where the hell he was – and then she heard his voice calling "Kate!" and she looked around through the little crowd of people and saw that he was there. Over at the business and first-class desk, well out of the way of most of the other passengers who were queuing, grinning broadly at her as he waved.

"What on earth are you doing over here?" she beamed as she made her way towards him, wheeling her trolley that was piled up like a forklift truck in front of her.

"Aw," he stooped to kiss her face, "I couldn't resist this little roped bit that they've sectioned off, with the little red carpet and stuff – and look, the airhostesses even have nicer uniforms down here –"

"No, they don't!" Kate laughed. "They are all exactly the same."

"Well, they have nicer smiles or something over here. Anyways, I couldn't resist the little rope, see?" He tugged at it, and she rolled her eyes. "So, I've upgraded us."

"*What?*"

"It's only business class, but if you play your cards right, shhh!" He put his index finger up in front of his mouth. "And then I pretended we were on our honeymoon. So they might be even nicer to us, see?"

She slapped his arm. "You big eejit!" she grumbled.

The check-in attendant looked at her with a look of cautious expectation.

"Kate Gilmore and Ronan Clare," said Kate, handing her a passport. "Both flying one way all the way to Johannesburg."

"A window or an aisle seat?" the attendant asked them.

"One of each," he replied. He looked at Kate. "No, you decide."

"Ronan!" she pushed him.

The attendant was waiting patiently.

"One for each of us," she said. "Definitely one of each."

THE END

If you enjoyed *Entanglement* by
Juliet Bressan, why not try
Snow White Turtle Doves
also published by Poolbeg?

Here's a sneak preview of Chapter One.

Snow White
Turtle Doves

Juliet Bressan

Chapter 1

May 2004

Isabella stood, arms crossed lightly in front of her clinging purple polo-neck sweater, at the long wall of windows that overlooked the campus, half-listening to the reading of a Pinter play. She let her gaze blur, over the tops of trees and paths and the open campus of a large suburban university. The small tutorial room was on the tenth floor of a domineering 1960's tower block of glass and concrete.

The top-floor rooms were warm and bright, catching all the delicate rays of sun that are so rarely and lovingly bestowed on Dublin by an otherwise disgruntled sky. In the distance the artificial lake didn't often shimmer or sparkle in the sun. Today, it simply sat there, blue beneath the trees. Cherry blossom was in flower.

"Project a little more. I can't hear you now!" Isabella spoke sharply with her back turned to the small drama group. They were beginning to shuffle their feet and doodle and cough. She had asked two of the first-year drama students to start a reading of *Old Times*.

"No acting, no motion, just read through the lines as if it were a radio play. I'll turn my back to you so that I can only hear the voice," she instructed them.

It seemed like a good way to get some work done on a day when her mind was just a sludge of anxiety, self-absorption and dense black mood.

"*Dark*," began the voice of one of the students.

"*Fat or thin?*" came the reply.

It reminded her immediately of this morning's conversation with Harry, which had ended so unsatisfactorily. So incomplete. Their conversations seemed to be becoming more unsatisfactory by the day. Conversations came and went but nothing was discussed. From day to day, she and Harry talked about each other's lives, asked each other questions, and demanded answers in return, but nothing was agreed.

Every sentence was a non-sequitur. Each question became rhetorical.

"What time did you get home last night?" she'd ask him.

"The meeting we had went very well."

"So who was there?"

"I think the Americans are planning on invading Syria as their next campaign after Iraq."

"Would you like some dinner, then?"

"Nothing on the news . . ."

For Isabella there were whole days, and increasingly many of them now, when she felt as though the entire dialogue of her life might well have been written by somebody else, who could only hear one side of the conversation. It was as if she and Harry had no relationship with one another at all, but they had somehow ended up in the middle of some bizarre party game where you had to make a conversation out of disconnected sentences that were being passed around on bits of paper.

She suddenly remembered a joke that used to make Harry and her snort with laughter when they were twelve in Mrs Glynn's class.

There are two pigs in a bath.

And the first pig says to the second pig:

"Pass the soap."

And the second pig replies:

"What do you think I am? A radio?"

In Pinter's plays the plot *grows out of* the dialogue between the characters, thought Isabella as she watched the sun straining to get out from behind thick clouds. The plot growing out of all the possible dialogues at that moment in Isabella Somerfield's life was becoming increasingly absurd.

The day had started badly. A horrendous row with Harry had left a cloud of gloom over her from the moment she had left the house. She felt wretched, and the familiar lump that rose from her chest to fill her throat was even more powerful than ever. Outside, many floors below, her tiny groups of students walking slowly along the pathways. To and from lectures, to the library, home to digs. Some worried, and some free.

I am free, thought Isabella carefully to herself. I have chosen this life. I have chosen this relationship, chosen this job, chosen this purple outfit. I have even chosen this room to hold my Thursday morning drama group because I like to be up here on top of the building. And yet I keep convincing myself that I am trapped. I feel as though my choices have all been *made* for me. As though everything I do is because of Harry, and everything I *don't* do is because of Harry. But the truth is, none of it is Harry's fault. It's the way I've always wanted it to be, she concluded miserably.

Isabella had always believed herself to be what she described as a deeply *hopeful* person. Harry described her as a pessimistic version of an optimist. Isabella believed that she had the goodness and reliability somewhere within her to make the most of her life. She knew that she was intelligent, caring, and capable of feeling great love, but she did not want to be a pushover. She liked to believe that she had the patience and fortitude to understand and tolerate other people's weaknesses and failings. But she also felt that her undying *tolerance* could sometimes be an easy way of avoiding self-reflection.

Harry, on the other hand, believed utterly in the goodness and virtue of all mankind. He questions nothing, thought Isabella guiltily to herself. He mistrusts nobody. He embraces the world with openness and love, and as a result he benefits personally every time.

"We don't *have* a personal relationship any more, Harry. All you care about is politics!" she had shrieked, when he dropped it on her that he planned to go to Venezuela next year.

"The personal *is* political!" Harry had laughed. "Even love is political, on many levels."

And he did love Isabella. She was quite sure of that. In as much as his love was possible, she tended to add to herself quietly but even then she knew that this qualifier was unfair. Harry did love her, very deeply. But Harry also loved the world.

"I am sick of having to share you with the rest of the *entire world*!" she had yelled. "The *world*, you know, Harry, *the world*, as such, can be a very, very large place!"

"The world is a global village," replied Harry dreamily.

And so Isabella just sat silent, furious and unmoving. The World Social Forum in Venezuela wasn't until next year but it was another plan for Harry to dream up, another series of fund-raisers to organise, another series of public meetings to plan, speakers to book, meetings to go to, articles to write. Another major part of his life that would totally, utterly exclude her.

From time to time, Isabella wondered if she envied Harry. This was not a pleasant thought at all. She did not believe, as it was not in the realms of her belief system, that it was possible to love someone whom one also envied. And yet she felt time and time again as though she was in some way losing, as though she *were* the loser in this relationship – even though at the same time she refused to believe that a relationship was like a *competition* and that one *could* either win or lose. But Harry *is* winning all the time, she thought. Winning friends, winning debates, winning arguments and winning support; and I feel as though I am slipping further and further away.

One of the students stopped the reading, and loudly cleared his throat.

"Sorry, Isabella, but I think it's probably well past one o'clock now."

The sound of ten chairs scraping rapidly off the floor was a sudden ear-splitting climax of relief. Isabella turned around. The students were rapidly shoving papers and books into bags and backpacks.

"Yes. Of course it is. I'm so sorry. Yes. Of course it is." She stepped forward briskly to stand at the front of the group, who were packing books and pencils away and edging hopefully towards the door, and raised her hands to corral them into listening mode.

"Good. Well, now: that was very interesting I think. Wasn't it?" she asked brightly.

Eleven dull, wretched faces looked back at her, grim-faced.

"So," she continued, searching their faces for some sign of forgiveness, "I think you will find this play is probably going to be a bit easier going than the Beckett we were doing last week, won't you? And there are parts of it that are quite funny too. So let's discuss it all a bit more during class next week. And meanwhile, perhaps you could write a short essay, let's say fifteen hundred words, about what you think might be the *underlying theme* of this play? Okay?"

She smiled a fake but bright smile at the sullen faces of the students while they pulled themselves together to leave the room. Oh God, she thought, I am such a dreadful teacher! They will probably kill themselves trying to write this essay over the weekend – when they should be out drinking and smoking and having coffee and making love. They probably hate me now for all of this. Her guilt burnt furiously on her cheeks.

Then again, they could stand up to me, she reminded herself. They could just say: Hey, look here, Isabella, this is rubbish! You couldn't be bothered doing any teaching. You are far too self-obsessed and your boyfriend is clearly getting bored with you. And now you think you can get away with staring out the window for a whole two hours while we read this and then expect us to write an essay about something you are far too lazy to teach us in the first place!

Well, they could say all that, she decided, and began to pack her own small brown leather briefcase with her papers. And so perhaps it is not *entirely* my fault.

Doctor Sinead Skellig sat at her desk alone for a just few more minutes, blowing on her coffee. Her desk was like a sanctuary to her. It was here she wrote to friends, phoned her mother, did her nails, ordered things online. The desk faced towards a wall. Sinead would have liked a view, but the surgery was very small and the only window in the consulting room was frosted, and overlooked a drain.

She glanced up at the clock now: it was just gone five past two. There was really only just enough time for one last quick look at her emails before the patients would start coming in. And so she clicked her mouse and opened up her inbox one more time, just as she had done every single morning for the past two weeks, desperate for a result.

And oh! There it was! At last. Oh, thank God for that! Sinead breathed in deeply, and then let her head sink into her hands, overwhelmed with sheer relief.

Moussa's email: finally sitting in her inbox after weeks of wondering. She paused a happy moment, just looking at it there before she clicked it open, almost triumphantly. But then her breathing slowed, and her heart thumped as she read.

My dearest Sinead,

I write to you quickly and in great fear. We are leaving Baghdad tonight to travel to Fallujah, some doctors and I. We have received short messages from there that the hospital is under siege. My doctors and I have obtained two cars to drive north with medicines and with food. The doctors in Fallujah are starving. One doctor who is a surgeon telephones me tonight and tells me that he has eaten the flowers in the garden around the hospital. I just can't bear to think my colleagues must be suffering so.

The Americans stopped the ambulances leaving the hospital to collect the dead. The doctors tried to leave the hospital in their cars. They tried to save those who died on the streets. But the Americans made them return, leaving many injured to die. Now the hospital has no food, no good clean water, and the medicines are almost gone. Communications are very bad. I have sent two emails to Jon Snow tonight, and I hope that he will understand them. Channel Four News does not always report the full truth but I hope that Jon Snow will try to speak about it on the news in England. I am very lonely here, Sinead. I know I will visit Dublin again. I hope you know it too.

Your old friend
Moussa.

It was horrendous. There was no other word to describe it. But the feeling that she felt most of all was guilt. Tense, uneasy, horrible guilt for Moussa and Baghdad. Oh God, why didn't he get out of that place a long time ago? What on earth was he doing, still living there? But she knew the answer far too well. He was there because it was his home. That was Moussa.

"Talk the talk, then walk the walk too," he'd laugh at her, when she held back from big decisions over patients.

But that kind of risk-taking was just a part of the big macho surgeon thing: it wasn't really dangerous. It was all bravado. "Get it into theatre, and open up! If you don't put your hands into it you put your foot in it!" Moussa used to say. "Not enough time to prep for theatre? Open up the chest in casualty, woman!"

Moussa had seen enough trauma surgery in his time to open up a chest with his two eyes closed. But he sounded frightened now. She held her forehead in her hands, leaning on her desk. *I am so lonely.* That wasn't her friend Moussa talking. It sounded almost as if it could be someone else. The most shocking thing of all though was the thought that Moussa's bullshit confidence might have gone. In his email he sounded almost as if he thought it were his last. *As if he might be saying goodbye.* Sinead sat very still and read it once again. She breathed out slowly, scrutinising every line. The phone rang twice but she ignored it as she printed out the email.

And then she felt tears begin to sting her nose. Tears of utter frustration. She shook her head fiercely to dismiss them.

She glanced up: it was well past two. Pins and needles down her back. She shivered and then standing up she folded Moussa's email printout, and put it in her bag. She gulped her coffee back and paced around the tiny surgery to compose herself. And then she suddenly caught sight of her tense expression in the mirror by the sink. Jesus Christ, I can't start the surgery in a state like this, she thought. She tried to smile instead at her pale reflection in the mirror.

She took her specs off, and bent forward to shake her head around so that her dark blonde hair bounced back when she stood up again. Bit better now, she thought.

I am going to write back to him tonight, she decided.

Her hair looked far too fluffy now. She flattened it down again and tucked it back behind her ears. After work she would read the email properly and decide then what she could do.

She took a deep breath in, glanced at the computer screen and bit her lip. It told her there were already two patients in the waiting room. She sniffed and fixed her glasses one more time and shrugged her shoulders round to ease them out. Okay. It was time to get back to work

Opening the surgery door, she called the first name on the list.

A small neat man with a rather juvenile beard stood up and smiled at her. A warm and generous smile. He looked to be about thirty, and was wearing a grey sweatshirt over faded jeans and carrying a satchel on his shoulder. Sinead held the door open and let him into the consulting room in front of her. Then she noticed that he had a little red and yellow badge pinned on to his satchel: *No War For Oil.* That's a good badge, she thought. He was nice-looking too. He looked intelligent and as if he might be rather fun.

"Take a seat," she said. "I like your badge."

"Thank you. I like your painting in the hall."

Sinead was thrilled that he had noticed it: her painting of a Baghdad street scene, in muted colours – grey, brown, black – that Moussa had given her just before she'd left Iraq; a group of bearded people walking, white-clothed, long and thin. Sinead had hung it in the waiting room so that it was the first thing she saw every morning when she arrived at work. It was her anchor in the world.

She offered him the other chair at right angles to her own. But he moved away and sat on the edge of the couch instead. She had to turn her whole body around in her swivel chair to address him at the back of the room. It was awkward, but she let him sit where he felt comfortable.

"So, what can I do for you today?" she asked, leaning back to look at him.

The young man coughed and wriggled a little as he sat on the edge of the couch. "This is a bit embarrassing," he began with a slightly red-faced smile.

Oh crap, Sinead thought gloomily. Please don't let him show me his arse. He's probably gay and he has piles. She was aware that her face had frozen into an expression of possible disgust, and that her cheeks had pinked up a little, and so she tried to look neutral again as the young man continued. The fact that she wore glasses with dark frames might distract from her expression at a time like this, she hoped.

Sinead's squeamishness was not something she was proud of. She tried to disguise it as much as possible, by suggesting to patients that they themselves might not want to be examined, that it would be much better to have a male colleague look at this. "For you own comfort, you understand?" And could they possibly make an appointment to see Dr Tom Fox on Friday? She cleared her throat and asked the young man whether he would like to wait until Friday when Dr Fox would – but he cut her off mid-sentence.

"Ah, no, not at all. I'm fine with a woman doctor. Thanks a million. No, it's not too embarrassing, actually.

I'm sure you're well used to this sort of thing. It's just that I'm in a bit of a hurry to have this seen to. I'm afraid that this is the only free time I've got this week, and so I'd really like to get it seen to right away."

"I see. So, what seems to be the problem?"

"It's my, er, ahem, my dick," he coughed.

Sinead breathed out slowly. "Okay. Well, let's have a look then, shall we?"

Men and their dicks, she thought. *Broken bones, broken hearts. Bring out the broken dicks, why don't you?* She pretended to straighten her glasses as he unzipped his trousers and lay back on the couch.

"It's all right. You can sit up," she offered, trying to sound bright, as she pulled on some rubber gloves.

"Oh. Okay. Thanks."

He swivelled round to sit perched on the edge of the couch again, and plopped it out.

He held it in his hand for her. Thick, round, wobbly and stub-like. Like the stump of a limb, with a pimple at the eye, winking back.

Sinead glanced at it as briefly as she possibly could, and prodded it a bit, and then let it go. Her visible relief was an antidote for his anxious face.

"You have nothing to worry about. It's only a pimple."

She snapped off her rubber gloves, and dropped them in the bin. "Any other spots, or lumps, or discharge? Pain? Itch? Burning?"

He was fiddling with his flies. "No, just this pimple. Is it common? Look, I know that this is probably really stupid, but I thought I'd better get a doctor to have a look at it in case it's contagious. I do feel very foolish about this. But I need to know whether or not I have to tell my girlfriend, and whether or not she should be tested or something . . ." his voice trailed off.

"Don't worry, it's eminently treatable." Sinead turned around again, and smiled at him from her desk. He was still perched anxiously on the edge of the couch. "You should put this ointment on it every day, and it will melt away. But if you're worried about infections, you really ought to go to the clinic and get a proper check-up, because they say that if you think you are at risk of one then you are at risk of another, and so on."

"Because they travel round in packs?"

"Something like that. Yes. That's a good way of putting it, I suppose," she giggled.

"So, I don't need to tell my girlfriend?"

"No – it's not contagious and it will clear up in no time."

"Great. She might think I'd caught it from somebody else, and that would really upset her. I think she feels monogamy is very important. She might think I was being unfaithful, or irresponsible, or something. She takes that kind of thing very seriously. Being faithful, I mean."

"Oh, everybody's faithful, give or take a night or two." Sinead couldn't help a grin.

"Hey! A doctor who likes Leonard Cohen! This must be my lucky day," he beamed back at her.

They looked at each other momentarily.

He is very slightly familiar, Sinead thought. His eyes, there is something familiar about his eyes. They really are rather beautiful. No wonder he's worried about picking up souvenirs of love.

"I'm sorry but I'm not sure whether I recognise you." She cleared her throat. "Have you been to the surgery before?"

"Oh God, no. I'm never sick. My office is just across the river and you were the handiest to come to. I have a meeting later and this is very convenient to the place I'm going."

Sinead handed him the prescription and he stood up. He looked at her, as if there was something else he wanted to say. She held his eyes for just a moment.

Nothing but their breathing.

"I just assumed you must be a Leonard Cohen fan. Because of the quote, you know. It's such a great song, that one, isn't it?"

"I guess it's one that tells the truth."

"Well, thanks. I think you've saved my life – well, not my *life*, of course. That's a gross exaggeration. But, you've saved my relationship anyway. Well, maybe for another week or two. I'd better go." He picked his satchel up. "Thanks again. Doctor. Thank you. Bye."

"Ah, yes. Well, it's thirty-five euros. Pay Dorinda at reception."

She watched him as he left the room.

It was his eyes: she felt there was definitely something about his eyes that she had seen before. And there was something familiar too about the way he moved his head forward slightly when he spoke, and looked up as if he were trying to see over his eyebrows. There is a lovely innocent sincerity about him, she thought. He seems kind. And there's a sort of passionate honesty about him too that I like. He looks like someone you could easily love.

His girlfriend probably gives him a hard time, she told herself, opening up another file.